continued . . .

Ace Books by Jack Campbell

THE LOST FLEET: DAUNTLESS
THE LOST FLEET: FEARLESS
THE LOST FLEET: COURAGEOUS
THE LOST FLEET: VALIANT
THE LOST FLEET: RELENTLESS

THE LOST FLEET

VALIANT

JACK CAMPBELL

WITHDRAWN

ACE BOOKS, NEW YORK

THE BERKLEY PUBLISHING GROUP
Published by the Penguin Group
Penguin Group (USA) Inc.
375 Hudson Street, New York, New York 10014, USA
Penguin Group (Canada), 90 Eglinton Avenue East, Suite 700, Toronto, Ontario M4P 2Y3, Canada
(a division of Pearson Penguin Canada Inc.)
Penguin Books Ltd., 80 Strand, London WC2R 0RL, England
Penguin Group Ireland, 25 St. Stephen's Green, Dublin 2, Ireland (a division of Penguin Books Ltd.)
Penguin Group (Australia), 250 Camberwell Road, Camberwell, Victoria 3124, Australia
(a division of Pearson Australia Group Pty. Ltd.)
Penguin Books India Pvt. Ltd., 11 Community Centre, Panchsheel Park, New Delhi—110 017, India
Penguin Group (NZ), 67 Apollo Drive, Rosedale, North Shore 0632, New Zealand
(a division of Pearson New Zealand Ltd.)
Penguin Books (South Africa) (Pty.) Ltd., 24 Sturdee Avenue, Rosebank, Johannesburg 2196,
South Africa

Penguin Books Ltd., Registered Offices: 80 Strand, London WC2R 0RL, England

This is a work of fiction. Names, characters, places, and incidents either are the product of the author's imagination or are used fictitiously, and any resemblance to actual persons, living or dead, business establishments, events, or locales is entirely coincidental. The publisher does not have any control over and does not assume any responsibility for author or third-party websites or their content.

THE LOST FLEET: VALIANT

An Ace Book / published by arrangement with the author

PRINTING HISTORY
Ace mass-market edition / July 2008

Copyright © 2008 by John G. Hemry.
Cover art by Peter Bollinger.
Cover design by Annette Fiore DeFex.
Interior text design by Kristin del Rosario.

ISBN: 978-0-441-01619-8

ACE
Ace Books are published by The Berkley Publishing Group,
a division of Penguin Group (USA) Inc.,
375 Hudson Street, New York, New York 10014.
ACE and the "A" design are trademarks belonging to Penguin Group (USA) Inc.

PRINTED IN THE UNITED STATES OF AMERICA

10 9 8 7 6 5 4 3

To Jack M. Hemry (LCDR, USN, retired)
and Iris J. Hemry, my parents.
One word I never said often enough: thanks.

For S., as always.

ACKNOWLEDGMENTS

I remain indebted to my agent, Joshua Bilmes, for his ever-inspired suggestions and assistance; to my editor, Anne Sowards, for her support and editing; and to Cameron Dufty at Ace, for her help and assistance. Thanks also to Catherine Asaro, Robert Chase, J. G. (Huck) Huckenpohler, Simcha Kuritzky, Michael LaViolette, Aly Parsons, Bud Sparhawk, and Constance A. Warner, for their suggestions, comments, and recommendations. Thanks also to Charles Petit, for his suggestions about space engagements.

And in memory of USS *SPRUANCE* (DD-963): launched 10 November 1973; commissioned 20 September 1975; decommissioned 23 March 2005; sunk as a target off the Virginia Capes 8 December 2006. The first and finest, she taught me about ships the hard way.

THE ALLIANCE FLEET

CAPTAIN JOHN GEARY,
Commanding (acting)

As reorganized following the losses suffered immediately prior to Captain Geary assuming command in the Syndic home system.

Ship names in bold are those lost in action, with the name of the star system of their loss given afterward.

SECOND BATTLESHIP DIVISION

Gallant
Indomitable
Glorious
Magnificent

THIRD BATTLESHIP DIVISION

Paladin (lost at Lakota)
Orion
Majestic
Conqueror

FOURTH BATTLESHIP DIVISION

Warrior
Triumph (lost at Vidha)
Vengeance
Revenge

FIFTH BATTLESHIP DIVISION

Fearless
Resolution
Redoubtable
Warspite

SEVENTH BATTLESHIP DIVISION

Indefatigable (lost at Lakota)
Audacious (lost at Lakota)
Defiant (lost at Lakota)

EIGHTH BATTLESHIP DIVISION

Relentless
Reprisal
Superb
Splendid

TENTH BATTLESHIP DIVISION

Colossus
Amazon
Spartan
Guardian

FIRST SCOUT BATTLESHIP DIVISION

Arrogant (lost at Kaliban)
Exemplar
Braveheart

FIRST BATTLE CRUISER DIVISION

Courageous
Formidable
Intrepid
Renown (lost at Lakota)

SECOND BATTLE CRUISER DIVISION

Leviathan
Dragon
Steadfast
Valiant

FOURTH BATTLE CRUISER DIVISION

Dauntless (flagship)
Daring
Terrible (lost at Ilion)
Victorious

FIFTH BATTLE CRUISER DIVISION

Invincible (lost at Ilion)
Repulse (lost in Syndic home system)
Furious
Implacable

SIXTH BATTLE CRUISER DIVISION

Polaris (lost at Vidha)
Vanguard (lost at Vidha)
Illustrious
Incredible

SEVENTH BATTLE CRUISER DIVISION

Opportune
Brilliant
Inspire

THIRD FAST FLEET AUXILIARIES DIVISION

Titan
Witch
Jinn
Goblin

THIRTY-SEVEN SURVIVING HEAVY CRUISERS IN SEVEN DIVISIONS

First Heavy Cruiser Division
Third Heavy Cruiser Division
Fourth Heavy Cruiser Division
Fifth Heavy Cruiser Division
Seventh Heavy Cruiser Division
Eighth Heavy Cruiser Division
Tenth Heavy Cruiser Division

minus

Invidious (lost at Kaliban)
Cuirass (lost at Sutrah)
Crest*, *War-Coat*, *Ram*, and *Citadel (lost at Vidha)
Basinet and ***Sallet*** (lost at Lakota)

SIXTY-TWO SURVIVING LIGHT CRUISERS IN TEN SQUADRONS

First Light Cruiser Squadron
Second Light Cruiser Squadron
Third Light Cruiser Squadron
Fifth Light Cruiser Squadron
Sixth Light Cruiser Squadron
Eighth Light Cruiser Squadron
Ninth Light Cruiser Squadron
Tenth Light Cruiser Squadron
Eleventh Light Cruiser Squadron
Fourteenth Light Cruiser Squadron

minus

Swift (lost at Kaliban)
Pommel, *Sling*, *Bolo*, and *Staff* (lost at Vidha)
Spur, *Damascene*, and *Swept-Guard* (lost at Lakota)

ONE HUNDRED EIGHTY-THREE SURVIVING DESTROYERS
IN TWENTY SQUADRONS

First Destroyer Squadron
Second Destroyer Squadron
Third Destroyer Squadron
Fourth Destroyer Squadron
Sixth Destroyer Squadron
Seventh Destroyer Squadron
Ninth Destroyer Squadron
Tenth Destroyer Squadron
Twelfth Destroyer Squadron
Fourteenth Destroyer Squadron
Sixteenth Destroyer Squadron
Seventeenth Destroyer Squadron
Twentieth Destroyer Squadron
Twenty-first Destroyer Squadron
Twenty-third Destroyer Squadron
Twenty-fifth Destroyer Squadron
Twenty-seventh Destroyer Squadron
Twenty-eighth Destroyer Squadron
Thirtieth Destroyer Squadron
Thirty-second Destroyer Squadron

minus

Dagger and *Venom* (lost at Kaliban)
Anelace, *Baselard*, and *Mace* (lost at Sutrah)
Celt, *Akhu*, *Sickle*, *Leaf*, *Bolt*, *Sabot*, *Flint*, *Needle*,
Dart, *Sting*, *Limpet*, and *Cudgel* (lost at Vidha)
Falcata (lost at Ilion)
War-Hammer, *Prasa*, *Talwar*, and *Xiphos* (lost at Lakota)

SECOND FLEET MARINE FORCE
Colonel Carabali commanding (acting)

1,560 Marines divided into detachments on battle cruisers and battleships.

ONE

TWO of the armored bulkheads surrounding hell-lance battery three alpha on the Alliance battle cruiser *Dauntless* shone like new. They were new, the broken fragments of the originals having been cut away and new material fastened into position. The other two sides of the compartment housing the hell-lance battery were scarred by enemy fire but in good enough shape to have been left in place. The hell-lance projectors themselves betrayed recent repairs, using improvised fixes that would never pass muster with a fleet inspection team, but the nearest fleet inspection team was a great distance away back in Alliance space. For now, with the Alliance fleet trapped deep inside Syndicate Worlds' space, all that mattered was that these hell lances were ready once again to hurl their charged-particle spears at the enemy.

Captain John Geary ran his eyes down the rank of the hell-lance battery's crew. Half of the sailors here were new to this battery, having been cannibalized from other hell-lance crews on the ship to replace losses suffered at Lakota Star System. Like their battery, two of the original crew still bore marks of combat, one with a flex-cast covering his upper arm and another with a heal-pad sealed over the side of her leg. Walking wounded, who should have been allowed to recuperate before returning to their guns, but that was a luxury neither *Dauntless* nor any other ship in the Alliance fleet could afford right now. Not with combat once again imminent and the fleet in danger of total destruction.

"They insisted on returning to their duty station," Captain Tanya Desjani murmured to Geary, her expression proud. Her ship and her crew. They'd fought hard and well, they'd worked around the clock to get this battery back online and ready to engage, and now they were ready to fight again.

He couldn't forget that the damage that had been repaired, the sailors who weren't here because their bodies awaited burial, were the result of his decisions.

And yet now those sailors watched him with eyes reflecting confidence, pride, determination, and their unnerving faith in Black Jack Geary, legendary hero of the Alliance. They were still ready to follow him. They were following his orders, right back to the place where this fleet had left a lot of destroyed ships. "Damn fine work," Geary stated, trying to put the right amount of emotion into his voice and no more. He knew he had to sound concerned and impressed but not overwrought. "I've never served with a better crew or one that fought harder." True enough. Before being rescued from a century of survival sleep and brought aboard *Dauntless*, his combat experience had consisted of a single, hopeless battle. Now he had a fleet of ships and sailors depending on him, not to mention the fate of the Alliance itself.

And maybe the fate of humanity as well.

No pressure. No pressure at all.

Geary smiled at the crew of the hell-lance battery. "In six hours we'll be back in Lakota Star System, and we'll give you something to shoot at." The sailors grinned back fiercely. "Get a little rest before then. Captain Desjani?"

She nodded to him. "At ease," she ordered the gun crew. "You're off duty for the next four hours, and authorized full rations." The sailors smiled again. With food stocks running low, meals had been cut back to stretch available supplies.

"The Syndics will be sorry we came back to Lakota," Geary promised.

"Dismissed," Desjani added, then followed Geary as he left the battery. "I didn't think we could get Three Alpha fully operational in time," she confessed. "They really did a fantastic job."

"They've got a good captain," Geary observed, and Desjani looked abashed at the praise even though she was a seasoned veteran of far more battles than Geary had fought. "How's *Dauntless* doing otherwise?" he asked. He could have simply looked up the data in the fleet readiness system, but preferred being able to talk to an officer or a sailor about things like that.

"All hell lances operational, null-field projector operational, all combat systems optimal, all hull damage from Lakota either repaired or sealed off until we can get to it," Desjani recited immediately. "We're at full maneuvering capability."

"What about expendables?"

Desjani grimaced. "No specter missiles left, twenty-three canisters of grapeshot remaining, five mines, fuel-cell reserves at fifty-one percent."

Ships were never supposed to go below 70 percent fuel-cell reserves, to leave enough margin of safety. Unfortunately, every other ship in the fleet was at about the same level of fuel-cell reserves as *Dauntless*, and he didn't know when he could get any of those ships back up to 70 percent even if they managed to fight their way out of Lakota again.

As if reading his mind, Desjani nodded confidently. "We've got the auxiliaries with us to manufacture new expendables, sir."

"The auxiliaries have been building new expendables and repair parts as fast as they can. Their raw-material bunkers are almost empty again," Geary reminded her.

"Lakota will have more." Desjani smiled at him. "You can't fail." She halted for a moment and saluted him. "I need to check on a few more things before we reach Lakota. By your leave, sir."

He couldn't help smiling back even though Desjani's confidence in him, shared by many others in the fleet, was unnerving. They believed he'd been sent by the living stars themselves to save the Alliance, miraculously found frozen in survival sleep but still alive, just in time to get stuck with command of a fleet trapped deep in enemy space. They'd grown up being told the legend of the great Black Jack Geary, epitome of an Alliance officer and a hero out of myth. The fact that he wasn't that myth didn't seem to have impressed them yet. But Desjani had seen enough of him firsthand to know that he wasn't a myth, and she still believed in him. Since Geary thought a great deal of Desjani's own judgment, that was very reassuring.

Especially in comparison to those officers in the fleet who still thought he was a fraud or the mere shell of a once-great hero. That group had been working to undermine his command since he'd very reluctantly taken over the fleet after Admiral Bloch was murdered by the Syndics. He hadn't wanted that command, still being dazed by the shock of learning that the people and places he had known were now a century in the past. However, as far as Geary was concerned, he hadn't had much choice but to assume command since his date of commission was also about a hundred years ago, making him by far the most senior captain in the fleet.

Geary returned Desjani's salute. "Sure. A ship captain's work is never done. I'll see you on the bridge in a few hours."

This time Desjani's grin was fiercer as she anticipated battle with the forces of the Syndicate Worlds. "They won't know what hit them," she vowed as she headed off down the passageway.

Either that or we won't, Geary couldn't help thinking. It had been an insane decision, to take a fleet fleeing a trap from which it had barely escaped and turn it to charge right back into the enemy star system in which it had narrowly avoided being destroyed. But the officers and sailors on *Dauntless* had cheered it, and he had no doubt those on other ships had as well. There were many things he was still trying to figure out about these sailors of the Alliance in a time a century removed from his own, but he knew they could and would fight like hell. If they were going to die, they wanted to do it facing the enemy, on the attack, not running away.

Not that most of them expected to die, because most of them trusted him to lead them home safely and save the Alliance in the bargain. *May my ancestors help me.*

VICTORIA Rione, Co-President of the Callas Republic and member of the Alliance Senate, was waiting in his stateroom. Geary paused as he saw her. She had access to his room at any time since she'd spent quite a few nights here at sporadic intervals, but Rione had mostly avoided him since Geary had ordered the fleet back to Lakota. "What's the occasion?" he asked.

Rione shrugged. "We'll be back at Lakota in five and a half hours. This may be the last time we get a chance to talk since the fleet could be destroyed soon afterward."

"I don't think that's a good way to inspire me before battle," Geary observed, sitting down opposite her.

She sighed and shook her head. "It's insane. When you turned this fleet around to go back to Lakota, I couldn't believe it, then everyone around me started cheering. I don't understand you or them. Why are the officers and crew happy?"

He knew what she meant. The fleet was low on fuel cells, very low on expendable munitions, damaged from the battle at Lakota and previous encounters with Syndic forces, the formation a tangle from the frantic retreat out of Lakota and the hasty reversal to head back to the enemy star system. Looked at rationally, it seemed insane to attack again, yet in one moment back at Ixion he had known it was the right move to rally his fleet. The fact that either trying to make a stand at Ixion or fleeing through that star system would have guaranteed destruction had made the decision easier. "It's hard to explain. They have confidence in me, they have confidence in themselves."

"But they're rushing back to fight in a place they barely escaped from! Why should that please them? It makes no sense."

Geary frowned, trying to put something he knew on a gut level into words. "Everyone in the fleet knows they're going to face death. They know they'll be ordered to charge straight at somebody else who will be doing their level best to kill them, and they'll be trying to kill the other guy. Maybe being happy to be going back to fight at Lakota doesn't make sense, but what else about what they have to do makes sense? It's about being willing to do that, to keep hitting longer and harder than the other guy and believing that will make a difference. They believe defeating the Syndics is critical to defending their own homes, they believe they have a duty to defend those homes, and they're willing to die fighting. Why? Because."

Rione sighed more heavily. "I'm just a politician. We order our warriors to fight. I understand why they fight, but I can't understand why they're cheering this move."

"I can't claim to really understand it myself. It just is."

"They cheered the orders, and obeyed them, because you gave them," Rione added. "What are these warriors fighting for, John Geary? The chance to get home? To protect the Alliance? Or for you?"

He couldn't help a small laugh. "The first and the second, which are really the same thing since the Alliance needs this fleet to survive. Maybe a little bit of the third."

"A bit?" Rione snorted her derision. "This from the man who's been offered a dictatorship? If we survive our return to Lakota, Captain Badaya and his like will make that offer again."

"And I'll turn it down again. If you'll recall, all the way to Ixion we were worried that I'd be deposed as commander of this fleet once we reached that star system. At least this is a better problem to worry about."

"Don't think your opponents among the senior officers in this fleet will stop just because you did something that has most of the fleet cheering!" Rione reached to tap some controls, and an image of Lakota Star System sprang to life over the table his stateroom boasted. Frozen on the display were the positions Syndic warships had occupied at the moment the Alliance fleet had jumped out of Lakota. A lot of Syndic warships, substantially outnumbering the battered Alliance fleet. "You told me we couldn't have survived if we tried to run through Ixion. All right. Why will things be different once we reach Lakota again?"

Geary pointed to the display. "Among other things, if we'd tried to run through Ixion Star System, the Syndic pursuit probably would have appeared behind us within a matter of hours. We'd had five and half days in jump space to repair damage from the battles in Lakota, but that wasn't enough. By turning and jumping back to Lakota, we gained another five and a half days for our damaged ships to repair themselves. There are limits to the repairs we can do in jump space, and I won't be able to get status updates from other ships until we enter normal space again, but every ship has orders to put priority to getting all of their propulsion units back online. At the very least, we'll be able to run faster once we emerge into normal space again at Lakota. That's not to mention the other repairs that ships are getting done, to weapons and armor and other damaged systems. By the time we emerge at Lakota, our ships will have had eleven days to repair the damage they suffered in our last encounter."

"I understand that, but we'll still be low on supplies and deep in enemy territory," Rione said. She shook her head. "Certainly we won't encounter the same size force of Syndic warships that we left at Lakota. They must have sent a powerful force in pursuit of us. But there'll be some Syndic warships there, and the ones that followed us surely turned around the moment they realized we must have turned and jumped back for Lakota. Those ships will still be only hours behind us."

"They had to assume we might wait in ambush outside the jump point at Ixion," Geary pointed out. "So they spent at least a few hours getting their own formation ready before they jumped after us. They must have come out at Ixion going a lot faster than we did, which means they'll take longer to get turned around, and since they have to assume we might ambush them at Lakota, too, they would've needed to keep their formation, which would also have taken more time than what we did, turning every ship in place. Give us three hours before the pursuit force arrives, and we might make it. Give me six hours, and there's a decent chance we can get this fleet to another jump point and safely out of Lakota."

"They'll still be right behind us, and we'll still be low on supplies."

"They've been running harder and maneuvering more than we have. If they don't stop to replenish their own fuel cells and weapons, they'll be in trouble, too. And if we get a breather in normal space, our auxiliaries can distribute to our warships the fuel cells and weapons they've manufactured in the last eleven days. That'll help. But you don't have to remind me that we're low on everything. *Dauntless* is barely above fifty percent on its fuel cells."

"Is that what you and your Captain Desjani were doing? Checking fuel-cell status?"

Geary frowned. How had Rione known he was with Desjani? "She's not 'my' Captain Desjani. We were inspecting a hell-lance battery."

"How romantic."

"Knock it off, Victoria! It's bad enough that my enemies in this fleet are spreading rumors that I'm involved with Desjani. I don't need you repeating them!"

It was Rione's turn to frown. "I don't repeat them. I don't want to undermine your command of this fleet. But if you continue to be seen with another officer with whom rumor links you—"

"I'm supposed to avoid the captain of my flagship?"

"You don't *want* to avoid her, Captain John Geary." Rione stood up. "But that's your affair, if you'll pardon the term."

"Victoria, I've got a battle coming up, and I really don't need distractions like this."

"My apologies." He couldn't tell if she was really sorry or not. "I hope your strategy of desperation works. You've been randomly alternating between cautious actions and wildly risky moves ever since you gained command of this fleet, and it's kept the Syndics off balance. Maybe that will work again. I'll see you on the bridge in five hours."

He watched her go, then leaned back, wondering what Rione was thinking now. Aside from being his off-and-on lover, this period being one of those "off" times, she'd been an invaluable adviser since she never hesitated to speak her mind. But she kept her secrets. The only thing he knew for certain was that her loyalty to the Alliance was unshakeable.

A century before, the Syndics had launched surprise attacks on the Alliance and begun a war they couldn't win. The Alliance was too big, with too many resources. But so were the Syndicate Worlds. A century of stalemate, of bitter war, of uncountable dead on both sides. A century of Alliance youth being taught to revere the heroic figure of John "Black Jack" Geary and his last stand at Grendel Star System. A century in which everyone he had once known had died, in which the places he had known had changed. Even the fleet had changed. Not just better weapons and such, but a hundred years of trading atrocities with the Syndics had turned his own people into something he hadn't recognized.

He'd changed, too, since being forced to take command of the fleet as it teetered on the brink of total destruction. But at least he'd reminded these descendants of the people he'd known what real honor was, what the principles were that the Alliance was supposed to stand for. He hadn't been remotely prepared to command a fleet of this size, let alone one crewed by officers and sailors who thought differently from him, but together they'd made it this far toward home. Their home, that is. His home wouldn't be recognizable. But he'd promised to get them home, his duty demanded it, and he was damned well going to get the job done or die trying.

His gaze came to rest on the display of Lakota Star System. So many Syndic warships. But the Syndics had been hurt during the last engagement, too. It had been impossible to be sure how badly hurt with the final hours a flurry of battles throwing out debris that blocked the views of sensors. He couldn't even know what losses the Alliance battleships *Defiant*, *Audacious*, and *Indefatigable* had inflicted in their last moments of life as they held off the Syndics long enough for the rest of the fleet to escape.

How confident had the Syndic commander been that the Alliance fleet was truly beaten this time and would only keep fleeing blindly? How many Syndic warships had pursued the Alliance fleet to Ixion, and how many had been left behind to guard against the unlikely (or insane, depending on the viewpoint) possibility that Alliance warships would quickly return to Lakota? The only way to answer those questions would be to stick the fleet's head in the lion's mouth and see what shape the lion's teeth were in.

He checked the time again. In four and a half more hours, they'd know.

DAUNTLESS'S bridge had grown comfortably familiar since his first time here in the wake of Admiral Bloch's death. Not the physical layout, which now seemed natural, but the equipment both more advanced than he'd once known and cruder in its outward appearance, the triumph of necessity over form. A century ago, on Geary's last ship, everything had been smooth, with clean lines and careful attention to outward show. But that ship had been designed and built with the expectation that it would serve for decades, one of comparatively few warships in a fleet not engaged in combat. *Dauntless*, on the other hand, reflected generations of warships constructed hastily to replace increasingly horrible losses, with an expected life span measured in a couple of years at best. Rough edges, ragged welds, uneven surfaces were good enough for a ship that might be destroyed in its first engagement, to be quickly replaced by another bearing the same name. Geary still hadn't gotten used to the expendable-ship philosophy born of ugly experience, which those rough edges broadcast.

Expendable ships and expendable crews. So much knowledge of tactics had been lost in a century of trained personnel dying before they could pass on their learning and experience to new generations of sailors. Battles had degenerated into slugging matches, with head-on charges and hideous losses. It had been far easier to accept the roughness of the edges on the ship than it had to been to accept the kind of combat casualties this fleet had regarded as routine.

But he'd kept *Dauntless* and her crew alive all the way from the Syndic home system to here, coming to know them until they were a comfort instead of a jarring reminder of those long dead. The watch-standers he had come to recognize and know by name, the amateurs he'd helped keep alive long enough for them to gain experience. Most of *Dauntless*'s crew had come from the planet Kosatka, a place Geary had visited once, literally more than a hundred years ago. Alone in this future, he'd come to see them as a family to partly replace what he had lost.

Captain Desjani smiled at him in greeting as Geary strode onto the bridge and dropped into his fleet command seat, positioned next to Desjani's own ship's captain command seat. She'd startled him at first, too, with her bloodthirstiness toward the enemy and willingness to accept tactics that appalled Geary. But he'd come to understand the reasons for her attitudes, and she'd listened to him and adopted beliefs closer to those of her ancestors. Besides which, his ancestors knew what a capable captain she was and how well she could handle her ship in action. Now Desjani's presence was undeniably the most comforting thing on this bridge. "We're ready, Captain Geary," she reported.

"I never doubted that." He tried to breathe calmly, look confident, speak with assurance. Even though he dreaded what might be awaiting this fleet when it left the jump point at Lakota, he knew he was always being watched by officers and sailors whose own confidence depended on what they saw in him.

"Five minutes to exit," the operations watch-stander announced.

Captain Desjani not only appeared calm and confident, she actually seemed to feel that way. But then Desjani always seemed to get more serene as combat and the chance to blow away Syndics drew closer. Now she looked at Geary and smiled tightly. "We've got some comrades to avenge in this star system."

"Yeah," Geary agreed, wondering whether or not Captain Mosko had survived the death of his battleship *Defiant*. Not likely. But Mosko was just one among many Alliance sailors who might have survived to be taken prisoner at Lakota. In addition to four battleships and a battle cruiser, the Alliance fleet had lost two heavy cruisers, three light cruisers, and four destroyers fighting the Syndics at Lakota. *Maybe we'll get a chance to liberate some of them. The Syndics shouldn't have been in any hurry to move those prisoners anywhere, so maybe some are still where we can reach them.*

The hatch to the bridge opened, and Geary looked back to see Rione taking the observer's seat in the back. Her eyes met his, she nodded at him with a cool expression, then Rione sat back to gaze at her own display. Desjani, apparently busy with her own work, didn't turn to greet Rione, and for her part the Alliance politician didn't seem to take notice.

"Two minutes to exit."

Desjani turned back to Geary. "Do you wish to address the crew, sir?"

Did he? "Yes." Geary paused to gather his thoughts. He'd had far too much experience with giving speeches before battles since assuming command of the fleet. Triggering the internal comm circuit, he put every effort into sounding upbeat. "Officers and crew of *Dauntless*, I am once more honored to be leading this fleet and this ship into combat. We expect to encounter Syndic defenders immediately upon exiting jump. I know we'll make them sorry they met us, and we won't leave Lakota without avenging our comrades who were lost here. To the honor of our ancestors."

Another announcement came on the heels of his closing sentence. "Thirty seconds to exit."

Desjani's voice rang through the bridge. "All combat systems active. Shields at maximum. Prepare to engage the enemy."

"Exit."

The gray emptiness of jump space went away in an instant's time, replaced by the star-filled darkness of normal space. The Syndic minefield was still there, of course, but *Dauntless* and the other Alliance ships were already turning upward sharply as they exited the jump point, maneuvering to avoid the mines. Geary scanned his display anxiously, praying that the Syndics hadn't laid more mines outside the jump point.

The star-system display had been frozen, showing the situation as it had existed in this star system when the fleet jumped out less than two weeks ago, the enemy-ship positions shown all tagged with "last-known-position" markers, which really meant "it could be anywhere except this exact location." Now the old ship symbols disappeared in a flurry of updates as the fleet's sensors scanned their surroundings and made identifications.

Geary squinted, trying to take it all in. There weren't any defenders right at the jump exit, but there were Syndic ships scattered all over the system it seemed. Lots of them. He had a momentary sinking feeling as he saw the numbers of enemy warships still within Lakota. Had he truly jumped right back into the teeth of superior enemy forces?

Then he focused on the identifying data and readiness assessments and saw a very different picture. The big cluster of Syndic ships located ten light-minutes from the jump exit consisted in great part of large numbers of repair ships, and the warships in it were all damaged significantly, with many systems evaluated as off-line while they were being fixed. The entire formation, a flattened sphere, was limping in-system at barely point zero two light speed.

The next largest formation, almost thirty light-minutes from the jump exit, had a mix of fully operational and slightly damaged warships, but only four battleships and two battle cruisers were among them.

All over the expanse of Lakota Star System between the jump exit and the inhabited world were other Syndic ships. Less badly damaged but still mauled Syndic warships crawling toward the orbital docks, freighters hauling supplies, civilian ships crossing between planets. Scores of sitting ducks, with too few guards standing sentry over them to stop the Alliance fleet from bagging every one within reach.

Desjani let out a gasp of pure pleasure. "Captain Geary, we are going to *hurt* them."

"Looks like it." His own formation was a jumbled mess, but he couldn't take time to sort it out now. He had a lead on the main Syndic pursuit force which had followed them to Ixion, but they'd come back through this jump exit sooner or later, and he didn't want the damaged Syndic warships and all of those helpless repair ships to get away.

As if reading his mind, Desjani pointed to the depictions of the enemy repair ships. "Preliminary assessments are they're pretty heavily loaded. They won't be able to run fast even if they can break away from the ships they've been fixing up."

"Too bad our own auxiliaries can run faster because they're *not* heavily loaded," Geary remarked, then he and Desjani exchanged a glance as the same idea apparently hit them both. "Is there any chance we can take those Syndic repair ships intact? We can't use any spares they've manufactured, but if they've got raw-material stockpiles on board, we can transfer those to our auxiliaries."

Desjani rubbed the back of her neck with one hand as she thought. "You'd think the Syndics would set the power cores on them to overload when they abandon ship. Lieutenant Nicodeom," she called to one of the watch-standers. "You're an engineer. Will they blow up those repair ships when we close to engage?"

The lieutenant frowned at his own display for a moment. "Blowing up a ship by core overload is done when recovery is judged highly unlikely, Captain. We don't blow up our own ships, no matter how badly damaged, in a star system we control. As far as I know, the Syndics follow the same policy."

"And this is a Syndic star system!" Desjani turned an enthusiastic look on Geary. "They'll abandon ship when we shoot them up, but leave the ships intact. They know we can't stay in this system, so they'll want the ships recoverable once we leave, and they don't know we want to loot them. We just have to make sure they don't realize we're seizing some of the repair ships intact until we've got as many as we need."

"Okay." Geary tried to calm himself. It seemed too good to be true, but it still wouldn't be easy to carry it out. "We can send most of the destroyers and light cruisers after the damaged Syndic warships proceeding independently, and send our battleships and battle cruisers toward the repair ships and the crippled warships with them. Some of those damaged Syndic warships could have substantial firepower available if they manage to get combat systems back online before we intercept. But we also need to hit the operational Syndic flotilla thirty minutes away hard, so they—" Something finally registered on him. "There's nothing at the hypernet gate. The Syndics pulled their guard flotilla out of there."

Desjani's breath caught. "Can we—? No, we can't reach the gate before that guard force does. They haven't seen us yet"—and they wouldn't until the light from the fleet's arrival reached them in about twenty-six more minutes—"but when they do, they'll still have too big a lead."

"I'm afraid so," Geary agreed. Normally, an enemy hypernet gate wouldn't be an option, impossible to use, but *Dauntless* carried a Syndic hypernet key provided by the supposed Syndic traitor who had helped lure the Alliance fleet deep into Syndic space and the ambush awaiting it in the Syndic home star system. The Syndics, knowing they couldn't allow the Alliance fleet to get home with that key, had already proven they would destroy their own hypernet gates before the Alliance fleet could use them.

Which wasn't merely disappointing but also very dangerous. "We could still risk it," Desjani argued. "If we do fail to stop them from destroying that gate, we could deal with it. The energy discharge from the collapsing gate at Sancere wasn't too much for our shields to handle."

Geary shook his head. "Nova, Captain Desjani," he stated very softly for only her ears. Desjani grimaced and nodded. According to the best estimates they had, the energy output released by a collapsing hypernet gate could vary from

effectively nothing to something equaling a nova, an exploding star. No ship could survive that, or outrun it. "No, the
gate isn't a realistic goal."

He hadn't told her yet that the Alliance fleet might have
its destination changed once within the Syndic hypernet system, hadn't told any of his ship captains. That would have to
change. Some of his other officers, including Desjani, needed
to know that they had other enemies besides the Syndics
actively working against them. "We've only got a short time
to do a lot before the Syndic pursuit force gets here from
Ixion. We need to overwhelm that big force of crippled ships
and auxiliaries, take out as many other Syndic ships as we
can, get our own auxiliaries in to loot the Syndic repair
ships, protect our auxiliaries from any desperate Syndic
counterstroke, and, uh . . ."

"That sounds like enough to start," Desjani observed.

His fleet, a disordered mass of ships, was "climbing"
up between the Syndic minefield and the jump point behind them, still moving at only point zero five light speed.
There wasn't any actual up or down in space, of course,
but humans needed those concepts to orient themselves. By
long-standing convention, the direction above the plane of
the star system was up, the direction beneath it down, toward the sun was starboard (or starward), and away from the
sun was port. Those conventions were the only way he could
give an order to all of his ships and have them understand
what he meant.

By the time the fleet reached a place where it could accelerate back "down" and toward the enemy, orders had to be
in place for them, telling each ship where to go. He had to set
everything up on the fly, with every moment critical. If only
he didn't have to do so much himself . . . Why the hell *did*
he need to do so much himself? Why not trust an officer he
knew was good at her business and had been watching him
work for months now? "Captain Desjani, would you set up
the maneuvering plan for the destroyers and light cruisers
while I take care of the heavies? We'll need to have our
boarding parties able to reach as many of the Syndic repair
ships as possible at about the same time."

Desjani's face lit up and she nodded without hesitation. "I'm on it, sir. I'll link our maneuvering displays so we're coordinating movements as we lay them out." She leaned forward and studied her display, then her hands began flying across her controls.

Focusing on his own display, Geary tried to sort out where his heavy cruisers, battleships, and battle cruisers were, where he needed them to go, and when he needed them to be there. His divisions were scrambled, further complicating the situation, and many ships still had limited combat capabilities from damage sustained the last time they were in Lakota. Practically all of them were back at full propulsion capability, but even with his experience with choreographing the movements of ships, he never could have sorted out the mess in the time available if not for the way the maneuvering systems provided simple intercept solutions as fast as he could designate a ship and an objective. While he did that, solutions appeared for light cruisers and destroyers as well, reflecting Desjani's work, and he found himself adapting to her inputs even as she adapted to his.

"*Audacious* is with that big group of Syndic repair ships and damaged warships," Desjani noted quickly. "What's left of her, anyway."

What was left of *Audacious* wasn't much, Geary saw as he focused on the derelict. His fleet's optic sensors were sensitive enough to track small objects across the length of a star system and could easily provide a sharp image of something only ten light-minutes distant. With all of its command, control, and combat systems dead, and its hull shape distorted by massive damage, the hulk hadn't registered immediately on the fleet's sensors as a friendly warship. The Alliance battleship, one of the three that had formed a rear guard as the fleet escaped Lakota, had been pounded badly. Her heavily armored hull had taken so many hits that it looked like sheet metal that had been pelted by acid rain and left to disintegrate. Either during the battle or afterward, every weapon on *Audacious* seemed to have been destroyed, and not a single propulsion unit was apparently capable of any thrust. But the Syndics were towing the hulk along with them. "What are they doing? Why have they got *Audacious* with them?"

Desjani frowned, then her expression cleared. "Prison barracks. See? There's heat and atmosphere leaking out, which means the Syndics have patched some compartments and kept life support up. I'd be willing to bet that *Audacious* is full of Alliance prisoners of war. They're probably using them for the heavy labor on those Syndic ships that need repair."

"Damn." Adjust the plan. They'd have to take what was left of the broken Alliance battleship, too, before . . . "Tanya, would they blow the power core on *Audacious*?"

She nodded, her face grim. "We've done it. They've done it. They're surely already preparing to do it again."

Nothing to lose, then. One of his greatest shocks had been seeing Alliance fleet personnel preparing to cold-bloodedly murder prisoners of war by blowing up their captured ship with them still aboard. This fleet, *his* fleet, would no longer do such a thing, but the Syndics hadn't had any such change of heart that Geary knew of. He need have no fear of putting a thought into the Syndics' heads that hadn't already occurred to them. Geary paused in his work and tapped the communications controls. "All Syndicate Worlds' personnel in Lakota Star System, this is Captain John Geary, the Alliance fleet commander. Be advised that if the Alliance prisoners of war on the battleship *Audacious* or on any other ship or location are murdered by core overload or other atrocity, I will ensure that every Syndicate Worlds' ship, shuttle, and escape pod in this star system is destroyed. Leave our prisoners alive, and I swear on my ancestors' honor that you'll be allowed to escape. Kill our prisoners, and I promise just as strongly that you will die as painful a death as I can arrange." It would take about ten minutes for that message to arrive at the Syndic formation containing *Audacious*, soon after the Syndics there saw the light announcing the arrival of the Alliance fleet. Hopefully that would be soon enough.

"That should get their attention," Desjani muttered, her eyes on her display again, her hands racing over the controls.

Geary refocused on his own task, now ensuring he had the remains of *Audacious* covered as well. The task seemed to take forever, great curves arching across the maneuvering display in an interleaving and intricate dance, even though he knew it was taking only seconds to plan the movements of numerous ships.

"Got it," Desjani gasped.

Tagging a last heavy cruiser and reading the maneuvering solution the system generated, Geary nodded. "Me, too. Double-check our work while I go over it, too, okay? Make sure we've got the heavies and the lighter ships coordinated enough to support each other where needed."

"Halfway done, sir."

He ran his eyes across his and Desjani's work, seeing the graceful arcs of projected ship courses streaking across space, the whole thing forming a picture of beauty that belied the deadly purpose behind it. The movements of the destroyers and cruisers didn't match the courses with the heavier ships perfectly, but everything worked and could be cleaned up in the time needed to close to contact with the enemy. He'd wondered if Desjani would just throw ships at the enemy, but she'd coordinated every movement so warships were working together in improvised formations that tried to maximize the combat capability of each ship. Clearly Desjani had not just been watching Geary control this fleet, but also learning from watching. Taken together, their work made the most of the current state of the fleet by dividing the bulk of it into about twelve subformations, each centered on at least one battle cruiser or battleship division. "Looks good. Looks very good."

"Same here, sir."

"Has that Syndic guard force reacted to us yet?"

"Not yet. They won't see us for another . . . nineteen minutes."

It was hard to believe that they had only been in Lakota Star System for eleven minutes. There wasn't any way to counter a reaction that hadn't happened yet, and waiting to see what the Syndics did would certainly be a mistake when every minute counted. Geary punched his controls again.

"All units in the Alliance fleet, this is Captain Geary. Maneuvering plan orders are being transmitted to you now. Execute immediately upon receipt. It is critically important that we gain control of as many Syndic repair ships as possible before they realize we're out to capture those ships instead of just shooting them up, so all units engaged in taking down enemy repair ships must adhere as closely as possible to the time line. It's also critical that we not accidentally trigger a core explosion on one of the Syndic repair ships. We assume there are Alliance prisoners of war aboard the wreck of *Audacious*, so ensure no fire hits the wreck. All other units, try to inflict maximum damage on Syndic units that come within range. We want to leave as little as possible for them to salvage. Use hell lances as much as possible and employ expendable munitions only when absolutely necessary."

He switched to another circuit, to the commander of the Marines embarked on his major combatants. "Colonel Carabali, work with the commanders of the warships going after the Syndic repair ships to ensure their boarding parties have Marine backup. Also prepare an assault force to retake the wreck of *Audacious* and liberate any prisoners. Time is critical. I've sent you a copy of the fleet maneuvering plan, so you'll know which of our ships are going near *Audacious*. You have authority to use shuttle assets from any of those ships except our own auxiliaries to get your Marines to *Audacious* and evacuate prisoners. Any questions?"

"No, sir," Carabali answered crisply. "I'll have my plan ready for your approval within half an hour."

"Thank you, Colonel. I may well be distracted dealing with Syndic warships and the overall situation. If you don't hear from me, assume the plan is approved and proceed with executing it."

"Command by negation, sir?" the Marine colonel asked in surprise.

"That's right. You're my landing force commander, and you've proven you're good at it. Get to work and let me know if you need more fleet assets dedicated to the task."

Carabali nodded, not quite suppressing a grin, then she saluted sharply. "Yes, sir!"

On to a third circuit, calling the commanding officer of *Witch*, who was also commander of the Fast Fleet Auxiliaries division comprised of *Witch*, *Goblin*, *Jinn*, and *Titan*. "Captain Tyrosian, we intend taking control of as many Syndic repair ships as possible. We need to loot their raw-materials bunkers as fast as we can. Is there some kind of conveyor we can run from our ships to the Syndic bunkers?"

Five light-seconds away, Tyrosian seemed dazed, blinking at Geary, then abruptly jerked into speech. "We have loading conveyors, but our systems won't mate with their systems, sir. Incompatible, by design of course. We'll have to use the Syndic conveyors to get the materials to a loading point, then transfer them to our conveyors. The transfer will cause a significant delay."

Geary gritted his teeth and turned to Desjani again. "The conveyor systems on our auxiliaries won't mate with the Syndic conveyors accessing their raw-materials bunkers."

"Blow the Syndic hulls open and run our conveyors right into the bunkers," Desjani suggested in a "the-solution-is-obvious" tone of voice.

"Excellent idea." Geary repeated it to Tyrosian.

"That will inflict some structural damage, sir—" Tyrosian began.

"We only need those Syndic repair ships to hold together until we get what we want off them! After that I don't care if they break into a million pieces because of the structural damage from the holes we blew through them. Hell, I want them to do that so the Syndics can't salvage them. Get your engineers ready to go. We need the raw materials onloaded fast. Will you need assistance from the Marines in blowing access holes through the Syndic ships?"

Tyrosian managed to look offended. "Engineers are better at demolishing things than Marines are," she declared.

"I'll arrange a contest sometime, Captain Tyrosian. Execute your orders and let me know immediately if you run into any trouble."

Geary slumped back, breathing heavily, amazed at how quickly they'd been able to put the plan together. He glanced over at Desjani again and saw her also leaning back, grinning at him, her face slightly reddened as if she'd just sprinted to finish a race. "Captain Desjani, has anybody ever told you that you're a damned fine fleet officer?"

Desjani's grin widened. "Thank you, sir."

As Geary caught his breath, he marveled at the experience. He and Desjani had worked together many times before, but never this well. Anticipating each other, supporting each other, setting up the movements for the fleet together. The closest thing he could compare it to was having sex without having sex.

He took another look at Desjani's flushed, happy face and wondered if that metaphor wasn't a bit too close for comfort. Her eyes caught his, her smile faded into an anxious expression, and she looked away. Great. Something in his own face had made her uncomfortable.

Now what? Find something else to focus on. Like the developing battle. "How long left until that Syndic guard force sees us?"

"Five minutes," Desjani replied, composed and professional again.

"The big formation of crippled ships and repair ships should have reacted to us by now."

"Some of them are. See this activity? Lines being severed between some of the warships and nearby repair ships. It looks like the Syndic warships in the formation that can fight are getting ready to fight or run."

"I hope the repair ships don't try to run, too." "Try" being the operative word. Even the so-called Fast Fleet Auxiliaries in the Alliance fleet were faster in name than practice, and they were purportedly designed to keep up with warships. Essentially mobile factories, most auxiliaries or repair ships weren't supposed to be able to maneuver anything like warships, with propulsion capabilities that accelerated them only sluggishly and couldn't come close to matching the velocities of combatants. Moreover, these Syndic repair ships were heavily loaded with the raw materials needed to manufacture replacement items, spare parts, weapons, and fuel cells, making them even more ponderous.

The leading elements of the Alliance fleet were clearing the top of the minefield that had prevented a direct run into or out of the jump point. As they did, each ship canted over and down and accelerated straight toward the enemy, the fleet seeming to be bending over the top of the mines like a waterfall in reverse.

Dauntless cleared the top of the mines, too, pivoting downward, the force of her acceleration obvious even though the inertial dampers were whining as they tried to block out the effects on the ship and crew. When it came to closing on the enemy, Desjani didn't waste time. "The Syndic guard force must have seen us by now," Desjani observed. "Since we're accelerating toward them, we'll see their reaction in . . . twenty or twenty-five minutes, depending on what they do in the meantime."

After the frantic activity they'd just gone through, those twenty minutes crawled by like a video playing in slow motion. At least the delay gave Geary time to go through the status reports streaming in from his ships, his first chance for a good look at their supply states and repair progress since the fleet had hastily jumped back for Lakota.

In the last fight at Lakota, *Warrior* had taken the brunt of fire from four Syndic battleships blundering past the Alliance auxiliaries that *Warrior* had been ordered to protect. Her crew had worked themselves to exhaustion patching up serious damage sustained at Vidha, so that the battleship could once again face the enemy, but now *Warrior* was once again barely combat-capable. Geary couldn't help shaking his head grimly as he viewed the latest status of the stricken battleship. She could keep up with the fleet, but *Warrior* would be out of the line of battle again for a long time.

The battleships *Orion* and *Majestic*, also badly damaged at Vidha, hadn't done nearly as inspired a job of fixing themselves up since then and remained barely combat-capable even though they'd taken little more injury the first time the fleet had been at Lakota. *Amazon*, *Indomitable*, *Vengeance*, and *Reprisal* were the next most badly damaged battleships, but all had made heroic repair efforts in the time allowed by the jumps away from and back to Lakota and were in good enough shape for combat.

The battle cruisers, which traded greater acceleration and maneuverability for the heavier armor and shields of the battleships, had paid the usual price for the bargain. Most of them had taken significant damage as the fleet had fought its way out of Lakota, but like *Dauntless*, most had been able to get at least the majority of their hell lances back online and their propulsion units functional. Only *Daring* and *Formidable* were still in bad enough shape that they needed to be kept back from any major fighting. Geary hoped he could manage to keep the commanding officers of those ships from nonetheless charging into the biggest fight they could find.

The rest of the fleet, the heavy and light cruisers and the many destroyers, were much the same though there hadn't been many badly damaged destroyers or light cruisers when they jumped out of Lakota with the Syndics on their heels. If the smaller combatants took major hits, they didn't have the size or armor to withstand the resultant damage and were usually blown apart or knocked completely out of action. Only Geary's attempts to protect his light combatants during the last battle had kept them from being decimated. As it was, four destroyers and three light cruisers hadn't survived the fleet's last visit to Lakota.

The four auxiliaries, vital to the fleet's survival, had emerged from the last encounter almost untouched, thanks in great part to *Warrior*'s stout defense. The one hit that *Titan* had taken had been patched up in the days since the battle.

As long as he didn't pay attention to the total lack of specter missiles among his ships, the almost exhausted supplies of grapeshot and the low fuel-cell states, the surviving ships of the fleet actually appeared to be in decent shape.

"Why haven't the Syndics done more repairs?" Geary wondered out loud. "They've had as long as we have, but their ships are still showing a lot of unfixed damage."

Desjani gave him a surprised look. "From what I know, they don't maintain the same onboard repair capability. It's more centralized with them. Supposed to be more efficient, I guess, and allows smaller crews on their warships. Odds are very little work was done before those repair ships showed up, and it would have taken them a while to be summoned after the battle even if they were in a nearby star system. They're close enough to where the last engagements were fought with us that I bet that formation has only been under way for a day or so."

"The Syndics were more like us before the war," Geary noted. "I guess they changed in response to their own losses. But what you're describing is something designed for peacetime, when there's the luxury of time and the ability to wait until you get to a repair facility or it comes to you. That may save the Syndics money in the short term, but it can't be helping their sustained combat capability in the long run."

She grinned. "Not today, for sure." Desjani paused as she noticed something. "We've got light from the Syndic guard force's reaction."

He hastily switched displays, seeing the images of two battleships on vectors accelerating toward the Alliance fleet. "Just two battleships? What about the rest?"

"We don't have light on their reactions, yet." Desjani checked something. "The two battleships are only twenty-two light-minutes away now since they're coming at us. When the rest of the force reacts, we should see it in the next few minutes."

It took a couple of minutes longer than expected, leading Desjani to predict that the rest of the guard force was accelerating away from the Alliance fleet. She turned out to be right. "They've split up."

"Split up?" As Geary watched the display, sensors throughout the fleet observed the time-delayed light showing the actions of the Syndic ships and provided rapid updates and estimates. Two of the battleships, both battle cruisers and the lighter Syndic warships, were accelerating like bats out of hell, on vectors clearly aimed at the hypernet gate. They were still twenty-eight light-minutes away and pushing their velocity up past point one light. Even though some of the lightly damaged warships in the guard flotilla were lagging slightly, it wasn't by much. He didn't need to run the figures to know the Alliance fleet couldn't possibly catch them. "They're going to defend and if necessary collapse that hypernet gate so we can't use it. But why split up a force that's already badly outnumbered? Why send those other two battleships toward us? Is it some sort of diversion?" He ran out the vectors for the two battleships, and the answer became obvious. The two battleships were headed for the large formation of damaged Syndic warships and repair ships.

"Going to defend their comrades," Desjani replied matter-of-factly. "It's a hopeless gesture, but that Syndic commander is making it."

Two battleships. Even counting out the badly damaged Alliance battleships like *Warrior*, he still had at least sixteen battleships to hurl against them, plus over a dozen battle cruisers. "It's what battleships do," Geary stated softly, remembering the words of Captain Mosko before he took *Defiant*, *Audacious*, and *Indefatigable* to their deaths holding off the Syndics closing on the rest of the Alliance fleet. "But this *is* hopeless. The other ships can't get away no matter what those two battleships do. The battleships can't even get to us until over four hours after we intercept that formation. They're being thrown away for no reason."

"Maybe the Syndic commander has orders to defend those other ships and the hypernet gate, too, and has to make the gesture."

That sounded entirely too likely to be true. A mission too great for the forces assigned, and so some of those forces would be sacrificed to satisfy the unreasonable expectations of the high command. In Geary's time a century earlier those sorts of things had only happened in exercises, fake losses in fake battles, but even then he'd wondered if things would truly be different in a real conflict as he was assured by his seniors, or if the same patterns would play out even though the costs were far higher. From what he'd learned of the war, and seen of it in person, too often the latter was true. "All right, Captain Desjani, let's make sure our fleet will be properly arrayed to take out those battleships without losing any of our own ships."

"Captain Desjani," the engineering watch-stander called. "*Dauntless* just went below fifty percent on fuel cell reserves."

Desjani nodded, then glanced at Geary. "The old girl's never been this low before."

The "old girl" had left her commissioning dock less than two years ago, but it was still a chilling thing to hear. If they didn't manage to loot those Syndic repair ships, the Alliance fleet wouldn't get much farther home. Warships couldn't run on prayers.

Forty minutes since they'd arrived in Lakota again. So far things looked very good. But how much longer would they have before the massive Syndic pursuit force came in behind them, determined to ensure that the Alliance fleet didn't escape again?

TWO

POURING over the top of the Syndic minefield, the jumbled warships of the Alliance fleet had accelerated onto individual vectors. For a moment, the sight of it had brought to Geary's mind the chaotic arrival in Corvus right after he'd assumed command, the Alliance fleet breaking into a wild scramble to attack a few weak Syndic warships. But this time was far different. This time the Alliance warships were following orders, tearing off on courses and speeds that would bring coordinated attacks to bear on every Syndic warship the fleet could reach. Even those officers who didn't like the way Geary fought shouldn't have any problems here, with so many targets available for the ships of the Alliance fleet.

With the orders given, the fleet reacting as it should, and no Syndic pursuit force yet showing up astern, Geary had one of those lulls created by the vast distances of a star system. Even with his ships accelerating to point one light speed, it would take more than an hour and a half just to cover the ten light-minutes separating the fleet from that big Syndic formation of damaged warships and repair ships.

But the Syndics were also moving away from the Alliance ships, though unable to do so nearly as fast the Alliance fleet was charging at them.

"Estimated time to intercept one point seven hours," Desjani grumbled. "They're running, but we'll still be on them well before those two Syndic battleships can reach us."

"We'll have to make sure those battleships are stopped dead before they can smash their way through to any of our auxiliaries." On Geary's display, paths arced through space as Alliance destroyers and light cruisers pulled ahead of the heavier combatants, aiming not only for the largest Syndic formation but also smaller groups and individual ships. "Call it two more hours before we take those Syndic ships. We'll be lucky if we achieve that before the Syndic pursuit comes in behind us."

"Do you suppose any more Syndic reinforcements showed up here after we left?" Desjani wondered.

"Good question. We can't assume the totals we saw at Lakota last time we were here reflect what the Syndics have available now and in the pursuit force. But it looks like what's here is going to fight." Geary watched some of the damaged warships that had been proceeding independently toward the inner planets alter their vectors to come around and head toward individual rendezvous with the two battleships, trying to build a scratch task force. Counting up the ships involved, and their states of repair, Geary shook his head. He knew how they were feeling, badly outnumbered and not prepared for this kind of battle. His own fleet had faced a similar situation when it had last been at Lakota.

Out of the almost eighty Syndic battleships and battle cruisers the Alliance fleet had once faced at Lakota, at least six Syndic battleships and ten Syndic battle cruisers had been destroyed during those battles. Alliance sensors had also been able to confirm twenty Syndic heavy cruisers destroyed then, as well as dozens of light cruisers and Hunter-Killers. But numerous Syndic warships had been badly damaged as well, some of them by *Audacious*, *Indefatigable*, and *Defiant* as they fought to the last. Those damaged Syndic ships had been left behind here when the Syndic

commander took a strike force in pursuit of the fleeing
Alliance fleet.

The large formation of crippled Syndic ships included
four battleships and no less than seven battle cruisers as well
as thirteen heavy cruisers. Trying to close with that formation of badly hurt warships right now in addition to the two
combat-effective battleships from the guard force were one
more battleship, two battle cruisers, and another three heavy
cruisers, all of which had suffered significant damage. Scattered around them were about a dozen light cruisers and
HuKs, which had been limping for repair docks, and some
of those were also trying to join in the defense of their helpless fellows.

He ran out the course vectors and the times. If all of those
ships managed to join together, it would create a weak but
dangerous flotilla. But with the distances involved and the
propulsion damage so many had suffered, the Syndic defenders could only arrive in staggered waves of a few ships
at a time unless they pulled back and tried to form up farther
away from the Alliance fleet, at the cost of letting the Alliance ships tear apart the big formation unhindered. That
would buy the Syndics a little time, but not enough to save
them unless the pursuit force came through that jump point a
lot sooner than Geary hoped.

A pair of tugs had been dragging a riddled Syndic heavy
cruiser only three light-minutes from the jump point. The
unlucky heavy cruiser must have been forced to wait the lon-
gest for a tow to show up. Now, with no hope of running
away from the Alliance destroyers and light cruisers heading
for them, the crews of the tugs abandoned ship, escape pods
spitting frantically from the slow, clumsy vessels. Several
escape pods erupted from the heavy cruiser itself as well,
marking the flight of the salvage crew left aboard the ship.

The Alliance destroyers *Jinto* and *Herebra* reached the
tugs first and blew them into fragments with close-in
hell-lance fire before altering course to head for their next
targets. Right behind them, *Contus*, *Savik*, and the light
cruisers *Tierce*, *Ward*, and *Lunge* rolled past above and to
port of the abandoned heavy cruiser, hell lances slamming

repeatedly into the hulk until it shattered into multiple fragments. "Let's see them recover that," Geary remarked.

"There goes another one," Desjani noted gleefully, as a solitary Syndic light cruiser whose remaining crew had also abandoned ship came apart under the fire of a half dozen Alliance destroyers.

Struck by a sudden thought, Geary sent out orders. "*Ocrea*, pick up some of the escape pods from that Syndic heavy cruiser. I want to know what the crew members from that ship can tell us about how long it took the pursuit force to jump after us and anything else they can tell us about the pursuit force." One of his own heavy cruisers, *Ocrea* wouldn't have interrogation facilities anything like those on *Dauntless*, but he didn't have the luxury of the time to get those prisoners to a capital ship for questioning. Hopefully some of the Syndic crew members would spill their guts after the shock of having the Alliance fleet reappear and destroy their ship.

It was also time to update the maneuvering plan based on what the Syndics were doing. The Syndic defensive moves had actually simplified the Alliance requirements. As Syndic warships came together, Alliance ships that had been dispersed to hit each one individually could also merge into larger formations. Geary frowned at the display, where the enemy flotilla filled with damaged warships had been tagged with the name Casualty Flotilla. The tactical systems automatically named enemy formations, so he was surprised that one had a specific status designator rather than a generic name like "Flotilla Alpha." It was always a little unnerving to him when automated support systems acted a bit too human.

He wasn't trying anything fancy that would require a lot of maneuvering. The subformations would be concentrated into loose, larger formations, which would sweep directly over the largest Syndic formation, the Casualty Flotilla, then onward to hit the less–badly damaged warships trying to form into their own flotilla, then soon afterward the two battleships racing outward from the guard force. "How's this look to you?" he asked Desjani.

She studied it, face intent. "A series of fast firing runs over the Casualty Flotilla to knock out the weapons on the Syndic warships that have any working? You don't want to destroy them right away?"

"Not until our auxiliaries are done looting their repair ships. I don't want to risk debris from destroyed warships messing up our pillaging operation. We can finish off everything when we pull away from the Casualty Flotilla. We'll have four of our battleships with the auxiliaries then."

Desjani nodded. "Even the Third Battleship Division should be able to handle destroying enemy ships with all of their systems knocked out. But you need to leave a couple of more battleships or battle cruisers with the formation containing the auxiliaries."

"Why? I know *Warrior* has been beat to hell again, but *Orion* and *Majestic* can put up a fight and *Conqueror* is in good shape. I'm sticking *Conqueror* with them since she's part of the same battleship division. Those four battleships should be able to handle anything that manages to get through the rest of the fleet."

Desjani kept her expression controlled and her voice bland. "That's true, if *Orion*, *Majestic*, and *Conqueror* do not have *difficulties* engaging the enemy."

Meaning that their commanding officers might find reasons to avoid battle. He had to admit that Desjani's diplomatically worded statement was justified. Captain Casia of *Conqueror* hadn't inspired any confidence. Commander Yin, acting commander of *Orion* since Captain Numos had been relieved of command and placed under arrest, made Casia look like a paragon of a combat officer by comparison. And *Majestic*'s acting commander, who had also gotten his job when his former captain (Numos's ally Captain Faresa) had been relieved for cause, was such a nonentity that Geary had trouble remembering the man's face. In a perfect world he would have replaced all of them by now, but a fleet fleeing for its life through enemy territory was far from a perfect world, especially when the fleet's politics left Geary's hold on command tenuous enough that he couldn't afford to be seen acting too high-handedly. Some officers might work against him more vigorously as a result, and other officers would believe such behavior meant Geary was on his way to accepting the role of the dictator they either hoped or feared he would become.

His frown deepened. "I hate to waste a couple of more capital ships just because those three battleships might encounter problems."

"If the wreck of *Audacious* does hold prisoners who need to be liberated," Desjani pointed out, "they'll need all the shuttles they can get to transfer them off, and ships nearby big enough to hold the liberated prisoners at least temporarily."

"Good point." But that still left the problem of two capital-ship commanders who wouldn't be thrilled to be told to stay back with the auxiliaries. Who might find ways to avoid following his orders, and if they were doing that to race into battle, most of their fellow commanders wouldn't condemn them for it or approve of Geary raising hell with them for abandoning their escort duty. The doctrine of all-out attack was still too thoroughly engrained in the fleet. He glanced back to where Co-President Rione was sitting, watching events with an unreadable expression. "Madam Co-President, I'd appreciate your advice on how to phrase some orders—"

"I heard you." Rione broke in. "Thank you for deigning to include me in your discussions." She paused just long enough for that to sink in. "You're sending these ships to ensure our own people, recently taken prisoner, are liberated and brought to safety. If any Syndic warships get through to the space near what's left of *Audacious*, they could disrupt that action, or even cause some of those prisoners to be killed. What more justification do you need to offer? What more honorable task can a ship be assigned than ensuring our people are safely recovered?"

Geary nodded. "Very well put, Madam Co-President." That left the question of who to send. He ran his eyes across the display, trying to decide who could be trusted and who wouldn't take exaggerated offense at what Rione had pointed out was indeed a highly honorable assignment even if it wasn't in the front of the engagement. He'd already heard indirectly that some officers were regarded as his favorites, and it wouldn't do to reinforce that impression even if it was in many ways true. He did like certain commanding officers because they were capable as well as aggressive, smart as well as brave, loyal to their duties to the Alliance rather than to political games meant to advance their careers. Captain Cresida, for example . . .

Whose battle cruiser *Furious* along with *Implacable* were the last surviving ships of the Fifth Battle Cruiser Division. And he needed two ships. "I'll send Cresida. Her ship and *Implacable*."

Desjani's eyebrows shot up, then hastily lowered again. "She's used to being in the thick of battle."

"Exactly. She's proven her ability to carry out this task."

"I'm glad I'm not the one who'll be telling her that, sir," Desjani responded dryly.

"We're almost a light-minute away from *Furious* now. That ought to be outside the blast radius," Geary noted. Desjani grinned.

He changed the plan, let Desjani see it again for a sanity check, then transmitted the changes. On the heels of that, he called *Furious*. "Captain Cresida, I'm giving *Furious* and *Implacable* the most important job in the fleet. I want you to make sure our imprisoned personnel, and our auxiliaries, are well protected."

Geary barely heard Desjani's low murmur. "Tell her that you're counting on her." She saw his reaction. "It's true. Say it. Sir."

The exchange had taken only a couple of seconds. Geary continued the same transmission. "I'm counting on you, Captain Cresida." It felt absolutely shameless to use that on Cresida. But it *was* true. Desjani was right about that.

Cresida's reply took a little over two minutes, given the distance between her ship and *Dauntless*. To Geary's surprise, Cresida sounded not angry but both pleased and determined. "Yes, sir. *Furious* and *Implacable* won't let our imprisoned comrades down, and won't let you down."

Geary stole a glance at Desjani, who was apparently absorbed in studying her display. Desjani had been giving advice that way almost from the first time he'd met her, Geary realized. Maybe she believed the living stars themselves had sent him, but if she thought there was something Geary needed to know, she'd tell him and keep repeating it until he paid attention. Just as importantly, Desjani wasn't blindly accepting his plans, instead telling him what she thought needed to be changed. He wondered now if she ever had shown total acceptance of his plans, or if her unquestioning faith in his mission had never gotten in the way of telling him when she thought something should be done differently. "Thank you, Captain Desjani."

She glanced his way and nodded with a slight smile. "Captain Cresida needs to be handled just so, sir."

"Just keep giving me advice when I need it."

This time Desjani looked surprised at the statement. "That's my job, sir. Though if I may say so, you take it much better than Admiral Bloch ever did."

He checked the time. Still no sign of the Syndic pursuit force and still over an hour left before the Syndic Casualty Flotilla was overhauled. This was going to be a long day no matter what happened.

"Captain!" a watch-stander called to Desjani. "We've spotted escape pods leaving the repair ships in the Casualty Flotilla."

"What?" Geary thought he and Desjani had said it simultaneously. But the display was indeed showing a swarm of escape pods leaving the Syndic repair ships. "They're punching out of their ships this early?"

Desjani was frowning, apparently trying to figure out what kind of Syndic trick this was. "Did they figure out how badly we need what's in the bunkers on those repair ships? Are they going to blow up all of them before we even get within a couple of light-minutes?" she wondered.

Before Geary could answer, his internal communications circuit buzzed urgently. Lieutenant Iger in the intelligence section. It was very unusual to hear from him during a battle since his work dealt with longer-term collection and analysis, everything of tactical importance being automatically shown on the displays before Geary and other commanders. "Yes, Lieutenant?"

Iger's head within the small pop-up window inclined diffidently. "Sorry to bother you during an action, sir, but—"

"Just tell me, Lieutenant. What is it?"

The intelligence officer looked startled, then spoke quickly. "We've confirmed these are standard Syndic repair ships."

Geary waited, but like the engineers on his own auxiliaries, the intelligence officer apparently expected him to just know things sometimes. "Meaning what? Why are they abandoning ship so early?"

"Because they're not military, sir."

"They're not military?"

Desjani, overhearing, gave Geary a surprised look.

"Yes, sir," Iger responded. "Syndic major logistics support isn't handled by combat arms. It's handled by a different directorate and contracted out to corporations. Our fleet never sees repair ships like these because they're never supposed to go where they can encounter Alliance warships."

"They're civilian?" Geary demanded.

"Yes, sir. Military-related civilian, of course. Totally legitimate targets. But no military personnel aboard, no combat training, no defenses. That's why they're abandoning ship. They and their corporations aren't paid to engage in combat. From what we know, the crews would get in trouble if their actions somehow caused us to inflict more damage on those repair ships. So they're punching out now."

"Wait a minute. They want to ensure as little damage as possible is done to those repair ships?" Iger nodded vigorously. "We know that?"

"Yes, sir. From captured records and prisoner interrogations. Most Syndic fleet personnel don't like the civilian contract people because they don't think they get proper support from them. The civilian contractors are also paid considerably more, which is probably the real main point of contention as far as Syndic military personnel are concerned."

"I'll be damned." Geary thought for a moment. "Then they won't have rigged any traps on those repair ships?"

Iger hesitated, clearly thinking, looked sideways as someone else in the intelligence section spoke to him, then nodded again. "I'd regard that as very unlikely, sir. They'd lose
their jobs if their corporations thought they had caused more
damage to those ships. It's safe to assume they've shut down
all systems and left the repair ships to coast in the hope that
we'll ignore them or just toss a few shots at them as we cruise
past."

"They're going to be disappointed. Thanks, Lieutenant.
Excellent work by you and your people."

As Lieutenant Iger's image vanished, Geary turned to
speak to both Desjani and Rione, then repeated what the
intelligence officer had said. "You've never seen these sorts
of repair ships?" he asked Desjani.

She shook her head. "Only in briefing documents on Syndic ship types. No, I've never encountered one and don't
think I ever ran a simulation with one in it, either."

Turning back to Rione, Geary addressed her. "Does what
Lieutenant Iger said make sense to you?"

"As a civilian?" she asked sardonically.

"Yes." More importantly, as a civilian after a century of
war. Geary's last experience with other civilians had been
almost one hundred years ago, before the war with the Syndicate Worlds began. He'd seen what a century of war had
done to the officers and sailors of the fleet, and wondered
how it had changed civilians.

Rione gazed at him, seeming to guess the reasons for
his question. "Certainly. As much as they'd like their military forces to triumph, as much as they've grown to hate
the enemy, civilians are still not prepared to stand up to
battle. Even if some individuals in those crews were ready
to resist, they would have been carried away by the mass of
their fellows who only wanted to avoid dying." Rione
caught the expression on Desjani's face. "They're *not* cowards," she added in a very cold voice. "Someone who isn't
trained or mentally toughened for combat isn't going to
stand and fight the way military fighting forces are. They're
surely smart enough to know they don't stand a chance
against us."

Desjani shrugged, her eyes on Geary. "Neither do those Syndic warships heading to intercept this fleet."

But Geary shook his head at her. "Staying with those ships when they lack any combat training or capability wouldn't accomplish anything. You or I would at least ensure they weren't captured intact if we had any suspicion the enemy intended doing that, but dying to no purpose wouldn't serve our cause." He jerked his chin toward the display, which showed the two Syndic battleships charging toward them, still hours away from contact. "The Syndic commander is throwing away those ships and crews because he or she can, because those crews will follow senseless orders, even though it's a total waste. May the living stars help me if I ever decide to waste lives like that just because I can."

Desjani frowned slightly, her eyes averted as she thought. It had to be a difficult concept for someone raised and trained to believe that honor demanded fighting to the death. For someone who already knew she would do that if necessary. But then she had made that commitment before joining the fleet and lived with it since then. "Yes, sir," she responded eventually. "I see your point. We expect obedience from those under us, and in return they deserve respect for their willingness to follow orders to the death."

"Exactly." She'd actually said it better than he had. He remembered Desjani once telling him that she'd been offered a job at her uncle's literary agency before she joined the fleet, and once again wondered what Desjani would have been like if she hadn't been born and brought up amidst a war already ancient to the Alliance.

Rione spoke again, her tone genuinely curious. "There's something I don't understand here. You watched the crews of the crippled Syndic warships we've already overrun hastily abandoning their own ships, yet didn't seem to find it dishonorable the way you did the civilians fleeing their ships. Why?"

Desjani grimaced but didn't turn or answer, so Geary did. "Because the warship crews waited until the last minute to abandon ship," he explained.

Co-President Rione eyed him for a moment as if judging

his seriousness. "Even though the action was inevitable, the fact that they waited made it better than if they'd left as soon as it was certain they couldn't escape our pursuit. *That* makes it all right?"

"Well . . . yeah." Geary looked toward Desjani, but she didn't seem interested in helping explain anything to Victoria Rione. "Something might happen. Something unexpected. Maybe we'll veer off. Maybe some big Syndic force will appear behind us at the jump point or come in through the hypernet gate again and cause us to run. Maybe the ships headed for them in particular will have something happen and drop their pursuit. Maybe they'll get another weapon working and be able to put up a decent fight. Maybe a lot of things. So you wait as long as possible, just in case."

"Just in case a miracle happens?" Rione asked.

"Pretty much. Yeah. Because they do. Sometimes. If you keep fighting or remain ready to fight even after it seems hopeless."

She frowned at him, then lowered her eyes for a few moments in thought. "Yes," Rione finally said. "Sometimes miracles happen. As long as you don't give up while any hope remains. I do understand. But at what point does the hope for a miracle change from inspirational motivation to suicidal insanity?"

How to answer that? "It depends," Geary finally stated.

Co-President Rione's eyes rose and locked on his. "And it's the job of the commander to judge the situation and decide whether continuing to hope for a miracle is sensible or insane?"

He didn't like thinking of it in those terms, but . . . "Yeah. I guess so."

Rione's smile appeared to be half-mocking. "Like coming back to Lakota instead of running through Ixion or trying to stand and fight there? I hope your judgment remains as sound in the future, Captain Geary. You seem to have a talent for sniffing out miracles."

He nodded back, unsure of how to respond to that, then faced forward again, noticing as he did so that Desjani seemed slightly baffled. "What's the matter?"

Captain Desjani shook her head. "Nothing, sir."

"Like hell. Is there something I ought to know?"

"No, sir," Desjani repeated, then twisted her mouth in annoyance before answering in a low voice. "I'm just . . . surprised to find myself agreeing with Co-President Rione on anything, sir."

"You're both crazy."

Desjani grinned.

"Update on Syndic warships in the Casualty Flotilla," the operations watch-stander announced.

Geary checked his display. Of the four Syndic battleships undergoing extensive repairs, only one showed signs of powering up any of its weaponry. The others apparently had their systems so badly damaged or extensively dismantled for repairs that they couldn't be activated on such short notice. Out of the seven battle cruisers in the formation, only two revealed indications that some of their hell-lance batteries were being charged. The twelve heavy cruisers seemed marginally better off, with five showing weapons activity.

One of the Syndic battle cruisers, its propulsion system less badly damaged than that of its fellows, had begun accelerating away at a painfully slow rate. "Running?" Desjani wondered, her fingers dancing across controls as she checked something. "Not on that vector. He's trying to join with the other damaged ships forming up ahead of the Casualty Flotilla."

The Syndics were obviously still hoping for their own miracle that would keep the Alliance fleet from annihilating all of the major Syndic combatants currently within reach.

An alert pulsed on his display, drawing Geary's attention. "The automated combat system is recommending we volley rocks at the Casualty Flotilla."

"Kinetic projectiles at ships? Those ships are too badly damaged to maneuver much, but it wouldn't take much to avoid rocks thrown at them from any significant distance." Desjani made a face, checking the recommendation herself. "We'd have to throw a lot of our supply of rocks out there to form a pattern that would have a decent probability of scoring any hits."

"Doesn't seem worth it to me," Geary agreed. "Hey, what about *Audacious*?"

"The recommended pattern would avoid hitting the hulk of *Audacious*, as long as *Audacious* didn't maneuver. Which she could if her tugs yank her off her current course, and walk right into one of our rocks." Desjani shook her head. "And what if the debris from some of the hits on the warships struck the repair ships that we want to loot? Only an artificial intelligence would think this was a good option. I'd give the combat system a 'disregard option' instead of just a 'recommendation noted.' Otherwise, it'll keep trying to refine the recommendation and annoying you with updated alerts about it."

"Good idea." He thumbed the right commands, hoping the disregard order would work since automated systems sometimes seemed able to ignore such commands and kept insistently pushing options they had already been told to forget about. Another case of automated systems acting a little too human at times. "Any idea what made that big hole in *Audacious*? It looks like something blew inside."

Desjani only glanced at her display. "That was her null-field projector self-destructing. The Syndics don't have null-field weapons yet, so there's a multiple-redundant self-destruct capability. Just like for Alliance hypernet keys. We don't want them to fall into enemy hands, either."

"Have any of them ever self-destructed when they weren't supposed to?"

"Not that I've heard of. The weapons-design bureau assured us that it can't possibly happen, so we don't worry about it." Desjani spoke with apparent total seriousness, but couldn't quite keep from smiling at the actual absurdity of her statement. While declarations from the weapons design bureau were supposed to be nonfiction, sailors soon learned from experience to treat them all as fantasy until confirmed by real-world events.

Geary barely managed not to laugh. "Of course not." His alert chimed to mark the arrival of Colonel Carabali's plan. He skimmed through it, stealing occasional looks at the display to make sure nothing unexpected was happening.

The Marine plan was simple enough, using detachments from all four of the battleships accompanying the Alliance auxiliaries, which were heading straight for the Syndic Casualty Flotilla of which *Audacious* was a part. Most of the Marines would assault *Audacious*, using every shuttle available from the battleships and Captain Cresida's battle cruisers. In addition, each boarding team from an Alliance auxiliary would be accompanied by a single Marine fire team to check for booby traps on the repair ships or some Syndic fanatic determined to die fighting.

He paused at the situation assessment. "I hadn't noticed the Syndics evacuating *Audacious*," he remarked to Desjani.

She checked her own display, tapping some recall commands, then nodded. "They pulled out when the other Syndics were bailing out of the repair ships. That's why we didn't notice it, but if you do a situation replay, you can see it clearly enough. There's no change in the readings from *Audacious*, so they didn't vent atmosphere or anything like that."

"Let's hope it simplifies things." He marked the plan approved and sent it back. Even though the Marines had been told they didn't need positive approval, a clean paper trail on orders usually made people happy.

Ten minutes later, as Geary watched for the arrival of the pursuit force and felt pressure building in his head from the growing tension, he got another alert, this time a high-priority communication. Geary barely suppressed a groan when he saw the identification tag. Captain Casia of *Conqueror*, one of the biggest openly pain-in-the-butt senior officers whom he had to deal with right now. But this might be legitimately important. Not likely coming from Casia, but he couldn't risk blowing it off. He tapped the acknowledge control and a window showing Casia's frowning face popped into existence. "Captain Geary," Casia stated heavily, "I've been informed that Marines attached to my ship will be employed in an operation to rescue presumed Alliance prisoners being held by the Syndics on the wreck of *Audacious*."

Geary glanced at *Conqueror*'s position. Ten light-seconds away. Not too annoying a delay in communications, even if the communication itself looked like it would be annoying. "That's correct, Captain Casia," Geary stated in formal tones, then waited to see what Casia's problem was this time.

"I've also been informed that there is no fleet command oversight for the Marines involved," Casia ground out.

Geary gave Casia's image a perplexed look. "That's incorrect, Captain Casia. I'm exercising command over Colonel Carabali, who is in turn directing the Marines according to my orders."

Twenty seconds later, Casia's image frowned even deeper as his reply showed up. "Perhaps oversight of Marines on fleet missions was much laxer before the war. I'm talking about the routine practice of fleet officers conducting direct supervision of Marine officers and senior enlisted who are engaged in ship-boarding operations."

"What?" The command and control systems allowed higher-ranking individuals to see and hear whatever any particular Marine in battle armor was doing, something that Geary thought an occasionally useful but usually dangerously distracting option. Geary muted his comm circuit and pivoted slightly to stare at Desjani. "Captain Desjani, is it true that fleet officers *routinely* look over the shoulder of Marines engaged in ship-boarding ops?"

Desjani rolled her eyes in aggravation. "Who brought that up?"

"Captain Casia."

"That figures. Sir," she added hastily as if suddenly remembering she was discussing the issue with her fleet commander. Desjani sighed, ran one hand through her hair, then spoke in a monotone. "Such oversight for warship boarding has been routine as long as I've been in the fleet."

"Why?"

"Because it's feared that Marines boarding a warship will punch the wrong buttons and wreck or blow up important things, including the ship."

"Am I wrong in assuming that the Marines have orders *not* to punch buttons unless they know what they're doing?" Geary demanded.

Desjani shrugged. "Of course they have orders not to punch strange buttons, sir. But they *are* Marines."

That was a point, Geary had to admit. Thousands of years of human technological advancement had yet to produce a single piece of equipment that was Marine-proof, or sailor-proof, for that matter. That was one of the main reasons why chief petty officers in the fleet and sergeants in the Marines had no fear of being rendered obsolete, since one of their primary functions remained to yell, "Don't Touch Anything Unless I Tell You To," at the more-junior enlisted whenever necessary. But because the Marines did have sergeants, Geary didn't see what purpose was served by having fleet officers tag along with the Marines via the command and control system. "What level of officers are we talking about? The ones assigned to this oversight of Marines?"

"Ships' commanding officers," Desjani replied in the same monotone.

"You're kidding."

"No, sir."

"Who's supposed to be commanding their ships while they're supervising junior Marine officers?"

Desjani's mouth twisted into a bitter smile. "I asked that same question of Admiral Bloch the last time I was assigned to stay on the shoulder of a Marine second lieutenant as he led a platoon aboard a Syndic warship. Admiral Bloch informed me that he had every confidence that an officer of my skills and experience could easily do both things at once."

Not for the first time, Geary felt a guilty sense of relief that Admiral Bloch had died before Geary had been required actually to serve as Bloch's subordinate. "I think I can already tell the answer to this, but do you personally see any good reason for doing that?"

Another shrug. "It's possible to find reasons, but there's plenty of reasons not to do it, too. I wouldn't ever do it by choice, sir."

"That's what I thought. I wouldn't, either." Turning back to front, Geary unmuted his circuit and gave Casia a serious but noncommittal look. "Thank you for bringing this to my attention. I'll ensure the Marines are aware of the need to consult fleet officers before taking any actions that might impact on the safety or security of the ship they're boarding."

Another twenty seconds or so, and Casia's frown was just as deep, but now accompanied by a slightly flushed face. "There are good reasons for current policies, Captain Geary. Failure to abide by experience gained in *wartime* could have deadly results for those prisoners we hope to liberate."

That was as pointed a barb as had been shot his way in a while, Geary reflected. It was true in a way, because he did lack the length of wartime experience of the other officers in the fleet. But also untrue, because he hadn't learned any wrong lessons. If there was one thing he was certain of, it was that senior officers had no business riding on the backs of junior officers trying to do their jobs. He'd had entirely too much experience dealing with that as a junior officer himself. "Thank you for your input, Captain Casia," Geary stated in a level voice. "It will be given full consideration, and any actions deemed appropriate will be taken." Maybe peacetime experience wasn't the same as wartime experience, but it had taught Geary how to say "get off my back" in totally professional and polite language.

From the look on Casia's face less than half a minute later, that officer hadn't had any trouble deciphering the meaning behind Geary's words. "After the disaster this fleet experienced during our last period in Lakota—"

Geary used his authority as fleet commander and activated his override. If he listened, he'd get mad, and he didn't want anger clouding his judgment. Wishing for a moment that Captain Casia had his own "disregard option" button, Geary spoke in a hard voice. "If you want to be relieved of command prior to combat, Captain Casia, you can retransmit your last message. Or you can stop beating a dead horse and get on with your job. If you wish to have a personal meeting after this engagement to discuss the command structure of this fleet and your place in it, I will be happy to oblige. Rest assured that the Marines are being competently supervised and that your concerns have been noted for the record. End of transmission," he added unnecessarily before breaking contact with *Conqueror*.

Captain Desjani was doing a very good imitation of someone totally unaware that her superior officer was unhappy. Around the bridge of *Dauntless*, the watch-standers were doing the same imitation with varying degrees of success. They couldn't have heard anything Geary had said within the sound-deadening field that gave privacy to his conversations with other ships, but any junior officer soon learned the essential art of reading a superior's mood by unspoken clues like body language.

Geary fumed a moment longer, then took a deep breath and called Colonel Carabali, who eyed him warily. "Colonel, I'm assuming that having fleet commanding officers directly supervising your people going aboard *Audacious* would be an unwelcome distraction."

"That's a safe assumption, Captain Geary," the Marine colonel agreed.

"I'm also assuming that your senior enlisted and junior officers are capable of preventing any Marines from pushing buttons at random or accidentally overloading *Audacious*'s power core."

"Yes, sir."

"And I'm assuming that if any Marine needs guidance or instructions from fleet personnel on how to deal with anything aboard *Audacious* they will have both the knowledge and ability to ask for those things."

"Yes, sir."

"In short, Colonel, I am assuming that your Marines have the experience, training, and intelligence to carry out their tasks without direct supervision from senior fleet officers."

"Yes, sir."

"Good." Geary felt himself relaxing, while Carabali watched him as if she were trying to spot an ambush. "I'd appreciate it if you were to help me demonstrate the truth of my assumptions. If your Marines can take *Audacious* without blowing up anything or venting the ship's atmosphere into space, I will be able to provide a solid example of their ability to function effectively without fleet officers breathing down their necks."

Colonel Carabali nodded. "Of course, sir. There won't be any screwups."

"Hell, Colonel, there are always screwups in any operation. Let's just keep them within reason."

Carabali finally grinned, then saluted. "Yes, sir. I'll let my people know of your confidence in them and reemphasize that they should ask for guidance if in doubt."

"And avoid pushing strange buttons," Geary couldn't help adding.

"Absolutely, sir. Because we'll be assaulting a ship that likely holds many Alliance prisoners of war, I've had my platoon and squad leaders instruct their Marines to exercise the highest level of fire discipline. They won't shoot at anyone or anything unless they know it's enemy."

"Good idea."

"They're all volunteers as well," the colonel added. "Since there's a chance the Syndics might have rigged the ship's power core to blow once our assault force is aboard."

Geary felt his teeth clench at the thought. "I can't tell you how much I appreciate their willingness to participate in the operation despite that chance, Colonel. I've warned the Syndics not to try anything like that, and warned what will happen to them if they do. Their escape pods can't outrun our ships."

The Marine colonel bared her teeth. "Thank you, sir."

"Thank you, Colonel. Let me know if anything significant about the plan changes." Carabali's image vanished, and Geary leaned back with a sigh.

"Another crisis averted?" Rione asked.

"Dealt with, anyway," Geary responded. "Have you heard anything I should know about now?"

She gave him an arch look, knowing he was referring to her spies within the fleet. "Nothing that can't wait." Rione hesitated, then stood up and walked close enough to speak softly. "Only a few of my agents have been able to get quick reports to me. They all say that those opposed to you were thrown off completely by your decision to return immediately to Lakota. Your opponents are now apparently waiting to see what happens before preparing their next moves."

"Thank you. What do you think? How does it all feel to you?"

"You want *my* advice?" Rione asked coldly. "Why not ask your flagship's captain again?"

Oh, for the love of my ancestors. "I ask her questions about fleet operations. Is there something wrong with that?"

"Of course not," Rione replied in tones that implied the opposite, then answered his first question without missing a beat. "Your enemies in the fleet are quiet and waiting. Until the situation in this star system is resolved, they won't act for fear that they themselves will be stuck trying to handle a dangerous Syndic trap."

Geary nodded, keeping his thoughts to himself. *If I fail, they have what they need to push for my replacement as fleet commander. Not that there's likely to be much of the fleet left to command if I fail. And apparently none of them want to try overcoming the Syndic presence in this star system.*

His eyes went to the display, looking again for what ought to be there by now. Still no Syndic pursuit force arriving via the jump point for Ixion. Geary's fingers drummed restlessly on one arm of his command seat. Why hadn't the pursuit shown up yet? They'd been in this star system for well over two hours now. Every additional minute was a gift, but he distrusted gifts that came for reasons he didn't understand. While he had told Rione of his hope for three hours' grace time and had been praying for that much, he'd actually assumed it would be less than two hours before the leading elements of the Syndic pursuit appeared. Even allowing for time needed to reorganize the Syndic flotillas, then to turn around at Ixion once they discovered the Alliance fleet had jumped back here, a decent pursuit should already have shown up in Lakota again.

Another high-priority message, this one from *Ocrea*, thirty light-seconds distant, which would make for a slow but not intolerable conversation. Geary wondered why the heavy cruiser would be calling him, then remembered that he'd asked that ship to pick up and interrogate some Syndics. "Geary here. Did any of the Syndics talk?"

Ocrea's captain nodded. "One did. Most of them just parroted the usual Syndic nonsense about it being a privilege to be a citizen of the Syndicate Worlds. But we got one senior enlisted who's apparently decided that this fleet can't be destroyed and that anyone trying is going against the will of the living stars. So he's spilling his guts about whatever he knows, thinking that's the only way to atone for helping to attack us." He paused for Geary's reaction.

"I like that attitude," Geary noted.

One minute later, *Ocrea*'s captain nodded. "Me, too, sir. This Syndic sailor doesn't know much, but he did know that we took out the Syndic flagship during our fight before the jump for Ixion. The senior Syndic CEO didn't make it off alive, and that left two CEOs of lower-but-equal rank arguing over who would get to command the force pursuing us to Ixion. Our source can't remember exactly how long, but he said it was at least four hours. Maybe even more than five, while the Syndic flotilla here hung around doing nothing." The other officer paused for Geary's reply.

"At least four hours?" Geary questioned. He'd targeted the center of the Syndic formation hoping for that, but hadn't known if he'd succeeded. "That sailor is certain?"

"Yes, sir. Unfortunately, he can't tell us anything more specific than 'big' about the size of the force that pursued us to Ixion. The only other thing he seems to know that's useful is that some of the badly damaged Syndic ships left behind here were required to transfer some crew members to the ships chasing after us. This guy thought they were to replace battle casualties, but said a lot of ships were undercrewed these days in terms of skilled personnel. The Syndics seem to have lost a larger than usual number of better-trained people lately, more than their training pipeline can replace for a while." This time *Ocrea*'s captain smiled in a very satisfied way.

"That's great work," Geary stated with total sincerity. "Do you think any of your prisoners are worth hanging on to for transfer to a ship with more sophisticated interrogation facilities?"

"I really doubt it, sir. Even the one who gave away everything he could doesn't really know anything beyond what I told you. In my opinion, they're not worth keeping." The commanding officer of *Ocrea* seemed struck by an unexpected thought. "I guess we could just put them back in their escape pods and relaunch them. We've done that with others lately, haven't we?"

Geary nodded, trying not to show his relief. Not too long ago *Ocrea*'s captain, like every other officer in the fleet, might simply have spaced the Syndic prisoners if dealing with them seemed too difficult. That he had on his own suggested a humane way of getting them off the fleet's hands was a very good sign that the concept of honor was returning to its old meaning. "That sounds like an excellent plan."

The other officer smiled. "Any messages from the living stars that we should give this guy to spread around?"

Geary almost jumped on that opportunity, then paused. It felt wrong in some indefinable way, as if someone was giving him a warning he couldn't hear or see but only sense. "That might not be such a good idea. His own ideas he can spread, but I wouldn't want to offend the living stars by presuming to speak for them."

The smile on the face of *Ocrea*'s captain disappeared. "I wasn't suggesting sacrilege, sir."

"I know that. But what we think is okay might not be in their eyes. Right? Better safe than sorry."

"True." *Ocrea*'s commanding officer nodded. "We seem to be in their favor right now, and I wouldn't want that to change. Thank you, sir. We'll relaunch the Syndic escape pods within the next ten minutes or so."

"Sounds good. Thanks again for outstanding work."

As the window showing *Ocrea*'s captain vanished, Geary turned to speak to both Desjani and Rione, filling them in on the news before adding his interpretation. "The surviving Syndic CEOs each wanted to be the one who could claim credit for destroying this fleet at Ixion, so they spent hours arguing over who would be in charge. Co-President Rione, don't the Syndics have some sort of seniority system like our date of rank?"

She shook her head. "CEO positions straddle both civilian and military commands. A CEO's standing is partially set by his level, but also by political influence."

"You're saying their command structure resembles . . ." He gave Desjani an apologetic glance. "Resembles what this fleet was like? I would have expected the Syndics to have a rigid command structure. Everything I've seen reflects that."

"Up to a certain point," Rione explained patiently, though with an amused glance at Desjani's discomfort. "Anyone below the rank of CEO had better do as they're told and not make waves. But once someone reaches CEO level, the knives come out. Among Syndic CEOs, it's constant political jockeying for position and higher-level assignments, culminating in those who manage to scheme, backslap, and backstab their way to the Executive Council."

"It doesn't sound all that different from our politicians," Desjani murmured as if to herself, yet loudly enough that Rione probably heard it.

But Rione just smiled coldly as she kept her eyes on Geary. "The CEO who can take credit for killing you will be on a fast track for that Executive Council. Small wonder the two surviving CEOs with the Syndic flotilla wasted precious time fighting for the post of commander. Contrary to what that Syndic sailor thought, they most likely weren't arguing with each other but each trying to convince the flotilla's commanding officers that existing orders and regulations meant that he or she should assume command of the flotilla. Those commanding officers would have been terrified of agreeing to follow the orders of someone without good bureaucratic justification that would allow them to claim they'd had no alternative."

"Not the same as this fleet at all, then," Geary observed. The Alliance fleet had looked for a leader after Admiral Bloch died, while the Syndic flotilla had tried to agree on what the regulations said. If the fleet had simply bowed to regulations, his own status as commander never would have been questioned since his seniority as a captain dated from a century ago when he received his "posthumous" promotion, considerably earlier by many decades than any other captain in the fleet could claim. But it was easy to imagine that the other problems ship commanders frightened of breaking the rules would have created would have more than balanced out the scales. "We lucked out, and it bought us at least four hours of delay in the Syndic pursuit, maybe more."

"We didn't 'luck out,' sir," Desjani objected. "You aimed our first attack on the Syndic formation at the point where you thought their flagship would be."

Rione spoke pointedly to Geary. "Don't forget that whoever is commanding the Syndic ships left here is the CEO who lost that dispute over who'd be in command of the pursuit force. That may influence how they're reacting to this fleet now."

"Good point," Geary agreed. "But how will it influence that CEO?"

"Whatever happens here is the fault of the CEO who assumed overall command and took off with the pursuit force. They wanted the command so they could gain the credit, but now it will position them to receive the blame. When that force gets back to Lakota, their CEO is going to be frantic to deal us a serious enough blow to make up for what you've done here."

At least four hours. The tense muscles in Geary's back relaxed a bit.

His fleet could do a lot of damage with a four-hour head start.

THREE

THREE more Syndic light cruisers were torn apart, then the major elements of the Alliance fleet converged on the Syndic Casualty Flotilla. A new swarm of escape pods marked many of the remaining crew members on the crippled Syndic warships without any combat capability abandoning their vessels. With the Casualty Flotilla inching away from its Alliance attackers, the engagement speed was a relatively slow point one light speed, or a mere thirty thousand kilometers per second. Fleet engagements often involved ships crossing paths at combined speeds of close to point two light speed, the limit beyond which targeting systems could not effectively adjust for relativistic effects, which warped the outside view of the universe.

As it was, even at point one light speed a firing pass came down to a mere fraction of a second in which weapons were in range, automated systems aiming and firing since human senses couldn't possibly react quickly enough.

The First and Seventh Battle Cruiser Divisions, totaling only three warships each, roared into range first. The Alliance ships were all approaching from behind and slightly above the big, flattened sphere of the Syndic formation. The sphere was a lousy combat formation but had probably been chosen as the most efficient for repair work. With the remaining Syndic ships in the Casualty Flotilla unable to maneuver, the Alliance warships could safely cut through the Syndic formation to attack any ship within it. Captain Duellos's *Courageous* led *Formidable* and *Intrepid* in a close pass over the single Syndic battleship in the formation that had been able to charge up some weapons. Normally a battleship could have slugged it out with three battle cruisers for some time, but in this case the damaged battleship had many systems only half-repaired. Its shields were spotty, its armor still had many penetrations unsealed, and most of its weapons were inoperable. The Alliance battle cruisers unleashed a devastating barrage as they tore past, hell lances aimed to knock out anything still working on the battleship.

As Duellos's battle cruisers raced onward, *Opportune*, *Brilliant*, and *Inspire* targeted one of the Syndic battle cruisers and a nearby heavy cruiser, which had managed to get some weapons working. A flurry of hits left both Syndic warships totally disabled as the Seventh Battle Cruiser Division followed Duellos's ships toward the crippled battle cruiser that had earlier left the Casualty Flotilla and was trying to join up with the two Syndic battleships charging on their futile mission to protect the damaged ships.

Several minutes later, Captain Tulev's *Leviathan* led his battle cruisers to knock out two more heavy cruisers and finish off the surviving weapons on the battleship.

Captain Desjani had slipped into her targeting mode, her eyes locked on her display as *Dauntless*, *Daring*, and *Victorious* closed the distance to the remaining Syndic Casualty Flotilla battle cruiser that still had working weapons. "*Dauntless* and *Daring* target weapons, *Victorious* target other working systems," she ordered.

The big Syndic formation flashed past too quickly for Geary's senses to register anything, but the display updated rapidly as the fleet's sensors evaluated the results of the firing pass. The Syndic battle cruiser was tagged with a mission-kill marker, all systems taken out, as *Dauntless*'s watch-standers called out the results of the enemy's weak defensive fire. "One hell-lance hit on forward shields. No damage. *Daring* reports two hits, no damage. *Victorious* reports no hits."

"It's too easy," Desjani grumbled.

"You'll get a decent fight out of those two battleships up ahead," Geary assured her.

"That's right." Desjani brightened up, focusing on her ship's next targets.

About five minutes later, the Sixth Battle Cruiser Division hit the Syndic Casualty Flotilla. Captain Badaya only had *Illustrious* and *Incredible* surviving in his division, but that was more than enough to handle the two injured Syndic heavy cruisers, which were the only warships in the Casualty Flotilla that still had any working weapons. As the last two Alliance battle cruisers smashed the Syndic heavy cruisers, a final burst of escape pods erupted from Syndic warships throughout the Casualty Flotilla, marking the last crew members abandoning their ships now that all hope of resistance was gone.

"They're not blowing up their ships, either," Rione observed.

"No," Geary agreed. "Same logic as with the repair ships. The Syndics own this star system and know we'll have to leave, so they're hoping to salvage those ships afterward if we don't have a chance to destroy them. We'll have to make sure they can't do that."

Duellos's battle cruisers overtook another Syndic heavy cruiser trying to join up with the surviving Syndic battle cruiser, lashing it with a barrage that tore the heavy cruiser apart. Not much farther onward lay the crippled Syndic battle cruiser limping frantically toward the oncoming but far-distant pair of Syndic battleships. Right behind Duellos's warships came the battle cruisers of the Seventh Division, which slapped the remains of the heavy cruiser with a few more hell-lance hits as they tore past.

The Syndic battle cruiser seemed in a hopeless position, but as Duellos brought *Courageous*, *Formidable*, and *Intrepid* in for a killing shot, the Syndic pivoted at just the right moment and accelerated downward and to port. Duellos's battle cruisers were moving so much faster than the Syndic that they couldn't react in time and could only hurl a few long-range hell lances at the enemy ship.

But *Brilliant*, *Inspire*, and *Opportune* were far enough behind the first Alliance battle cruisers to be able to react to the evasive maneuver, and close enough behind that the Syndic couldn't maneuver again before they got within range.

Geary tried to pull up mental images of the captains of *Brilliant*, *Inspire*, and *Opportune* and found himself oddly unable. Why hadn't those battle-cruiser commanders ever impressed themselves on him? The realization bothered him, and he tried to bookmark in his memory the need to look up all three when time permitted.

The Syndic battle cruiser rolled and pitched slightly under the push of its working maneuvering thrusters. The change in aspect allowed the battle cruiser to bring its surviving hell lances to bear, and the charged-particle streams shot out, targeting *Brilliant* as she, *Inspire*, and *Opportune* altered their own vectors slightly to pass just to starboard and above the Syndic warship. *Brilliant*'s shields flared from a few hits while she and *Inspire* hurled volleys of hell lances into the weak shields of the Syndic ship. The Syndic's shields collapsed under the barrage, then the Alliance hell lances lashed through the enemy battle cruiser, slicing apart hull, bulkheads, equipment, and any crew members unfortunate enough to be in the way.

By the time *Leviathan*, *Dragon*, *Steadfast*, and *Valiant* reached the Syndic battle cruiser, the enemy couldn't maneuver and could only fire back with a single hell lance. Tulev's battle cruisers battered the Syndic and went onward toward the battleships and lighter units trying to join up, leaving a silent hulk in their wake.

"His weapons and propulsion units are all dead, but something's still working on him, and his crew hasn't abandoned ship," Desjani remarked, her voice almost pleading for an order to swing *Dauntless* over and get in the death-blow on the Syndic warship.

Geary nodded, his eyes on the display. "*Daring* is in a better position to finish him off. Let's let her do it." Desjani nodded, barely hiding her disappointment.

Daring angled slightly up and over, flashing by the crippled Syndic battle cruiser in another flurry of hell-lance fire. As *Daring* raced onward, the Syndic ship abruptly exploded as its power core overloaded. "Did any escape pods get away?" Geary wondered, suddenly realizing he hadn't seen any.

A watch-stander shook her head. "A couple launched just before the core blew but got caught in the explosion."

"Bastard," Desjani muttered, clearly referring to the commanding officer of the Syndic ship who'd waited too late to allow the crew to abandon ship.

"You're unhappy about Syndics dying?" Geary asked, surprised at Desjani's being concerned about that. Tanya Desjani not only considered it her duty to destroy enemy ships and kill enemy military forces, but had usually seemed to derive a vengeful pleasure from the act.

Now she frowned at his question. "It's just as well those crew members won't be a threat to our people anymore," Desjani explained, "but their commanding officer still had an obligation to give them a fighting chance. You know what I mean."

He did, having given just such orders to most of his own crew to abandon ship a hundred years ago, as his fight at Grendel went from desperate to hopeless. "Yeah. I know."

The onrushing Alliance battle cruisers, totally in their element as their speed allowed them to run down lighter enemy combatants, gleefully shattered a succession of Syndic HuKs and light cruisers, almost as an afterthought blowing apart the two remaining operational Syndic heavy cruisers nearby. Watching his battle cruisers charging through space to smash enemy ships while the Alliance battleships were still just short of reaching the Syndic Casualty Flotilla, Geary finally understood why the best officers in the Alliance aspired to command battle cruisers. It was as glorious as a charge by ancient horse cavalry on a planetary surface. But even now he couldn't help wondering how many times battle cruisers had been ripped open in battle against more heavily armored battleships, and whether the number of engagements in which battle cruisers had been able to charge gloriously across the field of battle came anywhere close to the number times they had suffered from their lack of armor.

Behind *Dauntless* and the other battle cruisers, the Alliance battleships had altered courses slightly, aiming farther above the Syndic Casualty Flotilla and at an intercept with the two Syndic battleships still several light-minutes away. All around them, destroyers and light cruisers that had finished wiping out nearby Syndic ships were joining up with the battleships. In the very rear of what could loosely be called the Alliance fleet formation came the four fast fleet auxiliaries with their escorts of four battleships, Captain Cresida's two battle cruisers, and about twenty light cruisers and destroyers. Unlike the other Alliance ships, the auxiliaries had kept their courses aimed straight for an intercept with the Syndic repair ships in the center of the flattened bubble making up the Casualty Flotilla.

"Our leading battle cruisers are two light-minutes short of those two Syndic battleships," Desjani remarked. "They've been designated Syndic Flotilla Bravo. I wonder why the system didn't just call them the Syndic Suicide Flotilla."

She had a point, but Geary gestured to indicate the Alliance auxiliaries. "If they can somehow bull their way through to our auxiliaries, they could hurt us in a critical way."

Desjani shook her head. "If they manage to get past everything we've got headed for them, they'll be so weakened that Cresida's ships can handle them."

"I'm not happy with battle cruisers dueling with battleships," Geary noted, worried that his aggressive commanders might get carried away in the thrill of the battle so far. But he couldn't give orders telling them not to be too aggressive. None of them would listen. He tapped his communications controls again. "All Alliance battle-cruiser formations, upon completion of firing passes against Syndic Flotilla Bravo, brake your velocity to match that of the Syndic Casualty Flotilla and await orders. All Alliance battleship formations are also to brake velocity to match the Casualty Flotilla's speed as soon as Syndic Flotilla Bravo has been destroyed."

As he was speaking, shuttles sprang away from the Alliance ships bearing down on the Casualty Flotilla, each shuttle bending its course toward specific targets. Most were aimed at the wreck of *Audacious*, but others headed for Syndic repair ships and nearby warships to ensure they were truly abandoned and safe for the Alliance ships to approach.

The shuttles were still headed for their objectives when Duellos's battle cruisers and Syndic Flotilla Bravo tore past each other at a combined velocity just in excess of point two light speed. At that velocity, relativistic effects distorted the view of other objects enough to make targeting difficult, and the firing window when weapons were in range of the enemy was the tiniest fraction of a second.

As the two formations of ships separated again, Geary could see that the shields on the Syndic battleships had been weakened, but no hits had been scored. The Syndics, though, had concentrated their massive firepower against *Formidable*, doubtless having seen the damage that Alliance battle cruiser still carried from her last encounter with the enemy. *Formidable* had taken a flurry of hits, losing much of her combat capability, but had avoided taking any more damage to her propulsion units and kept up with her sister ships.

Brilliant, *Opportune*, and *Inspire* hit the Syndic battleships next, weakening the enemy shields a little more, *Opportune* taking several nasty hits in the process.

Tulev's four battle cruisers concentrated their fire on the Syndic battleship closest to them as they shot past just to port of the enemy, managing to cause some spot failures of the battleship's shields but taking a few hits to *Dragon*.

Desjani brought her battle cruisers in while Geary hoped she wouldn't push her firing pass in too close to the still–extremely dangerous Syndic battleships. The Syndics tried to concentrate their fire on already-damaged *Daring*, but Desjani had arranged the intercept so that *Daring* was farthest from the enemy, helping *Daring* to avoid the damage that *Formidable* had suffered. *Dauntless* and *Victorious* slammed shots at the Syndic battleship that still had the strongest shields, weakening the enemy's protection further while managing to avoid taking more damage themselves.

That left *Illustrious* and *Incredible* to hammer the first Syndic battleship again. As the last two Alliance battle cruisers finished their firing passes, the enemy battleships kept onward, their shields seriously weakened but their armor and all weapons and other systems intact, still headed on a curving intercept course aimed at the Alliance auxiliaries.

But bearing down on the Syndic battleships were the Alliance battleships of the Second, Fifth, and Eighth Divisions. Twelve to two would have been awful odds under any circumstances, but the Alliance battleships also had shields at full strength while the Syndics' shields were slowly recovering.

Geary grinned as he saw that the three Alliance subformations had stuck to the maneuvering plan that coordinated their movements. *Gallant*, *Indomitable*, *Glorious*, and *Magnificent* slashed by just above the Syndic battleships, followed milliseconds later by *Relentless*, *Reprisal*, *Superb*, and *Splendid* making a firing pass just beneath the Syndics, a few seconds after that *Fearless*, *Resolution*, *Redoubtable*, and *Warspite* pounding them from the starboard side. That much firepower hitting that quickly left the beleaguered Syndics without a chance. The Syndics fired back, scoring a couple of hits on *Glorious* and *Fearless*, but as the twelve Alliance battleships pulled away, they left behind them an expanding ball of debris that marked the destruction of one Syndic battleship and a tumbling mass of wreckage that had once been the second enemy battleship. A few escape pods spat from the ruin of the second battleship as it tumbled silently off to one side of its original vector.

By the time Captain Armus's Tenth Battleship Division reached engagement range thirty seconds later, all his four battleships could do was tear the remains of the second Syndic battleship into a lot of smaller pieces of wreckage.

Geary sighed with relief, then broadcast commands

again. "All Alliance ships with the exception of the Auxiliaries formation are to assume station on flagship *Dauntless* as indicated." On his display, the intended formation looked like a ragged ball extending outward in front of and slightly above the Syndic Casualty Flotilla, the subformations built around Alliance battle cruisers and battleships arranged roughly in a sphere. It wasn't pretty, but it would do.

Desjani gave him a questioning look, knowing that Geary favored neat formations. "Saving fuel cells?"

"That's part of it. This keeps maneuvering by our ships to a minimum. I was also thinking that if the fleet looks a little sloppy when the Syndic pursuit force arrives, they might think the Alliance fleet is still on the verge of falling apart like it appeared when we left Lakota the first time."

"Will they believe that after seeing what we've already done to the Syndics in this star system?" she asked doubtfully.

"The odds were good enough that even a disorganized force could have mangled the Syndics here. Maybe it won't fool the Syndics, but there's no sense in wasting fuel cells right now. Once the pursuit force shows up, we'll get moving fast and get everything neatened up then."

All the Alliance warships had pivoted to use their main propulsion units to slow down so they wouldn't get too far from the critically important Alliance auxiliaries, assuming their positions in the formation that Geary had mentally labeled the Big Ugly Ball. With that situation well in hand, the Syndic pursuit force still not having arrived, and the nearest operational Syndic combatants almost a light-hour distant and hauling ass away from the Alliance fleet, Geary gave in to temptation again and pulled up a view from one of the Marine officers retaking the *Audacious*.

The shuttles had mated not only with the remains of *Audacious*'s external air locks and shuttle dock but also with a few spots where big holes had been blown in the battleship's armor. Marine detachments had swarmed into the silent ship, ready for anything. Now, Geary's view from the combat armor of the Marine he'd chosen showed the battleship's interior rendered strange by tremendous amounts of internal

damage and a lack of regular lighting. The Marine lieutenant and his squad reached an internal air lock that had been
repaired just enough to function and passed through into
areas where temporary patches had been slapped on holes in
bulkheads to seal in atmosphere.

The Alliance Marines moved swiftly, their battle-armor
sensors scanning for booby traps, their weapons seeking targets as they came around corners and pulled themselves down
passageways cluttered with wreckage. No enemies revealed
themselves, and no traps materialized, which instead of being
reassuring just made everyone more nervous. Another hatch
loomed, this one locked. The Marines paused, most on guard,
weapons ready, while one of their number applied a mini
charge and blew the lock apart. "No stun grenades!" someone
barked over the Marine command circuit.

"But, Sarge, there might be—"

"There might be Alliance prisoners of war on the other
side of that hatch, and we don't know how bad off our own
people on this hulk might be. Even a stun charge might kill
'em. Aimed shots only, and nobody fire unless you have
positive ID on enemy targets. I'll personally shoot any bitch
or son of a bitch who puts a round into an Alliance prisoner
of war. Understand?" A chorus of assents sounded.

One Marine grabbed the hatch and tugged it open as his
comrades' weapons leveled to aim into the large compartment beyond.

For a moment Geary feared that the compartment was
stuffed full of dead Alliance personnel, but then he saw resigned, rebellious, and frightened expressions on the faces
turning to the hatch, each emotion changing to disbelief as
the former prisoners recognized Alliance Marine combat
armor. "The air in there sucks," the Marine lieutenant reported to his superior. "CO_2 is way too high."

"Get them out as fast as you can," the order came back.
"Third Platoon is rigging an evac tube from the last working
air lock to the shuttles. Get them moving!"

The uniforms on the prisoners showed insignia from a
mix of ships. In the front ranks Geary saw patches from
Indefatigable, *Audacious* herself, the heavy cruiser *Bassinet*,

and the destroyer *Talwar*. Some of the newly liberated Alliance personnel were grinning as the Marines hauled them out of the fetid compartment, some just seemed stunned as the Marines shoved them in the direction of the air lock. "First Squad! Line the passageways to direct these guys and keep them moving!"

A chief petty officer with a patch from *Defiant* and one arm in an improvised sling paused as he came out of the compartment. "First time I was ever happy to see a Marine," he gasped to one. "I could kiss you."

"I don't swing that way, Chief," the Marine replied. "Try my friend over there. But keep moving."

Another call on the Marine command circuit. "They found another compartment down this way, Lieutenant! Looks like it's full of space squids, too."

"Get 'em out here and on the way to the evac tube! Go, go, go!"

Geary broke the connection, wishing he could keep watching but knowing he had other responsibilities. Seeing Desjani watching him, he gave a nod. "The Marines are getting our people off of *Audacious*. It looks like a lot were on there."

"Good." Desjani nodded as well, toward the display before her. "Our auxiliaries are closing on the Syndic repair ships right now."

The four Alliance auxiliaries had overhauled four big Syndic repair ships, and now were gliding into position directly over the Syndic vessels, conveyor tubes extending outward and down from their undersides as if they were gigantic creatures intent on mating with even more enormous partners. Which, in a way, they were. It took a little playing with his menus, but Geary managed to bring up a diagram showing the activity inside the Syndic ships. Symbols representing Alliance engineers were blowing out bulkhead after bulkhead until clear paths existed into the raw-materials bunkers on the Syndic auxiliaries, then as each path was opened, more Alliance conveyor tubes extended down into the Syndic ships and began draining out their materials.

"Oddly disquieting imagery, isn't it?" Rione murmured

from over his shoulder. She'd gotten up and come to stand just behind him. "Or is that just a woman's perspective?"

Geary shook his head. "Not once the conveyor tubes started sucking stuff out of those Syndic ships. I guess we're not used to seeing parasites on that scale."

"Do they have what we need?"

"Some of it." Geary scowled at the display. Multiple overlapping windows showed exhaustive detail on fleet requirements and what had been discovered inside the Syndic repair ships. The mass of small type and unfamiliar terms made it impossible for him to figure out what was happening. "Why can't this just tell me how much we need of each material and how much we're getting? Captain Desjani, could you ask your engineering watch-stander to pop me up a display showing in simple terms where we stand on refilling our auxiliaries' bunkers?"

Desjani nodded and passed on the order, then smiled with satisfaction. "We've received two heavy resupply shuttles from *Titan*, sir. *Dauntless* will be back up to sixty-five percent fuel-cell reserves when the new ones are installed. We've also received sixty more canisters of grapeshot and seven new specters as well as some major spare parts we needed but weren't able to fabricate ourselves."

"Excellent. Is that all *Titan* is sending *Dauntless*?"

"Time permitting, we'll get a third shuttle, sir."

Even better. Geary felt himself smiling. "Now if we can only get food."

The engineering watch-stander had come up and now cleared his throat to attract attention. "Excuse me, sir. If I may . . ." His fingers tapped controls rapidly, then Geary saw a window appear with bar graphs showing total capacity of the bunkers on his auxiliaries, total materials found on the Syndic auxiliaries, and how much had been transferred. "Thanks. What's this column?"

"Food, sir," the engineer replied in that self-satisfied way of someone who'd already answered a question his superior hadn't yet asked him. "The Syndic ships we've boarded have all had food stocks on them. From what I've overheard, the stocks on the civilian ships are actually really decent food. It's not nearly enough, but we are acquiring more food here as well."

"Are samples being screened for contamination?" Rione demanded.

The engineer looked startled. "Yes, Madam Co-President. I'm sure they are, just like the raw materials we're pulling out of the bunkers. I'll double-check, though."

"Full screening. Macro, micro, nano, organic, and inorganic," Rione added.

"Yes, Madam Co-President. I'll ensure they understand, uh . . ." The engineer paused, clearly wondering if Rione was able to give orders to him and the four Alliance auxiliary ships.

"Make sure it's done," Geary said.

Relieved to have gotten an order from someone he knew could issue one, the engineer saluted and hastened back to his watch station to pass on the orders.

"My apologies for confusing your engineer," Rione stated. "I should have asked you to tell him to do that."

"No harm done, and I'm glad you brought it up. With everything else going on, somebody might have neglected to make every possible check of whether those Syndic food stocks were poisoned before their ships were abandoned."

"Sometimes it's good to have a devious politician around, isn't it?" Rione turned to go back to her seat, then paused as another message came in for Geary.

Colonel Carabali looked contented in a Marine sort of way. "We believe we've found all of the prisoner compartments on the remains of *Audacious*," she reported. "It's a wonder there weren't a lot of dead because of the crowded conditions and inadequate life support, but apparently the senior personnel in each compartment kept the prisoners rotating so none of them were overwhelmed. My scouts estimated that within another day or so the prisoners would've started dying from the conditions. They all need food, and most have barely treated injuries. Minor injuries were left untreated by the Syndics."

"How many?" Geary asked, thinking of the sizes of the crews on the Alliance warships that had been lost in this star system.

"We're still getting a count. Roughly nine hundred fleet personnel and eighteen Marines. Captain Cresida insisted on most of them going to *Furious*, *Implacable*, and the heavy cruisers with the formation even though the battleships wanted some. Captain Casia did intercept a few shuttle loads for *Conqueror*." Carabali's tone made it clear that she didn't consider it the Marines' job to straighten out disputes among fleet officers. "Apparently other Alliance prisoners were taken to other Syndic ships while we were gone from Lakota, so there are more somewhere in this star system. Merchant ships pressed into service as prisoner haulers, according to the ones we liberated. Any chance we can get them?"

"Not much, and getting less by the second." The Syndic pursuit force could appear at any moment, and the more time that passed, the more likely it would show up very soon. "We only overran two Syndic merchant ships near us, and both were full of supplies. There are a couple dozen more merchant ships visible in this star system, but they're out of our reach, and we can't tell what they're carrying. Since we haven't spotted any labor camps in this star system with Alliance personnel in them, our personnel taken prisoner might have been on other ships that quickly left this star system."

"I understand, sir. We're preparing to pull out of *Audacious*," Colonel Carabali reported. "What do we do with what's left of the ship?"

Geary grimaced. As much as he wanted to save that ship, what remained of *Audacious* couldn't possibly defend itself, couldn't possibly keep up with the fleet, couldn't be towed without hazarding the rest of the fleet, and probably couldn't be repaired at all even in the best shipyard imaginable. A brave warship now faced only one possible fate, the scrapyard. And there wasn't any sense in letting the Syndics have that metal. "Can we blow her power core?"

"Yes, sir. It's plenty strong enough to do the job."

"Then set it for overload in six hours and get out of there."

Six hours should be plenty of time. He couldn't imagine any circumstances under which the Alliance fleet would have more time than that to hang around the Casualty Flotilla.

"Wait!" That was Rione, leaning in to speak to Geary, her face intent. "Hold off on deciding to destroy *Audacious* that way."

Geary sighed and spoke to the Marine again. "Belay that. Don't set her for overload yet. Hold on a moment." Then he turned to face Rione. "Why not blow up *Audacious*? Why let the Syndics have her back?"

"I'm not suggesting giving that ship back to the Syndics," Rione replied coldly. "There are a great many Syndic warships in pursuit of us, and we could use any available weapon to balance the odds. Rig the ship so it will explode not at a set time but when the Syndics reoccupy it."

He couldn't avoid a grimace at the thought. Still, as distasteful as booby traps were, they were acceptable weapons in cases like this. Then another thought came on the heels of that. "Maybe we should rig all of the ships to explode their power cores when the Syndics reoccupy them."

Desjani, overhearing, twisted her mouth in an annoyed expression. "Too bad that won't hurt them until our battle in this system is over."

"Well, yeah," Geary agreed, "but it's not like we can . . ." His voice trailed off, and he gave Desjani a startled look.

Her eyes widened. "All of those abandoned Syndic warships with functioning power cores. If we can rig the Syndic ships to explode when we want them to—"

"Like mines?"

"Exactly like mines! *Huge* mines set for proximity detonations! We'd just have to lure the Syndic pursuit force close enough to the Casualty Flotilla."

"That'd be one hell of a minefield. Can we make it work?" he asked Desjani.

She spun to face her engineering watch-stander. "Lieutenant Nicodeom, give me an assessment of whether or not we can rig an abandoned Syndic warship to function like a mine, exploding its power core when a target enters an engagement envelope."

The engineering lieutenant looked surprised, then thoughtful. "The easiest way to do it would probably be to use a mine fuse rigged to the power-core control systems. It'd take some work, Captain, because they'd have to adjust the smart fuse's programming to reflect the estimated kill radius of the power core, factor in the time delay for bringing each ship's core to overload, run some control cables, and work out the interfaces with Syndic core control systems."

"Where are the resources in the fleet to do that?" Desjani demanded.

"The best weapons engineers in the fleet are on the auxiliaries, Captain. That's also where we'd get the mine fuses. You'd have to get the auxiliaries to the Syndic ship you wanted rigged with the fuse or else use shuttles to ferry personnel and gear from the auxiliaries to the Syndic ship."

Desjani's smile grew so broad it threatened to split her face. "Did you hear all of that, sir?"

Geary nodded, knowing that he was smiling, too. All four auxiliaries were with the Syndic warships of the Casualty Flotilla, right where they needed to be. "I think it's time to call Captain Tyrosian. Hopefully her engineers won't need specs for this rush job."

Lieutenant Nicodeom spoke up again. "Captain Geary, sir, it's a challenge. If they have to configure those fuses to individual Syndic ships and get them all rigged in a real short time, that's the sort of challenge any good weapons engineer would do just for the love of it. Making something really big blow up in a new way? It doesn't get any better than that."

"Thanks, Lieutenant." Geary punched the circuit to call Captain Tyrosian, then quickly explained what was needed. "Can you and your people do it, Captain Tyrosian?" he asked at the end. "I know this is a very difficult engineering challenge with a very short time line, and I'm told it's the sort of thing only the best weapons engineers can handle." He could scarcely be more blatant, but it didn't seem to be a good time for subtlety. Besides, he was dealing with an engineer, so subtlety might well be wasted anyway.

Captain Tyrosian's eyes, which sometimes seemed to glaze over when faced with operational matters, lit with enthusiasm. "Weaponize the abandoned Syndic ships? Proximity fuses? Do you want them linked and timed to create a mass detonation?"

"Yeah, that'd be great."

"Consider it done, sir," Tyrosian announced confidently. "When does it need to be in place?"

"About two hours."

The engineer jerked visibly at that, then nodded. "They'll be ready, sir."

As the image of Tyrosian vanished, Geary glanced over at Rione. "Thanks for the idea."

Rione raised both eyebrows. "Your idea seems to have considerably outstripped my modest proposal."

"We wouldn't have thought of it without your suggestion," Geary noted.

Desjani looked toward Rione and inclined her head slightly in silent agreement. Rione smiled stiffly back at her.

Pretending he hadn't noticed the byplay, Geary studied his star-system display, rubbing his chin with one hand. "The problem will be getting the Syndics to enter the danger area when it counts. We'll have to fool them without their knowing they're being led that way. It won't be easy."

"I'm sure you can manage it," Rione remarked.

"We already have decoys in place to lure them toward the Casualty Flotilla," Desjani pointed out.

He frowned at the display, knowing that she meant the auxiliaries. Without its auxiliaries, the Alliance fleet would be doomed, certain to run out of fuel cells as well as expendable munitions long before it could reach Alliance space again. It made them critically important to protect, and the best possible lures for an enemy attack. "We already did that once at Sancere. Will they be fooled again?"

"We just have to do it differently," Desjani argued.

"Got any ideas?" Geary asked.

As it turned out, she did. Not ideas that he completely liked, but enough to toss back and forth as they came up with a plan. Every once in a while he glanced at Rione to see if

she had anything to add, but Rione was just gazing stony-faced
at her own display.

"CAPTAIN Tyrosian, get any shuttles and personnel not engaged in looting Syndic repair ships or rigging up the hulks
to explode to work doing highly visible plundering of materials off other Syndic shipping in the Casualty Flotilla."

The engineer, doubtless ready to announce proudly the
progress of the pillaging so far, froze in midword and looked
confused. "Sir?"

"I want the Syndics to see us desperately grabbing everything we can," Geary repeated. "Food and anything else.
They need to think that you need to stay with the Casualty
Flotilla as long as possible to grab as much as you can. We
need to look desperate for supplies, Captain Tyrosian."

"We . . . are desperate for supplies, sir," Tyrosian protested.

Desjani barely avoided laughing, instead making a chok-
ing sound to one side that Geary ignored. "Captain Tyrosian," he explained patiently, "we're going to keep your
auxiliaries with the Casualty Flotilla long past the point of
safety once the Syndic Pursuit Flotilla shows up. They're
going to be focused on you anyway, since your four auxiliaries are the most critical parts of our fleet. The Syndics need
a plausible reason for your ships staying with the Casualty
Flotilla while the Syndics come right for you. If they think
you need to keep grabbing stuff off the Syndic hulks, it will
provide that reason."

Tyrosian took a moment to reply. "We're bait again?"

"Yes, Captain, you're bait again."

The engineering officer looked depressed, but nodded.
"Yes, sir."

"Needless to say," Geary felt compelled to add, "we'll do
everything we can to keep your ships from actually being
destroyed."

"Thank you, sir. We appreciate that."

"I will provide detailed maneuvering instructions for

your ships once the Syndic pursuit force arrives and we know their movement vectors. Thank you, Captain Tyrosian."

Twenty minutes later, with a few more Alliance shuttles out among the Syndic hulks and survival-suited sailors making a show of tossing looted supplies from Syndic ships into the open cargo bays of the shuttles, the alarms that Geary had been dreading finally sounded.

"The Syndic pursuit force has arrived at the jump point from Ixion," the operations watch-stander announced.

Geary held his breath as the Alliance fleet's sensors evaluated the enemy force appearing at the jump point, which was now fifteen light-minutes away, meaning the Syndics had already had fifteen minutes to decide what to do and to start doing it before the Alliance fleet had even seen their arrival in this star system.

The number of HuKs and light cruisers in the pursuit force was still impressive despite all of the losses that the Alliance fleet had managed to inflict. The ranks of the Syndic heavy cruisers, on the other hand, had been decimated during the engagements at Lakota the last time the Alliance fleet was here, with many destroyed and twenty-two heavy cruisers among the badly damaged ships that had remained in the star system. Nine of those twenty-two had already been destroyed, and the remainder were abandoned and part of the Casualty Flotilla. Only sixteen heavy cruisers remained with the Syndic pursuit force.

The Syndic capital warships flashed into existence, their numbers multiplying. Ten battleships. Fifteen. Thirty-one. Six battle cruisers. Thirteen battle cruisers.

"Thirty-one battleships and thirteen battle cruisers," Desjani murmured. "Not too bad."

"They're in better shape than ours are," Geary noted. He checked the numbers he already knew by heart. The Alliance fleet still had twenty-two battleships, the two scout battleships, and seventeen battle cruisers. Plus twenty-nine heavy cruisers. But a number of those Alliance warships had significant battle damage, and even though the Alliance ships had been resupplied with some new expendable munitions, the Syndics probably had much better inventories of missiles and grapeshot on hand.

Thirty-one enemy battleships. Geary took a moment to relax himself, knowing he had to respect that much combat capability and yet not get unnerved by it. "Our only advantage is in the number of heavy cruisers," he said out loud.

Desjani shook her head, "We've got another very big advantage," she corrected. "That Syndic commander last saw us running for safety and has had eleven days to fix that image in their mind. Now that commander is going to see how much damage we've done to the Syndic warships left behind here, which is going to create a lot of anger. Overconfidence and anger add up to recklessness, sir."

"I can't disagree with your math," Geary said. He couldn't help thinking that overconfidence on his part and his own anger at the more recalcitrant among his ship captains might have led him to make a reckless decision to come to Lakota the first time. That scarcely mattered now, though. What counted would be taking advantage of an enemy commander's own probable state of mind. "Let's see if he does what we expect."

As the minutes went past, it became increasingly obvious that the Syndic commander, whether reckless or not, was doing as they hoped. The Syndic formation altered slightly as it accelerated toward an intercept with the Alliance ships, the standard Syndic box formation adjusting into a deep rectangular shape with one broad side facing the Alliance fleet. The box was a decent multipurpose formation whose length, width, and depth could be adjusted for different tactical situations, but it had its limitations in terms of bringing firepower to bear on any point in any enemy formation and in adjusting its facing quickly. It seemed to be the only formation the Syndic commanders had been trained (or allowed) to use, though.

"Heading to intercept the Alliance ships with the Casualty Flotilla," Desjani noted with a smile.

Geary checked the estimated time to intercept. With the Alliance fleet slowed to match the Casualty Flotilla's velocity, all of the Alliance warships were headed away from the Syndic pursuit force at less than point zero two light speed. Coming on fast behind them and increasing velocity, the pursuit force had reached point zero seven nine light speed. Geary told *Dauntless*'s maneuvering systems to assume the Syndics would continue accelerating to point one light speed and came up with a time to contact of two hours and fifty-one minutes.

Assuming the Alliance ships didn't themselves maneuver. For a long time Geary's plan had been to run when the Syndic pursuit force showed up, because given the probable size of the Syndic force and his fleet's status, he didn't see any alternative. The plan for using the Casualty Flotilla as a weapon had changed that. Unless the Syndics inexplicably gave up the pursuit, he would have had to fight this force eventually anyway. Now he might be able to beat it.

"Will they believe that we're just waiting around here for them?" Rione asked.

"Hopefully they'll think we're trying to decide what to do," Geary explained. Just as at the Syndicate Worlds' home star system, when the Alliance fleet had wasted precious time debating who was in command and what they should do. "The Big Ugly Ball formation will make them think I may not be in command anymore."

"Big Ugly Ball? I see. You're going to simulate indecision and frozen panic."

"That's the idea," Geary agreed, hoping that both indecision and panic would remain simulated.

Rione came close again and ensured that the sound-deadening field around Geary's command seat was activated. "Even I can tell that this is a very risky battle. What are our odds of winning?"

"That depends," Geary said. He saw her aggravated reaction. "Honestly. If certain things happen as I've planned, we've got a good chance."

"And if they don't?"

"It's going to be bad. We'd have to fight them sooner or later."

She eyed him a moment longer. "I don't have to tell you

how important it is that *Dauntless* get back to Alliance space. Not the fleet as a whole. *Dauntless*. The Syndic hypernet key on her can tip the balance of this war even if every other ship in this fleet is lost."

He glared at the deck. "I know. Why'd you tell me that when you knew you didn't have to tell me that?"

"Because you're still focused on saving as much of this fleet as possible. You can't forget the bigger picture. If it becomes a matter of losing *Dauntless* while trying to save as much of this fleet as you can, or getting *Dauntless* home no matter how many other Alliance ships are lost, your duty demands that you focus on *Dauntless*."

"I don't need lectures on duty," Geary muttered. Rione was right in a big way, he knew she was right, but it wasn't a kind of right he could live with.

"The other ships could hold off the Syndic pursuit force while a fast task force built around *Dauntless* was loaded with as many fuel cells as they could carry and headed for Alliance space," Rione insisted, her voice unemotional.

"Run away, you mean. You're suggesting that *Dauntless* and a few other ships run and leave the rest of the fleet to its fate."

"Yes!" He looked at her again and saw in Rione's eyes that she wasn't liking what she suggested, either, but that she felt obligated to push for it. Duty. Her duty to the Alliance. "You have to remember the big picture, Captain John Geary! We all do! It's not about what we want, it's about what we have to do!"

He dropped his gaze to the deck once more. "Whatever we have to do to win. We're back to that, huh?" She didn't answer. "I'm sorry, but I'm the wrong hero for that. I can't do what you're suggesting."

"There's still time—"

"I didn't say it couldn't be done, I said *I can't do it*. I won't abandon these other ships to their fates. I won't allow the big picture to justify betraying the trust of the men and women who've placed their fates in my hands."

Rione sounded both pleading and angry. "They all took an oath to sacrifice for the Alliance."

"Yes, they did. So did I." He finally looked at her again. "But I can't do that, even if it costs the Alliance the war. The price would be too great."

Her anger grew. "We can pay any price that is necessary, Captain Geary. For our homes. For our families."

"I'm supposed to tell their families that? 'People of the Alliance, I sacrificed your parents, your partners, your children, for you.' How many people would really make that kind of bargain? Would anyone willing to make that bargain deserve to win?"

"We all make it, every day! You know that! Every civilian makes that bargain when they send their military off to war! We know they're risking their lives for us!"

She was right about that, too. But not entirely. "They trust us not to waste those lives," Geary stated heavily. "I will not trade the lives of the people of this fleet for a Syndic hypernet key. I will lead them and fight like hell to get that key home to Alliance space, but I will not write off the lives of my people as a necessary price for that. The moment I decide that any price is justified is the moment I betray my trust and what I see as my duty. We'll win or we'll die together, with honor."

Rione gazed back at him for a while, then shook her head. "Part of me is very angry with you, and part of me is very grateful that I couldn't convince you. I'm not a monster, John Geary."

"I didn't say you were." He jerked his head toward his display, where the movements of the warships in this star system were clearly shown. "But a lot of people are going to die today because of my decisions now and in the past. Sometimes I wonder what that makes me."

"Look in the eyes of your comrades, Captain Geary," Rione replied in a quiet voice. "The ones you wouldn't leave. Reflected in those eyes you'll see what you are."

Rione returned to her seat. Geary took a few deep breaths, noticing that Captain Desjani was acting totally absorbed in her own work. He wondered what she might have guessed about his and Rione's conversation.

As much to distract himself as because he needed to, Geary

called Captain Cresida. "I'm going to order the auxiliaries to break away from the Syndic Casualty Flotilla in two hours. Until then they're going to keep putting on a public display of frantically pulling everything they can off the Syndic ships."

Cresida nodded, only the rapidity of the gesture revealing her prebattle nerves. Those thirty-one Syndic battleships and thirteen battle cruisers were aimed straight at her force, and for protection of the auxiliaries she had only two battle cruisers, four battleships, of which three were in various states of disrepair, and a gaggle of escorts with varying degrees of damage. "We'll cover the auxiliaries, but we're going to need backup."

"It'll be coming," Geary promised. "Don't let *Furious* and *Implacable* get into a slugging match with those Syndic battleships. Try to disrupt their attacks instead of meeting them head-on." He was reciting advice from peacetime tactical workshops a century ago to someone who'd fought dozens of battles.

But Cresida nodded again as if Geary had imparted some piece of hidden wisdom. "*Warrior* can't maneuver well enough to dodge. She'll have to meet the attack. I don't know about *Majestic* and *Orion*."

Geary's ship status display showed that both *Majestic* and *Orion* had regained most of their maneuvering capability, so he guessed that Cresida was actually expressing doubt about what they'd do when confronted by the mass of Syndic battleships. He wasn't sure of that himself. "I understand. *Conqueror* shouldn't give you any trouble." Captain Casia was technically senior to Cresida, but Geary had painstakingly crafted orders which so limited Casia's role to close defense of the auxiliaries that he shouldn't be able to interfere with the actions of the much-more-capable Cresida.

"I hope *Conqueror* manages to give the enemy some trouble," Cresida observed.

"Me, too. We're going to disrupt the attack before it reaches you. Hopefully that'll do enough damage to make the plan work."

Cresida smiled, startling Geary. "If it doesn't, there's worse fates. I've got someone waiting for me."

It took him a moment to realize that she wasn't talking about someone waiting at home, but rather about what would happen if *Furious* was destroyed in the engagement. "We need you, Captain Cresida. Do your duty, but the Alliance already has too many dead heroes."

"Yes, it does." Cresida nodded again.

Geary ended the transmission and stared at his display, where the mighty Syndic pursuit force was still accelerating into its attack. He wondered how many more dead heroes the Alliance would have before this day ended.

FOUR

"YOU'RE not going to change the formation?" Captain Desjani asked again.

"No, I'm not going to change the formation!" Geary gave her an annoyed glance. How many times had she asked the question over the last hour? "We need to look like an easy, disorganized target."

"Sir, with all due respect, we *are* an easy, disorganized target in this formation." Desjani saw Geary's scowl deepen but kept speaking. "Our firepower is spread throughout a wide region. The Syndics will be able to overwhelm each of those subformations one after another, just like we overcame each weak Syndic formation we encountered."

She was stubborn, but she was smart, and under other circumstances she'd probably be right. Geary forced down his temper. "We can't engage them as a fleet. They have too great an advantage in firepower when you take into account that they probably have much bigger stocks of missiles and grapeshot on hand than we do."

"If we concentrate on one part of the formation like you did last time we were in Lakota—"

"Tanya, look." He gestured at the display. "Last time the Syndics let themselves get suckered into spreading out to catch us, which allowed us to concentrate and punch through. The CEO in command now was smart enough to learn from that. The Syndic formation is already concentrated into a fairly tight box."

"Then we can maneuver around it."

"Not with our fuel cell reserves in the state they are and not with the auxiliaries to worry about! They've taken on a lot of materials, and they're sluggish as hell again with all of that extra mass." Desjani glared at the display, clearly wanting to argue some more. Geary kept his voice reasonable with some effort. "The disadvantage of the Syndic formation is that it's so deep and dense that their CEO can't maneuver it easily. If our trap fails, we'll have to take what advantage we can of that by hitting it again and again on the edges."

"It would take *forever* to wear down that force that way," Desjani pointed out. "We don't have enough fuel cells to do that, either."

He took a moment to reply, looking at the display again, where the Syndic pursuit force was eight light-minutes distant. It had reached point one light speed and was still coming right for them, its box formation looking like a huge brick aimed at the Alliance fleet's bubble. Desjani was right, of course. He knew that. Sure, a head-on clash of concentrated formations would almost certainly result in the Alliance fleet being shattered against the much stronger Syndic force. But at least the end would happen quickly. What would be the purpose of drawing it out, losing ships one by one over a much longer period, with the same defeat awaiting them in the end?

The alternative would be to run, now, as fast as the fleet could go, jump to another star system ahead of the Syndics, knowing they'd be right behind this time, the Alliance fleet unable to stop to replenish the auxiliaries again. Sooner or later he'd have to turn and fight, and probably under worse conditions than this. He'd been forced to linger here to restock his auxiliaries, but the fleet would eventually run out of fuel cells if he couldn't replenish those stocks again, and he didn't know how that would be possible without first engaging the Syndic pursuit force.

"How do we want to die?" he finally whispered.

Desjani stared at him. "We're talking about how to win, sir."

"Then we fight here and try to minimize the Syndic advantages. If our plan works, our chances will get a lot better. If it doesn't work, we have to try to make the Syndics pay as much as possible for their victory. A head-on clash will too likely destroy us before we can wear them down at all."

She watched him, then nodded slowly. "Hit them again and again, knowing our time is limited, holding nothing back, because there'll be no reason to hold anything back. This will be as far as we get toward home."

"It might come to that, yeah." He took a long, slow breath, grateful that he'd been able to share that thought with someone.

Desjani flicked her eyes toward the back of the bridge for the barest moment. "Are you going to tell her?"

Her? Rione. "She's brave enough, but I think she'd have a little trouble understanding."

"I think you're right. Captain Geary, if we don't win, we're going to make sure this Syndic victory is one they wish they'd never achieved because it's going to cost them more than they ever imagined possible."

He felt a smile on his lips and nodded to Desjani. "Damn right we will."

"Estimated time to engagement range with Syndic Pursuit Flotilla one and one half hours," the operations watchstander announced.

IT all came down to timing again. His now-long-dead teachers, officers experienced in decades of fleet maneuvers, had drilled into Geary that the worst temptation a commander faced was to act too soon. Watching the enemy approach for hours or days, it was far too easy to jump the gun, make changes too early that should occur at the last moment before the enemy could see them and react. Make the changes too early, and the enemy would react, then you'd have to change things again, and they'd react again. He'd seen it happen in fleet exercises, as commanders drove ships and crews to exhaustion before the first shots could be exchanged.

Simulate indecision, simulate panic, while all the time real indecision and panic lurked ready to pounce. His fleet was waiting for orders. They trusted him, even though variations on his debate with Desjani were surely happening on a lot of ships. But they'd seen him snatch victory from the jaws of defeat before this, so they waited.

Most of them waited. Captain Casia wasn't happy. "The Syndic attack is less than fifty minutes away from contact! Why are my ships still at point zero two light speed and accompanying these Syndic wrecks?"

"Your ships are accompanying the Alliance auxiliaries," Geary pointed out.

"We are the closest to the enemy, and the nearest supporting formation is at least half an hour travel time distant!"

"That's correct, Captain Casia."

Casia's face reddened. "I will contact the other officers in this fleet and demand an immediate conference to decide on your competence to command. We need a fleet commander who will act, not one who lets this fleet sit idly while an overwhelming Syndic force approaches!"

It would be much easier to lose his temper with Casia, but he couldn't really afford to do that. Nor did he need the distraction of dealing with a call for a fleet conference right now. Fortunately, he'd learned enough about the way this fleet thought to know how to counter Casia. "Am I correct that you are declining the honor of being in the fore of the battle?" Geary asked, adding a hint of surprise to his voice.

"De—?" Casia broke off his words and swallowed, then spoke with a little less bluster. "That's not what's involved."

"I have arranged the fleet so that your battleship division will meet the enemy first. Do you wish me to inform the fleet that you decline that role?"

"I . . . my ship and my crew deserve a fighting chance!"

"They will have it, Captain Casia. I'm sure *Conqueror* and her crew will acquit themselves well."

Unable to contradict Geary without condemning himself in the eyes of his fellow officers, Casia abruptly broke off the transmission.

Slumping back, Geary rubbed his forehead, wishing the Syndics would hurry up and get here. He felt worn-out already, and the day had a lot left in it.

"Ration bar?" Desjani asked, offering one.

"Tell me it's not a Danaka Yoruk bar."

"It's not a Danaka Yoruk bar."

"Thanks." Geary took the offered bar, then read the label. "It is a Danaka Yoruk bar. Why'd you tell me it wasn't?"

"Because you told me to tell you that," Desjani explained, unable totally to suppress a grin. Her spirits always rose as action drew closer. "They're all we have left. They taste the worst, so everybody ate the others first. We've got some Syndic ration bars from Sancere that we're about to break out."

"What are those like?"

"The chief who volunteered to taste test them informed me that they have one great virtue." She indicated the bar Geary was holding. "They make Danaka Yoruk bars taste good by comparison."

"If I have to face death today, why does my possibly last meal have to be a Danaka Yoruk bar?" Geary complained. He ripped the seal, then bit off a chunk and tried to swallow without actually tasting the bar. It was only partially successful.

The ration bar did accomplish one thing, distracting Geary from the approach of the Syndic pursuit force while he choked it down. When he focused back on the display, it showed forty minutes until the Syndics closed to engagement range. *Five more minutes. Then it's showtime. Ancestors, I need everything you can give me today. Please guide me.*

He called Captain Tyrosian, Captain Cresida, and Captain Casia in a linked transmission. "Get your last shuttles recovered now. Captain Tyrosian, break contact with the

Syndic repair ships. In four minutes I'll provide maneuvering orders for your ships. Captain Cresida, Captain Casia, follow your orders but remember that your overriding priority is to maneuver the ships under your command in order to defend the fast fleet auxiliaries to the best of your ability."

He watched the final two shuttles still out dodge inside their docks on *Titan* and *Witch* as the grapples and conveyors still holding all four auxiliaries to the Syndic repair ships withdrew. Geary checked the latest vector for the Syndic pursuit force and ran out the maneuvering solution, making a small last-moment adjustment. The last minute ticked down, and Geary contacted the auxiliaries again. "Captain Tyrosian, accelerate your ships at their maximum capability. As soon as you clear the Casualty Flotilla, come port zero three degrees, down zero one degrees. Inform the commanders of *Titan*, *Jinn*, and *Goblin* that they are to maneuver as necessary to ensure the vector for the fastest intercept of them by the Syndic pursuit force passes directly through the center of the Casualty Flotilla."

"Yes, sir," Captain Tyrosian acknowledged.

"The success of this battle plan depends upon you and the other auxiliaries, Captain. I assure you that the rest of the fleet will be coming to assist in your defense."

Tyrosian managed a tense smile. "I know you have to make it a good show for the Syndics, sir. We won't let you down."

Geary checked his display again. The Syndics were three light-minutes away now, the time lag between what he saw of them and what they were actually doing at that moment growing steadily shorter. Was it time to move some more of his own ships? Not yet. He had to time it right, make it look like the Alliance fleet was reacting in piecemeal, disorganized fashion while actually bringing his ships in to hit the Syndics at close to the same time.

Titan, *Witch*, *Goblin*, and *Jinn* accelerated with painful slowness, their usual sluggishness now amplified by all the extra mass they'd taken on from the Syndic repair ships. He had factored that in and hoped the maneuvering systems and his own experience with the auxiliaries had been accurate enough to keep them from being overrun by the Syndic pursuit force too soon.

Between the four auxiliaries and the Syndic pursuit force, the four battleships and Cresida's two battle cruisers accelerated as well, maintaining their relative positions for now. Around them, the two heavy cruisers, twenty light cruisers, and destroyers also serving as escorts kept their speed down and held their position on the Alliance auxiliaries, too.

Geary felt an odd pang of regret as he watched the Alliance ships leaving the deserted ships of the Casualty Flotilla behind, the wreck of *Audacious* near the center of the formation seeming to protest this latest abandonment. *Don't worry, lady. We're not giving you back to the Syndics. They'll discover that you've got one punch left in you.*

As the auxiliaries cleared the Syndic ships making up the Casualty Flotilla and altered course, *Titan* began lagging and *Goblin* fell back to stay with her. "*Titan*'s acting as if she's lost a main propulsion unit," Desjani reported.

Given *Titan*'s record for suffering damage, Geary still felt a worry that the loss of a propulsion unit was real and not simulated, even though he already knew what the two auxiliaries were doing. "Nice job. It looks just like a real loss of propulsion capability, and along with *Goblin*, she's making sure the Syndic intercept path remains centered through the Casualty Flotilla."

"*Warrior* is falling back to stay with *Titan* and *Goblin*." Desjani didn't point out the obvious, that *Conqueror*, *Majestic*, and *Orion* had kept accelerating along with *Witch* and *Jinn*, putting them in a marginally safer position.

Geary thought through a number of comments or orders he could direct at the commanding officers of *Conqueror*, *Majestic*, and *Orion*, rejecting almost all of them as unprofessional even though venting them would have made him feel better. Tapping his controls, he called the battleships on a frequency the entire fleet could hear. "*Conqueror*, *Majestic*, and *Orion*, the fast fleet auxiliaries *Titan* and *Goblin* are deliberately putting themselves into greater danger and can use all of the close support available. Close on *Warrior* and assist her in defending *Titan* and *Goblin*." If that didn't shame the three battleships into doing their duty, at least he'd finally have unquestionable grounds for relieving their commanding officers. But he had a feeling that even such difficult subordinates as Captain Casia and Commander Yin would be more afraid of the contempt of their fellow officers than they would be of the Syndics, and so would feel forced to fall back to help cover *Titan* and *Goblin*.

"Where are those heavy cruisers going?" Rione asked.

Geary knew she had to mean *Ichcahuipilli* and *Rondelle*, which were now accelerating away from Cresida's battle cruisers *Implacable* and *Furious* as well as the Syndics. "They've been ordered to get clear because they're packed with as many of the wounded prisoners liberated from *Audacious* as they can carry," he told her.

"Getting them to obey that order must have taken some work."

"Yeah. They didn't want to avoid the fight, and neither did the wounded aboard them."

"We're seeing some vector changes on *Conqueror*, *Orion*, and *Majestic*," Desjani remarked. "Looks like they are finally dropping back toward *Titan* and *Goblin*."

Rione came close to Geary and spoke again, her voice low. "Can this fleet make it back if we save *Witch* and *Jinn* but lose *Titan* and *Goblin*?"

"If it comes to that, it'll have to," Geary replied with an outward confidence he didn't feel. All of the tactical success in the galaxy wouldn't save this fleet if it ran out of fuel cells. At best, he might end up having to decide which warships to abandon in the hope that the remainder could make it through to Alliance space.

Rione gazed back at him as if she had read his thoughts, then nodded and returned to her seat.

After a few moments, Captain Desjani spoke, her eyes on her display. "I wonder what it would be like on one of those auxiliaries, seeing that big Syndic flotilla heading for you, knowing that you had limited propulsion and maneuvering ability, limited defensive capability, and no real means of attack." She glanced over at Geary. "We look down on the auxiliaries and their crews, those of us in the warships, but it must take a great deal of courage to go to battle in ships like that." He nodded in agreement. "I'll take a battle cruiser any day," Desjani concluded, "but I owe those auxiliaries sailors some drinks when we get back."

"We can send over some cases paid for by the wardroom on *Dauntless*, Captain," Lieutenant Nicodeom suggested. "We'll all be happy to pitch in."

"Yes," Desjani agreed. "Remind me to do that, Lieutenant."

After the long, apparently slow approach of the Syndic pursuit force, the battle was reaching the point where events would begin happening with stunning speed. Even at point one light speed, the vast distances inside a typical star system took time to cover. But once ships traveling those velocities got close enough to their objectives, the remaining intervals seemed to vanish in the blink of an eye, which in fact they did. Human senses and reactions were made to deal with things moving at tens of kilometers per hour, not intercepts occurring at thousands of kilometers per second.

Geary took long, slow breaths, his own gaze fixed on the display. The Alliance fleet subformations, each built around one or two divisions of battleships or battle cruisers, remained scattered in the Big Ugly Ball formation. Captain Cresida's escort force, the four battleships, the other escorts, and the auxiliaries were at the back and bottom of the bubble. The flattened sphere of the Syndic Casualty Flotilla hung behind the fleeing auxiliaries, its aspect gradually tilting upward relative to the Alliance ships as they headed slightly downward in relation to it.

The surprise they had rigged in the Casualty Flotilla would hopefully substantially even the odds, but to ensure the success of that it was necessary to keep the Syndic attack focused on a line running through that flotilla. The scattered, irregular formation of the Alliance fleet made it hard for the enemy to identify a main axis of striking power to counter, which would have also offered an alternate target for the enemy attack. The Big Ugly Ball also had the virtue of appearing to show a fleet barely held together and ready to fall apart. To the Syndics, who as far as Geary could tell still judged military effectiveness by how precisely everyone maintained position and kept their ranks and files lined up perfectly, the Alliance fleet would look sloppy and therefore less of a threat than it really was.

As the Syndics drew closer, he'd concentrate his forces toward the auxiliaries, timing the movements of each formation to arrive close together. His battle cruiser subformations were farthest forward on the Big Ugly Ball, and therefore farthest from the enemy, so he'd have to turn them first and aim them to intercept the Syndic pursuit force. Fortunately, the sort of aggressive move being initiated by the battle cruisers was exactly what the Syndics would expect to see.

If the surprise worked, his concentrated forces would be able to hit the Syndics hard and at roughly the same time from multiple angles. If the surprise didn't work . . . then his subformations would have to make repeated fast firing runs on the edges of the Syndic box, avoiding offering a single strong formation for the Syndics to focus an attack on and hopefully wearing down the enemy before the Alliance ships took too much damage themselves and exhausted their fuel cells on all of those fast attacks. The chances of that working were slim to none, but it beat any alternatives that Geary had been able to come up with.

Geary knew that everyone on the bridge was watching him now, but no one spoke to him. They knew he needed to screen out distractions, feel the right moments to order each subformation onto its new vectors, taking into account the time-delayed picture he had of the enemy movements, the time needed to turn and accelerate for his different ship types, and the time delays in communicating with his own ships. "Alliance Formation Bravo Five." That was the one built around Captain Duellos's four battle cruisers. "Accelerate to point zero eight light speed and maneuver to intercept the Syndic pursuit force." He wouldn't have time to fine-tune each subformation's approach, but he could set their velocities to bring them into contact with the enemy at the right time and count on most of his commanders at least being able to follow maneuvering system recommendations for an intercept.

A few minutes later he called the subformation built around the Seventh Battle Cruiser Division. "Accelerate to point zero nine light speed and maneuver to intercept the Syndic pursuit force." Over the next several minutes he ordered the rest of his battle cruisers to turn toward the enemy and accelerate, then waited a short time before beginning to call out similar commands to his battleships in their subformations. The battleships were closer to the auxiliaries, but would accelerate at a slower pace.

On Geary's display, he could see the Big Ugly Ball formation collapsing in lopsided fashion like an irregular balloon deflating as subformation after subformation of the Alliance fleet moved inward toward points along the path the Alliance auxiliaries were taking. It didn't look like a fleet turning to fight, but rather like each individual subformation had independently decided to act.

"Very nice," Desjani said admiringly. "It looks terrible, but it's very nice. If I was outside this fleet, I'd think every subformation was calling its own shots."

"Let's just hope it all works," Geary muttered under his breath.

The action was playing out along a single path leading back to the jump point from Ixion, with the Alliance subformation containing the auxiliaries a moving target whose path was the aim point for the Syndic pursuit force's box formation coming from behind and slightly above, while the Alliance Big Ugly Ball formation was collapsing from slightly above and ahead toward roughly the same spot along the projected track of the Alliance auxiliaries. Between the Alliance forces and the Syndic pursuit force was the flattened sphere of the Casualty Flotilla. As the Syndic pursuit force's intercept of the Alliance auxiliaries drew near, Captain Cresida accelerated *Furious* and *Implacable* toward the enemy, knowing her battle cruisers would never survive a direct clash with the Syndic battleships but aiming to disrupt the enemy assault.

The Syndic path had been dictated by the paths of their targets, the lagging Alliance auxiliaries formation. The Alliance auxiliaries had kept to courses and speeds calculated so that the shortest, fastest path between them and the Syndics stayed straight through the drifting and now–totally abandoned Casualty Flotilla of badly damaged Syndic warships. Human instincts sought things to hide behind even in space and even when the objects screening them were woefully inadequate, so the auxiliaries' movements would seem perfectly natural, a desperate attempt to shield themselves using the only possible obstacle between them and the enemy.

An enemy commander less certain that Alliance forces were disorganized, running, and close to beaten, less focused on the glory and advancement that would come with finally defeating the Alliance fleet and less angered by the renewed losses inflicted on damaged Syndic warships in Lakota Star System might have wondered why the auxiliaries had seemingly been left lightly supported. But the obvious and frantic looting of abandoned Syndic ships in the Casualty Flotilla up until the last possible moment would match Syndic expectations of an Alliance fleet desperate for supplies.

Now the entire situation appeared quite natural to someone not looking beneath the surface appearance of fleeing Alliance warships trying to keep the false cover offered by the hulks of the Casualty Flotilla between them and the threat of the onrushing Syndic pursuit force. The Alliance battle cruisers turning to rush pell-mell into battle also matched expectations, as did the belated maneuvers of the Alliance battleships also to come to the aid of the auxiliaries. It was all no doubt exactly what the Syndic commander expected.

If everything looks like it's going according to plan, Geary's second commanding officer had liked to say, *try to spot whatever you missed that's about to bite you in the butt.*

Apparently not having had the benefit of such advice, the Syndic CEO was confidently charging along the straightest, tightest intercept his flotilla could manage, doubtless already imagining the sweet taste of victory. The abandoned ships in the Casualty Flotilla couldn't maneuver and had no weapons operational, and so posed no threat to warships that could safely cut very close to the predictable paths of the drifting wrecks.

If not for the inspiration provided by Victoria Rione's suggestion, the Syndic CEO might have been safe in assuming that was true. Minefields, after all, were supposed to be as well concealed as possible, not sitting out in plain sight. Mines were also supposed to be small enough to be hidden by stealth features, not as huge as the power cores of warships.

Geary watched the path of the Syndic pursuit force, the big box sweeping with its broad side forward on a vector that would cause the flattened sphere of the Casualty Flotilla to pass almost right through the center of the Syndic formation. Because the Alliance auxiliaries had headed slightly down, and the Syndic pursuit force was coming from above, the flattened sphere of the Casualty Flotilla was cocked slightly upward relative to the pursuit force's box, reducing the angle at which they'd meet. That box had greater length and width than the crushed sphere of the Casualty Flotilla, but slightly less depth. As the pursuit force raced toward its intercept of the Alliance auxiliaries, numerous Syndic warships inside the box formation made minor adjustments to their courses, in many cases aiming to skim just above or below the ships of the Casualty Flotilla, to let the Casualty Flotilla pass through the pursuit force's box.

The smart proximity fuses, which had been cannibalized from Alliance mines and mounted on the outside of the hulls of the hulks, their parameters adjusted to reflect the destructive effect of the improvised weapons they were now linked to, watched the oncoming enemy ships, calculating when to detonate their charges in order to catch targets moving toward them at almost a tenth of the speed of light. As the Syndic formation reached the right point, the fuses triggered overloads in the still-active power cores of the abandoned ships in a rippling mass of destruction into which the Syndics raced with no time to react.

An entire region of space lit up as so many power cores blew, including that of *Audacious*, the broken battleship striking one last deathblow against the enemy. A dense field of high-velocity debris, particles, and energy burst outward in all directions, reaching maximum intensity and size in the fraction of a second in which the Syndic formation sped through that area of space.

Geary watched, tense, as the center of the Syndic formation disappeared inside the massive explosions. The edges of the Syndic box were outside the zone of destruction, but its center had been caught almost perfectly.

Moments later the display updated, evaluating the Syndic pursuit force's status as it shot out of the still-expanding death throes of the Casualty Flotilla.

Muffled cheers erupted around Geary. Captain Desjani gasped a brief sound of glee. He simply stared, shocked at how much damage had been inflicted on the enemy.

Every ship in the Casualty Flotilla had disappeared, of course, totally destroyed by the explosions of their power cores. Most of the Syndic HuKs in the blast area had also vanished, those caught in the densest portions of the explosions blown into pieces too small to be worth tracking. Larger chunks of debris marked the remains of light cruisers and those heavy cruisers which had been caught dead on by the blasts. Two heavy cruisers emerged from the edges of the detonation field intact, but with their systems blown, falling off helplessly down and to port. Only five heavy cruisers survived in the outer parts of the Syndic formation.

Every Syndic battle cruiser in the zone of destruction had been knocked out, some literally broken into pieces and others still in one piece but with no operating systems. Of the thirteen battle cruisers the Syndic pursuit force had boasted, nine were either destroyed or out of commission.

Out of the pursuit force's thirty-one battleships, twenty had been caught in the blast zone. Eight of those were still intact but knocked out. Another nine were badly hurt, staggering onward with shields blown and many systems out. The other three were damaged but appeared still combat-capable.

"I think the odds just shifted in our favor," Desjani announced, her eyes bright with battle lust as the opposing forces began to come together.

Chances were the Syndic CEO in charge of the pursuit force had either died in the destruction of the Casualty Flotilla or was on a ship with all systems blown and unable to communicate with his own ships. Lacking new orders, the surviving Syndic warships stuck to their last commands, bearing down on the fleeing Alliance auxiliaries. Their formation now resembled the outline of a box, with the center torn out and trailing behind as crippled ships fell away.

Furious and *Implacable*, their hopeless charge now facing a much-diminished enemy, tore across one side of the now-empty Syndic box, concentrating their fire on the leading Syndic battleship as the moment of firing opportunity came and went in a flash. The Alliance battle cruisers' escorts focused their own fire on the lighter units with the Syndics, taking out a few HuKs and two light cruisers.

As Captain Cresida's warships rocketed away and began the vast turn required to make another firing pass at the Syndics, the enemy battleship, which had caught successive volleys of specter missiles, grapeshot, and hell lances, began sliding out of position, its aft propulsion systems still at full strength, but its forward sections torn and battered.

"*Furious* took several hits, one hell-lance battery and null-field projector out of commission," the combat watch-stander reported in a precise voice. "*Implacable* has lost two hell-lance batteries and suffered minor damage to one propulsion system. Both battle cruisers expended all of their missiles and grapeshot on that pass. *Utap* has lost all combat systems but remains able to maneuver. *Arbalest* and *Raven's Beak* have taken serious damage but can remain with their formation."

Less than two minutes later the Alliance subformations began arriving at their intercept points. Captain Tulev led *Leviathan*, *Steadfast*, *Dragon*, and *Valiant* against another edge of the Syndic formation. The Alliance battle cruisers once again concentrated their fire, and this time as they pulled away one Syndic battleship had taken severe damage and one of the remaining Syndic battle cruisers drifted with all systems dead.

Captain Duellos brought *Courageous*, *Formidable*, and

Intrepid in next, badly damaging another Syndic battleship, then the five surviving battle cruisers of the Sixth and Seventh Divisions ripped past and took out two of the last three Syndic battle cruisers.

Then it was the Fourth Battle Cruiser Division's turn. As important as it was for *Dauntless* to reach Alliance space intact, Geary hadn't been able to think of any way to keep her out of the battle. Even if he had told everyone that *Dauntless* held the enemy hypernet key, her crew would still have clamored to have their proper place in battle and been deeply ashamed if kept away from the engagement.

Not to mention the shame that Tanya Desjani would feel. Knowing her, she'd probably resign her command rather than endure such a disgrace.

They'd listen to him, they'd learn, but if he pushed too far, they'd rebel against what they saw as humiliation. Geary had to accept that.

Dauntless, Daring, and *Victorious* bore down on a portion of the Syndic formation holding an already-damaged battleship and the sole surviving Syndic battle cruiser. With the Alliance warships traveling at close to point zero eight light speed and the Syndics still just above point one light speed, the moment of actual battle was far too brief for human senses to register. The Syndics were ahead, then they were behind, *Dauntless* still shuddering from the hits on her during the millisecond in which she'd been within range of the enemy weapons.

"Spot failures on forward and port shields," the damage-control watch reported. "Hell lance battery one alpha has lost one weapon. Structural damage at frames forty-five and one twenty-seven."

"Very well." Desjani nodded, her eyes on the display where the results of the Alliance battle cruisers' firing pass were appearing. She grinned fiercely. "Got him!"

Geary felt himself smiling grimly as well. The last Syndic battle cruiser was spitting out escape pods, then blew up as its power core overloaded. The already-damaged Syndic battleship had taken more hits and was slowly losing speed.

Then his smile vanished. The Alliance battle cruisers

were all turning to make more firing passes, the battleships and the rest of the fleet were still coming on, and even though the Alliance auxiliaries and their escorts had put on a burst of speed and curved their courses up and to the side, the remaining Syndics were closing to firing range. With the fleeing auxiliaries and their close escorts going in the same direction as the oncoming Syndics, the relative speed of the warships was much slower. This encounter would play out slowly enough for human senses to observe.

Geary saw Desjani watching him and indicated the auxiliaries. "If we lose them, then it doesn't matter how many Syndic warships we kill today. We'll still have lost this battle."

"You had to risk it," she said in a low voice.

"I know."

Warrior, battered at Vidha and again at Lakota the first time the Alliance fleet was here, swung out to block the Syndics aiming at *Titan* and *Goblin*. A pair of Syndic HuKs apparently thought they could dart past the badly hurt Alliance battleship, but learned that *Warrior* could still punch as her few still-working hell lances ripped into the lightly protected HuKs. A Syndic light cruiser right behind the HuKs tried to trade fire with *Warrior*, only to be knocked out as well.

But behind the light cruiser came two almost untouched Syndic battleships. Missiles leaped from them, aiming for *Titan* and *Goblin*. *Warrior* and the Alliance destroyers with her targeted the Syndic missiles, taking out most of the missiles but leaving them unable to engage the battleships directly.

Moving almost painfully, *Warrior* swung again, sliding right across the path of the two Syndic battleships, which concentrated their fire on the Alliance battleship and in moments mangled the warship, knocking out every system on *Warrior*. Geary muttered a brief prayer as he imagined the havoc that barrage had inflicted on *Warrior*'s crew.

That left *Conqueror*, *Orion*, and *Majestic* along with the few heavy cruisers, light cruisers, and destroyers accompanying them. Having watched *Warrior* die, *Conqueror* seemed frozen, staying on the same course and speed as the two

Syndic battleships closed. *Orion* began sliding upward, then headed back for a spot close to *Conqueror* as if seeking the safety of a position near the undamaged battleship.

Geary would never know what *Majestic* started to do, whether the rearmost surviving battleship was trying to turn to engage the enemy or to flee. In charitable moments, he imagined that *Majestic*'s crew and commanding officer had been inspired by *Warrior*'s sacrifice, had finally found their spirit and tried to make up for past failures. Whatever *Majestic*'s intent, her crew finally paid the price for the slow pace of repairs they had made to her weapons and defenses.

The Syndic battleships volleyed their remaining missiles at *Majestic*, aiming to overwhelm her defenses. Three missiles got through and hit aft, wiping out the battleship's propulsion units. Then as *Majestic* spun out of control up and over, the Syndic battleships altered course to get within hell-lance range of the helpless target. Grapeshot from the Syndics collapsed *Majestic*'s remaining shields, then the enemy hell lances tore into inadequately repaired armor with too many weak spots.

Geary watched hits flaring repeatedly on *Majestic*, the image of the battleship momentarily vanishing under the flurry of impacts as more Syndic missiles, grapeshot, and an unrelenting storm of hell-lance fire tore the ship apart. Then a much bigger explosion lit space for a few moments as *Majestic*'s power core blew under the stress.

The light faded, leaving a growing field of debris through which a few surviving Syndic missiles quested vainly for a target.

"Damn them," Desjani muttered. Geary didn't know if she was referring to the Syndics who had just destroyed *Majestic* or the crew and officers of the Alliance battleship who had doomed themselves.

Conqueror, still fixed on the same trajectory, was lashing out at any lighter Syndic unit that came within range. *Orion* had drifted upward again while remaining as far forward as *Conqueror*, placing herself in an almost totally useless position as far as defending the auxiliaries went. The Alliance heavy cruisers, light cruisers, and destroyers had broken away from *Conqueror*, though, and were slashing through Syndic escorts trying to reach *Titan* and *Goblin*. The two auxiliaries were throwing out as much defensive fire as they could, which unfortunately was very little. A Syndic missile slammed into *Goblin* amidships, staggering the auxiliary. A HuK managed to get close enough to score two hell-lance hits on *Titan* before the Alliance destroyer *Reprise* rolled in from below and took out the HuK with several well-aimed shots.

It took Geary a moment to realize that *Majestic*'s death might not have been in vain. "When those Syndic battleships went for the kill on *Majestic*, it took them off their trajectory and slowed their intercept of *Titan* and *Goblin*."

Desjani took a moment from maneuvering *Dauntless* to scan her display. "The Fifth Battleship Division might make it in time," she agreed.

Might make it. He certainly couldn't count on *Conqueror* or *Orion* being of any use. Geary swung his own gaze to the other side of the Syndic formation. The remaining Syndics were altering course to come around at *Titan*, *Goblin*, and beyond them *Witch* and *Jinn*. As a result, the edges of the box formation whose center had been blown away were folding inward, the four sides of the box collapsing in toward vectors aimed at the four Alliance auxiliaries.

But coming down on the same edges were the Alliance subformations centered on battleships. Captain Armus in *Colossus* led *Amazon*, *Spartan*, and *Guardian* straight toward one edge of the Syndic formation anchored on three Syndic battleships that had been mostly untouched up to this point. As the huge ships lumbered into contact, the four Alliance battleships volleyed everything they had at the leading Syndic battleship, then hit the second as they flashed past. In their wake, the Alliance battleships left the leading Syndic battleship a pile of junk and the second with significant damage. In exchange *Colossus* and *Spartan* had taken several hits, but none critical.

At the same time, the lighter units on both sides clashed, the now-superior numbers of the Alliance ships telling as Syndic light cruisers and HuKs reeled from repeated blows.

Soon afterward, *Relentless, Reprisal, Superb*, and *Splendid* wiped out the two Syndic battleships and their escorts holding another edge of the increasingly chaotic Syndic formation, battering the enemy but losing the heavy cruiser *Vambrace* in the exchange.

Titan took another hit, then a Syndic light cruiser made a firing run on *Goblin* while Alliance destroyers flashed past, trying to knock out the attacker.

A surviving Syndic heavy cruiser led two light cruisers and several HuKs straight for *Titan*. "Damn," Geary whispered.

He hadn't been watching *Furious* and *Implacable*, which had finally completed their long, wide swing through space and instead of aiming for more Syndic capital ships had focused on the closest threat to the auxiliaries. Now the two Alliance battle cruisers tore past, riddling the Syndic heavy cruiser, blowing up one light cruiser and shattering the second, while the battle cruisers' escorts wiped out the HuKs.

"Not bad," Desjani praised, her own battle cruiser division still curving up and around. "I told you Cresida would stick with the auxiliaries if she knew you were counting on her."

In trying to avoid the other attacks, *Orion* found itself directly between *Titan* and *Goblin* and the two Syndic battleships that had annihilated *Majestic*. Having expended all of their remaining missiles on *Majestic*, the Syndic battleships were trying to close within hell-lance reach while *Titan* and *Goblin* poured on all of the acceleration the damaged auxiliaries could manage in an attempt to stay out of range.

Orion started dropping back out of the line of fire between the Syndic battleships and the auxiliaries as if she had lost propulsion, even though Geary couldn't see any damage reported to *Orion*'s propulsion units. "That does it. If Commander Yin survives this battle, she's out as commander of that ship." His eyes focused on *Conqueror*, still far enough ahead of *Titan* and *Goblin* to be unable to defend them from the two Syndic battleships. "Captain Casia, too. I'll court-martial both of their worthless asses."

Desjani stretched her mouth in a humorless smile. "Cowardice before the enemy. You can just have them shot by order of summary execution. No one could complain with the records of this engagement as the official proof."

At the moment, with the fate of *Titan* and *Goblin* teetering in the balance, that option sounded entirely too good to Geary. If he lost those two ships because of Casia's and Yin's avoidance of battle, he knew he might not be able to resist the temptation to follow Desjani's advice.

Hell lances from the Syndic battleships began reaching out at extreme range, licking at the shields of *Titan* and *Goblin*. Geary knew the shields on the auxiliaries couldn't long withstand the punishment that a pair of battleships could inflict even at maximum range.

Flanconade weaved between the Syndic battleships and the Alliance auxiliaries, drawing Syndic fire for the few moments needed to tear apart the Alliance destroyer.

The sacrifices and the maneuvers finally added up to a decisive number as *Fearless*, *Resolution*, *Redoubtable*, and *Warspite* came within weapons range of the two Syndic battleships. The four Alliance battleships split their fire, two hammering one Syndic battleship and the other two hitting the remaining one as the Fifth Battleship Division finally engaged the enemy.

As the Alliance battleships drew away, both Syndic battleships staggered and slowed dramatically because of blows aimed at their propulsion systems. *Titan* and *Goblin* slowly pulled out of range as the hobbled Syndics tried to keep targeting them, then Tulev's four battle cruisers came in from another angle on their second firing run and smashed the trailing Syndic battleship.

Geary blinked, trying to take in events all through the region of battle. Desjani was leading *Dauntless*, *Daring*, and *Victorious* against a hurt Syndic battleship. Elsewhere, *Vengeance* and *Revenge* were bearing down on the remaining Syndic battleship that had nearly destroyed *Titan* and *Goblin*. The other Syndic battleships still capable of fighting had been stripped of their escorts and were being slammed by repeated firing passes from Geary's subformations. The Syndic formation had completely fallen apart, replaced by a trail of damaged ships and debris leading back to where the

Casualty Flotilla had once existed. The only remaining organized Syndic naval force in Lakota Star System was the guard force, a mere two battleships and two battle cruisers with their escorts, far away and heading for the hypernet gate at a fast clip. "We won."

Dauntless's hell lances tore into the targeted Syndic battleship, then null fields from *Dauntless*, *Daring*, and *Victorious* dug huge holes in the enemy vessel. Desjani let out a long breath as *Dauntless* left her broken enemy behind, then nodded to Geary. "Yes, sir. You did."

"*We* won," Geary repeated. "This fleet won this victory, not me."

"You did help," Rione pointed out dryly.

Taking a deep breath, Geary called his fleet. "All ships in the Alliance fleet, general pursuit. Break formation and ensure no Syndic warships escape. Destroyers and light cruisers not engaged with the enemy are to recover escape pods from Alliance ships."

Space in Lakota Star System was now filled with wreckage and hundreds of Syndic escape pods. Geary's warships were pouncing on surviving but damaged Syndic warships, overwhelming them and adding to the quantity of both debris and escape pods as the remnants of the Syndic force were wiped out.

But the victory hadn't been painless. *Majestic* was gone, along with the heavy cruisers *Utap*, *Vambrace*, and *Fascine*. The defenders of the auxiliaries had taken heavy losses. In addition to *Flanconade*, the light cruisers *Brigandine*, *Carte*, and *Ote* had been destroyed, as well as the destroyers *Armlet*, *Kukri*, *Hastarii*, *Petard*, and *Spiculum*. Most of the other ships in the fleet had taken various degrees of damage and lost crew members. Measured against the Syndic losses the price was insignificant, but Geary had to fight off depression as he thought of his own fleet's dead.

"Sir, *Warrior* can't be saved," Desjani stated somberly.

He couldn't argue that even though he wanted to debate it. *Warrior* had fought so well, her crew going beyond the call of duty to protect the auxiliaries. *Warrior* deserved to survive, to return proudly to Alliance space. But the already-damaged battleship had been riddled, its propulsion systems destroyed, every weapon knocked out, and life support left spotty throughout the hull. Looking at the readouts and images of *Warrior*, Geary was forcefully reminded of how the wreck of *Audacious* had looked. "Commander Suram," he ordered, "you and your crew have performed in a manner that brings all possible honor to your ancestors, but *Warrior* is now beyond repair. Abandon ship."

Long before a reply could have come, the communications watch called out. "We're receiving a voice-only emergency circuit call from *Warrior*. It's very weak, but we've enhanced it."

Geary punched *accept* and listened to the message, the voice of Commander Suram oddly distorted by the electronic enhancements required to make the message understandable. "All systems are out except for emergency controls on the power core. We're attempting a safe core shutdown. *Warrior* cannot continue the fight. Many escape pods damaged or destroyed in the last engagement. Those members of the crew who can be held in the surviving pods are abandoning ship. To the honor of our ancestors."

"Continue the fight?" Geary wondered.

"With all systems out they're blind," Desjani answered. "They can see some explosions and signs of battle with the naked eye and the minor enhancement gear on their survival suits, but have no idea that's just us mopping up the Syndics. We need to get some ships there to pull off the rest of *Warrior*'s crew," she added quickly, "I'd recommend—"

"Sir," another watch-stander called in an alarmed voice. "We're picking up indications that *Warrior*'s power core is fluctuating. The emergency control systems must have been damaged, too, and are failing."

"How long until it blows?" Desjani snapped.

"Impossible to predict, Captain. It could hold until they manage a shutdown, or it could have already blown, and we haven't seen the light from it."

Desjani gave Geary a somber look. He nodded, knowing this was his call. Any ship trying to close on *Warrior* to rescue her trapped crew members would risk being caught in a core explosion. "Who were you going to recommend for crew recovery?" he asked Desjani.

"Ships from the Twentieth Destroyer Squadron," she responded immediately. "They're still close together and well positioned, but *Warrior* drifted away from the battle after she got knocked out, or rather the battle kept going and *Warrior* stayed about where she was. Our destroyers will require close to half an hour to get there and match speed to the wreck."

"Okay." Geary tapped his controls, thinking through his words. "Twentieth Destroyer Squadron, members of *Warrior*'s crew are trapped on board. *Warrior*'s power core is fluctuating uncontrollably and may blow at any time. Request to know which destroyers in your squadron will volunteer to close *Warrior* and attempt to take off her remaining crew."

The reply took only a little while, though it seemed agonizingly long. "Sir, this is Lieutenant Commander Pastak on *Gavelock*. *Arabas*, *Balta*, *Dao*, *Gavelock*, *Kururi*, *Sabar*, and *Wairbi* volunteer to assist *Warrior*'s crew. All ships proceeding to intercept *Warrior* at maximum acceleration."

Geary checked his display. Every surviving destroyer in the squadron. "Don't let me forget this," he murmured to Desjani.

"I won't," she replied. "Did you expect anything else?"

"I don't know. I do know I am proud as hell to command this fleet."

"Estimated time for destroyers to reach *Warrior* is twenty-three minutes," the maneuvering watch announced.

"Try to get a message through to *Warrior*'s survivors that the destroyers are on the way."

"Yes, sir. We are now in communication with the escape pods launched from *Warrior* and will try to relay through them."

Geary nodded almost absently, his mind's eye too easily imagining the scene on *Warrior* right now, the few sailors who could work on the power core trying to keep it under control, the rest waiting in the ruin of their ship for rescue or death. "Is Commander Suram on one of the escape pods?" he asked, already guessing the answer.

"No, sir. The highest-ranking officer on one of the pods is a Lieutenant Rana, who is badly wounded."

He felt curiously detached as he saw the symbols of the escape pods racing away from *Warrior,* his mind numb after all of the other losses this day. Escape pods were designed to boost rapidly away from their ship on the assumption that distance would be critical, and in this case that was certainly true. "How much longer until the escape pods are outside the estimated danger zone for *Warrior*'s power-core blast radius?"

"Five minutes, sir. That's the estimate based on the known state of *Warrior*'s power core and the readings we're picking up on it."

Seven minutes later, with the destroyers of the Twentieth Squadron still sixteen minutes away, Geary watched the image of *Warrior* blossom into an irregular sphere of light and debris. He confirmed that the escape pods were far enough outside the blast area to be able to ride out the shock wave, then closed his eyes, took a long, slow breath, and called *Gavelock.* "Lieutenant Commander Pastak, please alter your mission to recovery of the escape pods from *Warrior.* They were close enough to the core overload that many probably received some damage. Thank you, thank all of your ships, for your efforts."

Pastak's somber acknowledgment came a few minutes later, then Geary leaned back and closed his eyes again. "Sir?" Desjani whispered. He shook his head, denying any conversation. After a moment, her hand closed over his wrist and squeezed tightly for a second in wordless comfort before being withdrawn. She knew how he felt, and somehow that made it a little easier to bear.

FIVE

GEARY sighed as the tensions of worrying about the upcoming battle were replaced by the pains of dealing with the aftermath of that engagement. He felt incredibly weary, as though he had been on the bridge of *Dauntless* for most of a week instead of most of a day.

"The Syndic guard force is still about thirty light-minutes from the hypernet gate," Desjani reported, her own voice tired. "If they keep up their speed, they'll reach it in about four and a half hours."

"Fine." Geary rubbed his eyes, then looked back at his display. That Syndic guard force was now almost two light-hours away from the Alliance fleet. If it had been a lot, lot closer, he might have had to worry about a suicide charge against *Dauntless* or the auxiliaries, but at this distance the Syndics would take almost a day to get here after they started such a charge. "I guess we can decide what to do about them later."

There didn't seem to be much to worry about for the moment. The guard force was clearly going to stick close to the hypernet gate, just as it had last time the Alliance fleet was here, and that gate lay about two and a half light-hours off to port of the Alliance fleet. The habitable world that Lakota boasted was orbiting on the opposite side of its star from the Alliance fleet, almost two and a quarter light-hours to starboard. The Syndic military assets there wouldn't be any threat unless the Alliance fleet came close to that world, and Geary had no intention of doing that.

Otherwise, the Syndic presence here seemed rapidly to be going to ground as the light from the latest engagement reached different parts of Lakota Star System. Merchant ships were fleeing for whatever sanctuary they could find, and colonies and mining operations on outer planets were shutting down equipment as they sent their populace to whatever shelters existed. Accustomed to having Alliance forces bombard Syndic worlds, the people in the system expected the worst from the victorious fleet. It wasn't going to happen, but Geary didn't feel like explaining that to them at the moment.

All around *Dauntless*, the now–widely dispersed ships of the Alliance fleet were making emergency battle repairs and running down Syndic warships knocked out but not destroyed in the battle, to ensure that their power cores were overloaded. Nothing was to be left for the Syndics to salvage. Shuttles flew between Alliance ships, carrying critically needed replacement parts for those warships requiring them. Destroyers and light cruisers darted around, finding and picking up every Alliance escape pod ejected by ships lost during the battle. Geary had already heard of one such pod, containing sailors who had abandoned the battleship *Indefatigable* during the first engagement in Lakota Star System weeks ago, been captured by the Syndics and taken to the wreck of *Audacious*, been liberated by Alliance Marines earlier today and taken to the heavy cruiser *Fascine*, then had to abandon *Fascine* when the heavy cruiser was shot up, and finally been rescued again by the light cruiser *Tsuba*. He wondered if those sailors regarded themselves as lucky or unlucky, and whether or not they were worried by the fact that they'd kept ending up on progressively smaller warships.

Rione stood up with her own heavy sigh. "I need to check on a few things. Let me know if you need me," she told Geary.

Needing her could mean a number of different things. The ambiguity of the phrase made him wonder if Rione had decided it was time for them to share a physical relationship again. Then Geary spotted Desjani's teeth clenching for a moment, her eyes rigidly fixed on her display before she relaxed herself. Apparently Desjani had interpreted the phrase the same way and hadn't liked it. He hadn't noticed that kind of reaction from her before and wondered if Desjani was more worried about Rione's influence on him than he had realized.

He could scarcely discuss that now, though, so Geary turned toward Rione and shook his head. "I'll be fine. Get some rest."

"That's not too likely, but I'll try."

Desjani visibly relaxed after Rione had left. "You should get some rest, too, sir."

"There's a lot of after-battle mess to clean up," Geary replied.

"We can handle that. You've already ordered our ships to return to their places in Fleet Formation Delta Two once they finish their postbattle operations. They can do that without you watching them. Even *Orion* and *Conqueror* can carry out tasks reliably if they're not being shot at."

"Yeah, I guess they can." Geary stood, surprised by how unsteady on his feet he felt. "Are you going to get any rest?"

Desjani shrugged apologetically. "I'm the captain of *Dauntless*, sir."

"And captains of warships never get to rest." He hesitated, then asked the question he had wanted to avoid. "How many did *Dauntless* lose?"

She took a deep breath, then answered in a steady voice. "Twelve. We were lucky. Another nineteen wounded, two critically."

"I'm sorry." Geary rubbed his forehead, meaningless phrases about honoring their sacrifices rolling through his brain. Twelve more sailors who would never again see Alliance space, never again see their homes, families, and loved ones. Twelve more just on this lightly damaged ship. Multiply that across the fleet, and the great victory suddenly felt even less worthy of celebration.

Maybe Desjani felt the same. As if reading his mind, she shook her head. "I guess we're all a little shell-shocked, sir. Tomorrow I'll be able to appreciate what we did here. Right now I'm just trying to keep going."

"You and me both." He frowned down at the deck. "What was I doing?"

"Rest, sir," Desjani prodded.

"If you can remember that, you're in better shape than I am. I'll be back up here in a little while."

"Yes, sir."

"Call me in an hour or so."

"Yes, sir."

"I mean it, Captain Desjani."

"Yes, sir."

He left the bridge, somehow certain that Desjani had decided that she wouldn't actually call him unless another emergency erupted but too tired to debate the issue any longer.

HIS stateroom comm alert buzzed angrily, jerking Geary awake. He'd fallen asleep in a chair and took a moment to orient himself before acknowledging the call.

"Captain Geary," Desjani reported, "there's a problem at the Syndic hypernet gate."

His stomach turned to lead. "Reinforcements for the Syndics?" His fleet wasn't in any shape to fight another major engagement. The aliens on the other side of Syndic space had diverted a big Syndic force to Lakota the last time the Alliance fleet was in the star system, baffling the Syndics but giving them an opportunity to destroy the Alliance fleet. They'd come far too close to succeeding. Somehow the aliens had known the Alliance fleet would be at Lakota the first time, but his immediate jump back should have thrown off even whatever means of tracking the aliens were using.

"No, sir." Geary's initial relief at Desjani's words vanished as she continued speaking. "The Syndic guard force is destroying the gate."

Geary took the distance to the bridge in record time, coming to a halt beside his command seat and staring at the images on his display. It took him a moment to accept what he was seeing. As Desjani had reported, the Syndic guard force at the hypernet gate had opened fire on the gate. "They're taking down the gate. While we're still light-hours away." His disbelief must have been obvious.

Desjani was checking her own display and made a gesture of contempt. "The Syndic commanding that guard force has panicked. He or she has orders to ensure you don't use that gate, so they're acting long before they have to act."

"But this fleet is so far away, we're much less likely to be damaged by the resulting energy discharge!" Geary stared at the representations of the Syndic guard force. "And his or her own ships are right there. Why commit probable suicide if you don't have to?"

Rione answered, her voice sharp. He hadn't noticed her coming onto the bridge, but she must have been right behind him. "Obviously because the Syndic commander doesn't know what's going to happen when that hypernet gate collapses. The commander wasn't informed, either because of a misplaced emphasis on secrecy or because no one thought to do so in the wake of this fleet's apparent defeat in this same star system almost two weeks ago."

Desjani spoke as if to herself. "Or because the Syndic Executive Council didn't want their on-scene commander knowing what would happen and deliberately kept that commander in the dark to ensure their orders would be followed."

Geary had a sick feeling that Desjani's guess was the right one. The Syndic leadership would have wanted to ensure that the Alliance fleet couldn't use the hypernet gate, and would have decided to withhold any information that might have caused their own commander to hesitate in carrying out orders to destroy it.

"Therefore," Rione continued as if Desjani hadn't spoken, "that commander is playing it safe, terrified that this fleet will once again do something that is supposed to be impossible, not realizing that playing it safe is actually dooming them."

Geary turned on her. "The Syndics are playing it safe because they think this fleet can do the impossible?" he demanded.

She met his gaze coolly. "Don't blame me. *You're* the one who keeps achieving the impossible."

Arguing with Rione would obviously be as futile as usual. He took a moment to think, then called *Furious*. "Captain Cresida, can you give me an estimate of how long it would take the Syndic guard force to cause that hypernet gate to collapse?"

Several seconds later, Cresida's image appeared and nodded. "Just a moment, sir." She looked to one side, her eyes examining something, then back at Geary. "Assuming they continue firing and destroying gate tethers at their current observed rate, my calculations indicate that it would take between twenty and thirty minutes more for the gate to begin uncontrollable collapse. I'm sorry I can't be more precise, but it's mostly theory since we just don't have enough actual gate-collapse data to reference."

Twenty or thirty minutes. And the gate was two and a half light-hours away. "So it probably collapsed a little over two hours ago."

A few more seconds, then Cresida nodded again. "Yes, sir."

"Is there any way to estimate the level of the energy discharge before it gets to us?"

"The energy pulse is going to propagate outward at the speed of light, Captain Geary." Cresida shook her head. "We'll find out when it hits us. Which could happen in about twenty minutes."

There was very little time left to react. Geary spun to Desjani. "Get me a course directly away from the hypernet gate's location." While she was coming up with that, he studied his display, looking at the disposition of his ships and realizing he had no time to rearrange them.

"Port one four zero degrees, down one two degrees," Desjani announced.

Geary slapped the fleetwide command circuit. "All units in the Alliance fleet. Immediate course change. All ships come port one four zero degrees, down one two degrees, and accelerate to point one light. I say again, immediate execute turn port one four zero degrees, down one two degrees, and accelerate to point one light. The Syndic guard force has caused the hypernet gate in this system to collapse, generating an energy discharge of unknown scale. The energy discharge is theoretically capable of a nova-scale level. In one five minutes all ships are to cease acceleration, pivot to place themselves bow-on to the Syndic hypernet gate's location, reinforce bow shields to the maximum strength possible, and set maximum preparation levels for damage control and repair."

He slumped backward as Desjani rapped out orders and *Dauntless* swung onto the new course, her propulsion units kicking in hard enough once again to make the inertial dampers whine in protest. "Captain Desjani," Geary asked, "can this ship survive a nova-scale burst of energy at this distance from the source?" He was pretty sure he already knew the answer and pretty sure it wasn't a happy one, but he wanted to be certain.

"I seriously doubt it." Desjani frowned, then glanced around the bridge, focusing on one watch-stander. "Assessment?" she demanded.

The watch-stander tapped a data pad frantically, then shook his head. "No, ma'am. As the burst expands away from the source, its single-point intensity is going to be dropping rapidly, but not nearly fast enough. A battle cruiser's shields and armor, even at full strength, couldn't withstand it even with maximum preparations. Destroyers, cruisers, they'd be totally overwhelmed. Battleships might have a chance at this distance. Not a big one, but some might make it through, though they'd be completely crippled." He paused and tapped a couple of more times. "The battleships' crews would all be killed by the radiation, though, after it collapsed their shields, so I guess it wouldn't matter."

Desjani blew out a long breath, then looked to Geary. "We'd better hope it's not nova-scale."

"I was thinking the same thing," he agreed.

Desjani seemed to hesitate, then turned back to the same watch-stander. "What about the inhabited world in this star system?"

Geary stared at her. In his concern for the fleet, he hadn't yet considered what would happen to that world. Yet Desjani had, or at least had realized that he would care.

The watch-stander rubbed his brow with one hand and tapped his data pad again. "There's a lot of uncertainties. If the energy wave is nova-scale or anywhere near that, the planet will be turned into a cinder. If it's something a great deal lower than that, the side facing the hypernet gate's former location when the shock wave hits will be fried, but the sheltered side might be able to ride it out though they'll face horrific storms. Whether the planet will be habitable after that is hard to say."

"What about the star itself?" Geary asked. "What'll be the effect on Lakota?"

"That's impossible to determine without knowing how much energy will hit it, sir." The watch-stander shook his head. "If it's nova-scale, the star will be really messed up, but then no one will be left around here to care. Anything less than that, it's just too hard to estimate. Stars have incredibly complex internal reactions going on constantly. They're remarkably self-regulating, but even the most stable star has some variability in output. If I had to guess, I'd say that if this energy burst we're expecting is at all significant, it will cause enough problems inside the star Lakota's photosphere to make it experience more variability at shorter intervals."

"So even if the habitable world remains able to support life, the star Lakota may render it uninhabitable in the near future."

"Yes, sir. I can't say that will happen, but I'd regard it as a probable outcome."

Desjani frowned and checked her display. "That world is almost five light-hours from the hypernet gate and two and a quarter light-hours from this fleet. If we sent a warning message, they would get it in time to at least order people into shelter, though that's unlikely to matter to those on the side of the planet that gets hit."

The woman warrior who had once expressed regret that null-field weapons couldn't be used against enemy planets was now willing to warn enemy civilians. "Thank you for thinking of that," Geary told her.

"We need survivors, sir. People who can tell other Syndics that the Alliance fleet didn't do this."

Desjani was just being pragmatic, then. Or justifying her actions on pragmatic grounds. He wondered which it was. Geary's eyes strayed back to the display of Lakota Star System. He looked at the data for the main inhabited world, at the representations of colonies on other worlds or moons, at the orbital facilities and the civilian space traffic that hadn't yet reached a place where the crews could take refuge if the Alliance fleet sent warships after them. And at the clusters of small symbols that marked escape pods from Syndic warships and repair ships fleeing for safety. Hundreds, probably thousands of Syndic personnel in those escape pods, but Geary didn't want an estimate of their numbers. They wouldn't stand a chance if the energy discharge from the collapsing gate had any power at all, and there was nothing he could do about it. "I need a broadcast to the entire star system."

How do you tell so many people that death may already be on its way? Geary tried to speak calmly, but knew his voice sounded bleak. "People of Lakota Star System, the Syndicate Worlds' warships at your hypernet gate have opened fire on it to prevent its use by the Alliance fleet. By the time you receive this message, the hypernet gate will certainly have collapsed. When it does so, a burst of energy will be released, a burst which could be powerful enough to wipe out all life in this star system. If we're fortunate, the energy burst will be much weaker than that, but it could easily be extremely dangerous to all human lives, ships, and installations in this star system. I urge you to take all possible measures in the very short time available to protect yourselves."

Geary paused, then spoke slowly. "I don't know how many of the humans in this star system will survive this. May the living stars watch over all here, and may their ancestors welcome all who die this day. To the honor of our ancestors, this is Captain John Geary, commander of the Alliance fleet."

The silence afterward was broken by Victoria Rione. "They were already anticipating bombardment by us and taking shelter. Maybe that will help."

"Maybe. It's not going to help all of those Syndics in escape pods." It only took the briefest look at the display to confirm that the Syndic escape pods were all too far distant for any Alliance ships to reach in time. "Unless the energy discharge is almost nothing, they won't stand a chance."

"Thank the living stars we already got all of ours recovered," Desjani murmured.

"Two minutes to turn, Captain," the maneuvering watch advised.

The initial moves to speed away from the Syndic hypernet gate's location had taken place ship by ship as Geary's order reached them, the farthest ships turning last. But the next maneuver was based on the time Geary had sent the first order, and so exactly fifteen minutes after Geary's message, the Alliance fleet turned as one, ship after ship swinging its bows to face the place where the Syndic hypernet gate still appeared intact but wavering as its tethers were blown away by the Syndic guard force. But the light showing that was over two and a half hours old, an image from the past. For well over two hours that gate had been gone, replaced by a discharge of energy of unknown intensity. The Alliance ships were facing the source of the energy burst with their heaviest shields and armor, and still heading away from it stern-first at close to point one light speed, which would reduce the force of the impact. "Forward shields at maximum strength," the combat-systems watch reported to Captain Desjani. "All compartments sealed, crew braced for damage, repair capabilities at highest readiness levels."

"Very well." Desjani bent her head for a moment, her eyes closed, her lips moving silently.

A prayer right now was a good idea, Geary reflected. He

also took a moment to say a few words noiselessly, pleading with the living stars to preserve this fleet and its crews, and with his ancestors for whatever aid they could provide.

"Standing by for earliest assessed possible impact time," another watch-stander announced. "Three . . . two . . . one . . . mark."

The moment passed without any change, the image of the distant hypernet gate still there, still fluctuating as the tethers holding the energy matrix in place were destroyed one by one. It had been absurd to think that Cresida's earliest estimate would be accurate to the second, but it was human nature to lock on to that time as critical.

Another minute went by, everyone on the bridge of *Dauntless* staring at their displays as if they would somehow provide advance warning, when in fact the wave front would hit at the speed of light, providing no notice before it struck.

Geary stared at the distant image of the hypernet gate, the fluctuations in energy levels inside it obvious to the fleet's sensors even from this far away. He would never forget how it had felt close to a collapsing gate, as *Dauntless*, *Daring*, and *Diamond* had fought to keep the gate at Sancere from frying the star system it had served. Space itself had been warping inside the gate as the forces within it were unleashed, causing effects echoed within nearby human bodies even through the shields and armor of the warships. Only Captain Cresida's theoretical firing plan for causing the gate to collapse in a way that minimized the resultant energy discharge had saved the three Alliance warships and who knew how many other ships and inhabitants in the Sancere Star System.

He wondered how the crews of those Syndic ships destroying the gate in this star system had felt, whether they'd experienced those forces and questioned their orders, whether they'd had time to realize that their obedience to commands was dooming not only them but also a great many other inhabitants of Lakota. He'd never know. Unaware of what they were unleashing, those ships had almost certainly been destroyed more than two hours ago, their crews forever silenced.

One more minute. Two more. Geary heard others muttering to themselves, the words inaudible but the tones clearly pleading. *The words of the prayers change, but they always mean the same thing. Have mercy please, because there's nothing else that human skill or device can do now.*

The shock wave slammed into *Dauntless*. Geary fought down a surge of fear as the ship jerked and lights dimmed, his mind knowing that if the energy burst had been great enough to destroy *Dauntless*, then the battle cruiser would have been shattered before he had time to be afraid.

"Forward shields down thirty percent, no hull damage, minor energy leak-through affecting ship systems." The reports rolled in while Geary waited for the display to clear and reveal the state of his fleet, whether his lighter ships had been able to survive the blow.

"Preliminary estimate places the energy output at the source at point one three on the Yama-Potillion Nova Scale."

"Point one three," Desjani murmured, then she ducked her head again and her lips moved without a sound for a moment.

Geary did the same, breathing his own quick thanks that the energy output had been so much lower than it could have been.

The display cleared, symbols updating rapidly. Geary ran his eyes across his ship-status reports, searching for red-lined systems. The hardest hit had been the destroyers since their shields were weakest, but none seemed to have suffered major damage. A lot of subsystems blown and a few cases of hull damage, but otherwise even the fleet's smallest ships had come through intact.

Where the image of the Syndic hypernet gate and the nearby Syndic warships had been, there was now nothing. It took the fleet's sensors a few moments to find what was left of the Syndic guard force. Whatever remained of the smaller warships was in pieces too small for the system to find immediately. Large pieces of debris tumbling away from the former site of the hypernet gate were assessed as the remains of the two Syndic battle cruisers. One of the two battleships had also been shattered into several large fragments, while the other had broken into two segments that seemed very badly torn up. As Geary watched, one of the big segments blew up. Or rather, he finally saw the light from two and a half hours ago showing the segment explode back then. "They never knew what hit them. That close to the energy discharge, even reinforced shields wouldn't have been enough."

Desjani nodded. "That's what would've happened to us at Sancere if Captain Cresida's calculations hadn't worked, isn't it?"

"Yeah."

"I owe that woman a drink when we get home."

Geary couldn't help a short laugh born of relief. "I think we owe her more than that. A bottle of the finest booze we can find. I'll go halves with you on it."

Desjani's mouth widened in a brief, tight smile. "Deal." The smile vanished. "Where now?"

"Let's head toward the jump point for Branwyn. What should our course be if we hold this speed?" He could have worked it out himself easily but didn't trust his thinking at the moment.

Desjani glanced toward her maneuvering watch, who hastily worked out the solution.

Geary paused a moment longer to ensure that his voice would be steady, then punched his command circuit again. "All units in the Alliance fleet, return to positions in Fleet Formation Delta Two. At time three five all units turn together starboard one zero six degrees, up zero four degrees."

Now that they were behind the shock wave, they could watch it sweep over those parts of the star system that hadn't yet been hit. It was like watching a terrible before-and-after presentation. Ahead of the shock wave, before it struck each region, Lakota brimmed with life and activity. As the shock wave expanded across the star system and swept over human habitations and ships, it left behind a field of broken debris and death.

The Syndic escape pods had been simply annihilated by the shock wave, wiped out like a swarm of gnats in the path of a heavy, fast-moving vehicle, the sailors inside them dying instantly. A couple of freighters, too far from anywhere to reach safety, had been torn apart. One colony on the moon of a gas giant had been sheltered by the gas giant itself, though the giant had shed a fair amount of upper atmosphere as the shock wave passed by. That colony was an exception though. Two other colonies, on the fifth planet, were badly damaged, and a third on another moon was possibly wiped out.

Hardest to watch had been the impact of the energy discharge on the habitable world. On the side of the planet facing the shock wave when it hit, huge amounts of atmosphere had been scattered and blown off, the surfaces of oceans, seas, rivers, and lakes flashing to vapor. Forests and fields burst into momentary flame, the heat so intense that they were almost instantly reduced to charred remnants. Cities became melted, flattened fields of wreckage. Towns were so badly crushed by the wave of energy that many to all intents and purposes vanished.

Half a world died in the space of seconds.

"It's possible that people in deep enough shelter on the exposed side might have survived the shock wave's hitting," a watch-stander reported.

"What about the aftermath?" Rione demanded.

The watch-stander grimaced. "A lot of them will be trapped. Food supplies are gone, the atmosphere appreciably thinned worldwide, all that water vapor and ash blown into the air. There are going to be some horrendous storms. I don't know, Madam Co-President. The people on the sheltered side might stand a chance even though life will get awfully rough. The ones who got hit . . . Well, I wouldn't want to have been there when it hit, and I wouldn't want to be there trying to survive."

Geary nodded. "And that was only a point one three nova-scale output of energy. Way toward the low end of the possible output."

Desjani had her eyes on the display, her face rigid, but she said nothing as she gazed at the image of a ruined world.

"Seeing this," Rione observed in a quiet voice, "it's hard

to see them as enemies. They just look like people who need help."

Geary nodded again, silently.

"Can we render any assistance?" Rione asked.

This time he shook his head. "Unfortunately, I have experience with this. When I was a junior officer, the star in the Cirinci system spat out a big flare that fried most of the facing parts of the primary inhabited planet in that star system." No one on *Dauntless*'s bridge seemed to recognize the event, a more-than-a-century-old tragedy lost to popularly remembered history in the wake of the many disasters that had followed as war raged for decade after decade.

Fighting off the old feeling of being lost among strangers, his own life vanished in time, Geary used one hand to indicate the display. "Cirinci wasn't this bad, from what I can see, but we had to run out the disaster-relief requirements to see what the fleet could do, and the answer kept coming up not very damn much. The Alliance government had to requisition lots of civilian freighters to carry the relief-and-rebuilding supplies, and even then it all took too long. I think the only military assets that ended up being used were some of the big troop transports to bring in relief workers and haul out evacuees. Even if this fleet was fully stocked, and it's far from that, everything we could do would be a drop in the bucket compared to what the surviving people in this star system need. And we couldn't expect much in the way of gratitude from the Syndic leaders. They'd still do their level best to destroy us if we lingered here."

Rione sighed. "There's nothing that can be done?"

"We'll tell every Syndic system we pass through that they need help here." Geary pointed to his display. "Some Syndic merchant ships survived the shock wave. They sheltered behind available worlds, either by luck or because they got our warning in time. Those ships can go for help."

"Yes. They'll tell everyone what happened here." Rione's eyes met his, and Geary nodded once more.

It was no longer a matter of trying to keep secret the destructive potential of collapsing hypernet gates, but rather a matter of dealing with the results of the knowledge of that spreading as fast as humans could pass on reports of disaster.

Desjani finally spoke again. "The Syndic leaders." She turned a hard gaze on Geary. "After Sancere, some of them surely suspected what destroying this gate could do to this star system. But they ordered it here anyway, and apparently told no one what to expect. If the energy burst had been strong enough, everyone in this star system would have died and no one could have reported what really happened." Her eyes returned to the display of the devastated world. "This isn't war. It's an atrocity, committed on these people by their own leaders in an attempt to destroy this fleet."

There wasn't much he could say to that except to nod once more in silent agreement.

Desjani spoke again, her tone abrupt. "There could be Alliance prisoners of war on that world. Some of them could've been brought there after our battles here nearly two weeks ago."

Geary's eyes went back to the image of the ruined world. He forced out an answer. "If they were on the side of the planet that got hit, they're beyond finding and beyond help."

"What if they're on the other side?" Desjani swung on her watch-standers, barking out orders. "I want a fine-grain analysis of that world prior to the shock wave hitting for any signs of a prisoner-of-war encampment or indications of Alliance personnel being held anywhere. Optics, communications, everything!"

"Captain, analysis of the planet prior to the shock wave's hitting it didn't reveal any such indications—"

"*Do it again!* If there's an Alliance flea alive on that world, I want to know it!"

Desjani's voice echoed on the suddenly silent bridge, then her watch-standers hastily acknowledged the orders and jumped to their tasks. As Desjani slumped in her captain's chair, glaring at her display, Rione eyed her somberly, then left the bridge without another word. Geary hesitated, reading Desjani's mood of frustration and outrage at what had happened in this star system, then left silently as well. Sometimes even the closest friends needed distance.

Geary wandered through the passageways of *Dauntless* for a while, feeling depressed and restless. He'd just been coming out of his postvictory low caused by the inevitable cost of any victory when the sight of the destruction wreaked by the hypernet gate's collapse had made him dejected again.

The crew members he met were subdued as well, but also giddy with the relief of survival and victory. In days to come, the extent of the victory would sink in and elation would follow, but for now everyone was mostly just glad to be alive and still have a chance of getting home. They seemed to regard Geary with even more awe than he'd encountered on any previous occasion. Not able to stand much of that, Geary retreated to the only sure shelter available.

When he finally reached his stateroom, craving some time alone, Rione was already there and staring at the star display, her attitude distant. "My condolences on the losses to the fleet," she stated in a low voice.

"Thanks." Geary sat down, keeping his own eyes fixed on the display, not wanting to be around anyone else at the moment or to talk about his fleet's latest losses. Not when memories of the destruction caused by the hypernet gate's collapse were still fresh in his mind as well.

"As far as I can tell," Rione continued, "Captain Faresa died on *Majestic*."

"Nobody got off that ship," Geary responded shortly.

"And Captain Kerestes died on *Warrior* along with Commander Suram."

That stung. Kerestes had been aggressively passive, something Geary had once thought impossible, so afraid of making a mistake that he took every effort to avoid doing anything. By contrast, in his short time as captain of *Warrior*, Commander Suram had motivated her dispirited crew and fought well. "I intend doing everything I can to ensure that Commander Suram receives the credit he deserves as commanding officer of that ship. Captain Kerestes had no role in the matter." Geary wondered briefly if Kerestes had even survived long enough to be among those trying to abandon ship. It was just as likely that he'd died in his stateroom as Syndic hell lances ravaged *Warrior*, a career dedicated to avoiding any action that might look bad ending at the hands of enemy warships that didn't care whether or not Captain Kerestes had a service record unblemished by any obvious blunders.

"And Captain Falco?" Rione asked.

Geary almost winced, thinking of the insane Captain Falco, confined to his quarters as *Warrior* fought her final battle. He hadn't yet discovered what Falco's last moments had been like, or even if anyone knew. "I hated what that man did, but that's no way for anyone to die."

"Most likely he was safely wrapped in his delusions," Rione suggested. "Believing he was commanding the battle, going down to heroic defeat, fighting to the last. Not realizing how little he really controlled his fate."

Geary didn't look at her. "Are you mocking him?"

"No. I sometimes wonder how different Falco's delusions would be from what you and I are doing." She paused. "Faresa, Kerestes, and Falco have died in battle. At least that spares you the worry of three court-martials if we make it back to Alliance space."

His temper boiled over. "Dammit, Victoria, if you're trying to find a silver lining in this, you're not doing a very good job! I didn't want two ships to die so those three could find some measure of justice! I don't even know what the hell justice would be for Falco!"

She stayed silent for a moment after his outburst. "I know you looked at records from Falco's past, before he was captured by the Syndics. You saw his speeches. Triumphantly celebrating so-called victories in which dozens of major Alliance warships were destroyed in exchange for at best equal numbers of Syndics. Do you think he would spend a single moment worrying about the loss of a few battleships?"

"That's not the point," Geary objected bitterly.

"No, of course not. You don't judge yourself in relation to people like Falco." Rione exhaled slowly. "As far as I can tell, all three of those officers did indeed die on their ships."

The idea that they might not have hadn't even occurred to Geary. "Is there some reason to think they didn't?"

Her smile held no humor. "A suspicious mind. Had Captain Faresa had time, I think her sympathizers among the crew would've helped her get off *Majestic*. But no one had such an opportunity. Those seeking to use Falco might have tried to get him off of *Warrior*, but . . ." She paused. "A fool and insane, but his last act was to refuse the chance to be evacuated from *Warrior*. You hadn't heard? A few witnesses survived. Falco declared it his duty to remain with *Warrior*, though it's hard to say if he truly realized what was happening. I suppose we can be charitable to the dead and assume he did."

Geary had no trouble believing it. He could see in his imagination Captain Falco moving dramatically through the shattered passageways of *Warrior*, Falco's practiced expression of confident camaraderie being turned to the officers and sailors with him awaiting their doom. The perfect theatrical role, and if Falco had recovered any of his sanity long enough to realize the fate that awaited him in Alliance space, perhaps a welcome chance to find his end as a dead hero rather than in disgrace at a court-martial. But, knowingly or not, he had chosen to die well and given his space in an escape pod to someone else who had lived as a result. "No one living knows what his last thoughts were like, so I don't see any reason not to grant him that." Geary frowned slightly as a thought occurred to him. "Is that right? There's no one alive who saw enough of him to tell?"

Rione frowned back. "How would I know?"

"You've obviously heard from eyewitnesses. You must have had some of your spies on those ships, too."

Her expression twitched, then settled back in emotionless lines. "Had. Past tense. One got off *Warrior*. Nobody got off *Majestic*, as you already noted."

Hell. "I should have realized that your spies on those ships died along with everyone else that didn't get off. I'm sorry."

She nodded once, still revealing no feelings. "They ran the same risks as everyone else in this fleet."

Geary glared at her, his nerves stretched to their limit. "Sometimes you act like a cold-blooded bitch."

Rione returned an impassive glance. "And you prefer your bitches warm-blooded?"

"Dammit, Victoria—"

She held up one hand. "We all deal with our pain in our own ways, John Geary. You and I handle that very differently."

"Yeah, we do." He looked down at the deck, knowing he was still frowning. Something else was bothering him, something he hadn't connected yet. Something about the Alliance fleet's losses. *Majestic, Warrior, Utap, Vambrace . . . Vambrace?*

He must have reacted as realization hit, because Rione spoke in a gentler tone. "What's the matter now?"

"I just remembered something." The heavy cruiser *Vambrace*, the ship to which Lieutenant Casell Riva had been transferred from *Furious*. A Syndic prisoner for almost ten years, liberated from a Syndic labor camp by this fleet and brought to Lakota, perhaps dead now. He tried to recall how many crew had gotten off *Vambrace* before she blew up. Had Riva been among them? Desjani hadn't said anything, even though she'd surely realized much sooner than he had.

"Something?" Rione pressed.

"It's a personal personnel issue." He had to pronounce the words carefully so they made sense to her. "I'm sorry for blowing up at you." Rione stayed quiet for so long that Geary looked up finally, seeing her watching him. "What?"

"Can you keep going?" she asked.

"Of course I can."

"Of course?" Rione shook her head. "We took significant losses again, and I know the havoc created on the inhabited world in this star system by the destruction of the hypernet gate weighs heavily on you. For a long time after assuming command of this fleet, you were balanced on a knife-edge, ready to fall off if the pressure grew too great. You weren't used to the sort of combat losses the Alliance has become accustomed to, so each ship lost weighed very heavily on you. You needed someone to prop you up, to keep you going, and for a while I filled that role, both as an ally to turn to and as an adversary to be bested. I don't anymore."

"Excuse me?" He studied her, trying to figure out what Rione was saying.

"Why are you fighting?" Rione asked, turning to face the star display again.

"For the people in this fleet. For the Alliance. You know that."

"I know that those things are abstractions. You don't know a fraction of the people in this fleet. The Alliance you knew is changed, your own home altered in ways I know have worried you." Rione glanced his way again. "You're not fighting for abstractions. No one does. Humans pay lip service to that, to big causes and great purposes, but any politician of any skill soon learns that what really motivates people is the small, personal things. Close friends, family, the small area they call home. They wrap those things around ideals and call them precious, but they're precious for the smallest and closest of reasons. Soldiers may swear to fight for their flag, but they really fight because of the soldiers next to them. You've found something like that, John Geary. Here in this fleet, some personal connection that gives you the strength and resolve to continue."

Geary eyed her. "And just what is that connection?"

"Not what. Who. Someone besides me." Rione was back to studying the stars. "I know who. I don't think you know yet. Or you haven't admitted it to yourself yet."

"Then tell me."

"No. You'll figure it out eventually. Then you'll have to deal with it. For now, I and this fleet need you at your best, so I just accept what is." She took a deep breath, then turned to face him. "Where are you taking the fleet next?"

The sudden shift in topic startled him, but Geary wasn't interested in pursuing whatever Rione's idea of his personal connection could be, so he just pointed to the display. "You heard. We're heading for the jump point for Branwyn."

She raised one eyebrow. "That didn't mean you were going to use that jump point. Your old objective from the first time we were in this star system. As close to a straight shot for Alliance space as you can manage."

"That's right. The Syndics should have enough major combatants left to bring us battle, and we know they're building replacements for their losses despite what we did to the shipyards at Sancere because they have a lot of other shipyards in other star systems. But after what we did here, they'll have to gather those ships. We should be able to transit Branwyn without much trouble, then go from there to Wendig. Branwyn is supposed to have a minimal Syndic presence left, and the records we've captured from the Syndics say that Wendig was completely abandoned almost thirty years ago. From there we'll have a couple of options, but I'm leaning toward Cavalos. There's a strong Syndic presence there, so they'll probably expect us to avoid it."

Rione nodded slowly. "I see. Will the mines the Syndics laid across the jump point to Branwyn during our first time in this star system be an obstacle?

"No." Geary pointed to the display. "They laid those mines so close to the jump point they couldn't maintain a stable position. We knew that then, but also that it would take a few weeks for the mines to drift away from the jump point, so it didn't do us any good at that time." He paused and gave a pained smile. "Hell, I'm an idiot. That energy discharge will have fried all the mines at all of the jump points in this star system. It wouldn't matter if they were still in position or not."

"Sadly, you're surely right. If only that had been all the shock wave destroyed. Do you believe we'll face many mines in the systems where you want to go?"

"Probably not. According to our intelligence people, if our estimates of the Syndic mine inventories are anywhere near accurate, they used up everything in their attempt to trap us in or near Lakota. They'll have to manufacture a lot more and get them to where they think we'll be before they can try that again."

"Good." She turned a demanding look on Geary. "That takes care of the Syndic threat. What about the aliens?"

"I don't know." Geary scowled at the virtual stars. "The aliens have actively intervened against us, and somehow they're tracking this fleet's movements, but I'm out of ideas at the moment."

"As am I. You need to make more people aware of them and see what ideas they can contribute." She obviously saw

Geary's surprise at the suggestion. "There are officers you can trust in this fleet. We can't try to solve a problem like this alone."

"That makes sense. A few have already been made aware of it, but I haven't really had any chance to talk it over with that group."

Rione nodded, obviously unsurprised by the news.

Geary shook his head as he considered the implications of the alien attempt to destroy his fleet. Whatever they were, they clearly had technology superior to humanity's. "I'm not sure whether to be glad that we haven't detected any more moves against us by them or worried that we haven't spotted anything those aliens are up to."

"I'd suggest worried," Rione stated.

"I thought you might. Is there anything else?"

"Yes." Rione briefly smiled sardonically at Geary's aggravated expression. "Your internal foes, the senior officers in this fleet who've been plotting against you since you assumed command."

If he really hated any part of his current situation, having to deal with disloyal officers who remained in the shadows had to be it. "Is there something specific you know? Something they're planning?"

"No. But I know they must be planning something, and they must be intending to act before much longer."

"Why?" Geary leaned forward. "Your spies must have told you something concrete to have you reach that conclusion."

"I've heard nothing!" Rione stepped closer, her face angry now. "Don't you understand? With every victory, with every star system you get this fleet closer to Alliance space, your legend grows and your standing in the fleet becomes stronger. Defeating the Syndics in this system was an amazing achievement, and if you want to partially credit my minor suggestion for that victory, then feel free, but even listening to such suggestions is a worthy accomplishment. This fleet believes in you. Sailors on every ship in this fleet are whispering that the living stars themselves intervened to prevent that energy discharge from destroying us, intervened because *you* are in command of the fleet."

He stared at her, aghast. Did that explain the looks he'd gotten from *Dauntless*'s crew recently? "You can't be serious."

"I can show you the reports I've received, or you can walk around this ship some more and listen to the crew talk. Even the ones who don't credit divine intervention with saving us believe with plenty of justification that your recognition of the danger and quick reaction saved many ships and personnel. Those in this fleet who didn't believe in Black Jack Geary the myth are coming to believe in Black Jack Geary the man, and those who always believed in you now have unshakeable faith. Your enemies in this fleet can see that as well as I can. After what you've done here, returning to annihilate a Syndic force that outnumbered you and had this fleet on the run, your enemies will be growing desperate. Despite their own disbelief in you, they have to be coming to the conclusion that you might actually get this fleet home. They know they must discredit or stop you soon, or their chance will be lost."

Geary nodded, his eyes narrowed in thought. "What do you think they'll do?"

"I don't know. I'm trying to find out. They can nibble away at your standing with accusations of personal scandal, but that alone can't dislodge you from command of this fleet. Not anymore. Their chosen figureheads like Casia are thoroughly discredited, not only because of your latest victory but also by their own recent actions. You have to assume that your real opponents among this fleet's senior officers will finally have to make themselves more publicly known. Because your opponents have to strike, and they have to do it before much longer. Somehow."

"You make it sound like they may actually attack me."

"They might. Fortunately, on this ship you're surrounded by the faithful, most notably your special captain, who would gladly sacrifice herself for Black Jack." Rione saw his angry reaction. "Don't try to claim otherwise. Just be grateful. She and I have our differences, but right now we are fully committed to ensuring that nothing happens to you."

Of all the strange things that had happened since he was

woken from survival sleep, the idea of Victoria Rione and Tanya Desjani standing on either side of him as bodyguards was perhaps the strangest. "I need to hold a conference with the ship commanders. Will you attend?"

"Not this time," Rione answered. "I will monitor events remotely, but I'd like to see what people say without me there."

Geary gave her a look. "The fleet conferences are conducted under a tight security seal. No one not present is supposed to be able to observe events."

"Ah, well, another illusion shattered. Any security lock a human can make can be broken by another human, John Geary." She went to the door. "I'll be watching. What will you do with Captain Casia and Commander Yin?"

"I'm still trying to decide," he replied truthfully.

"You don't have to be Black Jack to have them shot, you know. Even Admiral Bloch could have done it with a simple order."

"I know. I just don't know if I want to do that. Do you think they should be shot?"

"Yes, and as soon as possible, Captain Geary," Rione stated with total seriousness as she left.

SIX

GEARY walked steadily into the conference room. Although it was actually an average-sized compartment inside *Dauntless* with an unimpressive table anchored on one side, the conferencing software created the illusion of a room big enough to hold the commanding officer of every ship in the fleet, arrayed down the length of a table virtually expanded to accommodate them all.

Even though that table was now crowded with hundreds of officers, the only other person physically present in the room was Captain Desjani. The others were images, allowing officers to remain on their own ships and attend the meeting at the same time. Aside from the seconds-long delays in reacting that afflicted those officers on the ships farthest away, the images otherwise acted just as if every officer were actually here.

He'd never liked these conferences, and part of the business he had to do today was distasteful enough to make him look forward to this one even less than usual. Deciding to start on a high note, Geary nodded to the assembled officers. "May I open this meeting by congratulating the officers and enlisted personnel of this fleet on a great victory. We've not only more than avenged our losses from the last time the fleet was in Lakota Star System, we have in battles from Kaliban to here evened the score for all of the ships lost by this fleet since arriving in the Syndic home system. You have every right to feel proud of these great achievements, purchased by the courage and fighting spirit of everyone in the fleet."

Smiles appeared nearly everywhere. Geary noticed Captain Casia frowning into the distance and Commander Yin staring nervously at the table's surface. "Unfortunately," Geary continued, "not everyone in this fleet can honestly share in that praise. In our last engagement, two ships avoided battle. Or rather, two commanding officers avoided battle." The atmosphere in the room had suddenly grown extremely tense, the silence so profound it seemed the slightest noise would deafen everyone. Captain Casia's face had reddened, while that of Commander Yin had paled. No one else was looking at them. Whatever support they had once had was gone.

Geary faced Casia. "Captain Casia, you are hereby relieved of command of *Conqueror.* Your current executive officer will serve as acting commander. Commander Yin, you are relieved as acting commanding officer of *Orion. Orion*'s operations officer is appointed acting commanding officer, effective immediately. Both of you are to transfer to *Illustrious,* where you will be assigned to whichever tasks Captain Badaya finds appropriate." He'd wondered what best to do with Casia and Yin, who had openly opposed him in meetings like this, and the idea of sticking them on the same ship with Badaya, who was supporting Geary for the wrong reasons had a certain simplicity to it.

Commander Yin's mouth worked, but no sound came out. Captain Casia, though, stood up and spoke loudly. "You cannot relieve a senior officer without good cause!"

Geary somehow kept his voice level. "Your ship avoided combat. You had orders to protect this fleet's auxiliaries, and instead you remained too far from them to defend those ships, engaging only those enemy warships that came close enough to you to constitute a threat to your ship. You refused to engage enemy ships when both duty and honor required it."

"Are you accusing me of cowardice?" Casia almost shouted.

"Yes."

The single word rang through the room. In a fleet so obsessed with honor, to state such a charge openly was almost unthinkable.

Captain Tulev spoke into the silence that followed Geary's answer. "I am unhappy to be forced to agree that the records of the engagement fully support Captain Geary's charge."

"If so," Captain Armus noted, leaning forward, his face and voice hard, "and I agree with Captain Tulev that it *is* so, then simply relieving Captain Casia and Commander Yin of command falls far short of the punishment expected for such acts."

"Shoot the cowards," someone muttered.

Noise erupted as everyone began shouting, many seconding the suggestion, others protesting. Geary tapped the control that let him silence everyone, one of the best features of the conferencing software in his opinion, then waited a few moments for attention to return to him. "I am aware that fleet regulations permit me to order death by firing squad on the battlefield for any officer who clearly displays cowardice before the enemy." He looked to Casia again and was surprised that Casia met his eyes even though fear was apparent on the other officer's face. He felt a grudging measure of respect for Casia that the man hadn't collapsed.

"Fleet regulations *require* a firing squad," said Captain Kila, the commanding officer of *Inspire*. Why had she chosen now finally to speak up at a fleet conference?

Whatever the reason, she had challenged him, trying to force Geary to take an action he didn't want to take. So he shook his head. "That's incorrect."

Kila seemed not hostile but puzzled. "The regulation in question is clear and does not allow exception." Heads nodded around the table. Commander Yin appeared ready to pass out.

Geary shook his head again. "Surely every fleet officer is still familiar with standing fleet regulation thirty-two? 'In any situation, a fleet commander is expected to exercise independent judgment and take necessary and appropriate action regardless of the letter of preceding regulations, as long as such action does not violate Alliance law or the fleet commander's oath to defend the Alliance against all enemies foreign and internal.'"

"But was that intended to apply in cases like this?" Captain Armus asked.

"I assure you it was." Geary looked around the table again. "That fleet regulation was adopted about one hundred and ten years ago. I was a lieutenant, and required to attend briefings by the officers who had drawn up the new regulations."

Captain Kila had been about to speak again but hastily subsided.

To Geary's surprise, Cresida spoke up. "Sir, I accept that you have the right to deviate from regulations in this case, but I don't understand why. Why show mercy to officers whose failures contributed to the loss of other ships? If they'd supported *Warrior* and *Majestic*, both of those ships might have survived this battle, to say nothing of the cruisers and destroyers lost defending the auxiliaries."

It was a fair enough question. "To put it bluntly, Captain Cresida, I chose not to order a field execution of those two officers because I wasn't feeling merciful."

That brought looks of surprise and bafflement, including from Cresida. "You were *not* feeling merciful?"

"No." Geary looked toward Casia and Yin. "Sending these two officers to the arms of their ancestors would end their suffering in this world. As long as they live, they'll have to face some of the officers and sailors they failed. Officers and sailors who know what they did. Every living moment they'll have to face those who know they chose cowardice."

A long silence followed before Tulev spoke again. "Are you certain, Captain Geary, that these two officers will feel that scorn and contempt as harshly as you and I? Will they not simply be grateful that their lives have not been given either in the line of duty or as punishment for their failures?"

Another fair question. Geary looked again to where Casia was glaring at him, his eyes haunted, and Yin was almost shaking as she avoided everyone else's eyes. "Do they look grateful, Captain Tulev?"

Armus frowned at the two. "I suggest they be given the right to appeal, Captain Geary. I'd like to hear what they want."

"That's a reasonable request, Captain Armus, and in light of your service, I have no trouble granting it." Armus had been a pain in the butt for Geary more than once, but in battle he'd fought well and with honor. Now Armus responded to Geary's words with ill-concealed satisfaction as Geary turned to Casia. "Well?" he asked. "What do you feel is an appropriate punishment?"

Casia looked around the table, straightening himself, then back at Geary. "I demand a fleet officer's death. You call me coward. I see agreement in many of my comrades' eyes. I'll prove you all wrong when I face the firing squad."

Another surprise. Geary examined the other officers, seeing approval on their faces. They wanted this.

He looked down for a moment, wondering why it was so hard to make a decision that regulations, honor, and the fleet's officers all agreed was right. He had ordered this fleet into action numerous times, sending ships into combat where death was a constant possibility. Twelve sailors had died aboard *Dauntless* alone in the last battle. By his orders. Yet that was a far different thing than this, deliberately to order an officer to die.

Geary looked up again. Casia was waiting, his eyes pleading now. *Let me die with honor.*

"Very well." Geary nodded slowly. "Your request is granted, Captain Casia. I will approve execution by firing squad."

Casia's mouth twitched into a ghastly smile. "In Lakota. I want it done before the fleet leaves Lakota."

"Very well," Geary repeated. "Colonel Carabali, please canvass your Marines for volunteers for the firing squad." He took a deep breath, then fixed his gaze on Commander Yin. "Commander, do you also wish to appeal?"

He thought she might break down completely, but Yin suddenly leaped to her feet. "I was following orders!" she shouted.

A moment of baffled silence followed. "Not my orders," Geary finally stated.

"You are not competent to command this fleet!" Yin answered, her eyes wide. "You're only a figurehead for those using you against the Alliance! They want to bring you home with all of these victories to your 'credit' and install you as a dictator! You and your . . . your female companion!"

It had been a little while since the last attack on Co-President Rione, so Geary wasn't surprised that Yin was dragging her into this. But then he realized that everyone in the conference was either looking at or obviously not looking at Captain Desjani. In turn, Desjani had her eyes fixed on Yin. If Desjani's eyes had been hell-lance batteries, there would have been nothing left of Commander Yin but drifting ash.

The rumors of his being involved with Desjani clearly hadn't died. There wasn't any good way to address those now, however. Geary focused instead on the rest of Yin's accusation. He'd been assuming that those opposed to his command of the fleet had been motivated primarily by personal ambition or personal dislike or distrust. Instead, if Yin's words were to be trusted, at least some of them were motivated by fear that Geary or those backing him intended to overthrow the government of the Alliance. Those enemies might be working against him for reasons he could respect.

He was still thinking that through when Captain Duellos spoke sharply. "Commander Yin, whose orders were you following if not Captain Geary's?"

She wavered, gulped once, then answered unsteadily. "Captain Numos."

"Captain Numos is under arrest," Duellos observed. "He is not able to issue orders. You know that."

"I know that the arrest and all orders pertaining to it were themselves unlawful!"

Commander Neeson of *Implacable* spoke in a puzzled voice. "Does the charge of cowardice before the enemy stand if Commander Yin claims to have been following orders she believed to be legitimate?"

"She knew they weren't legitimate," Captain Badaya of *Illustrious* argued. "Commander Yin had to know that."

"But if she's saying she avoided action for that reason, it's not the same as cowardice. Or is it?" Neeson appeared frustrated now.

Geary rapped one fist on the table to draw Commander Yin's attention again. "Commander, I understand you to be claiming that you avoided engaging the enemy in accordance with orders from Captain Numos. Are you denying the charge of cowardice?"

Yin visibly quivered, but choked out one word. "Yes."

Tulev shook his head. "That still amounts to disobedience of orders in the face of the enemy, which is also a battlefield execution offense."

Low conversations broke out all along the table, officers debating the issue. Geary thought about it himself for a moment. "Commander Yin, there are issues here that don't have simple answers. I am hesitant to order the execution of an officer in circumstances under which she may have thought her actions justified." Everyone was listening intently. "Nonetheless, by your own admission you have violated orders from me, not only on the battlefield but also in conferring with Captain Numos. That alone is more than adequate grounds for relieving you of command. However, I will not unilaterally order the execution of an officer who claims to have believed her behavior was required by duty. You will be held under arrest, Commander Yin, until such time as this fleet returns to Alliance space, there to have proper charges lodged against you in a court-martial in which you can defend your actions and receive such justice as is considered appropriate by the judgment of your peers."

No one called out objections. Captain Armus frowned, then nodded unenthusiastically. Commander Yin made to sit down again, but it looked more like she fell into her seat as her legs gave way.

Geary turned back to Captain Casia. "Captain, were your actions in command of *Conqueror* in the last battle also the result of following orders from someone other than the acting fleet commander?"

Casia hesitated, then shook his head roughly. "No one is responsible for my actions but me."

Why did Casia have to display admirable behavior now? "All right, then. Colonel Carabali, please instruct your Marines on *Conqueror* and *Orion* to take Captain Casia and Commander Yin into custody and prepare them for transfer to *Illustrious*. Captain Casia, Commander Yin, please leave this conference."

Casia took a moment to glare around in defiance, then reached for the controls at his location and disappeared. Commander Yin, her hand visibly shaking, followed suit quickly.

After that, discussing movements of the fleet seemed anticlimactic. Geary brought up the star display, a three-dimensional image of nearby space hovering over the table. "We're going to take advantage of our victory here to continue toward Alliance space. Our next objective will be Branwyn. I don't expect to encounter any resistance there, but we'll be prepared for mines at the jump exit and a possible Syndic delaying force." He pointed onward, to a dim red star a few light-years from Branwyn. "After that, we head for Wendig. That star system is supposed to be totally abandoned. Unless something unexpected happens in Wendig, we'll then continue on to Cavalos."

"Why not Sortes?" Captain Armus asked.

Geary indicated the star system in question. "Because it has a Syndic hypernet gate. We've inflicted serious losses on the Syndics at Kaliban and since, but we're low on a lot of supplies and many of our ships have sustained damage. I'd prefer to avoid another major battle until our auxiliaries have had time to manufacture all of the fuel cells, expendable weapons, and replacement parts they can using the raw materials we've acquired here, and until our warships have had time to repair as much damage as possible."

"But we can still try to use that hypernet gate to get home," Armus argued. Apparently Geary's earlier praise wasn't going to incline Armus to accept Geary's plans quietly.

"I believe, Captain Armus," Geary stated patiently, "that the Syndics will ensure that they have sufficient means on hand at that hypernet gate to destroy it before we could reach it."

"It's worth a try, isn't it?" No one answered him, causing Armus to frown and look around impatiently. "We easily survived the collapse of the hypernet gate in this star system."

"We were very, very lucky," Captain Cresida replied. "Next time, every ship in this fleet might be destroyed."

Duellos nodded. "Not to mention what the gate collapse did to this star system. I won't speak for anyone else, but I have enough on my conscience as it is."

"Will the Syndics follow orders to destroy another gate after what happened here?" Commander Neeson asked.

"I would think that would depend on whether they hear what happened at Lakota," Duellos speculated. "And whether they believe it. Some surviving Syndic civilian ships are already headed for jump points to spread the news and ask for help, but we have to assume that the Syndic leadership will attempt to downplay the disaster here, censor the news to the maximum extent possible, and to the degree it admits something happened, blame it on our actions."

"They've shown us a weapon," Captain Kila spoke again. "We can still use it. If we send out detachments to destroy hypernet gates in every Syndic star system with them that we pass near, we can—"

"We can *die*," Captain Tulev interrupted. "You saw what happened to the Syndic warships that destroyed the hypernet gate in this star system. How many suicide missions do we launch until we run out of ships?"

"We ask for volunteers," Kila noted calmly. "This is an

unprecedented opportunity to inflict incalculable damage on the Syndicate Worlds."

"Damage?" Commander Landis of *Valiant* shook his head. "I want those Syndic bastards to suffer as much as anyone, but wiping out star systems at one blow?"

"You've bombarded Syndic worlds," Captain Armus pointed out.

"Yes, I have," Landis agreed. "But this was different. I felt sick watching it, and I'm not ashamed to admit it. I've fought damned hard for the Alliance. I'll keep fighting for it as long and as hard as I have to. But I don't want to see that happen to any more habitable worlds, theirs or ours."

Kila's lips bent upward in a brief smile. "That's all right, Commander. I'm sure we won't have trouble finding enough volunteers."

"Even assuming we could find such volunteers," Geary cut in, "I will not approve or allow suicide missions as long as I command this fleet."

Commander Vendig of *Exemplar* spoke quickly. "We could use robotic ships, crewed by artificial intelligence. Pull off the crews, and—"

A chorus of yells drowned out Vendig, one voice rising above the others. "Unleash armed AIs with instructions to wipe out human-occupied star systems? Are you insane?"

Captain Badaya was shaking his head and spoke into the renewed quiet that followed the outburst. "Commander Landis brought up an ugly truth. What happened at Lakota could happen at any Alliance star system with a hypernet gate. If the people of the Alliance see our records of what happened in this star system, they'll demand that our own hypernet system be shut down. Who wants a bomb that big sitting in their backyard?"

"We can't just shut the hypernet down," Captain Cresida interjected. "It's a finely balanced net of energy. There's no way just to turn it off."

"Why the hell did we build it?" someone demanded.

For some reason everyone looked at Geary. He gazed back at them. "Don't ask me. I wondered the same thing, and

I wasn't around when it was built. But we're stuck with it, and so are the Syndics."

"There has to be a solution," Commander Neeson insisted. "As long as those gates are up, they're potential weapons. If we could figure out a way to employ them as weapons and hold that threat over them, the Syndics wouldn't dare—" He paused, looking stricken, and stared around. "They could figure it out, too. The destructive potential of the hypernet gates is vastly greater than any weapons we or the Syndics have been able to employ before. We and the Syndics could literally wipe each other out."

That cat was now completely out of the bag. Geary nodded. "That had occurred to me. Who wants to start a war of species extinction? Captain Kila?"

Kila looked steadily back at Geary but said nothing.

Captain Tulev pointed one finger toward the star display. "Show us, please, Captain Geary. Play back the recording of what happened after the hypernet gate collapsed."

He didn't want to view that again, even in miniature, but Geary brought up the records, setting them to play at a vastly accelerated speed so that the shock wave rolled across the image of Lakota Star System in about thirty seconds.

It was quiet after the recording finished, then Tulev indicated where the images of the ruined star system had played out. "We should send this to the Syndics. They don't have anything like it because so many of their sensors were destroyed by the energy wave. Send it to the ships leaving this star system for help, and to as many others as we can, and make sure they can send it onward."

"So they can figure out what the gates can do sooner?" Armus asked sarcastically.

"They don't need our help to do that," Cresida answered. "They've already got records of what happened at Sancere, and even the dimmest mind can look at the damage to Lakota Three, calculate the amount of energy it took to do that, and work back the planet's orbit and rotation to confirm that what hit it came from the hypernet gate location. But if we send what we have out now, which we can sanitize of any data about the collapse of the hypernet gate that we want to try to keep from the Syndics, it will prove that we didn't cause all of that destruction." She glared around the table. "My reputation, like Commander Landis's, speaks for itself. I don't want to be blamed for what happened here. It's over the line. I'll kill as many Syndics as I have to kill to win this war. I don't want to kill any star systems."

"Yes," Tulev agreed. "It's important the Syndics know we didn't do this, so there will be no popular demand for retaliation in kind. Also important is the impact it will have on the Syndic population." He gestured at the star display again. "They'll see it, all over, no matter how much the Syndic leaders try to suppress it. They'll see what can happen to a planet with a hypernet gate in the same star system. What do the Syndic leaders say then? If they try to blame us, their people in star systems with hypernet gates will fear we could do the same to their worlds. If those leaders try to claim they can stop us, their people will want to know why they didn't stop us in Lakota. If they say their people need not fear Alliance attacks of this nature because it was not an Alliance attack that caused it, then their people will demand to know what did cause it."

Everyone thought about that, and grim smiles started appearing on a lot of faces.

"They'll be in an impossible position," Badaya noted approvingly. "That's a brilliant suggestion, Captain Tulev. It will generate intense public worry all through Syndic space and confront the Syndic leaders with serious problems in how to handle mass fear of the hypernet gates."

Commander Neeson, looking concerned, shook his head. "But what happens when our people hear about it? We can't keep that news from crossing the border into Alliance space. We'll face the same problem."

"*Our* leaders need to know this problem exists," Captain Badaya stated. He gave Geary a meaningful look. As far as Badaya was concerned, Geary should be the only leader of the Alliance, a dictator backed by most of this fleet. Commander Yin hadn't been totally paranoid in her worries, though Geary himself wanted nothing to do with the idea.

"We need to figure out what to do, too," Badaya continued, "before the Syndics decide to attack *our* gates."

Geary frowned, worried again about what the Alliance's elected leaders might decide, then saw Captain Cresida nodding.

"I think we can counter this threat," she stated. "I've been thinking. We have two experimental results to draw on now, the only two known cases of collapsing hypernet gates. This fleet has the only full sets of observations from both incidents. With that data, I can refine the targeting algorithm we used at Sancere, make it more reliable and more certain to minimize energy output from a collapsing gate."

"What good does that do?" Badaya demanded. "We can't get close enough to a Syndic gate to stop them in time, and we don't want to destroy our own gates."

"But if the Syndics tried to destroy one of our gates," Cresida replied, "and we had attached self-destruct charges to all of the gate tethers, tied into an automated safe-collapse program that would trigger if the gate suffered enough damage—"

The wave of relief was almost palpable. "We could make sure none of our gates destroyed their own star systems!"

"Maybe," Geary cautioned. "We have no way of knowing how reliable the algorithm is because we only have two gate collapses to draw on for data. If it wasn't as reliable as we think, we wouldn't want to find that out the hard way. It's also going to take time to get such a design finalized, approved, and installed on every hypernet gate within reach of the Syndics."

Captain Cresida grimaced but nodded. "That's true, sir."

"But it's better than nothing," Tulev added.

"Much better," Geary agreed. "Captain Cresida, please continue work on that concept. If we can offer that when we return to Alliance space, it will protect our homes from what happened here." His eyes went back to the star display, realizing how far they had yet to go. A fleet still low on supplies, still pursued by Syndic forces able to destroy it if the fleet was caught in a bad position, still too deep in enemy territory.

No one else seemed worried about that. No one questioned Geary's use of "when" they got back instead of "if" they got back. He found himself unnerved by the fear that this fleet (or most of it, at least) would do whatever he asked now, all of them certain that whatever Geary ordered would succeed. That would have been fine if he were some sort of genius, but he'd already made plenty of mistakes. *Ancestors, I want their confidence, but I don't want their faith.* Unfortunately, it seemed he would get both whether he liked it or not, and this was coming on top of his distress over ordering Casia's execution.

"Thank you," Geary stated. "Thank you and all of your crews again for achieving the sort of victory that will be remembered as long as the Alliance endures." He caught Duellos's eye, then Badaya's, sensing that both intended staying after the conference for private talks. Right now he couldn't handle that and shook his head subtly to each to indicate they'd speak later. "I'll see you all in Branwyn Star System."

The images of officers vanished, and the room seemed to shrink with incredible speed. Geary sat down heavily as the last image disappeared, his eyes on the star display, wondering how long he could keep from making a mistake fatal to the entire fleet, wondering if he could really help defuse the hypernet gate bombs that the unknown aliens had succeeded in tricking humans into seeding throughout the regions of space they occupied.

"We'll make it."

Geary hadn't remembered that Desjani was physically present, or realized that she had stayed in the room and was now watching him.

"I know it's hard, sir. But you've brought us this far." She indicated the display.

"I can't do miracles," he noted in a bleak voice.

"If you provide the right leadership, then this fleet will perform the miracles. You saw that here at Lakota."

He laughed shortly. "I wish I could believe that! But the fleet has certainly done an amazing job. I won't argue with you there." The laugh died, and he nodded toward the stars.

"I almost made some lethal mistakes at Lakota the first time around. I can't afford to make any more, and that's scary, Tanya."

"You don't have to be perfect."

"Don't the living stars expect that of me?" Geary asked, hearing his voice get tense.

She frowned. "I'm not wise enough to know what they expect, but I'm smart enough to see that they wouldn't have chosen a human agent if they wanted perfection. Sir, winning is usually a matter of making one less mistake than the enemy or just getting up one more time than you get knocked down. You're doing both."

He gave her an appraising look. "Thank you. I know you've told me on a few occasions that you know I'm human, but sometimes I still think you expect me to be some perfect, godlike being."

Desjani's frown deepened. "That would be blasphemy, sir. And unfair to you."

"But you still think I can do it?" It was one thing for Desjani to say that if she believed him perfect, but if she knew he wasn't perfect and still believed in him, it would mean much more.

"Yes, sir." She looked down for a moment. "My ancestors tell me to trust you, that we were meant to . . . to serve together."

He took a moment to answer, trying to make sure he didn't say the wrong thing. "I'm glad we're serving together. You've been invaluable."

"Thank you, sir."

He didn't know why, but he suddenly felt the need to bring up something. "*Vambrace* was destroyed in the battle. I saw Lieutenant Riva made it off. He's on *Inspire* right now."

"I'm sure he'll be happy there," Desjani responded, her tone notably cooler. "There are any number of attractive female officers on *Inspire*, assuming he doesn't try for an attractive enlisted this time." She saw his reaction and shrugged with every appearance of uncaring. "Lieutenant Riva burned his bridges with me a decade ago, sir, though I didn't fully appreciate that until recently. I'd regret the loss of any member of the Alliance fleet, but on a personal level, I really don't care if I never hear his name again."

"Sorry," Geary offered, "for bringing it up, I mean."

"That's all right. I've learned a lot about men since I was involved with him, a lot about what a man should be." She looked down and bit her lip. "But we were talking about getting home, about you being able to do that."

"Yeah."

She must have heard the lack of enthusiasm in Geary's voice, and somehow knew what it meant. "It's still your home, too, sir."

"Is it?" Geary fell silent again but knew Desjani was waiting for him to say more, as if she knew he had more he should say. "How much has changed in a century? The people I knew are gone. I'll be greeting their now-elderly children and grandchildren. The buildings I last saw new will be old. Old ones will be torn down, with something else in their place. On this ship I can pretend not much time has passed, but once we get back to Alliance space, then everywhere I look there'll be reminders that my home is dead and gone."

Desjani sighed. "You won't lack for friends."

"Yes, I will. What I won't lack for is people wanting to be near Black Jack Geary," he answered, letting the bitterness he felt at the thought enter his voice. "They won't be interested in me, just in the great hero they think I am. How can I avoid that? How can I get to know anyone when that will be following me everywhere?"

"It won't be easy," Desjani admitted. "But people will get to know you. Just like people in this fleet did. Who you really are besides being a hero, and I see how you react when I say that, but I'm sorry, you *are* a hero. Everyone in this fleet would be dead or in Syndic labor camps long ago but for you. You have to accept that."

"I could still screw up so badly that we'll end up that way anyhow," Geary noted. "Look, I wish you wouldn't call me a hero."

"The fleet knows—"

"Not the fleet. You."

She stayed silent for a moment, then nodded. "You need to be able to escape that at times. I understand. But I do believe you'll be happy once we get home. You'll get to know people. People will get to know you," Desjani repeated. "Just as some of them know you now."

"Sure. People in the fleet know me. People I'll have to leave." She didn't answer this time, and Geary looked over to see Desjani staring at the deck, her face rigid with suppressed emotions. For the first time he really thought of leaving her, of not seeing her every day, and felt as if he'd been punched in the gut. Geary wondered how his own expression looked as he realized that. "Tanya—"

"Please don't. It'll just make it harder."

He wasn't sure what she meant, but in some way knew that she was right. "Okay."

"You'll have Co-President Rione," Desjani added in a rush.

"No. I don't have her now. Not like that." He shrugged, hoping he wasn't sounding callous. "We're using each other. I need someone who is skeptical of me and willing to speak openly her every doubt to me, and she needs . . . I'm not sure what she needs."

Desjani spoke in a very low voice. "It seems that you're giving her what she wants."

Geary barely managed not to flinch. Desjani had a point. A very good point. Why was he having sex with a woman when he wasn't even remotely sure of his feelings about her? "Not lately. But maybe that should stop completely."

"If the fleet needs it—"

"That's a fine justification for me to use, isn't it? Just the sort of abuse of power I'm supposed to be avoiding."

She smiled slightly. "Yes."

"It's not like Rione and I get along that well. Especially when—" He broke off, suddenly realizing that he'd been about to say "when she acts jealous of you."

But Desjani looked even farther away for a moment, as if she'd actually heard those words. "I've given her no grounds for that. Nor have you."

"She seems to think so," he noted in frustration. "So does

most of the fleet, apparently. What the hell are we going to do, Tanya?"

She knew that he wasn't referring to the Syndics or the fleet this time. Desjani gazed toward a corner of the room for a while before answering in a calm and controlled voice. "We can't *do* anything. Sir."

"No. We can't." The carefully emphasized "sir" was meant to remind him of their relative positions. She was his subordinate, he was her commander, and nothing could be done about either of those things. He looked down, trying to understand the feelings inside himself and wishing Desjani hadn't gotten dragged into the politics surrounding him. "I'm sorry."

"Thank you," she replied. "I'm sorry, too."

It was only after she left that it occurred to him to wonder exactly what she felt sorry for, and only then because he wasn't entirely sure that he'd meant it the way he'd thought he had.

"CAPTAIN Geary, this is Captain Desjani. The accounting of prisoners liberated from *Audacious* was scrambled by the subsequent engagement and the losses of some of the ships involved in the recovery, but a preliminary list is now available. They're working on verifying it and hope to have a finalized list before we reach the jump point for Branwyn."

Geary felt a sense of satisfaction at the news, a reminder that he had succeeded in liberating some of the Alliance sailors captured during the first battles in Lakota Star System, as he reached out and tapped the comm unit in his stateroom. "Thank you, Captain Desjani. You didn't need to track that for me. You're not my chief of staff." He didn't have a chief of staff, of course. Admiral Bloch's had died along with Admiral Bloch in the Syndic home system, and Geary hadn't wanted to pull any officers out of badly needed primary duties on any of his ships. The automated systems available could do most of the work staffs used to do, anyway.

"I'm happy to help however I can, sir."

Geary smiled and broke the connection, then turned to see Victoria Rione glowering at him. She'd come here to discuss the fleet conference she had observed but not attended, but had been interrupted by Desjani's call. "Now what?" he asked. "That was good news."

"Yes," Rione agreed in an icy voice, "eagerly delivered by your happy little helper."

He felt heat rising to match her coldness. "Are you talking about Captain Desjani?"

"Who else? Everyone in this fleet knows how she feels about you. You don't have to flaunt it in front of me."

"Those are rumors, and you know it! I've never seen her act that way, and I don't act that way with her," Geary objected. "No one I meet in the passageways of *Dauntless* gives me looks of disapproval. If the crew of this ship thought Captain Desjani and I were even thinking of that, they'd—"

"No, they wouldn't!" Rione gave him a look mixing anger and exasperation. "If you and that woman were screwing on the bridge of this ship, the watch-standers would politely look away and joyfully approve that their respected captain and their legendary hero had found happiness together! How can you not know that?"

"That's ridiculous. They know you and I are together."

"We may walk together at times, but anyone can see that we're no more emotionally tied to each other than we were the day you were defrosted from survival sleep!"

He started to object, then thought better of it. Rione was right about that. Even when their bodies were joined, their spirits were separate. Lust and love were two different things. He knew which of those motivated him to desire Victoria Rione, and he couldn't pretend otherwise. "We've still publicly been companions. If I left you for Desjani—"

"They'd applaud! I'm a civilian and a politician! They don't trust me, they don't think I'm one of them, and I'm not!"

"That doesn't mean—"

"Yes, it does! If an election on the matter were held

tomorrow in this fleet, the officers and sailors would overwhelmingly vote to shove me into an escape pod and eject it in the direction of the nearest Syndic labor camp, and for her to move into this stateroom to warm your bed and body for the foreseeable future and fleet regulations be damned! She knows that! Why do you think she's so uncomfortable when the subject is raised?"

"She has every right to feel uncomfortable!" Geary shot back heatedly. "She's never done anything to justify the impression that she'd want that."

Rione stared at him for a long moment. "Of course she hasn't *done* anything. Neither have you."

"What? Are you implying something about my feelings for her?"

"No, I'm not implying anything, I'm stating it! It's clear you prefer her company to mine or anyone else's. Moreover, she returns the feeling, and you know it!"

"I know nothing of the kind!" Geary roared. "We have to work together! She has a good military mind and good instincts, so of course I want to consult with her! Why the hell are you so jealous of Desjani anyway?"

"Because you like her better than me, you idiot! If not for your honor and her honor, which I will freely admit are impeccable, and both of your refusals to violate regulations because you're both so damned dedicated to your duties and responsibilities as officers, you and she would be spending every waking moment together! And every sleeping moment, too! And if it came to that, she would feel the kind of bliss she's previously only gained from destroying Syndic warships! And if you don't know all of that, then you're even more oblivious than I thought any human male could ever possibly be!" Rione glared at him as if trying to decide whether to say anything else, then threw up her hands in apparently total frustration and stormed out.

The obvious reply came to Geary right after the hatch shut. *Maybe I like her better because she doesn't yell at me as much as you do!* But there wasn't much sense in wasting the comeback by saying it to an empty room, and there was no way he was going to chase her down the passageway to deliver it, and in any event he didn't think he'd believe the retort nearly so wise once his own anger had cooled.

Besides, he knew a totally honest answer would be different. *I like Desjani because she understands me. Even though she thinks I'm some great hero on a great mission, she seems to know who I really am, too. And because we work so well together, like we just instinctively know what the other needs. We like the same things, we can talk, I can relax with her in ways I can't with anyone else.* Which made Desjani a great captain for his flagship, a great companion to discuss things with, a great person to be around, a great—

Damn.

Rione's right.

He sat there a while, trying to figure out what to do. In a way, though, he and Desjani had already discussed it. They couldn't, and wouldn't, do anything that wasn't appropriate for a commander and one of his subordinate officers. That didn't mean they couldn't have a close working relationship, and indeed, recent events had emphasized how important her assistance was to him during critical situations. But he'd have to make sure not to push beyond that, not to seem to pressure her in any way that wasn't professional. She hadn't invited his feelings for her, and he had no right to even state them to her.

Never mind Rione's angry accusation that Desjani had feelings for him. He couldn't assume that was true and certainly couldn't act as if it was true. It would be better for all concerned if it wasn't true.

Geary finally recalled what had started his (latest) argument with Rione, and called up the preliminary listing of Alliance personnel who had been liberated from *Audacious*. The list was gratifyingly long, though he didn't want to compare it to a list of the total crews of all of the Alliance ships that had been lost in this star system. For that matter, he didn't want to linger on the knowledge that those liberated prisoners would be needed to make up combat losses on his surviving ships. Most of the former prisoners were enlisted personnel, of course, with a decent number of junior officers among them. Only one officer above the rank of lieutenant was listed. Geary's gaze lingered on Commander Savos's name for a few moments, then he noted that Savos was currently aboard the battle cruiser *Implacable* and called that ship. "If Commander Savos is up for it, I'd like to speak with him."

Ten minutes later, *Implacable* reported that Savos was standing by for his interview. Geary stood up, made sure his uniform looked decent, then told *Implacable* to activate the link.

The image of Commander Savos, former commanding officer of the light cruiser *Spur*, which had been destroyed during the Alliance fleet's first visit to Lakota Star System, looked like hell. His uniform appeared new, obviously provided by someone on *Implacable* to replace the one Savos had worn while abandoning his ship, then being captured and imprisoned, but the rest of the man reflected what he'd been through in recent weeks. Commander Savos appeared slightly gaunt, his face lined with the strain of his time as a prisoner. One side of his head was covered by a flex-patch, and his eye on that side bore the remnants of a nasty bruise. Commander Savos nonetheless tried to stand at attention and salute. Geary returned the salute quickly, feeling guilty for having summoned the man and wondering why no one had bothered telling him that Commander Savos wasn't in good shape. "At ease, Commander. Sit down. Are they taking good care of you on *Implacable*?"

Savos sat down carefully, keeping himself slightly stiff as if trying to sit at attention, then nodded. "Yes, sir. *Implacable*'s been wonderful for all of us, sir. Excellent treatment, though the captured Syndic food leaves a bit to be desired."

"You don't have to tell me that. I'm already starting to miss Danaka Yoruk bars, and I never thought that would be possible." Geary paused. "How are you doing?"

"Happier than I imagined I could be a couple of days ago, sir," Savos stated with a grin that quickly faded. "The Syndics didn't feed us enough and worked us hard at times. We'll be okay now, though."

"You're the senior surviving officer among the liberated prisoners."

"Among those on *Audacious*, yes, sir," Savos confirmed. "I heard some things that make me think one or more captains may have been captured but taken to Syndic warships for interrogation." The commander paused, looking distressed. Geary knew what he was thinking, the same pain that troubled Geary at the very real possibility that some of the Syndic warships they'd destroyed had held Alliance prisoners of war. There had been no way to know and no way to save them, but the thought would still disturb Geary whenever he thought about the battles here.

Savos began speaking again. "After I had to order *Spur* abandoned, I'm afraid I was knocked out for a while when the ship suffered some more hits. My crew helped get me off in one of the escape pods, but it took me a few days to get thinking again. That may be why I was left on *Audacious* instead of being taken for interrogation like other senior officers."

"What do our medics say about your concussion?"

"Nothing they can't fix, sir." Savos gave a smile that was almost a grimace and raised one hand toward the bandage on the side of his head. "If it hadn't been treated, I'd have developed serious problems down the road, but I'm told everything should be fine now."

"Good. I'm sorry about *Spur*."

Savos looked distressed again before answering. "She wasn't the only ship lost, sir."

"No. But she also didn't go without making the enemy pay. Your ship fought well." He knew that was what any good commanding officer would want to hear. "The battle with the Syndic pursuit force scrambled up the released prisoners with crew members from other ships we just lost. We're getting the liberated prisoners sorted out, and once we have a list of those from *Spur*, I'll make sure you get a copy."

"Thank you, sir."

"We'll probably distribute them around the fleet on ships that need replacements for battle casualties," Geary told him. "Let me know if there are any you'd like to be on the same ship with."

Commander Savos nodded. "Thank you, sir."

Geary regarded the officer for a moment. Savos had impressed him, and he needed a new commanding officer for *Orion*. Could Savos handle it? Going from a light cruiser to a battleship might be too big a step, especially if Savos was suffering aftereffects from combat injuries. It would be best not to push him. He'd see what shape Savos was in when the fleet reached Branwyn and make a decision then. "I know intelligence is debriefing all of the liberated prisoners, but is there anything you think I ought to know right away?"

Savos pondered that for a moment. "We heard very little. They'd haul us out in small bunches and put us into working parties, but otherwise we were kept in our compartments. There is one thing you probably ought to know."

"What's that?"

"We didn't know what was going on yesterday, but the Syndics knew I was the senior officer among the prisoners on *Audacious*. A bunch of their Mobile Assault Forces guys hauled me outside the compartment, stuck their weapons in my face, and asked me if you were really in command of the fleet and whether it was true that you'd forbidden the killing of Syndic prisoners." Savos shrugged. "I didn't know why they were asking, but I told them the truth, yes and yes. I told them that you'd insisted on following the old rules of war and that all of us were following those orders. I said you always did what you promised. Then one of them said something like 'screw our orders,' they shoved me back into the compartment, and that's all I knew until the Marines broke the hatch open. Our Syndic guards must have bolted for their escape pods right after they talked to me."

Geary wondered what the "orders" had been. Shut off life support to the prisoner compartments? Set *Audacious*'s power core to overload? Apparently his threat, backed by his record, had worked in this case. "Thank you, Commander. Get yourself some rest. You've earned it. I'll talk to you again at Branwyn."

"Yes, sir." Savos made a gesture toward the controls at his location, then paused. "They're scared, sir. They're scared of this fleet. They're scared of you. I could feel it."

"Huh." How did he respond properly to that? He'd never led by fear, though it was one thing for your own personnel to be afraid of you and another for the enemy to fear you. Still, it wasn't how he saw himself. "Well, they ought to be scared of everyone in this fleet, Commander Savos, because I couldn't have done a single blessed thing without every man and woman on every ship in this fleet." Savos looked grateful, as if, Geary thought, he couldn't have been expected to state the obvious. Then Commander Savos's image disappeared, leaving Geary alone once more.

"THE shuttle carrying Captain Casia and Commander Yin to *Illustrious* is on its way," Desjani reported, as if transporting one senior officer to meet a firing squad and a second to be imprisoned were the most routine event in the fleet.

"They're both on one shuttle?"

Desjani's image on his stateroom communications display nodded. "*Conqueror* and *Orion* are still close to each other, so there wasn't any sense wasting fuel with two shuttle flights. The bird should be at *Illustrious* in twenty-five minutes."

Which would leave about four and a half days before the fleet jumped to Branwyn. Plenty of time for the firing squad to do its work at Lakota just as Geary had promised Casia, but somehow the time available still felt rushed.

It felt wrong to sit in his stateroom, working or not, while that shuttle was en route to *Illustrious* with its small cargo of prisoners and Marine guards. Geary made his way up to the bridge and sat down near Desjani, noting that the shuttle was now twenty minutes from *Illustrious*. He wondered if Colonel Carabali had managed to find enough volunteers for Captain Casia's firing squad yet but decided he wasn't ready to ask. He didn't want to think about it at all, but couldn't stop thinking about it.

Ten minutes later an alert pulsed.

"Accident on shuttle flight Omicron Five One," a watch-stander called out.

Geary was still focusing on his display when Desjani

gasped in recognition. "That's the bird with Casia and Yin on it."

He stared at the display with a sick feeling. "The bird that *had* them on it." Images and text presented the same picture, that the shuttle had blown up. "It's gone?"

Desjani was scowling now, tapping controls. "Shuttle accidents are uncommon but not impossible. But that level of failure—our systems say it must have been the shuttle's fuel cell suffering a catastrophic containment failure. What the hell could've caused that?"

"Destroyer *Rapier* is closest to the accident site," the operations watch called out. "She's requesting permission to proceed to the area in search of survivors and to collect physical evidence."

He should have already thought of the need to send a ship to do that. "Tell *Rapier* that permission is granted," Geary stated, still trying to grasp what had happened.

Desjani shook her head, looking angry. "Chances of survivors are nil, but maybe *Rapier* can find something in the wreckage that will help explain what happened."

Rapier was still on her way to the field of debris that had been shuttle flight Omicron Five One when Rione came quickly onto the bridge, then bent down close to Geary to speak in the barest whisper. "A very unusual accident, and two officers who might have named names are now dead."

He stared at her. "You think—?"

"Casia might have made a final statement when he faced the firing squad. Yin might have crumbled or revealed something if we decided to interrogate her. What do *you* think?"

He didn't want to accept the idea, but the coincidence of a deadly accident on that particular shuttle flight made Rione's suggestion too convincing to ignore. Someone had escalated their efforts against Geary into the realm of deadly force. He hadn't really believed Rione's warning before. Now there seemed little doubt. Whoever they were, they were willing to kill Alliance personnel in the name of contesting Geary's command of the fleet. Though if what had turned out to be Commander Yin's final statement was to be believed, they also wanted to prevent him from becoming a

dictator if the fleet made it home, and, like Rione, were willing to kill to keep that from happening. Unlike Rione, they
had not merely threatened such actions but carried them out,
and, unlike her, they had struck not directly at Geary but at
other officers in the fleet.

Which meant they were doubtless willing and able to
commit more such attacks. The only questions were where,
when, and how.

SEVEN

HE hadn't seen Captain Numos since after the battle at Ilion. Numos didn't get up when Geary's image appeared in his stateroom/cell, instead eyeing Geary with the same mixture of contempt and dislike that he'd shown from their first meeting. "What do you want?"

Refusing to let Numos get to him, Geary shook his head. "As I'm sure you've already heard, the crew of a shuttle, four Marines, and two fleet officers are dead. Do you think I care right now how you act?"

"Are you accusing me of being involved?"

"No." The direct answer seemed to startle Numos. "I just want you to consider the implications. Captain Casia and Commander Yin were silenced to prevent them from saying things. If you could say anything, you should be worried about what your alleged friends were planning."

Numos snorted derisively. "I'm supposed to trust you instead? How do I know you didn't arrange that little accident to get rid of two officers who had challenged your authority?"

"If I had wanted either of them dead," Geary pointed out, "I had full justification to order it openly under fleet regulations. Captain Casia was on his way to face a firing squad. Why would I have destroyed a shuttle to kill a condemned man?"

"You've already eliminated Captain Franco, Captain Farcsa, Captain Midea, Captain Kerestes . . . Have I missed anyone?"

Geary sat down, gazing intently at Numos. "You aren't that stupid. You know those deaths happened in action. You know that Midea caused her own death. I've been wondering how you kept her under control."

Numos shrugged. "She respected legitimate authority."

He'd wondered if his dislike of Numos had tinged his memories, making them worse. Apparently not. "Maybe you are that stupid. Your friends have cold-bloodedly murdered members of the Alliance fleet."

"I thought you said it was an accident."

"Actually, no, I never said that. You've used the word repeatedly. Funny that you should be so certain." Geary's thrust went home as Numos's eyes glittered with anger. "I don't know whether you think there's some tiny chance that you would be accepted as fleet commander if I were gone. There isn't. I don't know whether you think I plan on making myself dictator when we return to the Alliance. That isn't going to happen."

"I'm supposed to believe you?"

Geary studied Numos for a few seconds. "I did think you'd show a little more emotion over the deaths of fellow officers." Numos gazed back impassively. "If any more accidents happen, you're going to be in an interrogation facility, Captain Numos. I know you've received training on wording your replies to fool even brain scans, but we've got some very good interrogators in this fleet. I also know that while I can't justify subjecting a fleet captain to interrogation without some grounds right now, another accident will arouse enough concern for me to do so." Numos reddened but remained silent. "Tell your friends."

Geary stood up, triggered his controls, and vanished from Numos's stateroom.

"I told you that it would be a waste of time," Rione remarked, lounging back in her seat. She hadn't been part of the virtual meeting, but she'd been able to observe the entire thing.

"I had to try." Geary shook his head. "I don't know how I've managed to avoid ordering Numos shot and dumped out of the nearest air lock."

"Black Jack could do it." Rione seemed thoughtful. "Black Jack gets to make his own rules. I think Black Jack should order Numos into interrogation now."

"So you told me." Geary sat down, rubbing his forehead. "I've sounded out some other officers. They all agree that I could get away with it, but it would both frighten those who think I want to be a dictator and encourage everyone who wants me to be a dictator. Both things could trigger more events that I really don't want. I need more justification."

"That justification may involve more deaths," Rione emphasized.

"I know that. Acting prematurely might cause even more. I take it your spies still have nothing to report?"

"No." She frowned. "The fleet is buzzing over the shuttle accident, but it all seems to be surprise and conjecture over how the fuel-cell failure could have happened. No one seems to be openly implying that you might have had a role in it, since everyone else seems smarter than Numos and knows you didn't need to blow up a shuttle if you wanted Casia and Yin both dead. The silence is deafening among your opponents in this fleet. I wish I knew what that meant."

He studied her for almost a minute before asking a question that had been bothering him. "Why didn't you ever tell me that some of those opposed to my commanding this fleet were motivated by fear of my becoming a dictator?"

Rione made a dismissive gesture. "Because their exact motives didn't make any practical difference."

"*You* were willing to kill me to prevent me from becoming a dictator." She didn't answer, and Geary felt the need to amend his statement. "I suppose you still are willing to do that if you think it becomes necessary. But I think their exact motive did matter if it was the same as yours. Why didn't they contact you since your loyalty to the Alliance is so well-known? Or did they contact you?"

She laughed. "Getting paranoid? I'll make a politician of you yet. No, John Geary, they didn't. I'm convinced that our motives only partly coincided at any point. That is, both they and I don't want you to be a dictator. But I also want the elected government of the Alliance to remain in power. I suspect that your foes such as the late Commander Yin and her friends believe in the need for a military dictator. They just don't want you to be that dictator."

That made sense. "Like Falco. Some other senior officer who thinks the way to save the Alliance is to overthrow its government." Rione nodded. "I have increasing trouble believing that they are backing Numos though. That interview just confirmed for me that he's too arrogant to make a decent pawn, and too dumb to function on his own. But he makes trouble for me, and that probably makes him useful to them."

"That could well be true," she said. "I think your assessment is right, that the conspirators are happy to take advantage of Numos's hostility to you but that Numos is too prideful and unimaginative ever to work as a puppet for them. I suppose in that light there's not much sense in pushing to have him interrogated quickly."

"Yeah. I'll bet he doesn't know a thing that'll help us." Geary stared at the star display, feeling a need to bring something else up. "How many officers in this fleet are willing to back a dictatorship? I've been told it's a strong majority, so maybe I should ask how many *aren't* willing to do that, since that seems to be a much smaller number. Duellos wouldn't, I don't think Tulev would, or Cresida—"

"Don't be so sure about Cresida," Rione objected. "And I'm a little uncertain about Tulev now. Even before you miraculously returned from the dead, the civilian government was increasingly worried about the loyalty of its officer corps. It's our own fault. We know that. They're on the front lines, watching their friends and comrades die, and we can't tell them that it's bringing us any closer to victory. It's been that way for a century. Their grandfathers and grandmothers, their fathers and mothers, watched comrades die or died themselves in the same war. I'm sometimes surprised that our elected government has managed to survive a war this long."

"Has our government made that many mistakes?"

She waved an angry hand. "It's made its share of mistakes. So has the military. But it's not about that. It's about frustration. A century of war and no end in sight. People want something, anything, that would hold out hope for an end to it." Rione shook her head at Geary. "And then you show up. The hero who legend decreed would return to save the Alliance in its hour of greatest need. Do you wonder that so many are looking to you?"

"That hero is a myth," Geary insisted.

"Not entirely, no, and in any event, what you think scarcely matters. It's what everyone else thinks. You can save the Alliance. Or you can destroy it. It took me a while to put that together. You embody the ancient duality, the preserver on one side and the destroyer on the other. I saw the destroyer at first, then I saw the preserver, and now I see both." She shook her head again. "I don't envy you having to personify those two contrary roles, but that's what comes with being the legendary hero."

"I never volunteered to be a legendary hero!" Geary stood up and began pacing angrily again. "You did this to me, the government, while I drifted around Grendel Star System in survival sleep, making me into every schoolkid's greatest idol so you'd have something to keep inspiring people to fight."

"The Alliance government created a myth, John Geary. You're real, and you have the real power to preserve or destroy the Alliance. If you haven't fully accepted that yet, do it *now*."

He stopped pacing and gave her a sour look. "I've never been the type to believe I was sent by the living stars to save the universe, or even just the Alliance."

Rione raised an eyebrow at him. "That may be the only thing that keeps you from destroying the Alliance. Maybe that's why you were chosen."

"Don't tell me that you're starting to believe that, too!" Geary made a frustrated gesture. "I get too much of that as it is."

"I thought you liked it when your special captain gazed at you with those worshipful eyes," Rione observed.

"No, I don't, and no, she doesn't. And why the hell are we talking about Captain Desjani all of a sudden?"

Instead of answering, Rione simply stood up. "I have some other business to attend to. You're still going to jump the fleet to Branwyn as scheduled?"

"Yes," Geary snapped, still aggravated with her. "We'll be at the jump point in four days, barring any more 'accidents.'"

She was heading for the hatch but paused to look back at him. "I would have tried to stop it if I'd known someone was going to sabotage that shuttle. Yes, I thought Casia and Yin should die because of their actions and because I saw them as a threat to the Alliance, but I wouldn't have let a number of innocent people be killed."

He stared at her. "It never occurred to me to think you would have."

"Sooner or later, it would've occurred to you."

Geary kept looking at the hatch after she had left, realizing that she was right, and wondering why sometimes his allies scared him as much as his enemies.

THE transmission from what had once been the habitable world in Lakota Star System was streaked with interference, the sound portion garbled by static. Geary tapped the control to apply enhancement filters, and the image cleared, the sound now audible, though with occasional odd gaps as attempts by the software to guess which word to use came up blank.

A man stood in the front of the image, behind him a table at which a half dozen other men and women sat. All of them looked as if they'd been wearing the same clothing for days, and as if those days had been arduous ones. They were in some room without visible windows, whose construction and fittings conveyed a feeling of being an underground shelter.

The man spoke with weary desperation, blinking with fatigue. "We are appealing to any ships in this star system to carry news of our disaster to authorities who can provide aid. Lakota Three is undergoing intense storm activity. Estimates are that between ten and twenty percent of the atmosphere is gone. Lakota star's output may be fluctuating, causing more havoc on this world. Most electrical systems on the planet were destroyed by the energy pulse that struck us. We're incapable of estimating the number of dead but it surely runs into many millions. We've been unable to establish contact with anyone in the hemisphere that faced the energy pulse. The survivors in this hemisphere are in desperate need of food, shelter, and other necessities. Please notify anyone who can help."

The image stuttered, then the message began repeating.

Geary shut it off, letting out a long, despairing breath. "There's nothing we can do."

Desjani nodded gloomily. "We can't even run shuttles down into that atmosphere right now without risking their loss."

"Did you find any signs of Alliance prisoners of war on the planet?"

She shook her head, looking depressed now. "A few marginal indications. But even if they were there, we couldn't get to them. The planet is going to be a hellhole until the atmosphere stabilizes again."

Geary tapped his communications controls. "Authorities on Lakota Three, this is Captain John Geary, commanding officer of the Alliance fleet. We deeply regret our inability to offer immediate assistance, but have no capability for disaster relief. We will notify any and all Syndicate Worlds' entities encountered of your need." It occurred to him that with so many electronic systems destroyed, the authorities on Lakota Three might have no idea what was going on above the world's atmosphere. "Be advised that a few Syndicate Worlds' civilian ships survived the energy pulse and are heading for jump points out of this star system. I have given orders that they not be engaged by my units and have provided them with clear records of the disaster here to assist authorities in other Syndicate Worlds' star systems in responding to your need. May the living stars provide for you and may your ancestors offer you what comfort they can."

He ended the transmission, then looked to the communications watch. "Try to punch that through to the origin of the distress message, and set it to repeat until we leave this star system. Also forward that distress message to the Syndic merchant ships heading out of the star system." With a fleet configured for war, there wasn't much else he could do. "Captain Desjani, I'm going to hold a small meeting in one hour. I'd like you to be there."

"Of course, sir," Desjani acknowledged. "Is there anything I should do to prepare for the meeting?"

"Just bring your brains and your common sense."

ONE hour later, Geary looked around the conference room, where he, Captain Desjani, and Co-President Rione were physically present and Captains Duellos, Cresida, and Tulev were virtually present. To the naked eye, all six figures appeared identical, but the occasional extra couple of seconds' delay in reactions from the three who were attending via conferencing software betrayed their virtual nature. "I wanted to talk to you because you've all been told about our belief that there's a nonhuman sentient species on the other side of Syndic space."

"Belief?" Captain Cresida questioned. "From the evidence I've seen, it's a lot stronger than a belief."

"And there's more evidence that I haven't had a chance to share before this." Geary paused, uncertain how to say it. "You know we were on our way to defeating one of the Syndic flotillas in Lakota when a much larger Syndic force arrived via the hypernet gate. This fleet was almost trapped and destroyed as a result." Rione knew what he was talking about, but none of the other officers did, and they were all watching him, plainly trying to figure out the connection to the aliens. "Intelligence on *Dauntless* intercepted a number of signals from the Syndic ships that had arrived via the hypernet gate, messages that clearly revealed that the Syndics were shocked to be in Lakota. They'd entered their hypernet system with a destination of Andvari Star System."

He let them absorb that for a moment. Cresida, perhaps the fleet's best expert on the hypernet, responded first. "They made that big a mistake? No, it's impossible to make that kind of mistake. There's no way to set one destination on the hypernet and end up in another."

Geary nodded. "So I was told. No way that *we* know of."

Desjani got it first, her face reddening with rage. "They did it. Whatever they are. They changed the destination of those Syndic ships so we'd be confronted by an overwhelming force."

"That's the only conclusion that makes sense," Geary agreed. "They intervened in an attempt to destroy this fleet."

"Why?" Tulev, not surprisingly, had been the first to look past the outrage of the aliens' actions and search for a reason.

"Damned if I know. They don't want us to get home. Is it because they want the Alliance to lose? I don't think so. If they wanted to help the Syndics defeat us, they could provide the Syndics with more of their technology, but as best we can tell, they secretly gave the hypernet technology to both the Alliance and Syndicate Worlds at about the same time several decades ago."

"What are they?" Desjani demanded. "What do we know of them?"

This time Geary shrugged. "Shadows and scientific wild-ass guesses. We see signs of them, apparent proof they're out there and intervening in this war, but nothing about them directly. If they did redirect that Syndic flotilla, it not only means they can mess with a hypernet in ways we don't understand, it also means they can covertly monitor where this fleet is and where it's going, and get that information somewhere at something close to real time over interstellar distances." The others stared at him as the implications of that struck home, but none of them denied his logic.

"The Syndics certainly know more about the aliens," Rione added to the group. "But that knowledge has apparently been kept very close, and even the existence of the aliens kept secret from most Syndic citizens. Only the Syndicate Worlds' highest leaders may know everything there is to be known. We've found nothing in captured records."

"Are they human?" Tulev wondered.

"I don't think so," Geary answered. "If they were human, why would the Syndics have kept them secret? And how could another human power strong enough to hold the Syndics on a border exist without us knowing something? They would have had to come from somewhere."

"Not human." Tulev shook his head. "How do they think? Not like us."

"Surely we can still figure out their intent," Desjani insisted.

Duellos was frowning in thought. "My grandmother taught me an ancient riddle when I was quite young. That riddle might help us understand what we're dealing with."

"Really? What is it?"

Duellos paused dramatically. "Feathers or lead?"

Geary waited, but nothing else came. "That's it?"

"That's it. Feathers or lead?"

"What kind of riddle just asks you to chose between two things?" Cresida asked, then shrugged. "I give. What's the answer?"

"It depends." Duellos smiled as everyone looked aggravated. "The one asking the riddle is a demon, you see. The demon chooses which answer is right. In order to guess the right answer, you have to know what the demon thinks it should be that particular time."

"How are you supposed to know what a demon thinks?" As soon as Geary said the words, he got Duellos's point. "Like the aliens."

"Exactly. How do we answer a question posed by something that isn't human, when we have no idea what the question means or what the ones asking it want the answer to be?"

"And what do they expect from us? Honor or lies?" Captain Cresida asked. Everyone turned to look at her. "Who have these aliens been in contact with? The Syndics."

Rione nodded. "Whose leaders have broken every agreement made with us, even when abiding by those agreements would have been in the long-term interests of the Syndicate Worlds."

"The Syndic leaders don't think long-term," Duellos pointed out. "Short-term gain is all that matters to them."

Geary shook his head. "Would they have been stupid enough to use those kinds of tactics against an alien species that clearly has technological superiority over the human race?" He saw the answer on every other face in the room. "Yeah. Maybe they would have." After all, those same leaders had repeatedly broken agreements with this fleet, even knowing that the fleet could easily retaliate by wiping out entire worlds.

"The superior technology would have been irresistible bait for them," Rione observed bitterly. "They would have been willing to try to acquire it by any possible means, leaving the aliens to conclude that the human race could not be trusted. Anything the aliens have done could have been seen by them as defensive, a means to neutralize humanity."

"But if the Syndics were dealing with aliens," Cresida argued, "and unsuccessfully dealing with them apparently because they've never surfaced with any technology far in advance of the Alliance except the same hypernet we got, why would they turn around and attack us? We know from the disposition of Syndic hypernet gates on the far border that the Syndics fear the aliens. Why start a war with us?"

"Because they were surrounded?" Duellos offered. "The Alliance on one side and these aliens on the other side. That leaves the Syndicate Worlds pinned between two powers. They must have feared being crushed between us once we learned of the existence of the creatures."

"Then why start a war with us?" Cresida demanded. "Why make their nightmare come true?"

Geary shook his head. "During peacetime, Alliance ships traveled through Syndicate Worlds' space. Only occasional warships carrying out diplomatic missions, but more frequent freighters. Alliance citizens also traveled through the Syndicate Worlds on business or pleasure. Any of those might have found clues to the existence of the aliens or been contacted by them directly."

"Well enough, sir, but starting a war to prevent occasional Alliance traffic through their territory seems like massive overkill. It's not like the Syndics ever invited much Alliance shipping into their areas of control. They could have choked it off completely using any number of excuses, and what could the Alliance have done? Besides, how could they know the aliens wouldn't attack them while they were involved in fighting the Alliance?"

Duellos shrugged. "Maybe the Syndic leaders thought they could defeat us quickly."

"That's irrational!" Cresida objected. "Even the Syndic leaders couldn't have been so stupid as to believe they could do that!"

"They thought the Alliance would crack under the first blows," Desjani cut in. "That we wouldn't have the spirit to rebound from the initial losses and hit back."

"We don't *know* that," Rione replied with a slightly but unmistakably dismissive tone. "That was the argument used to rally the Alliance after the first attacks. That was why the Alliance made the most of whatever heroic examples existed, as proof that any such Syndic belief was wrong."

Which was where the legend of Black Jack Geary began. Fighting to the last against overwhelming odds. A heroic example to inspire everyone else. Geary tried not to notice everyone not looking at him.

Tulev shrugged. "It may have been a useful rallying argument for the Alliance, but that doesn't mean it wasn't true," he suggested with a glance at Desjani, whose eyes had narrowed in response to Rione's tone. "What other explanation exists?"

"Perhaps they reached some sort of agreement with the aliens," Rione suggested. "Doubtless planning to go back on it as soon as they'd dealt with us."

"What kind of agreement?" Geary wondered, his mind going back to a time that was the recent past for him but a century old for the others here. "A nonaggression pact might temporarily secure their border with the aliens, but the Syndics couldn't have decisively beaten the Alliance. They didn't have military forces large enough to overcome the sheer size of the Alliance, any more than the Alliance could muster enough force to defeat the expanse of the Syndicate Worlds. We knew that as well as they did. That's why the surprise attacks, including the one in Grendel, came as such a shock."

"Maybe there's the answer," Desjani declared, her expression shadowed with an emerging idea. "What everyone's been saying made me think of something." She tapped some controls and an area of space that Geary found heartbreakingly familiar was displayed above the table. "Alliance space along the frontier with the Syndicate Worlds," Desjani explained to Rione as if she couldn't be expected to recognize a display of the area, causing Rione's expression to harden slightly this time. "I've spent some time recently studying the start of the war. This shows the initial Syndic attacks a century ago. Shukra, Thabas, Diomede, Baldur, Grendel. Why did they hit Diomede instead of Varandal? Why Shukra instead of Ulani?"

Geary frowned. He didn't know this, hadn't ever known it, because he had been lost in survival sleep since that first Syndic surprise attack at Grendel. In the months after his awakening, he'd avoided studying the early Syndic attacks closely since he still felt the pain of knowing his crew from those days had all died in either that battle or later battles or, if lucky, from old age, while Geary's survival pod drifted among the other debris of battle at Grendel. "Good question. I just skimmed those events and assumed they must have hit the Alliance base at Varandal."

"They didn't," Duellos confirmed, studying the display. "Varandal was a major base back then as well?"

Desjani nodded. "The primary command, repair, supply, and docking facility for the Alliance fleet in that entire sector of space."

"That seems a far-more-critical target than some of those that were hit. Does anyone know why they didn't strike Varandal?"

Once again Desjani answered. "Our histories all say that it was assumed Varandal, Ulani, and other high-value star systems were intended for a follow-up wave of attacks that didn't happen because of Syndic losses suffered in the first wave. Assumed," Desjani emphasized. "It's obvious they made that assumption because everyone on the Alliance side agreed the Syndics shouldn't have had any expectation that their first wave of surprise attacks to start this war could have inflicted enough damage on the Alliance to be decisive. The Syndics didn't have enough forces on hand, as Captain Geary says, to hit everything they needed to hit all at once."

"What's your point?" Rione demanded.

Desjani gave her a cold look in return, but her voice stayed professionally calm. "Perhaps the Syndics expected to have more forces than we knew of. Suppose the Syndics had reached an agreement and expected to have help? Suppose they expected an ally, a very powerful ally, to hit places like Varandal while they hit Diomede?"

This time the silence was longer. Rione's face hardened again, but now her feelings weren't directed at Desjani. "The aliens double-crossed the Syndics."

"By promising to help attack the Alliance."

"And then didn't show up, leaving the Syndics to fight alone. They suckered the Syndic leaders, who thought themselves the masters of cunning behavior, into an unwinnable war with the Alliance. But the Syndic leaders couldn't admit they'd been fooled on such a huge issue, and they'd enraged the Alliance, and so couldn't get out of the war they'd started."

Cresida was nodding now. "The aliens don't want either side winning. That's why they intervened at Lakota. Captain Geary was doing too well, inflicting enough losses to, perhaps, eventually decisively tip the balance against the Syndics, and getting closer and closer to getting the Syndic hypernet key back to Alliance space. The aliens want humanity at war, and they want us to remain totally absorbed in this war. But is that purely defensive? Or are they waiting to see how much we can weaken ourselves before they move in?"

"We think that they can wipe us out at any time using the hypernet gates," Geary noted.

"But they haven't yet," Cresida argued. "If they're watching us as the events here at Lakota seem to prove, they must know from the collapse of the Syndic hypernet gate at Sancere that we're at least learning about the destructive potential of the gates. If they *want* to use the gates to wipe us out, why haven't they triggered them already?"

"Feathers or lead?" Duellos asked, studying his fingernails.

Frustrating as it was, Geary had to admit Duellos had a point. "We can speculate endlessly and not reach conclusions because we don't know anything about what we're dealing with."

"We know they've figured out how to trick us," Desjani insisted. "Sir, look at the pattern. They intervene in hidden ways, and they know how to get us to do things that either hurt or have the potential to hurt ourselves."

"Good point," Duellos conceded. "Which means they very likely adopt such tactics among themselves. They seem to favor causing an enemy to make mistakes that result in self-inflicted injury."

Rione nodded. "By figuring out what that enemy wants, then offering it to them. They must have formidable political skills."

"And the Syndics tried to mess with them," Geary noted angrily. "They poked a hornet's nest with a stick, and all of humanity got stung."

"Why haven't the Syndics come clean?" Cresida wondered. "They don't have any hope of winning this war and haven't for a long time. Why not say they were tricked by the aliens, claim the aliens told them we were going to attack, whatever. Get us on their side against whatever these things are."

Rione shook her head. "The Syndicate Worlds' leaders can't afford to admit they made that kind of mistake. Heads would roll, possibly in a very literal way. Even though the predecessors of the current Syndic leaders actually made the errors, the current leaders derive their legitimacy by claiming to be the chosen successors of past leaders. And all Syndic leaders are supposedly chosen for their competence and abilities. Admit to horrible errors by one generation of leaders and it calls into question the legitimacy of their chosen successors and the entire system. It is much easier and safer for them to continue on a ruinous course of action than it would be to admit to serious errors and try to change the situation."

"They're that stupid?" Cresida asked.

"*No*. It's *not* stupid. If they admit to mistakes made by leaders of the Syndicate Worlds, mistakes so serious they have trapped the Syndicate Worlds in an apparently endless war, then it is certain they will lose power, and if they lose power, they will at worst die either quickly or slowly, and at best lose every bit of their status and wealth. But as long as they continue the current policies, they can hope something will change. It's not about what's best for the Syndicate Worlds or the Alliance or humanity as a whole. It's about what's best for them as individuals. They'll fight to the last warship and ground soldier, because that's someone else paying the price for their mistakes and putting off the day when they'll personally be called to account."

Geary noticed the other officers were trying not to stare at Rione. He knew what was bothering them. Not just the rationale the Syndic leaders were probably using, but also that Rione understood it and could explain it, which meant she could think the same way.

Clearly seeing the same thing, Rione glared around at the others. "I forgot. You're all so noble and honorable. No senior military officer would ever allow people to die rather than admit a mistake, or cling to a foolish course of action in order to maintain their position."

This time a lot of faces reddened. Geary spoke before anyone else could. "Point taken. But no one here engages in that kind of thing. And, yes, I include Co-President Rione in that. She came along on this mission, risking her own life along with the sailors of this fleet. Now, let's redirect our anger at our enemies, not each other."

"Which enemies?" Duellos wondered. "We've spent all of our lives knowing that 'enemy' meant the Syndics. They were the ones attacking us, bombarding our worlds, killing our friends and family members. And all that time we had another enemy, one none of us knew about."

"Is that true, though? *Do* our leaders know about them?" Desjani asked.

Every eye turned again to Rione, who flushed slightly but gazed back defiantly. "*I* don't. As far as I know, no senator knows of the aliens."

"What about the Governing Council?" Duellos questioned.

"I don't know." Rione looked at the others and obviously saw doubt there. "I don't have any reason to lie," she snapped. "I know there are extremely sensitive matters of which only members of the Governing Council are apprised. Supposedly some of those matters are passed verbally to new members and never written down, but I don't know that's true. Only the members of the Governing Council know, and they *don't* discuss their secrets."

Geary nodded. "I can easily believe that. What would be your guess, though, Madam Senator?" He used the title deliberately, wanting to emphasize for the others the political rank that Rione held. "If you had to make a guess, is there anything you know or have heard about the Governing Council that would lead you to think they might know?"

She frowned, bending her head in thought. "Maybe. It would depend upon how you interpreted things."

"Things?"

Rione's frown deepened. "Questions that you're told to stop asking for Alliance security reasons, private statements regarding plans or budgets, that sort of thing. But there are plenty of other explanations for any of that. Listen, I'm as suspicious as any politician. I parse everything I hear for possible interpretations. If the Governing Council has any clue as to the existence of these aliens, they've done a very good job of keeping it quiet. I certainly never suspected it until Captain Geary showed me what he'd figured out."

"But then we'd all stopped asking that question," Cresida observed. "Hadn't we? No nonhuman intelligent species had ever been discovered or contacted us, that we knew of, and the war had us all focused on other matters. Captain Geary had a fresh perspective."

"More like a fresh-frozen perspective," Geary replied, and everyone smiled at the reference to his long period in survival sleep. He hadn't thought that he'd ever be able to joke about that. "Here's the question: Do we keep them secret? Or do we start telling lots of other people?"

This time the silence stretched, then Rione spoke in a world-weary voice. "We fear that humanity will use the power in the hypernet gates to wipe itself out because of the hatreds generated by this war. If humanity learned that the war had been caused by a trick from another intelligent species, and that the same species had fooled us into planting the means for humanity's extinction throughout the star systems we control, what would the mass of people do? What would they demand?"

"Revenge," Tulev answered.

"Yes. War on an even greater scale, against an enemy of unknown strength, unknown size, and with unquestionably superior technology."

Cresida clenched her fists. "I don't particularly care how many of those things died. They've earned it. But the thought of how many more humans would perish . . ."

"I think my question has been answered," Geary stated heavily. "We have to keep the secret, too, yet also figure out how to counter these aliens without starting an even bigger war."

Duellos pursed his lips as he frowned in thought, the fingers of one hand drumming silently on the table near him. "One enemy at a time. That's what I'd recommend. We have to deal with the Syndics before we can have a hope of dealing with the aliens."

"But how can we beat the Syndics if the aliens are actively helping them?" Cresida demanded.

Duellos's frown deepened. "I'll be damned if I know the answer to that."

For some reason everyone else turned to look at Geary.

He stared back at them. "What? Do you think I know how to do that?"

To his surprise, Cresida answered. "Sir, you have shown an ability to see things the rest of us take for granted or just haven't thought about. Perhaps it's because you've got an outside viewpoint in many ways, or perhaps you're, um, being inspired to see things the rest of us cannot."

Being inspired? What could that mean? Geary looked around at Cresida and the others, and saw the meaning, from Cresida's slightly embarrassed expression to Desjani's calm belief to Rione's measuring glance. "You believe the living stars are telling me things? I'd think I'd know if that was happening."

Duellos frowned slightly again. "No, you wouldn't," he corrected. "That's not how they work. Or not how they're supposed to work."

"No one knows how they work! Why after all we've been through would you think I'm getting divine inspiration?"

Desjani answered. "You keep telling us in private deliberations that you're just a normal man, not exceptional. But you keep doing exceptional things. Either you are an extraordinary man, or you're receiving extraordinary assistance, and I'm not vain enough to believe any aid I provide is that special."

That was a neat little logic trap. "Captain Desjani, all of you, any extraordinary assistance I'm getting is from you." Every face somehow conveyed disagreement. "You can't risk the fate of this fleet, of the Alliance, on some vague belief that I'll receive divine inspiration whenever I need it."

"We're not," Tulev stated. "We're basing it on what you've done so far. Just keep doing it." A rare smile showed on his face as Tulev signaled that he understood the half-joking/half-unreasonable nature of his statement.

Just keep doing it. Save the fleet. Win the war. Confront and deal with a nonhuman foe of unknown characteristics and power. Geary couldn't help laughing. "I'll try. But no inspiration is coming to me right now. I need all of you to keep doing what you've been doing, providing invaluable support, advice, and assistance."

Cresida shook her head. "I wish I could think of some advice for dealing with the aliens. At least thinking about that will give us something to do while the fleet is in jump space en route to Branwyn."

Three days later, Geary gave the order to jump, and the Alliance fleet left Lakota Star System for the second and, hopefully, last time.

AFTER the many stresses of recent weeks and the struggles within Lakota Star System, the days spent in jump space on the way to Branwyn proved a welcome though brief period of recovery. Everyone kept working hard to repair battle damage, but they were able to relax a bit emotionally and mentally. Despite the eeriness of jump space, Geary found himself regretting the return to normal space when they reached their destination.

The star-system-status display, loaded with information from captured Syndic star-system directories, updated itself with actual observations as the Alliance fleet's sensors evaluated the human presence at Branwyn. Surprisingly, the star had more Syndic presence than expected. Most star systems bypassed by the hypernet had declined either slowly or quickly as the space traffic that had once been required to pass through them using the jump drives had instead used the hypernet gates to go directly between any two points on the hypernet.

But here in Branwyn the mining facilities that made up most of the human presence were significantly larger than in the decades-old Syndicate Worlds' star-system guides the Alliance fleet had captured at Sancere. "Why?" Geary wondered out loud.

Desjani shook her head, apparently baffled as well. "There's no Syndic military presence here. No picket ships, no force guarding against us. I've never seen an occupied Syndic system without at least an internal-security-forces facility."

Information kept updating on the display, revealing a few cargo ships running to and from one of the other jump points in Branwyn Star System. "Where does the jump point lead?"

He saw the answer even as a watch-stander called it out. "Sortes Star System, sir."

A robust Syndic presence in a hypernet-bypassed star system, with apparently regular traffic to another nearby star system with a hypernet gate. But there didn't appear to be anything being mined here that wouldn't also be present at Sortes. "What the hell?" Geary muttered.

Victoria Rione laughed, drawing his attention. "None of you understand this? Don't you realize what you're seeing? This is all unauthorized, a pirate facility if you will, set up by Syndic corporations seeking to bypass central controls and taxation. Everything they pull out of here hasn't been regulated or taxed, which more than makes up for the extra costs of smuggling the material into hypernet-linked star systems and covering up its origin."

"How would you know that?" Geary asked.

"Because similar operations spring up in Alliance space from time to time. It's illicit, but it's profitable. One of the hobbies of the Alliance Senate is passing laws trying to ensure that no one can get away with it, but people are always looking for and finding loopholes."

An illicit operation. Geary wondered whether the people of Branwyn would provide aid to the stricken Lakota Star System or simply hunker down to avoid being caught. "Let's send them the recording of what happened at Lakota and the plea from the habitable planet there. What will happen if the Syndic authorities or their military find out about this place?"

Rione shrugged. "Some of them surely already know. I imagine bribes to the right people keep that knowledge secure. Having us pass through here might draw too much attention to cover up, though."

He checked the maneuvering display. "It'll only take four days for us to reach the jump point for Wendig. The auxiliaries are already drawing down the raw materials we looted at Lakota. Do you think we can trust the Syndics here to provide unsabotaged raw materials if we demand them?"

"Trust a pirate operation? How much profit could you offer them?"

"None," Geary replied.

"Then that's how much trust you could have in them."

WITH the Syndic presence in Branwyn showing every sign of hasty emergency evacuation and no threats toward the Alliance fleet, Geary found himself restless. Unable to sit still and think, he started taking more long walks through the passageways of *Dauntless*. Battle cruisers were large ships, but not so large that such walks didn't often encounter Captain Desjani doing her own thinking and maintaining a constant presence among her crew. Ironically, being openly seen with Desjani was a far better defense against rumors of unprofessional conduct than avoiding her would be, because if they weren't seen walking and talking together, then gossip would assume they were together in places where they couldn't be seen doing things they didn't want seen.

Most of the conversation kept to professional topics. The war, ship-handling, the merits of different classes of ships, tactics, logistics, personnel matters, and where the fleet should go next. Not the sort of thing anyone overhearing could possibly construe as social conversations, though Desjani did have a passion for those topics. She truly did love being a fleet officer.

But as time went by Desjani spoke more of her home planet Kosatka and Alliance space in general, of her family, and gradually drew Geary out on the same topics. He found himself bringing up memories that had been too painful to consider, thoughts of people and places now vanished, surprised that he could speak of them with her and feel a sense not only of melancholy but also of release.

"You told me a while ago that you knew someone on *Dreadnaught*," Desjani brought up once, as they walked through a long passageway running toward the propulsion spaces. It was well into the ship's night, and only an occasional sailor or officer went past on an errand through the darkened passage.

That brought up a whirl of more recent painful memories, centered on the Syndic home system. "Yeah," Geary agreed softly. "My grandniece. Captain Michael Geary's sister. He gave me a message for her."

Desjani was looking at her data pad. "Commander Jane Geary? She's not just on *Dreadnaught*. She's the commanding officer." Then Desjani frowned. "A battleship commanded by a Geary. There's something odd there, but I never heard any negative stories about her."

Geary tried not to snort. The modern fleet assigned its best officers to battle cruisers, where they could charge into battle first, and die first. "Maybe she's being judged by an impossible standard."

"That of her legendary great-uncle?" Desjani asked, then smiled. "It's possible." The smile went away. "And when we get back, you'll have to tell her that her brother is probably dead. I'm sorry."

"It won't be easy."

"But you have a message for her from him?"

"Yeah. Just about the last thing he said before *Repulse* was destroyed." He thought about it, then decided if there was anyone who would comprehend that message who wasn't a Geary, it might be Desjani. "He told me to tell her that he didn't hate me anymore."

She looked briefly shocked, then the expression faded into thoughtfulness. "The impossible standard. Michael Geary hated you for what he'd been forced to live with?"

"That's what he said." In the very brief time that Geary had been granted to speak with his grandnephew, there hadn't been much opportunity to say more.

"But he changed his mind." Desjani gave Geary a long look. "Because he was using *Repulse* to hold off the enemy. A last-ditch rearguard action to allow the rest of the fleet to escape, the same sort of action that you became legendary for. He understood then, didn't he?"

"Yes." He felt a great sense of relief at being able to share the story. Tanya Desjani got it. Of course she did. "He realized I hadn't done it because I thought I was a hero or because I wanted glory. I did it because so many others were counting on me. That's all."

"And he had to do the same." She nodded. "It *does* take a hero, sir."

"No, it doesn't." Geary shrugged, feeling old pain rising to the surface as he thought of the death of his old ship a century ago and more recent sorrow from ships in this fleet that had been lost fighting the same sort of hopeless rearguard actions. "It's pure chance who ends up in a situation like that."

"Maybe." Desjani gave Geary a serious look. "But what someone does when faced with that situation isn't pure chance, sir. They make choices, as we all do. Those choices define us. I know you don't like me to say it, but you are a hero, sir. If you were a fraud, people would have seen that by now."

"I'm *human*, Tanya."

"Of course you are. That what makes it heroic. Humans fear death and pain, and when we reach beyond that fear to protect others, we have done something to be proud of."

Startled, Geary walked silently for a moment before replying. "I'd never thought of it that way. You're pretty good with words, you know. No wonder your uncle wanted you to be part of his literary agency."

She looked down at the deck and smiled in a slightly wistful way. "My fate lay among the stars, Captain Geary. I think I've always felt that way."

"Any idea why?"

"No. They just always called to me. Strange that I should gaze up at the vast emptiness of space since I was little and believe that the emptiness would hold what really mattered to me, but that's how it always felt."

"*Dauntless*?" Geary teased. "I can tell you love being on the bridge of a battle cruiser."

Desjani laughed, something so rare that Geary wasn't certain if he'd heard it before. "I hope not! I adore *Daunt-*

less, but battle cruisers are very demanding queens to their captains. It's an extremely one-sided relationship, as you know. I was hoping for something a little more balanced." She was smiling, still, and despite himself, he wondered what such a relationship with Desjani would be like. But he couldn't, of course, and she couldn't, of course, so they walked on down the passageway, the conversation safely turning to the latest modifications in hell-lance targeting systems.

When he reached his stateroom he was surprised to find Rione there despite the late hour, standing before the star display as if she'd been studying it for a long time. "Is something wrong?"

"I wouldn't know," Rione said. "I'm just your former lover. You've been talking to her."

Geary frowned at Rione. "Captain Desjani, you mean. She's my flagship captain—"

"And you weren't just talking about your beloved fleet," Rione finished, but she didn't sound angry this time, just defeated.

"There won't be anything between us, Victoria. You know why there can't be anything between Tanya Desjani and me."

Rione kept her face averted for a while, then looked back at Geary, her expression unreadable. "There's already something between you. Nothing physical. No. No improper actions of any kind. I freely admit that. Neither of you would do that. But there's an emotional bond, feelings that go far beyond professional, and you *know* that's true, John Geary." She exhaled slowly, looking away again. "I won't be any man's second choice."

He wondered what to say. "I didn't think—"

"No. You didn't. Not that I ever encouraged you to think I'd be interested in anything more than the physical relationship we've sometimes enjoyed. But a strong woman needs a strong man, and I've found myself wanting more from you than sex. But I can't have that. Admit it. You don't love me. You lust for my body, but you do not and cannot love me."

"I can't honestly say I love you," Geary admitted. "But I wouldn't lust after you if I didn't admire who you were."

Rione directed a pained smile to a corner of the stateroom. "That's just what every woman wants. To be lusted after and admired."

"I'm *sorry*. You always said we were promising each other nothing."

"True. I broke the bargain. In part. Don't flatter yourself that I'm madly in love with you. But I will not be your second choice," she repeated. "I have my pride." Walking to the hatch, Rione paused before opening it and looked back at him. "Once I leave here, change your security settings so that I no longer have free access."

Geary nodded. "If that's what you want."

"What I want scarcely matters anymore. But you must know that I mean what I say. I will not be back here except as an adviser."

"Thank you. Your advice has been more valuable than I think you ever realize."

She twisted her mouth, then shook her head. "The Alliance needs this fleet, and it needs you. I will remain your ally and confidant as long as you remain true to your beliefs and the Alliance. But I will not come to your bed again, and I ask you not to come to mine, because I know that while you were making love to my body you'd be thinking of her, and *that* I will not endure."

He sat for a long time after the hatch closed, realizing the truth of Victoria Rione's words. The one woman he could have in this fleet wasn't the woman he wanted, and Rione had every right to refuse to accept any lesser place with him.

Getting up, he went to the hatch controls and reset them to eliminate Rione's free access to his stateroom. Somehow the finality of that gesture served to make it certain that this time Rione would not be returning except for talks about the fleet's situation. He couldn't help feeling both guilty and relieved.

EIGHT

TWO days in Branwyn, two days left until they reached the jump point. The Syndics here continued pulling up stakes as fast as they could. There hadn't been any acknowledgment of the messages the Alliance fleet had sent about the situation at Lakota, so Geary could only hope that the people in the system would react somehow to help provide relief. "And what do your spies tell you these days?" Geary asked, slumping into his seat.

The virtual image of Captain Duellos looked offended as it lounged in a seat. "Politicians have spies, but I have sources, my good Captain Geary."

"My apologies."

"Accepted. I don't honestly have that much, but I thought you could use a talk."

"You thought right. Thanks. So what do we talk about?"

"Pressure." Duellos waved toward the star display. "If we make it through Cavalos, this fleet will be within five or six jumps of a Syndic border star system from which we can jump into Alliance space. The casual thinker might assume you're feeling relieved at how close we are to home. I'm inclined to think you're increasingly waiting for the sword to fall."

Geary nodded. "Good guess. Every step closer to home makes me wonder if I'm being set up for a disaster at the last moment. I make it six jumps past Cavalos, by the way, since we have to avoid Syndic star systems with hypernet gates."

"True." Duellos eyed the depiction of the stars. "The Syndics have to be increasingly desperate. They'll be pulling in everything they've got left to stop you."

"To stop *us*."

"Correct, although it's natural to personalize something as impersonal as a fleet."

"I suppose that's true." Geary made a face as he looked at the display. "Having the Syndics concentrating their remaining warships against us should create some real opportunities for the Alliance warships that were left behind when this fleet headed for the Syndic home system. At the very least they'd be able to send reinforcements to meet us in whatever Syndic border system we aim for. But there's no way to tell our people back in Alliance space what's happening or where we are."

"Too bad the aliens won't tell them, but I suppose we'll have to be grateful if they don't tell the Syndics where we are."

"Yeah." Geary pressed his palms against his eyes, feeling a headache threatening. "Let's talk about something else."

Duellos seemed to be thinking. "Do we want to discuss personal matters?"

"Yours or mine?" Geary asked dryly.

"Yours."

"I was afraid of that. What now?"

Duellos frowned slightly, looking downward. "You and Tanya Desjani."

"No. We're still not involved with each other, and we won't be."

"The fleet is increasingly certain that you are. Everyone knows that Co-President Rione has ceased spending nights in your stateroom and that she and Captain Desjani remain on barely civil terms with each other." Duellos shrugged.

"The assumption is that the better woman won, the fleet naturally accepting that Tanya Desjani is better than any politician."

Geary gave an exasperated sigh. "She's a wonderful woman. But she's also my subordinate. You know the regulations as well as I do, and as well as she does."

"You could get away with it, you know," Duellos suggested. "You're a special case. You're Black Jack Geary."

"The almost mythical hero who can do anything he wants. Right. I can't afford to believe that about myself." Geary stood up and began pacing restlessly despite his sense of weariness. "If I break that regulation, why not others? Where along that path do I find myself accepting the offer of Captain Badaya to become dictator because I can? Besides," he added, "Tanya wouldn't do it. She won't do it herself, and she wouldn't let me do it."

"You're probably right," Duellos agreed. "But you'll have to work at not getting that longing look in your eyes when you say her name."

Geary pivoted to stare at Duellos. "I hope you're joking. Do I really?"

"Enough for me to notice, but don't worry. It only seems to happen when you say 'Tanya.' Just saying 'Captain Desjani' you appear thoroughly professional." Duellos grimaced. "And it's not as if she doesn't get the same look sometimes when watching you."

She did? "I swear we've done nothing—"

Duellos held up one hand in a forestalling gesture. "You don't need to. I never doubted it. Jaylen Cresida and I know Desjani well enough to tell that she feels not only anguished but also guilt-stricken over her feelings for you. To become emotionally involved with her commanding officer goes against all she once believed in." Duellos shrugged. "Now, of course, she believes in you."

Feeling his own share of anguish and guilt, Geary rubbed his face with both hands. "I should leave *Dauntless*. I don't have any right to put her through that."

"Leaving *Dauntless* wouldn't accomplish anything. As Captain Cresida remarked to me, 'Once Tanya locks on to a target, she doesn't let it go. She *can't*.' And Jaylen is right. You can't leave Tanya's focus just by leaving this ship, and not being able to sight her target might just increase her distress. Besides which, frankly, the crew of *Dauntless* has taken quite a pride in having you aboard. I'd advise against leaving her."

Geary nodded in response, then wondered whether Duellos's last "her" referred to Tanya Desjani or *Dauntless*. "But if the fleet thinks there's something going on between us—"

"They don't. Not that way. Despite a sustained whispering campaign claiming otherwise, most of the fleet believes you two are thoroughly involved yet remaining professional with each other and at properly chaste arm's length."

"Even that is wrong," Geary insisted, dropping back into his chair.

"True, by a strict reading of the regulation, but there's a certain romantic aura to the love that cannot be fulfilled, and I believe the fact that you two are abiding by the rules despite your feelings is actually enhancing your standing. It's like one of those ancient sagas." Duellos smiled as Geary gave him a sour look. "You asked, and I'm telling you."

"Don't a lot of those ancient sagas end tragically?"

Another shrug from Duellos. "Most of them, anyway. But this is your saga. You're still writing it."

For some reason that made Geary laugh briefly. "I need to have a long talk with myself about the plot, then."

"Sagas wouldn't be interesting if terrible things didn't happen to the people in them," Duellos pointed out.

"I never wanted my life to be interesting, and I sure as hell don't have any right to make Desjani's life interesting that way."

"She's writing her own story. You can command Tanya Desjani on the bridge, but she doesn't strike me as the sort to let someone else, *anyone* else, dictate how her personal saga goes."

He couldn't argue that point. "It's all speculation, anyway. Let's get back to nonpersonal matters," Geary grumbled. "I hope people aren't giving Tan—Captain Desjani a hard time about this."

"She's fully capable of returning fire if they do. I have to admit to being surprised at your apparent preference for dangerous women, but then they seem to prefer you as well."

Unable to come up with a decent response to that observation, Geary changed the subject. "I didn't know that you and Cresida were friends."

Duellos shrugged. "We weren't. We barely knew each other. But since you've assumed command, we've had reason for many talks. She's quite impressive. I'm not sure if she has the temperament for a larger, independent command, but Jaylen Cresida is a brilliant scientist. One wonders what she might have done in peaceful pursuits if not for this war." He looked thoughtful. "My wife and I have some friends back home we'll have to contrive to introduce her to. They and she could do much worse."

"That's easy to believe." He'd avoided looking into his ship captains' personal-data files, but it was long past time he learned more about them as individuals. "So, getting away from my non–love life and your desire to fix up Captain Cresida . . ."

Duellos grinned momentarily and leaned back himself, thinking again and quickly looking unhappy. "I can't find out what Captain Numos is up to. Surely he hasn't finally accepted being under arrest. But any messages he's sending out to supporters are now being kept so closely that not even the rumor of them is reaching anyone willing to pass that on to me."

"What about Captain Faresa? Did anything trace back to her before *Majestic* was destroyed?"

"Nothing that I could find. Faresa always followed Numos's lead in any case. Captain Falco made occasional clumsy attempts to send out orders, but even if he were still alive, he couldn't serve as a figurehead now." Duellos frowned deeply this time. "Your enemies need someone to rally around, some officer respected enough to appear an alternative to you. I haven't been able to find out who that is, and it worries me."

"Surely we can make guesses," Geary noted, glad that the talk had veered firmly away from his personal life.

"I'm not so sure. The figurehead who replaces you has to appeal at least a little to those who believe in you. That means someone who isn't known as an opponent of yours and someone who's at least a decent commanding officer."

Geary mentally ran through the officers he knew. "Someone we likely trust, then?"

"Not Tulev or Cresida, certainly. Not Armus, though we don't trust him. But he's a blunt instrument, speaking and doing things forthrightly. He couldn't carry off the deception. Badaya has been increasingly vocal, but his loyalties are locked on you as long as he believes you will seize power when this fleet returns to Alliance space."

"That leaves a lot of possible candidates."

"It does," Duellos agreed. "I'm working it. Hopefully we'll learn something that will help."

"Thanks. I'll ask Co-President Rione to see what her spies can find out." Duellos made another face. "You don't trust her?" Geary asked.

"That's not it. I trust her to do what's best for the Alliance. But I'm worried about what she might decide is best for the Alliance."

It was a legitimate concern. Geary nodded, then a memory struck him. "What about Caligo on *Brilliant* and Kila on *Inspire*?"

Duellos pondered the question for a moment. "What brought them to your mind, if I might ask?"

"The recent realization that I'd hardly noticed either of them even though they're both battle-cruiser captains. Kila finally spoke up at the last conference."

"That's the way Caligo is," Duellos explained. "He and I have never talked much. He mostly sits and watches. He likes to stay in the background." Duellos's thoughtful expression shaded into a frown. "Interesting, given the sort of officer we think is working against you."

Geary couldn't help thinking the same thing. "But what's he like?"

"I haven't heard bad things about him, or all that many good things for that matter," Duellos observed. "He does his job and doesn't make waves, yet he's impressed people enough to earn command of a battle cruiser."

Under other circumstances, that would have sounded like the sort of officer Geary liked to have working for him. Now it left him wondering, and feeling angry with himself for worrying about the loyalty and intent of a fellow officer based on such nebulous information. "What about Kila?"

"Kila. She's been unusually quiet, now that you mention it." Duellos looked slightly embarrassed. "I'm a bit biased. She and I were involved as ensigns. It didn't really last past our training. Once we went our separate ways, she made it clear that we had separated in more ways than one."

"Ouch," Geary said sympathetically.

"I was eventually very grateful," Duellos responded. "Sandra Kila is ambitious and aggressive. Smart, too."

"She sounds a bit like Cresida."

"Ummmm, more like Cresida's evil twin. Kila tends to impress superiors but isn't well liked by her peers or subordinates because her aggressiveness shades too easily into ruthlessness, even in matters of competition for assignments or ranking in evaluations."

It didn't fit. Geary shook his head. "That doesn't sound like someone who'd just sit quiet and remain essentially unknown to her fleet commander. She won't earn good marks that way. Why isn't she in the forefront of argument and debate? Why hasn't she tried to suck up to me? The points she brought up at the last conference weren't pressed hard and seemed aimed at pressuring me, not supporting me in a way that would impress me."

"Perhaps she has a larger goal in mind." Duellos let that sink in, then spoke pensively. "But too many officers don't like her because of personal experience or her reputation. If she were an animal, Kila would be known as one of those which eats its young."

Geary raised an eyebrow at Duellos. "Did you say you were a *bit* biased?"

"Just a bit," Duellos admitted. "But my opinions are far from unique. Kila would never be accepted as acting fleet commander, and she's smart enough to know that."

"Why would an officer that ambitious suddenly recognize a ceiling above her? I've known officers like that. They want to reach the top. They don't aim to get so high and no higher, but don't realize that their tactics often eventually get them tarred so that they can't rise any further in the ranks."

"Yes, but . . ." Duellos made an annoyed gesture. "This isn't the fleet you knew. If Kila could continue impressing superiors, she could hope to be promoted to command despite the wishes of those serving under her. Diplomatic skills are far more important for anyone aspiring to the highest levels of command."

"Don't you mean political skills?" Geary asked sarcastically.

"There's no need to be insulting." Duellos sat silent for a moment, then nodded. "As much as we refuse to confront the issue, you're right. Admiral Bloch was a much better politician than he was an officer, and that served him well enough for promotion and eventual command of the fleet. It didn't serve the fleet or the Alliance nearly so well, of course. Maybe we've been increasingly hostile to people like Co-President Rione because we look at them and see a mirror of what we've become."

"Rione's not that bad," Geary objected almost automatically. Duellos just gazed back at him. After a long pause, Geary nodded in turn. "Maybe she is sometimes. But she's on our side."

"Let's hope she stays there."

Time to change the subject again. "Do you have any idea whether or not Caligo or Kila is among those supporting Badaya's bid to make me a dictator?"

Duellos thought for a while. "I would have said Caligo was, but can't recall a single thing that makes me think so. Kila . . . well, I don't think Kila would be happy at accepting any other officer as a dictator. It's less a matter of her support for the elected government and more a question of her own ego. I'll see what I can find out. You sound worried, if I may say so."

Geary blew out a long breath. "I suspect the accident that killed Casia and Yin wasn't an accident. Either one might have chosen to name other officers, but the shuttle explosion eliminated that possibility." Duellos's face froze for a moment, then he slowly nodded. "And if the people who oppose me, who want someone else in command of this fleet or someone else as dictator, were willing to do that, then they might do worse next time."

"I'll see what I can find out. You have more friends and supporters in this fleet than ever. Perhaps one of them can tell us something."

"Something tells me that it's my enemies we need to start telling us things," Geary replied.

THEY were nine hours from the jump for Wendig and in the middle of *Dauntless*'s night cycle when the pinging of a message alert woke Geary. He hit the acknowledgment button, then frowned as he saw that the message was from Commander Gaes on the heavy cruiser *Lorica*. Why would she be sending him a high-priority message under maximum security lock?

There wasn't any video, just Commander Gaes's voice, sounding strained. "Drive fleet jump in worms systems." The message cut off, leaving Geary frowning a lot more heavily. What the hell had that meant? The sentence sounded scrambled, as if the words had been mixed up.

Which they would be if someone was trying to confuse software monitoring fleet transmissions and scanning for word combinations. Nothing should be able to spy on messages under high-security lock, but Geary now had a lot less faith in the protection rendered by security systems than he'd had a few months before.

Which words obviously went together? Jump and drive. Jump-drive systems. Fleet jump-drive systems. In. Worms.

The phrases suddenly strung together properly. "Worms in fleet jump-drive systems."

He rolled out of bed, pulled on his uniform, and called Desjani. "Captain, I need to see you and your systems-security officer as soon as possible."

Less than ten minutes later, Desjani was at the hatch to his stateroom, accompanied by a tall, lean lieutenant commander whose eyes seemed permanently focused in front of his face rather than on the outside world.

Geary ensured the hatch was sealed and his stateroom's security systems were active, then repeated the message he'd received.

Desjani sucked in her breath. "Who sent you this, sir?"

"I'd rather not say. Can you confirm whether or not it's true?"

"On *Dauntless*? Yes, sir," Desjani promised, turning to her systems-security officer. "How long?"

The lieutenant commander's mouth twisted as his eyes studied a virtual display only he could see. "Give me half an hour, Captain. We're assuming the worm is malware?"

"Until we learn otherwise, yes."

Twenty minutes later, Desjani was back in Geary's stateroom along with the lieutenant commander, who now looked very upset. "Yes, sir. It was there. Very well hidden."

"What would it have done?" Geary asked.

"When we jumped, it would have initiated a series of destructive system failures." The lieutenant commander's face seemed paler than before in the low nighttime lighting of Geary's stateroom. "*Dauntless* never would have come out of jump."

Geary wondered how pale he himself looked. "How did someone manage to plant something like that?"

"They had to know our security systems backward and forward, sir. Whoever they are, they're very good, too. It's a sweet design for something created to cause that much damage."

Geary glanced at Desjani, who looked ready to break out enough rope to hang every person she even suspected of imperiling her ship that way. But the message had said the fleet's systems were infected. Had every ship been sabotaged for destruction, or was this aimed at him alone? He could get a better idea of the threat by checking on the ships of officers known as his closest allies. "Captain Desjani, I want you and your systems-security officer to notify the commanding officers of *Courageous*, *Leviathan*, and *Furious* under maximum-security seal. Tell them what was hidden inside *Dauntless*'s jump-drive system and ask them to examine their own jump systems immediately and tell me whatever they find as soon as they find it."

"Yes, sir." Desjani's salute was as rapid and sharp as the swing of a sword blade, then she left quickly with the lieutenant commander.

Half an hour later, Geary was in the fleet briefing room, looking at the angry and determined faces of not just Captain Desjani, but also Captains Duellos, Tulev, and Cresida, who were there in the virtual conference mode. Tulev, seeming unusually rattled, spoke first. "A worm. Yes. When *Leviathan* tried to make our next jump, the worm would have instead taken the jump system off-line."

Duellos nodded in confirmation. "*Courageous* as well. We couldn't find any destructive component, just a worm designed to disable the jump drives for a while."

Cresida spoke uncommonly quietly, as if trying to maintain extra control. "*Furious* had malware similar to that on *Dauntless*. We would have jumped and never come out."

Desjani's face reddened. "Then whoever was behind this wanted at least *Dauntless* and *Furious* destroyed, and at least some of the rest of the fleet left behind."

"Those seeking to end Captain Geary's command have decided to declare war on their comrades in the Alliance fleet," Duellos observed, his harsh tone at odds with the measured words. "This isn't just politics. It's sabotage. It's treason. *Furious* must have been targeted because Captain Cresida is known as a strong supporter of Captain Geary."

"Then why not you and Tulev as well?" Desjani asked.

"An interesting question, and one to which I have no certain answer. I can guess that Captain Cresida is more impulsive than I and Tulev, and those responsible for this might have feared that she would take aggressive action against anyone trying to assume command if she even suspected they had been responsible for the loss of *Dauntless*."

"And they would have been right! We need to make an example of them!" Cresida added, one hand flexing as she already had a pistol in it.

"We will when we find them," Geary promised.

"Arrest alone won't be sufficient," Cresida insisted. "This is far worse than what Casia and Yin did. It's possible to argue that the actions of Falco or Numos were meant in good faith, but there can't be more than a handful of people in this entire fleet who would accept the idea of deliberately trying to destroy at least two of our own battle cruisers. Especially that way, trapped in jump space forever."

Geary nodded, feeling his own guts tighten again at the idea. "*If* we positively identify those responsible, I *will* have them shot." That was a big if, yet Geary found himself surprised by how calm he felt this time while promising summary executions of fellow members of the fleet. But as Cresida said, this was the sort of stab in the back that would horrify most of the personnel in the fleet. Captain Casia had let down his comrades, but he hadn't tried to kill them. "How do we find the ones responsible?"

Everyone sat silent, looking angry or distressed.

The room security system chimed, announcing someone who wanted to enter. Geary checked. "Co-President Rione is here. Did anyone tell her?" The other officers all shook their heads. Desjani seemed ready to say something, then subsided. "Are there any objections to letting her in here and telling her about this? If none of us have good ideas for nailing our saboteurs, maybe she will." Once again Desjani appeared on the verge of speaking, but finally shook her head again along with the others.

Geary told the hatch to allow Rione's entrance, then watched as she came in, swept the small group with her eyes, and sat down in an empty seat. "What's happened?" Rione asked quietly, even as her eyes focused on Geary with another unstated question—*and why wasn't I told and made part of this group?*

No one else spoke, so Geary filled Rione in, watching as the news hit her. Rione's eyes widened only slightly, but her skin also flushed a bit. Geary wondered if the others, not nearly as used to judging Rione's reactions, would even notice those things or if they would believe that Rione hadn't responded at all to the information.

When he was done, Rione inhaled deeply and closed her eyes. "Tell everyone."

"What?" The incredulous question popped out of Cresida but could have come from any of the officers present.

Rione's eyes flew open, and she looked at each captain in turn. "I know the military mind-set. This is a secret so far, you think secrets must be kept secret, and you believe the best way to keep a secret, to keep people from trying to find out more, is for no one to know the secret exists. That's not what you want here."

"You want us to tip off the people who did this that we know they did it?" Cresida demanded.

"They're going to find out anyway in eight hours when this fleet's next jump is scheduled! Either you delay the jump without explanation, which will tip them off and create problems with everyone else, or you deal with that malware in every ship so you can make the jump safely." Rione looked around at the others. "Tell everyone what was done. In politics and in the military we keep secrets because we don't want people digging for more information. In this case we *need* more information. Once people know or suspect wrongdoing, many eyes and minds focus on the issue of learning more, of finding out who's involved."

Her expression hardened. "Tell everyone. You'll have thousands of sailors and officers trying to find out anything they can, and racking their memories for anything they might have seen or heard that could have been related to this. They'll be searching for more sabotage, and for all we know, there's more out there. Our enemies in this fleet have made a serious error by doing something that will arouse outrage in nearly everyone and alert everyone to the threat they pose."

Duellos frowned. "What if our enemies in this fleet claim

that what we're saying isn't real, that we somehow set this up ourselves?"

"The longer you try to hide it, the more people might suspect that." Rione slammed a palm onto the surface of the table. "Tell them now! Let your initial reactions show, your own shock and horror and outrage. Do exactly what you'd do if the Syndics had planted these worms."

Tulev nodded. "Send out a high-priority alert to all ships. Order a full system scrub to ensure that there's nothing else lurking inside any of our automated systems."

"And," Rione added, "bring up the loss of the shuttle in Lakota. The rare accident which killed two officers who might have named coconspirators. Few now will question that the fate of the shuttle wasn't the work of the same ones who tried to destroy entire warships."

One by one, Duellos, Cresida, and Desjani nodded in agreement as well. Geary turned to Desjani. "Please have your systems-security officer draft an alert, along with what we know of the worms. *Dauntless* and *Furious* may not be the only ships in the fleet with a worm designed to cause the loss of the ship. Run it by me when it's ready, and we'll get it out at highest priority."

"Yes, sir."

"The rest of you, thank you for your inputs and for keeping this quiet until we decided what to do. See if you can discover any leads on your ships to who did this and how they did it."

The shapes of the other officers winked out as they broke the software connection, leaving only Rione, Desjani, and Geary present. Rione stood up, her eyes focused only on Geary, as if no one else were there. "I can help you if you let me." Then she left almost as quickly as those whose virtual presences had simply vanished.

Geary frowned at Desjani, who very uncharacteristically hadn't leaped up to carry out her orders as fast as possible. "What?"

Desjani hesitated, then spoke in low tones, looking toward another part of the room. "My systems-security officer found something else."

"Another worm?" Geary asked, wondering why Desjani hadn't brought this up earlier.

"No. Unauthorized modifications to security settings." Desjani took a deep breath. "The hatch to my stateroom. The security settings had been recently modified to allow free access for Co-President Victoria Rione."

Geary just stared for a moment, trying to grasp the implications. "Why would she do that? She can't get in my stateroom anymore—"

"Can't she?"

He hesitated, then called up a remote readout. "My settings have been recently changed, too. To allow Victoria Rione free access again." He remembered Rione's comments, admissions that she would kill Geary if necessary to protect the Alliance. But why now? "She did it? She caused those modifications?"

"We can't prove that," Desjani admitted reluctantly. "But why would anyone else do it?"

"Why would she want to get access to your stateroom?"

Desjani bit her lip, her face reddening with what might be anger or embarrassment, or maybe a mix of those, then spoke with forced calm. "We both know that she sees me as a rival."

"Surely you don't believe that she'd—"

"I have no idea what actions Co-President Rione is capable of, sir."

What could he say to that? When Rione had frankly told him that she was willing to kill for the right reasons? But those had been very big reasons, having to do with the fate of the Alliance, and if she still intended such a thing, why had she demanded he change his security settings to deny her access? Geary thought hard, trying to separate out his feelings from everything he had seen of Rione, everything he had learned about her in both public and private. "I know she suffered that meltdown at one point, but I find it very hard to believe that Co-President Rione would plot your murder as a romantic rival. She was willing to walk away from me, Tanya."

"How kind of her," Desjani muttered, her face definitely showing anger now.

If only there was a way to know for certain. And Geary realized there was such a way. "I'm going to see if she's willing to be asked about this matter while in one of the interrogation rooms."

Desjani looked startled. "You intend ordering a senior civilian elected official of the Alliance to submit to interrogation by military-intelligence personnel?"

"No, I intend *asking* her to do so." He stood up, feeling something sour in the back of his throat. "If she's truly crazy enough to plot murder, that request should send her clawing for my throat. But if she agrees, it can clear her." Desjani looked troubled and disapproving as she stood as well. "I don't believe that she's a danger to me." *Not right now, anyway.* "Or to this fleet."

"With all due respect, sir, you can't afford to let misplaced loyalty or lingering personal feelings get in the way of a detached assessment of the danger any individual might pose to you or this fleet."

He felt a little angry himself now, but then he didn't really have any right to since he had let himself get involved with Rione. "My loyalty to Rione as an individual doesn't come close to being as strong as my duty to this fleet and the Alliance. And there are no lingering personal feelings." Desjani somehow conveyed disagreement without saying or doing anything. "Give me some credit for being able to make that kind of judgment."

"Yes, sir."

"I'm going to follow up on this. I'm not discounting your information or your assessment."

"Yes, sir."

"Dammit, Tanya—"

"*Yes, sir.* It's your decision."

He considered possible responses, most of which would be unfair or unprofessional or simply unwise. "Thank you."

"Then I will carry out my own orders, sir. I'll have the message you requested ready as soon as possible, sir."

He wanted to yell at her, but she was being perfectly professional and proper. "Thank you," Geary repeated, letting his aggravation show. As Desjani left, her back either at attention or just stiff, Geary spent a moment contemplating the unfairness of having to deal with relationship problems with a woman he couldn't have a relationship with.

VICTORIA Rione didn't go for his throat, but she did seem to be thinking about doing that. "Do you have any idea what you're asking?" He hadn't heard her voice that icy for a long time. "Do you actually believe that I would imperil this fleet by having anything to do with the worms you found?"

"Why do you have unrestricted access to Captain Desjani's stateroom?" Geary asked bluntly. "The settings were altered recently, without Captain Desjani's knowledge."

"I have no idea!" Rione seemed on the verge of shouting with anger. "Perhaps *she*—"

"My stateroom security settings were also altered to allow you free access again."

Rione choked off her next words and stared at him. "Damning. Definitely damning. Do you think I'd be stupid enough to do something that so obviously pointed to me, Captain Geary?"

"No," he replied. "I've been thinking about it, and if you could've changed those settings, you could have also made up some false identity and allowed it access. You're too smart to have generated such clear evidence of guilt against yourself. But I want it undeniably known that you're not involved."

She gazed back at him for a while before answering. "Because the other fleet officers would be willing to believe the worst of me. A politician."

"I fear so. That's why this was done, I'm sure. To discredit you, as a political representative of the Alliance, and to deny me your counsel."

Rione finally relaxed slightly, running her hands through her hair. "Very good. I have taught you a few things. Do you really want the intelligence personnel involved in this, though?"

"Yes. I need them to certify to others that you told the truth, and I need them to help us deal with these problems.

Traitors and aliens. Both groups have stepped up their attacks on this fleet, and that means we need to ensure that some other people know what we're dealing with."

Rione spent a moment thinking, then nodded and began walking toward the intelligence area as Geary called ahead to alert the personnel.

When they reached the high-security hatch at the entry to the intelligence area, Lieutenant Iger was waiting, his uniform showing signs of hasty dressing and his expression worried at this very-early-morning summoning. As Geary and Rione walked up to him, Captain Desjani and the systems-security lieutenant commander came hastening from the other direction, Desjani offering Geary a data pad, her face as emotionless as Rione's.

He read the alert quickly, then added a further order: *All indications are that this sabotage was carried out by someone within this fleet. All personnel with any knowledge of the matter should contact the flagship as soon as possible. It is critical that those responsible for attempting the destruction of at least two of our own ships and the deaths of their crews be found before they try to commit further treason against the Alliance and their comrades in this fleet.*

Desjani read the addition and nodded her approval wordlessly. Geary hesitated, then offered it to Lieutenant Iger to read. The intelligence officer skimmed the message quickly, his face reflecting shock as he took it in. Then Geary tapped the approve button and the message went out. Within moments, the commanding officers of every other ship in the fleet would be getting roused from sleep with very unwelcome news. Geary couldn't help wondering how many of them would secretly be distressed not by the sabotage but by its discovery. "Thank you, Captain Desjani."

"Yes, sir." Desjani's eyes swept over Rione, then settled back on Geary. "Is there anything else, sir?"

Yes. Stop being so damned cold and formal. "We'll have a fleet conference in a few hours."

"Yes, sir." She saluted rigidly and left with her systems-security officer.

Geary turned back to Rione and gave her a momentary

glare, seeing the amusement Rione couldn't quite hide as she watched Desjani's still-stiff-backed departure. "Lieutenant Iger, we need an interrogation room."

Iger's lingering shock changed to surprise. "You already have a suspect, sir?"

"We have someone who will likely be identified as a suspect, Lieutenant. I don't think she's actually involved, but evidence was planted implicating her so she's agreed to answer any questions in a controlled interrogation environment."

Lieutenant Iger nodded, his puzzlement still there, then his eyes shifted to Rione and widened in renewed shock. "M-madam Co-President?"

"Let's get it over with," Rione ordered.

Looking very much out of his depth, Iger led them into the intelligence spaces, past more high-security hatches and the enlisted intelligence personnel standing watch at this hour, who eyed the unusual procession with ill-concealed concern. A chief petty officer came up to Iger to see if he needed help and was waved off.

Iger sealed the hatch leading to the interrogation room behind them, then looked nervously at Rione. "Madam Co-President, if you would please enter that hatch and seat yourself in the red chair."

Rione nodded haughtily and stalked off, while Iger directed Geary into the neighboring observation room. One wall acted like a one-way mirror, giving them an unobstructed view of Rione as she sat down and stared ahead rigidly at what to her was a blank wall. Iger tapped controls, activating the devices that would not only monitor Rione's external physical signs but also conduct remote brain scans and other measures to provide clear evidence if the person in the interrogation room was lying or telling the truth.

Iger turned to Geary. "Sir, uh, who . . . ?"

"I'll ask."

The lieutenant tapped another control and nodded to Geary.

Geary composed himself, then spoke clearly, knowing his words were being repeated inside the interrogation room.

"Co-President Victoria Rione, did you have any prior knowledge of the worms found within the jump systems of *Dauntless* and other Alliance fleet ships?"

"No." The single word was as hard and direct as a grapeshot volley.

Readouts before Geary glowed green.

"Do you have any knowledge of any malware on Alliance fleet ships?"

"*Now* I do," Rione replied coldly.

Geary winced. He'd have to phrase his questions better. "Did you have any knowledge of any kind regarding the modifications to the security settings on either my or Captain Desjani's staterooms prior to my telling you?"

"No."

"Did you have anything at all to do with those modifications?"

"No."

"Have you taken any actions which might harm any ship in the Alliance fleet?"

"No."

"Do you know of anyone else who is taking or planning such actions?"

"Not for certain. I only suspect certain individuals of being involved."

Geary paused, trying to think of other questions, then glanced at Lieutenant Iger. Iger nodded, licked his lips nervously, then spoke with the emotionless calm of a trained interrogator. "Co-President Rione, would you notify proper authorities if you had any suspicion of any harmful actions directed toward the Alliance or any ship or person in this fleet who is carrying out their duties toward the Alliance?"

"Yes, I would."

"Would you harm or allow to come to harm this ship?"

"No."

"Would you harm or allow to come to harm anyone on this ship?"

"That would depend upon whether or not I had good reason to believe they were acting against the Alliance."

Every indicator still glowed green. Iger tapped a control

again, then spoke to Geary. "Sir, all indications show truth-fulness in every answer. She's, uh, not happy, but in her own mind she's being truthful, and her answers are short and direct."

Geary took a long look at the readouts. All confirmed Iger's words, though "not happy" was a nice way of saying that the readouts indicated high levels of anger. He wondered how much of that anger was directed at him, how much at Desjani, and how much at the enemy. *I've got Rione in the one place where I could know what her every answer meant. Just how much did you get emotionally involved with me? How do you feel now? Would you justify trying to harm Tanya Desjani by thinking of her as a danger?* But he couldn't ask those questions. Even if Lieutenant Iger weren't here, asking them would break the implicit bargain under which Rione had agreed to enter an interrogation room. "Thank you, Lieutenant. Let's get Madam Co-President out of there. There'll be a fleet commanding officers conference in a few hours. I want you present."

"Yes, sir." Lieutenant Iger seemed baffled this time. Such conferences had become political meetings over the course of the last century, backroom gatherings where deals could be cut and senior officers jockey for support from more junior commanding officers. Lesser beings were excluded so they couldn't be aware of the political maneuverings their seniors were debating.

"You looked at the things I asked you to examine? On the far side of Syndic space?"

"Yes, sir." Iger's expression shifted to worry again. "Who are they? Who's on the other side of Syndic space, sir?"

"No idea, Lieutenant. The most-senior Syndic leaders know. Do you agree with me that whoever or whatever they are, they've intervened actively against this fleet?"

"Yes, sir," Iger repeated. "They must have been responsible for diverting that big Syndic flotilla to Lakota. But why?"

"We don't know, can't know, for certain. The best guess is that they want humanity tied down in this war, and they were afraid we'd get the Syndic hypernet key home and gain a decisive advantage. But that's still just a guess." Iger nodded unhappily. "We won't discuss that at the conference, and I don't want you informing anyone else. But I need you thinking about it, and about anything you might see or have seen within intelligence channels that might provide more information about the threat."

"I understand, sir."

After Rione joined them, Lieutenant Iger led her and Geary back out into the passageway, where the dim night-cycle illumination and lack of other traffic came as a slightly jarring reminder that the official day was still a few hours away from starting.

Rione waited until they were alone, then spoke in a voice so soft Geary could barely hear. "Who framed me?"

"If we knew that, we'd know who planted those worms."

"Not necessarily. It could be a totally separate action. I know what you were thinking. I'm not the only woman on this ship capable of acting out of jealousy."

It took him a moment to realize what Rione meant. "Captain Desjani would not act that way."

"I'm glad you're so confident of that."

Geary glared at Rione. "Tanya Desjani is a very direct person. If she wanted to hurt you, she'd hunt you down and beat you up. She'd confront you face-to-face. You've been on this ship long enough to know that."

Rione glared back for a moment, then dropped her gaze. "Yes. She's not the sort to stab someone in the back."

"I've really got enough problems right now without you two sniping at each other."

"Are you going to tell her that?"

Geary realized for the first time that Rione had long since stopped referring to Tanya Desjani by her name. "I did, and I will. I need both of you."

Rione raised her eyes to Geary's, her expression sardonic. "You need both of us? Tonight, perhaps? I'm shocked."

"You know what I mean."

"I know what you think you mean." Rione shrugged. "My loyalty is to the Alliance, Captain Geary. I'll do what's necessary to support that. Right now, that means supporting you to the best of my ability. Neither you nor she need fear me unless you start acting against the Alliance. You know I'm telling the truth."

He did, Geary realized, since a slight variation on that statement had registered as true in the interrogation room. "Thank you. I know this isn't easy."

"You'd better be referring to the fleet's situation."

He eyed her, wondering if he should admit he was also talking about personal issues.

Her eyes blazed as she stared back. "Don't you *dare* pity me. *I* left *you*." Rione spun on one heel and walked quickly away.

THE atmosphere inside the conference room was different this time. The tension wasn't from politics or worry about the Syndics. It was focused inward, with every virtual commanding officer's presence eyeing those around it as if hoping to see clear signs of who had tried to sabotage the fleet. But eyes also kept going to Lieutenant Iger, who was looking uncomfortably out of place, and to Victoria Rione, who sat so silent and expressionless that she might have been carved from stone.

Geary stood up, and all eyes went to him. "You all know the reason for this conference. I've received reports from all of your ships and confirmed that every single one had been sabotaged by the placing of a malware worm in the jump-drive systems. The great majority of those worms would have simply kept your ships from jumping the next time it was ordered and kept your systems off-line for some time while it was neutralized. Three ships, the battle cruisers *Dauntless*, *Furious*, and *Illustrious*, had worms which would have allowed the ships to jump but then stranded them in jump space forever." He paused to let that sink in.

"Someone intended removing me from command of this fleet by destroying a warship of the Alliance and her crew. Someone attempted also to destroy *Furious* and *Illustrious*." Geary glanced at Captain Badaya, whose face was rigid with anger. "Whoever did it knew the daily changing security access codes for the system filters and had access to the means to transfer the malware to every ship in the fleet. That means it had to be the work of individuals wearing the uniform of the Alliance. This is not dissent, this is not debate or professional differences or the act of someone loyal to the Alliance. It's the act of traitors. The act of cowards. Has anyone found any information that might help identify them?"

He ran his eyes over the long, long virtual table, meeting the gaze of each commanding officer in turn. He almost lingered on Commander Gaes but remembered in time not to. She'd been a critically important informant this time, and he couldn't afford to risk compromising her. *Lorica* had been one of the ships that followed Captain Falco, and apparently whoever was continuing to conspire against Geary thought Gaes was still mutinous enough to be part of the plot. Either that or Gaes had managed to maintain enough contacts among the plotters to discover what they were doing.

Captain Caligo and Captain Kila didn't betray anything other than the same feelings shown by others.

It was impossible to tell if any of the faces reflected guilt rather than anger or fear. Geary gestured toward Iger. "Lieutenant Iger is the senior intelligence officer on *Dauntless*. He has some information regarding Co-President Rione."

The commanding officers of the ships of the Callas Republic and the Rift Federation gaped at Rione, their expressions shocked, but she unbent enough to give them a reassuring look.

Lieutenant Iger spoke in his briefing voice. "I was made aware of unauthorized security software modifications aboard *Dauntless* that implicated Co-President Rione."

"Why is she sitting here?" Captain Armus of *Colossus* demanded. "She should be—"

"Let Lieutenant Iger finish," Geary broke in, his voice like ice.

Iger continued as if totally unaware of any interruption. "Co-President Rione volunteered to be questioned inside a Class Six interrogation cell. She was asked a series of questions to determine if she had actually been involved in those or any other software modifications, and registered as absolutely truthful in her denials of any knowledge or involvement."

Silence reigned for a moment, then *Warspite*'s commander spoke up. "Class Six? Is there any way to deceive or mislead a Class Six?"

"Specialized training can suggest ways to avoid answering questions in deceptive ways, sir, but I and my personnel have been trained to identify when someone is using those techniques," Lieutenant Iger replied. "We might not be able to pin someone down into saying what we want, but we can tell if they're evading the real question so they don't register as deceptive. Co-President Rione did not employ such methods. Her answers were direct and unambiguous."

"So, what does that mean? Someone tried to frame Senator Rione?"

"That would be my conclusion, yes, sir."

"'That's treason, too." *Warspite*'s commanding officer leaned back, shaking his head in disbelief.

Geary leaned forward slightly and spoke louder than he usually did. "I've known ever since assuming command of this fleet that some officers did not approve of my command, that some have spread rumors about me, that some have tried to generate opposition to me. But this is not just politics over who commands this fleet. Someone tried to destroy three major warships. The ships your friends and comrades are serving on, the ships that have fought beside you. I don't care how much any of you might have been involved in speaking against me in the past, nor at this point do I care about past actions. This isn't about me. Whoever did this was striking at the fleet as well, and at ships I wasn't present on. If any of you have been rendering support in either passive or active form to the people behind this, please rethink your allegiances. I promise in front of all of you that anyone who comes forth with information regarding this treasonous sabotage will not be subjected to disciplinary action as long as they were not actively part of the creation and planting of these worms or were not aware of their content and intended use."

Silence again, but then he hadn't really expected anyone

to leap up, point a dramatic accusing finger, and cry, "Captain X did it!" That would have been a nice outcome in a work of fiction, but things just didn't resolve themselves so neatly in the real world.

Captain Badaya spoke for the first time. "Someone willing to kill Alliance personnel and destroy Alliance ships. We lost a shuttle before we left Lakota to a supposed accident." He glared around the table. "A very rare sort of accident, but believable in the absence of evidence of wrongdoing. Captain Casia and Commander Yin died on that shuttle, and I now suspect they died because of fear that they would identify some of those with whom they were working against Captain Geary. Anyone involved in this should consider that whoever is leading the effort is willing permanently to silence possible weak links. If you have to be caught, I'm certain that the fleet commander will have you shot. If you remain silent, you run the risk of being silenced forever by your coconspirators. The only chance you have is to reveal yourselves." Badaya subsided, his angry gaze traveling around the table.

"Why would anyone do this?" *Intrepid*'s commanding officer asked. "Everyone knows some people have been unhappy with Captain Geary being in command. I had my own doubts. But he's proven himself. Most of the doubters, myself included, are now very pleased to be led by him."

Captain Duellos answered. "You may have stated the reason for this. Those responsible can no longer hope to convince this fleet's ship captains to oust Captain Geary from command. Their only chance of success is to eliminate Captain Geary."

"But anyone even suspected of murdering him and the crews of three other warships—!"

"Consider what would have happened if these worms hadn't been found. *Dauntless*, *Furious*, and *Illustrious* would have disappeared into jump as if their drives had worked normally. The rest of us would have found the worms preventing our jump drives from working, and jumped as well once our systems were back online. This would have taken a few hours at least. We would have assumed that for some reason the worms found in our systems didn't work on the three ships that jumped as scheduled. When we arrived at Wendig, the other three ships wouldn't be there awaiting us as we'd expected. No trace of them would ever be found, no evidence that their jump drives had been infected with a very different worm from that in the rest of the ships."

Commander Neeson nodded, his face like granite. "No evidence of the deliberate destruction of three warships. Very neat. Most of us would be grief-stricken by the disappearance of the three ships and Captain Geary, but we'd have to choose a new fleet commander. I wonder who would have stepped up to fill that job?"

"What about Numos?" Captain Armus asked.

Geary shook his head. "In light of the seriousness of the attempted sabotage against this fleet, I've ordered that Captain Numos be interrogated for any knowledge of whoever is behind this. I suspect, however, that he won't be able to tell us anything."

"Why not?" Badaya asked.

"Because *Orion* didn't have the same worm as *Dauntless*, *Furious*, and *Illustrious*. Numos wouldn't have a prayer of being accepted as fleet commander, but if Numos did know who was behind the loss of those three ships, he'd be able to blackmail those individuals. They would've tried to get rid of him."

Rione gave Geary a surprised look, then nodded to him with a trace of a satisfied smile, like a teacher whose pupil has revealed unexpected attention to lessons.

"Numos tried to leave Captain Falco to swing," *Warspite*'s captain agreed. "You think he's not actually connected to whoever planted the worms?"

"I think those people might have been willing to use Numos," Geary explained, "but that they wouldn't have trusted him." He gave another look down the virtual length of the table. "Every ship is making additional scrubs of its systems to ensure that there's nothing else dangerous hidden among them. When we have a clean bill of health reported for all ships, we'll jump to Wendig. Before we jump, I strongly urge anyone who knows anything to inform me or someone else in authority whom they trust. Our enemies are the Syndics. Not each other. Some individuals in this fleet have forgotten that, and now they're on the side of the Syndics."

Captain Badaya nodded firmly. "*Anything* Captain Geary chooses to do will have the backing of this fleet."

A flicker of unhappiness crossed Duellos's face, but he said nothing.

For his part, Geary knew he couldn't afford to offend Badaya's powerful faction right now, not when he had another internal danger to this fleet to worry about. "May our actions remain those which our ancestors will look upon with favor," Geary stated carefully. "As we approach the time for jump to Wendig, I'll inform all ships whether the jump will take place as scheduled."

Images of commanding officers vanished in a flurry, Lieutenant Iger gratefully hastening out of the room, with Co-President Rione following haughtily. Captain Desjani, her eyes on Rione's back, went out as well.

One unexpected figure remained. Geary checked the identification. Lieutenant Commander Moltri, commanding officer of the destroyer *Taru*. "Yes, Commander?" Geary asked.

Moltri swallowed, then averted his eyes as he spoke. "Sir, I think I know how the worms were propagated through the fleet and were able to bypass security."

"Were you involved in that?" Geary kept his voice calm with some effort. Moltri seemed not only frightened but also extremely embarrassed, which didn't make sense.

Lieutenant Commander Moltri shook his head very quickly. "No, sir. Not . . . not knowingly." He closed his eyes, visibly nerved himself, then focused on Geary and spoke steadily. "There are . . . certain programs that get passed around to those . . . interested in them. Because of their nature, they have to be passed through means that avoid fleet security checks. There's a whole subnet within the fleet that handles those programs covertly."

Pulling out his data pad, Moltri tapped a few commands, his face grim and his hand shaking. "I've sent a sample to you, sir. Your security personnel will be able to use it to identify the means by which it was being passed. I swear, sir, that

I had no idea that someone might use the same means to propagate a dangerous worm, but I think that's what must have happened."

"Thank you, Commander Moltri," Geary stated. "I'll take a look at it. You may have done this fleet a great service."

Moltri gritted his teeth in what seemed to be pain. "Please don't reveal my connection to the content of what I sent you, sir. I'm not proud of it. Not at all. I've never really hurt anyone. I swear."

"I understand."

"I know there'll be some disciplinary action, sir. Please, don't let the full reason be part of the record."

Geary, increasingly disturbed by Moltri's distress and statements, spoke evenly. "If it's not germane, it won't be. Thank you, Commander."

Moltri's image vanished as if the man were fleeing. Geary checked his message queue and found what Moltri had just sent him. He called up the program in it, then stared, his stomach roiling, at the images displayed. No wonder Moltri and the others interested in this kind of thing had distributed it by undercover means. Hastily shutting off the program, Geary called Captain Desjani and her systems-security officer.

Desjani hadn't gotten far and was back quickly, but it took the security officer a few minutes to get there. Geary offered his data unit. "Take a look."

The security officer seemed first outraged, then both sickened and resigned. "They keep finding new ways to spread this stuff, sir. May I forward it to my address?" Geary nodded. "I'll be able to use this message to locate and monitor the subnet it was originally sent on," the security officer advised.

"Will you be able to tell if that's how the worms were spread?"

"We're unlikely to be able to prove it, sir, if this subnet is typical of what I've seen before, but I'd lay bets that this is what was used. This subnet would have been set up to access every ship in the fleet."

Geary's reaction surely showed. "There's someone on every ship in the fleet who likes this kind of thing?"

"No, sir," the security officer corrected hastily. "Subnets that handle this sort of material are designed not to leave fingerprints when stuff is uploaded or downloaded. It automatically spreads to every communication node on the net, meaning every ship. Anyone on any ship who knew about it could get to it, but it'd be almost impossible to identify anyone who actually had done it or even what ship they were on."

The implications of that were clear enough. "So the odds that we'll be able to figure out who put the worm into this subnet are pretty dismal."

The security officer made a helpless gesture. " 'Dismal' is probably an optimistic term in a case like this, sir. We can monitor this subnet now that we have its characteristics identified, and that means it can't be used for that again."

"Monitor it? Shut it down. Are we sure there aren't other covert subnets active?" Desjani demanded.

This time the security officer appeared surprised by the question. "We know there are, Captain. The net linking the fleet is riddled with unofficial subnets, handling anything that's not authorized officially, like gambling."

"Why haven't they been shut down?" Desjani pressed.

"Because my people are responsible for security, not law enforcement, Captain. As long as we know where the subnets are, we can monitor them and know what people are doing on them. If we shut one down, it'll eventually reappear and have to be found again, and until we find it, we can't know what's going on in it. Like this one. If we'd known about it, we'd have picked up the worm when it was introduced into the subnet, so whoever used this particular subnet probably did it for that reason." The lieutenant commander held up Geary's data unit. "But you told me to shut this one down, so I will. The people who like this will have to set up a replacement, and that takes time."

Geary pondered the moral difference between allowing material like that to be spread through the fleet so worse misuse could be tracked and shutting it down at the risk that the replacement would be used for sabotage as well. "How much time?"

"For a replacement subnet, sir? Under current conditions?" The security officer's eyes went distant. "Half a day."

"Half a day?" Geary exchanged an aggravated look with Desjani. The choice didn't really exist, given the nature of the threat to the fleet posed by another worm like that. "Keep it up and make sure it's monitored."

Captain Desjani gestured to her security officer. "Get on it. But give me that first." The security officer hesitated, looking to Geary, who also hesitated, then waved a quick, reluctant assent.

"This one?" Desjani opened the file on Geary's data unit, staring dispassionately for a few seconds, then clicked it off. "Is what it shows real?"

The security officer shook his head. "Usually not. Producing this stuff is bad enough, but if they used real people, the producers would find themselves facing eternity in prison. They use very realistic computer-generated images."

"But it looks real," Geary stated, feeling unclean for having viewed it.

"Yes, sir. That's, uh, the point."

"Thanks. Take care of it." He shivered when the security officer had left.

Desjani looked as if she'd swallowed something vile. "I know why you agreed to leave the subnet up, but I also know how you must feel about that. Where'd you get that download?"

"From someone I never would have guessed would like that kind of thing, judging by appearances."

"Whoever it is needs a full psych workup."

"Yeah." Geary drummed his fingers on the table surface. "Can I order a psych workup confidentially?"

She nodded. "Yes, though I don't know why you'd want to protect whoever this is. Just possessing that is a serious violation of regulations."

"Because that person was willing to let me know this about himself so I could protect the fleet," Geary explained.

Desjani made a face. "That can't have been easy. I won't ask who it was."

"Had you ever seen something like that before?"

She shook her head this time. "I'd heard about it, but never seen it."

"Me, neither." Geary rubbed his face with both hands. "Excuse me, Tanya. I need to call the fleet psychs and a fleet officer, then I need to take a shower. Let me know what your security officer finds out."

"Yes, sir." Desjani paused at the door and turned back to face him. "I wish to apologize for not trusting your assessment of Co-President Rione, sir."

"That's all right, Captain Desjani. It never hurts to have someone keeping me honest. And at least you'll say her name."

"Excuse me, sir?"

"Nothing. Please let me know when the rescrub of *Dauntless*'s systems is completed."

Three hours later, every system in the fleet triple-scanned and certified as malware-free by security officers who knew their lives might well depend on not missing anything, Geary ordered the fleet to jump for Wendig. Despite a tight feeling in his gut as *Dauntless* entered jump space, nothing went wrong.

NINE

IT wasn't hard at all to figure out why Wendig hadn't gotten a Syndic hypernet gate, nor why Syndic records indicated the star system had been abandoned once the Syndic hypernet had been constructed. The only puzzle was why anyone had actually remained in the system. Only three worlds orbited the star, along with a mess of asteroids. Two of the planets were in distant orbit, frozen balls of rock orbiting more than five light-hours from the feeble warmth of the dim red star. The world nine light-minutes from the weak star had too little atmosphere, and what it did have was poisonous to humans, but it had once boasted at least two covered cities. Taking another look at the data, Geary decided that even at their biggest, "town" had been a better description than "city" for both of them.

Absolutely no other trace of humanity remained in the Wendig Star System. Now one of those towns was dark and cold, but the other was still inhabited even though many portions of it seemed inactive. "They, or their parents, might have been abandoned here when the Syndic corporations employing them pulled out of the system," Desjani remarked.

"Yeah. I can't see any other reason they might have stayed."

"Captain?" The communications watch-stander gestured toward his display. "There's a distress signal being broadcast. It's from the inhabited world."

That brought up unpleasant memories of Lakota. Desjani frowned as she and Geary both punched their own displays to bring up the signal.

It was audio only, a voice speaking with labored calm. "Anyone passing through or near Wendig Star System, this is the town of Alpha on the world Wendig One." The corporate minds of the Syndic leaders hadn't tended to grant poetic names to worlds or towns, Geary reflected for maybe the hundredth time, unless the names had been created for advertising purposes. "Our remaining life-support systems are at risk of imminent failure," the message continued. "We've cannibalized everything left on this world to keep them working, but all resources are now exhausted. There are over five hundred and sixty remaining inhabitants who require emergency assistance and evacuation. Please respond." A pause, then a universal time and date register, then the message began repeating.

Geary checked the date on the message again. "They've been sending this for a month."

"Anyone near Wendig?" Desjani asked. "They must know that no one would be closer than the nearest inhabited star systems, and this message will take years to get to those. Even then, it's too weak to be heard across interstellar distances. Unless an astronomical researcher scanning that frequency band picks it up, it'll go unheard, and researchers avoid bands used for human communication systems because they're so full of noise."

"Maybe these people have been sending rescue requests for years, then, which have gone unheard. Are they still alive?" Geary wondered.

Another watch-stander answered. "That city isn't at a comfortable temperature for humans, but it's still got some heat, and the atmosphere inside reads out as breathable. Their air-generation and recirc systems must be in bad shape, though, from the amount of contaminants we're seeing on spectral analysis."

Geary looked over at Desjani, who was grimacing. She noticed his regard and shrugged uncomfortably. "It's not a nice way to die, sir. Even for Syndics."

"Five hundred and sixty. Families, surely. Adults and kids." Geary had the automated billeting assistant on his fleet database run the figures. "We could hold them."

"Hold them?" Desjani stared at him.

"Yeah. Like you said, it's an ugly way to die, slowly freezing and feeling the air get worse and worse. We could take them somewhere else."

"But—" Desjani stopped and spoke slowly. "Sir, it's the smallest drop in the bucket. Yes, it's . . . tragic. Even though they're Syndics. But that many people die in this war every second. At this very moment there's a good chance that an Alliance world is being bombarded by Syndic warships, and thousands of our civilians are dying."

Geary nodded to show he knew the truth of her words. And yet . . . "What was the Third Truth?"

She looked back at him for a long moment before answering. "Only those who show mercy can expect to receive it. It's been a very long time since I heard the Truths recited."

"I guess we used to do that more often a century ago." Geary looked down, gathering his arguments. "I know what's been done. I know what Syndic ships may be doing at this moment. But how can we just sail by and let those people die? Anything we could have done at Lakota would have been insignificant against the scale of the tragedy. Here we can make a difference."

"Sir, any delay could be fatal. We don't know what kind of Syndic force might be in pursuit of us, or what forces are moving to block us in other star systems. Going to that world will cost at least an extra day in this star system. Maneuvering to pick them up will cost fuel-cell reserves we can't afford to burn. Not a lot, but some. They'll eat our rations while aboard our ships, and we're already short on food, too. On board they'll have to be guarded constantly to ensure that they don't commit sabotage. And then we'll have to find a way to drop them off in the next star system without costing too much time and fuel-cell reserves, possibly while dodging an enemy flotilla." Desjani laid out each point in turn, then spoke firmly. "Sir, the cost of this gesture could well be more than we can afford."

"I understand." And he truly did. What would be the morality of hazarding the many thousands of personnel in this fleet, and the fate of the Alliance itself, in the name of saving a few hundred enemy civilians? It wasn't like he didn't have other things to worry about, like whoever had placed the worm in the fleet's jump drives, and might take advantage of any focus on these Syndics to commit more sabotage. He'd hoped that once the fleet returned to normal space someone who had searched their conscience during the transit to Wendig would have contacted him with important information, but no such informant had appeared. Nor had Rione's or Duellos's sources within the fleet discovered anything new. But was that a critical factor in deciding whether or not to help these people? "Co-President Rione, what is your opinion?"

Rione took a while to answer. "I can't dispute the arguments laid out against offering assistance," she finally replied in an unemotional voice. "But you want to do it anyway, don't you, Captain Geary?" Geary nodded. "Then my advice would be to follow your instincts. Every time you've done so, you've been right."

Desjani turned enough to glare at Rione, then her expression changed as she thought. "Co-President Rione is right, sir. About your instincts. You are guided in ways we are not."

Geary managed not to groan. Guided. By the living stars themselves. Or so Desjani and a large portion of the fleet believed.

"But, sir," Desjani continued, "it's still a very large risk. My advice has not changed. Besides, it's very likely that another Syndic pursuit force will come through this system after us. They'll hear the distress message, too."

He nodded, grateful at the realization that a humane

alternative existed. Then another insight hit. "Would a Syndic force in pursuit of us divert to assist those civilians?"

Desjani's lips compressed into a thin line, then she shook her head. "Probably not, sir. Almost certainly not. Their commander would be sent to the labor camps for wasting time."

Give Desjani full credit. She didn't want to divert to help those people, for a long list of good reasons, but she'd given him an honest assessment even though it hurt her case. He thought about the people on Wendig One. It was entirely possible that some of them, even adults, had never seen any ship in their star system. Why would any ship come here once the hypernet had been constructed? Now, with their means of life failing, they would look up and see this fleet and watch it pass by and leave. Then they'd maybe see a Syndic flotilla and watch it pass by and leave. Then there'd be no more ships. While the air got colder and harder to breathe. While the elderly and the youngest children died one by one, the strongest citizens clinging despairingly to each other as death came slowly for them each in turn, until Wendig Star System was as devoid of human life as it had been for uncounted millennia before the first starships came here.

Geary drew in a deep breath. The vision he'd seen of the dying colony had been so real, as if he were there. Where had it come from?

Maybe he was being guided. He knew what his heart said, and he knew what everything he'd been taught said. Measured against that was the cruel reality of war and the necessities of command. But there wasn't a Syndic flotilla right on this fleet's tail, no imminent threat to measure against those innocent lives.

Everyone was watching him, waiting. Only he could decide. And that knowledge tipped the balance, because he had a responsibility to make hard decisions, and going onward and leaving the colony to its fate didn't require a decision, just the absence of one until the option became too hard to carry out. "I feel," Geary began, "that we have a duty to help those people. That this is a test of us, one we must pass to prove we still believe in the things that made the Alliance great. We will pass that test."

It felt like all those on *Dauntless*'s bridge had been holding their breath and now let them out all at once. Geary looked to Desjani, dreading to see a look of disapproval there. He knew how Desjani felt about Syndics. And now Geary wanted to risk her ship to rescue some of them.

But Desjani didn't seem angry. She was watching him as if trying to see something not apparent to the naked eye. "Yes, sir," she said. "We will pass that test."

THE video message feed from Wendig One was broken by static, another ugly reminder of what they had left behind at Lakota. "I can't trace it to interference. It's probably because their equipment is patched together," the communications watch explained.

A man looked out, his expression baffled. "Alliance warships, we are in receipt of your message. We're incredibly grateful for your assistance. Is the war over? How do you come to be this deep in Syndicate Worlds' space?"

Geary checked and saw that the fleet was still almost two light-hours from Wendig One. Not the best circumstances for a conversation. Extremely annoying circumstances for a conversation, really, when his reply would take two hours to reach the Syndic and the Syndic's next answer another two hours to reach Geary. "This is the Alliance fleet commander. We won't deceive you. The war is not over. This fleet is on a combat mission, on its way back to Alliance space. But we do not war on civilians or children. We will divert from our course through this system far enough to be able to send shuttles down to evacuate your people. There must be no delays. You have my word on the honor of my ancestors that you will be treated properly while aboard Alliance ships and dropped off safely in the next inhabited Syndicate Worlds' star system we reach. Provide an accurate count of people involved, broken down by families so we can ensure that no families are separated during the transit. We've identified the landing pad on the northwest side of your town as the best location for our shuttles to land. There's some drifting sand covering part of it that needs to be swept clear by your people if possible. Everyone must be standing by at the nearest access to that landing pad when our shuttles arrive. No weapons of any kind are to be brought, nor anything that could be used as a weapon. Personal luggage must be limited to ten kilos per person. Are there any questions?"

Geary leaned back and closed his eyes. If there were any questions, he wouldn't hear them for at least four hours.

Less than two hours later Captain Desjani took a message, then got up from her command seat and stepped close to speak to Geary, activating his sound-deadening field. "My systems-security officer reports that the subnet we were told about before leaving Branwyn was used again to try to plant a worm. The worm was identified and blocked, but all attempts to ID the originator have failed."

"Messing with our system jump drives again?"

"No, sir." Desjani tilted her head toward the star-system display. "It would have infiltrated the combat systems of two warships and caused the targeting and launch of kinetic bombardment munitions aimed at the town occupied by the Syndic civilians. A systems-security alert has been sent to all warships in the fleet to scrub their combat systems for any worm that might have gotten through by other means."

That took his breath away for a moment. "So our saboteurs are willing to kill helpless Syndics as well as unsuspecting Alliance comrades. Which ships?"

"The munitions would have been launched from *Courageous* and *Furious*, sir."

"Ships commanded by two of my strongest supporters in the fleet." Geary felt a slow burn of anger. His fleet and shuttles never could have reached the Syndic survivors before those munitions struck. "Someone has a sick sense of vengeance and a very ugly willingness to do anything."

Desjani's expression showed she agreed with him. "In half an hour they'll know the worm was blocked. That's when the munitions were supposed to launch."

"Thank you, Captain. I have a couple of people to talk to." Geary left the bridge and waited until he was in his stateroom,

with all security features active, before calling Rione and filling her in. "I don't know if anyone will react when the worm
doesn't work, but you might have your sources watching."

Rione, her face pale, nodded.

Geary passed the same information to Captain Duellos,
then waited, wondering what he'd do if somehow another
worm hadn't been blocked or detected, if some of his ships
did launch bombardment munitions against that dying Syndic colony. Nothing happened, though, and no one called.
He hadn't really expected anyone suddenly to rage in disappointment when the set time passed, but apparently not even
subtle signs of frustration had been spotted in anyone. The
only thing he could be certain of was that whoever had
planted the worms would now be aware that their chosen
subnet path had been compromised.

That and whoever had tried to destroy three Alliance
warships earlier was now also opposed to Geary's aiding
these Syndics. At least that helped reassure him that he was
indeed doing the right thing.

After all of that a reply finally came from the Syndic
colony.

The Syndic he'd seen before was now anxious. Geary
couldn't help thinking how much more nervous the Syndic
would be if he'd known how close his town had come to being turned into a large crater. "Sir, my people are very worried. Please don't take this wrong, but many don't trust the
Alliance. Unless things have changed a great deal since our
last news from outside, and it has been decades, there has
been very little consideration for civilians in this war. I'm
trying to convince them to trust you, because I can't think of
any reason why you'd bother to kill us aboard your ships
rather than just letting us die here. No reason except . . . the
women . . . the girls . . . all the children. I'm sorry, but you
must understand what we fear. What can I tell them, sir?"

Geary pondered his reply. This man clearly wanted and
needed to be convinced himself if he was to argue effectively with his own people. "Tell your people that Captain
John Geary commands this fleet by the grace of his ancestors, and that he will never dishonor those ancestors by

harming the helpless or breaking his word. I tell you again that I give you my personal word of honor that you will not be harmed as long as you do not attempt to harm these ships. Any person in this fleet who tries to assault any one of you will be dealt with under the wartime provisions of the fleet code of justice. I could have lied to you about the war, about this fleet's mission. I didn't. Your people have no military value whatsoever. But they are people. We won't let them die if we can save them. Please provide the information we need as soon as possible."

The next half day passed with a normalcy that felt almost surreal. Geary authorized the release of information about the latest worm despite fears that it might garner support for the saboteurs from officers who opposed his decision to aid the Syndics, but instead there was another wave of revulsion at the idea of hijacking ships' combat systems. Humans had never fully lost their mistrust of automated combat systems, so anyone messing with their software to cause weapons systems to act on their own ended up on the wrong side of the fence as far as just about everyone was concerned.

Shuttles soared between warships, bringing new fuel cells and expendable munitions, replacement parts and anything else the auxiliaries had manufactured to meet the needs of the fleet during the period since leaving Lakota. Geary was pleased to see his fleet's average fuel-cell reserves climb back up to 65 percent. Not great by a long shot, but better than it had been. Commander Savos was brought to *Orion* as her new commanding officer, fully aware of the challenge he faced there. Maybe he could turn *Orion* around as Commander Suram had done with *Warrior*.

The next reply from the Syndics didn't come until the Alliance fleet was less than a single light-hour from Wendig One and about ten hours at its current velocity from reaching the planet. "We will trust you because we have no choice. Some of our people are using the few working survival suits we have left to try to sweep clear the landing pad you indicated. All of us will be standing by when your shuttles arrive."

Desjani listened to the message with a resigned look.

Rione's expression masked her thoughts. Everyone else Geary could see seemed puzzled, trying to figure out why he was doing this. In a way, that was very depressing. But none of them were objecting anymore, and that was at least hopeful.

The shuttles launched as the fleet approached Wendig, the Alliance warships braking their velocity to allow time for the shuttles to reach the surface, load, and rejoin. Geary monitored the action from the bridge of *Dauntless*. Every shuttle had a detachment of Marines in full battle armor aboard just in case. He hadn't been thrilled by that since it meant reducing the passenger capacity of the shuttles and requiring using more of them, but Colonel Carabali had been insistent, and he'd recognized the wisdom of her strongly worded suggestions.

"All birds down," the operations watch-stander reported.

On his display, Geary could see an overhead image of the grounded shuttles, the Marines spilling out to stand sentry and screen the passengers, evacuation tubes being run to the air lock on the civilian town. He toggled briefly to the video feed from one of the Marines. The outside of the Syndic town already looked long abandoned, drifts of toxic snow and sand piled up against its walls, broken and cannibalized equipment littering the lifeless landscape. Geary couldn't help shivering at the cold, empty image of desolation. "Can you imagine being trapped in a place like that?" he asked Desjani.

She viewed the feed, frowning, but said nothing.

"Loading complete," Colonel Carabali reported. This was a landing expedition and therefore a Marine operation, she had insisted. "Evac tubes being withdrawn into shuttles. Shuttle liftoff estimated in zero three minutes."

"Any problems, Colonel?" Geary asked.

"Not *yet*, sir." Confronted with well over five hundred Syndics, Carabali obviously believed it was only a matter of time before problems arose.

"Birds in the air on schedule," the operations watch-stander reported. "Rendezvous with warships projected on time in twenty-five minutes."

Desjani tapped her own controls. "Colonel Carabali, please confirm all Syndics were searched for weapons and destructive materials."

Carabali sounded slightly insulted at having a fleet officer ask if Marines had done their jobs. "Absolutely. Full scans. They're clean. They don't *have* much."

Geary and Desjani went down to the shuttle dock to see the Syndic civilians destined for *Dauntless* arrive. The Syndics filed off the shuttle between ranks of Marines in full battle armor with weapons at guard position. Some of the civilians were trying to look brave, but all appeared frightened. Fifty-one of them, their civilian clothes a mix of styles and types that Geary realized must reflect raiding old stockpiles and closets as their supplies of clothing wore out. All of them seemed slightly gaunt, reflecting what must have been short rations in recent years as the amount of food available also ran low.

They were also trying not to stare around at the ship and at the Alliance personnel in the hangar deck. It struck Geary as he watched them that these people had never encountered strangers before, never actually been anyplace unfamiliar. Far in time and space as they were from mankind's origins, these Syndics were like the ancient inhabitants of a small island encountering their first ships from the outside. Not just ships, but warships carrying people who were supposed to be their sworn enemies.

Desjani stood beside him, her posture rigid, her face revealing nothing as she watched the enemy civilians walk onto the deck of her ship.

Geary recognized the man he'd spoken with and stepped forward. "Welcome to the Alliance fleet flagship. We'll have to keep you all under guard, and a warship isn't designed for a lot of passengers, so your accommodations will be pretty cramped."

The man nodded. "I'm the mayor of . . . Well, I used to be the mayor of Alpha. We can't very well complain about conditions here. It's warm, and we can breathe. We honestly didn't know if our life-support systems would hold out until your shuttles reached us." The man's eyes were still troubled by the memories of what must have been an agonizing wait. "But at least we knew you were coming. There haven't been any ships here since the corporations pulled out. Before we got your call, we were getting ready to draw lots, though some argued the oldest shouldn't even draw since we wouldn't last long anyway."

It was all too easy to imagine how these people had felt. "Why weren't you evacuated from this star system along with everyone else?"

This time the mayor made a baffled gesture. "We have no idea. All of us who were left worked for subsidiaries of the same corporation, and our senior staff left on the last ship sent by another company. We were told the ships for us would arrive soon. They never did."

"We're taking you to Cavalos, so I guess your ships finally did arrive."

The mayor grinned nervously. "Better late than never, right? You said you're Captain John Geary? We know the name. It's in our histories, though I expect they say different things than yours do. You're his grandson?"

Geary shook his head. "No. I'm him. It's a long story," he added, as the mayor stared at him in disbelief, "but suffice it to say I fought at Grendel in the first battle of this war, and the living stars willing, I'll see the last battle of it as well."

The man leaned back involuntarily, his eyes wide.

A woman stood beside the mayor, her eyes constantly shifting from him to Geary, then to three children hanging on to her. The oldest of those, a young boy, saw his father recoil slightly and eyed Geary defiantly. "Don't you dare hurt my father!"

Before Geary could answer he became aware that Desjani was beside him again, gazing down at the boy, her face still expressionless but her eyes showing inexplicable sadness. "Your father will not be harmed on my ship as long he does not attempt to cause any damage to my ship."

The boy moved slightly, putting himself between Desjani and his mother. "We can't believe you. We know what you've done."

To Geary's surprise, Desjani went to one knee so her head was on a level with the boy's. "Man of the Syndicate Worlds," she addressed the boy as if he were his father's age, "under the command of Captain John Geary, the Alliance fleet no longer wars on the innocent or the helpless. Even should he leave his command, we would not do so again because he has reminded us of that which honor demands of warriors. You need not protect your family from us."

The boy, wordless with surprise at being spoken to that way, nodded.

Desjani rose and looked down at the boy, then at his mother, exchanging some wordless message. The mother nodded, seeming reassured. Then Desjani gazed around and spoke in her command voice, her words ringing through the shuttle dock. "Citizens of the Syndicate Worlds, I'm Captain Desjani, commanding officer of the Alliance battle cruiser *Dauntless*. You are not combatants and will be treated as civilians in need of humanitarian assistance *unless* you try to harm my ship or members of my crew. Follow all instructions and orders given you. Anyone who violates orders or attempts to damage this ship or harm any Alliance personnel will be regarded as an enemy combatant and treated accordingly. We will require about three more days to reach the jump point to Cavalos, then just under nine days in jump space before arriving at Cavalos. According to the latest Syndicate Worlds' star-system guides in our possession, that star retains a robust human presence. Once there, we'll identify a safe place to deliver you."

Desjani frowned as she studied the Syndic civilians. "I'll have my medical personnel check you for serious problems. You'd be wise to cooperate with them to the best of your ability. Your rations will be equivalent to what my own crew is eating. At this point that's mostly expired Syndic rations, so don't expect any fine meals. Are there any questions?"

One woman, late middle-aged, called out. "Why?"

Desjani flicked a glance at Geary, but he indicated she could answer if she wanted. Facing the woman, Desjani spoke crisply. "Because only those who show mercy can expect to receive it. And because the honor of our ancestors demands it. Marines, escort the civilians to their accommodations."

Despite Geary's fears, no more sabotage attempts occurred over the next two days as the fleet covered the distance to the jump point for Cavalos. The Syndic civilians were so terrified, none of them had caused any problems. As he sat on the bridge of *Dauntless* waiting to give the jump command, Geary noticed Desjani gazing morosely at her display, where an image of Wendig One floated. "Something wrong?" he asked.

Desjani shook her head. "I was just thinking about how I'd feel if we were about to jump, and they were still there. I've had to think a lot about it, but you did the right thing, sir."

"*We* did the right thing, Captain Desjani." She glanced at him and nodded. Geary took one last look at Wendig One, lifeless again as it had been for uncounted years before humans came, and gave the order. "All ships, jump for Cavalos."

NINE days, a fairly long stretch in jump space that couldn't help but evoke thoughts about what would have happened if the worm in the jump drives hadn't been discovered. Geary found himself staring at the drab grayness of jump space and the mysterious lights blooming and fading there, feeling the familiar sense of discomfort as if his skin didn't fit right, growing each day, and wondered how long humans could remain sane if stuck there.

The Syndic civilians remained quiet and scared, crews worked continuing to repair internal battle damage to their warships, the auxiliaries manufactured more necessities for the fleet, and Geary found himself worrying more about his internal foes in the fleet than he did about the Syndic military. That was a first, but then his internal enemies had never before posed deadly threats to him and the ships of the fleet.

Five days along in jump space, he got the sort of brief message that was all that could be transmitted there. *Making progress,* from Captain Cresida. If she could figure out how to defuse even partially the threat of human-species extinction via hypernet gate collapses, it would remove a great weight from his shoulders.

Nine days, one hour, and six minutes from the time they jumped from Wendig, the Alliance fleet flashed into normal space at the Syndic star system Cavalos, its weapons ready for action and its sensors scanning for targets. But no mines awaited here, nor a Syndic flotilla or picket ships at the jump points. Apparently the unexpected Alliance victory at Lakota had badly thrown off the Syndics.

Cavalos did indeed have a decent human presence remaining. A halfway-comfortable world orbited about eight light-minutes from the star, and an even half dozen other significant planets swung around the star farther out, including a typical number of three gas giants, one with a fair amount of activity still apparent at mines and an orbiting facility. Near the inhabited world an obsolete Syndic light cruiser and a couple of even-more-obsolete "nickel" corvettes orbited.

Geary studied the situation, then looked to Desjani. "Just a standard self-defense force for a system deep in Syndic space. No threat to us."

She shrugged. "We should take them out if the chance arises. They are legitimate targets."

"I know. But I don't expect them to be dumb enough to charge us, and they're not worth the time or fuel cells it'd take to try to chase them down."

Desjani nodded this time. "They're junk anyway. As far as internal threats go, all of the systems-security officers in the fleet are on full alert, but nothing has popped up yet."

No apparent threat to the fleet. That left room to worry about the Syndics from Wendig again. "This star system doesn't seem to have suffered much deterioration since the hypernet was built. Should we drop our passengers off at that orbital facility? It's not too far out of the way and won't take us far into the star system." The Syndic facility orbiting the gas giant was one and a quarter light-hours distant from the Alliance fleet, a bit off the track the fleet would have followed if going directly to the jump points for the next two stars Geary had to chose from, Anahalt or Dilawa. Not too far off, though. The main cost of dropping off the Syndic civilians would be the need to slow the fleet down again while the shuttles made their deliveries, a small loss in time and a small but real price in fuel cells.

Desjani pursed her lips as she checked the reports from the fleet's sensors. "It's got a fair amount of cold areas, which means they've got the ability to expand back into those if they need to. Either that, or they've got excess life support in the still-occupied areas. They should easily be able to absorb all of the civilians from Wendig."

"Co-President Rione?" Geary asked.

"I defer to your professional judgments on the matter," Rione replied.

"All right then." Geary organized his thoughts for a moment, then activated his comm circuit. "This is Captain John Geary, commanding officer of the Alliance fleet, making an open broadcast to the inhabitants and authorities of the Syndicate Worlds' star system Cavalos. We do not intend engaging in any military actions in this star system unless attacked. If we are attacked, we will reply with all necessary force."

He paused. "This fleet carries five hundred sixty-three civilian citizens of the Syndicate Worlds whom we evacuated from Wendig Star System in response to their plea for rescue as their life-support systems failed. We will deliver those civilians to the main facility orbiting the gas giant five point three light-hours out from your star. Any attack on this fleet during our transit may result in injury to your own citizens, so you would be wise to exercise restraint."

He took a deep breath before continuing. "This fleet was present in Lakota Star System when Syndicate Worlds' warships destroyed that star system's hypernet gate and unleashed a destructive wave of energy that inflicted serious damage on the habitable world and all other human presence in the star system. We will transmit to all ships and occupied planets in this star system copies of our records of that event and of the pleas for assistance from the survivors on Lakota Three. The survivors at Lakota are in desperate need of aid, so we request that you forward this information as fast as possible."

"I repeat, any attack on this fleet will be met with over-whelming force. To the honor of our ancestors." He leaned back and glanced at Desjani. "Threatening enough?"

"If they're smart."

To no one's surprise, the Syndics didn't directly respond to Geary's message or to the information from Lakota. Syndic shipping in the star system followed the usual pattern of fleeing for jump points or facilities, but otherwise no response to the Alliance fleet's presence could be spotted aside from obvious civil-defense activity on the habitable world. Similarly, nothing happened from the fleet's internal saboteurs, which didn't so much cause relief as fear that something had been missed.

As the Alliance fleet bore down on the Syndic orbiting facility, less than two hours' travel time remaining, someone finally reacted. "We have a transmission from the Syndic facility," *Dauntless*'s communications watch-stander reported.

Geary called it up, seeing the image of a woman with gray hair and nervous eyes. "Do not approach this facility. You cannot land shuttles here," she declared.

"We're going to," Geary assured her. "We're going to drop off Syndicate Worlds' citizens, then we're leaving."

"We'll defend ourselves if you attempt to invade this facility."

"We have no intent to invade any facility in this star system. Our shuttles will be accompanied by Marine security personnel. You are to ensure that no armed presence is nearby when our shuttles drop off your citizens. Once your citizens have been delivered, our shuttles and Marines will depart."

The woman shook her head, fear coloring her expression. "I cannot authorize or allow an Alliance presence on my facility. We will defend ourselves."

Geary had never liked bureaucrats, especially bureaucrats who seemed unable to adjust when reality collided with the rules they lived by. "Listen. If any attempt is made to attack my ships, my shuttles, or my personnel when we're dropping off your civilians, I will hit that station of yours so hard that the quarks making up its component atomic particles will never find their way back together. Is that clear? If anyone fires on the civilians we drop off, I'll do the same thing. They're your people. We rescued them at risk to ourselves, we're taking time we don't have to spare to drop them off here, and you'd damn well better take good care of them after we do!" Geary's voice rose as he talked, ending in a roar that seemed to terrify the Syndic station administrator.

"Y-yes, I . . . I understand," she stuttered. "We'll prepare to receive them. Under duress. Please, we have families aboard this station . . ."

"Then let's not have any trouble," Geary replied, trying to get his voice's volume back to normal. "Some of the people we rescued from Wendig have long-term health problems they couldn't treat there. We've done what we could, but they'll need more assistance from you. I'm going to be blunt that I find it appalling that your leaders would abandon human beings to eventual deaths when their life-support systems failed."

"You're not going to kill us? Or destroy this station?" The administrator seemed to be having a lot of trouble grasping the idea.

"No. Any military value it has doesn't outweigh the suffering such actions would cause civilian inhabitants of this star system."

"And you truly saved people from Wendig? We thought no one was left there." The woman seemed about ready to break down. "Everyone was supposed to have been removed when the system was abandoned."

"The people we evacuated told us that the corporation they or their parents were employed by never sent ships. They had no way of finding out why, of course. Perhaps you can help them with that," Geary added pointedly.

"H-how many?"

"Five hundred sixty-three." He could see the question on her face, the same question all of the Syndics, and many of the Alliance personnel, kept asking. Why? Irritated at again having to be faced with a question whose answer he thought obvious, Geary spoke roughly. "That's all."

Desjani was once again pretending to be absorbed in something on her own display.

"When are we loading the Syndics into the shuttles?" Geary asked, his voice angry still.

"They should be on their way to the shuttle dock now," Desjani replied in a tone that sounded suspiciously soothing to Geary. He was trying to decide whether to get irritated by that, too, when she stood up. "I was about to go down to see them off."

Calming himself, Geary stood as well. "May I come along?"

"Of course, sir."

The same scene as from eleven days ago was playing out on the shuttle dock, though in reverse as the column of Syndic civilians shuffled onto the shuttle, some pausing to wave quickly to individual members of *Dauntless*'s crew who had come to the shuttle dock and stood to one side, watching silently. The Marines seemed as menacing as ever in their battle armor, but the Syndics appeared to be less terrified of them.

The former mayor of Alpha turned to Geary and Desjani as they walked up. "Thank you. I wish I knew what else to say. None of us will forget this."

To Geary's surprise, Desjani answered. "If given the chance in the future, offer the same mercy to Alliance citizens."

"I promise you that we shall, and we'll tell others to do the same."

The mayor's wife moved forward to gaze intently at Desjani. "Thank you, lady, for my children's lives."

"Captain," Desjani corrected, but bent one corner of her mouth in a crooked smile. She looked slightly down and nodded to the boy, who gazed back at her solemnly, then saluted in the Syndic fashion. Desjani returned the salute, then looked back to the mother.

"Thank you, Captain," that woman stated. "May this war end before my children have to face your fleet in battle."

Desjani nodded wordlessly again, then watched with Geary as the last of the Syndic civilians walked quickly into the shuttles. As the last hatch sealed, she spoke so quietly only Geary could hear. "It's easier when they don't have faces."

It took him a moment to realize what she meant. "You mean the enemy."

"Yes."

"Have you ever met a Syndic before?"

"Only prisoners of war," Desjani replied in a dismissive tone. "Syndics who'd been trying to kill me and other Alliance citizens a short time before." Her eyes closed for a moment. "I don't know what happened to most of them. I do know what happened to some of them."

Geary hesitated to ask the obvious question. A short time after assuming command of the fleet, he'd learned to his horror that enemy prisoners of war were sometimes casually killed, the outgrowth of a hundred years of war in which atrocity had fueled atrocity. He'd never asked Desjani if she had participated in such a crime.

But she opened her eyes and looked steadily at him. "I watched it happen. I didn't pull any triggers, I didn't issue any orders, but I watched it, and I didn't stop it."

He nodded, keeping his own eyes on hers. "You'd been taught that it was acceptable."

"That's no excuse."

"Your ancestors—"

"Told me it was wrong," Desjani interrupted, something she rarely did with Geary. "I knew it, I felt it, I didn't listen. I take responsibility for my actions. I know I'll pay the price for that. Perhaps that's why we lost so many ships in the Syndic home system. Perhaps that's why the war has kept going all of these years. We're being punished, for straying from what was right because we believed wrong to be necessary."

He wasn't about to reject her, or condemn someone who'd already accepted a full measure of blame. But he could stand alongside her. "Yeah, maybe we are being punished."

Desjani frowned. "Sir? Why would you be punished for things done while you weren't with us?"

"I'm with you now, aren't I? I'm part of this fleet and

loyal to the Alliance. If you're being punished, then so am I. I didn't suffer through all the years of war that you have, but all I knew was taken from me."

She shook her head, frowning deeper. "You just said this is your fleet, and the Alliance has your loyalty. *Those* things weren't taken from you."

Geary frowned back at her, surprised to realize he'd never thought of it that way.

Desjani gave him an intent look. "They sent you when we needed you. They gave us a second chance. They gave *you* a second chance, instead of letting you die in the battle at Grendel or afterward, when your escape pod's systems would have eventually given out. We're being offered mercy if we can prove ourselves worthy of it."

She had startled him again, with a point of view he'd never considered, and by including him as part of them all. Not a separate hero out of myth but one of them. "Maybe you're right," Geary stated. "We can't win this war by destruction unless we go all out with the hypernet gates and commit species suicide. If this war is ever to end, we'll not only have to beat them on the battlefield but also be willing to forgive the Syndics if they're willing to express real remorse. Maybe we're being given an example to follow."

She was silent for a few moments, and he stayed quiet as well. The shuttle dock internal doors sealed between them and the shuttle, then the external ones opened, and the bird lifted off, carrying its passengers to the Syndic facility. Finally, Desjani looked back at him. "I've spent a long time wanting to punish the Syndics, to hurt them as they've hurt us."

"I can understand why," Geary said. "Thanks for going along with me on helping those civilians. I know it went against a lot of what you believe."

"What I believed," Desjani amended. She was quiet for a moment longer, but Geary waited, sensing that she had something else to say. "But that cycle of vengeance never ends. I realized something. I don't want to have to kill that boy someday, when he's old enough to fight."

"Me, neither. Or his father or his mother. And I don't want that boy trying to kill Alliance citizens. How can we end this, Tanya?"

"You'll think of a way, sir."

"Thanks."

He meant it sarcastically, and was sure it sounded sarcastic, but Desjani smiled slightly at him. "Did you see how they looked at us? They were afraid, then they were disbelieving, and finally they were grateful." She stopped smiling and looked outward. "I like fighting. I like going head-to-head with the best the Syndics have. But I've had enough of killing people like those. Can we convince the Syndics to stop bombarding civilian targets?"

"We can try. Our bombardment weapons are accurate enough that we can certainly continue to keep taking out industrial targets while minimizing civilian losses."

Her face was grim now. "They kill ours, and we don't kill theirs?"

"It'll have to be a mutual deal. When we get back, we'll tell them, stop bombarding our people, and we'll continue not bombarding yours."

"Why would they—?" Desjani stopped talking in mid-question, then gave Geary a long look. "And they might believe we'd abide by that since you've been demonstrating the willingness to do so."

"Maybe."

"And if they don't stop?"

"We keep taking out their industry and military targets." Desjani grimaced. "Listen, Tanya, if there's nothing for those people to build or fight with, they're a burden to the Syndics who have to worry about feeding them and taking care of them."

"They'll build new industrial sites. New defenses."

"And we'll blow those away, too." Geary jerked his head to indicate roughly the space outside of *Dauntless*'s hull. "Ever since humanity achieved routine space travel, we've had the ability to destroy things with rocks tossed from space far faster and easier than humans on planets can build things. The Syndics can sink endless effort and resources into rebuilding and never catch up."

She thought about that, then nodded. "You're right. But that same logic applied a long time ago when we started bombarding civilian populations as well as military and industrial targets. Why did we start, all those decades ago?"

"I don't know." Geary cast his mind back, trying to imagine the point at which the people he had known a century earlier had changed to become people like those now. But there hadn't been any point, any single event, rather what Victoria Rione had called a slippery slope in which one seemingly reasonable decision to escalate led to another. "Maybe revenge for Syndic bombardments of Alliance worlds. Maybe a tactic of desperation when the war kept going on and on. An attempt to break the enemy morale. We studied that when I was a junior officer, but as a lesson in what hadn't worked. Time and again in history people tried bombarding enemies enough to make them quit. But when the enemies thought their own homes or beliefs were in danger, they never quit. Totally irrational, but then we're human."

"Syndic bombardments never made us want to give up," Desjani agreed. "We're very frustrated with our leaders, but we want them to win. We don't want them to surrender. But not many people, especially in the fleet, still believe our leaders can win this war. That's why—"

He glanced at her as she stopped speaking again. "Why I got a certain offer from Captain Badaya? You know about it, too?"

"Yes, sir. Of course, sir. It's being widely talked about."

"I won't, Tanya. I won't betray the Alliance that way, by accepting the offer to become a dictator. I told Badaya that." She looked at the deck, her face expressionless. "It wouldn't work, and it'd be wrong."

Desjani spoke very, very quietly. "I have to ask you, have you been offered something else? If you agreed?"

He tried to remember, because whatever it was seemed to bother her a great deal, but couldn't come up with anything.

"No. Nothing specific. It's all been couched in very general terms."

"You're certain?" Her voice was angry now though still very quiet. "You haven't been promised anything else, Captain Geary?" He shook his head, letting his puzzlement show. "Any*one* else, Captain Geary?"

Anyone else? What could—? He was certain his shock showed. "You mean you?" he whispered, too stunned to speak in euphemisms.

She looked at him again, studying his face, and seemed to relax. "Yes. I've been urged by some individuals to . . . offer myself. I've wondered if they had offered me on their own."

Geary felt heat in his face, embarrassment and anger rising in tandem. He couldn't remember the last time he'd been so filled with rage. "Who?" he whispered savagely. "Who the hell had the bloody nerve to dare suggest such a thing to you? You're not some prize or playing piece. Tell me who they are, and I'll—" This time he had to choke off his words, aware that even a fleet commander couldn't threaten to rip subordinates into tiny pieces and vent them out the air lock.

Desjani gave him a thin-lipped smile. "I can defend my own honor, sir. But thank you. Thank you very much."

"Tanya, I swear, if I find out—"

"Let me deal with it, sir. Please." He nodded reluctantly. "We should get back to the bridge, sir, to monitor what's going on." Another nod. One corner of Desjani's mouth bent farther upward. "You wouldn't make a good dictator, would you?"

"Probably not."

"Perhaps there's a reason for that, too."

He kept waiting for something to go wrong, but the Alliance shuttles dropped off every Syndic civilian and lifted off again, then returned to their ships without any Syndic attempts to interfere with the operation. "Did we actually carry out an operation without the Syndics trying to double-cross us and booby-trap everything in sight?" Desjani asked.

"Looks like it. And so far our own double-crossers haven't sprung any more traps on us, either." Geary studied the display, as unwilling to believe it as Desjani. The shuttles all recovered, the Alliance fleet was cutting across one arc of Cavalos Star System toward the jump point that could access either Anahalt or Dilawa. "Three more days to the jump point?"

"Yes, sir. Unless something else happens." Desjani clenched her jaw as alerts sounded. "And something just did."

Syndic warships were becoming visible at the jump point they were heading toward.

TEN

"**TEN** Syndic battleships, twelve battle cruisers, seventeen heavy cruisers, twenty-five light cruisers, forty-two Hunter-Killers," the operations watch-stander announced.

"Roughly half our strength," Desjani observed, "though we've got a much bigger advantage in lighter units. Will they avoid action or fight?"

"They've got to have orders to stop us or delay us," Geary pointed out. "To do either of those things, they have to fight."

"They might be too frightened to fight after what this fleet did at Lakota." Then Desjani paused as something occurred to her. "They may not know what happened at Lakota. They may assume the pursuit force we destroyed at Lakota is still after us and may appear at any moment."

"You're probably right, since they came from either Anahalt or Dilawa." Geary watched as the eight-light-hours-distant images of the Syndic formation could be seen coming around onto a new vector. The Syndics had already had eight hours to decide what to do and get started doing it. "It's a standard Syndic box formation so far."

"Maybe this CEO will be as stupid as the one at Kaliban,"

Desjani suggested. That enemy commander had simply charged head-on at the superior numbers of the Alliance fleet, allowing Geary to annihilate the enemy forces by bringing all of his firepower to bear.

"That'd be nice," Geary agreed, "but we can't count on it. I've got a suspicion that we're killing stupid CEOs faster than the Syndics are promoting them."

"I've found it hard to overestimate the ability of any system to promote stupid people."

With the promise of combat looming, Desjani was in a good enough mood to crack jokes, although Geary had to admit she had a point. "Let's assume he or she isn't stupid. Do you think they'll try hitting our flanks with fast runs, or if I have the formation divided, will they try to hit one of the subformations head-on?"

Desjani considered that. "They've been taught to fight like we used to fight, with head-on charges. Even if they try something fancy, it's more likely to be a charge against one portion of our formation rather than a firing pass against a flank or corner like you taught us. That's what I'd expect."

Ideally, he'd just concentrate his own fleet into one big formation for the Syndic to charge toward. But such a big formation wouldn't allow all of his ships to engage the smaller enemy formation, negating a lot of his superiority. On the other hand, if the Syndic was going to aim for a subformation rather than going straight for the main body of the fleet, tactics like those at Kaliban wouldn't work either. He'd have to use something different.

Rione reached the bridge then, pausing to look at the display before her seat before addressing Geary. "What do you plan on doing?"

Geary indicated his own display, where the sweeping arc of the Syndic formation's projected course and speed was coming around and steadying on a vector that intercepted the arc of the Alliance fleet's own path, the two curved lines bending across light-hours of distance to join like twin sabers clashing. "I plan on meeting the enemy, Madam Co-President, in a little less than a day and a half."

Rione looked from her display with its readout of the

enemy's numbers, then to Geary, and shook her head. "It's like fighting a hydra. No matter how many Syndic warships we destroy, there are always more."

"They keep building them, and unlike us, they can get reinforcements," Geary pointed out.

"I'd recommend trying to capture this CEO alive, Captain Geary. He or she may be able to answer some questions for us."

"I'll do my best, Madam Co-President."

"**CAPTAIN**, we're receiving a very tightly focused transmission from the direction of the primary inhabited world. It's addressed to Captain Geary."

Desjani gave him a wary look. They were still almost eight hours from contact with the Syndic flotilla, not having assumed their combat formation yet. "I'll take it," Geary advised. "Let Captain Desjani see it, too."

The window that popped up before him showed an older woman seated at a desk, wearing a midrank Syndic CEO uniform. "I suppose you're wondering why the senior Syndicate Worlds' officer in this star system is communicating with you, Captain Geary, and doing it in a manner that minimizes any chance anyone else will discover that she did so."

She gestured to a picture on the desk, of a young man Geary vaguely recognized. "I had a brother, long dead in an accident, I thought. Now I *have* a brother, and the knowledge that a corporation tied to a very senior Syndicate Worlds' leader wrote off actually removing him and hundreds of his coworkers from Wendig because it shaved a small amount off the expenses column in that corporation's annual report. I also have a sister-in-law and some nieces and a nephew I'd never known of, all of whom owe their lives to you."

The face in the picture suddenly clicked in Geary's mind. It was the mayor of Alpha, though decades younger.

The Syndic planetary CEO shook her head. "Not to mention all of the lives that would have been lost in this star system if you had chosen to bombard this planet. But I've heard from people in places like Corvus and Sutrah and even Sancere, so I know you've been behaving the same way everywhere, striking only at military targets or industrial sites in retaliation for our own attacks on you. I don't know how many millions or billions of Syndicate Worlds' citizens you might have easily killed, but I do know you didn't do it."

Now the Syndic planetary CEO smiled grimly. "Now I find myself thanking the Alliance fleet for all of those lives even though my orders are to take any actions that might cost you any ships or delay you in any way, regardless of the potential loss to the inhabitants of this star system. I'm well aware of the situation you find yourself in. We've been told a half dozen times that your fleet was trapped and soon to be destroyed. How you've made it this far the living stars alone know. That you came to be in command, Captain Geary, and the identification the Syndicate Worlds have been able to do on you seems positive, leads me to wonder if the living stars have actually intervened in this war. That you took a force built for war and used it to save the lives of your enemies causes me to be grateful that they have.

"I owe you, Captain Geary, and I believe in repaying debts. Your fleet is headed for an engagement with a substantial Syndicate Worlds' force, but one you outnumber significantly. Even though our leaders are trying to keep everything about you and your fleet highly classified, there are plenty of credible unofficial reports circulating. Based on those, I don't expect the Syndic force to prevail here, but based on your actions to date, that expectation does not fill me with fear. Your fleet will be less a threat to the people here than one answering to the Syndicate Worlds' Executive Council."

The Syndic CEO shook her head again. "I won't forget what you did, Captain Geary. A lot of us have come to the understanding that this war stopped making sense the day it began. We're tired of trying to hold things together in our star systems while our leaders squander the wealth of the Syndicate Worlds in a war that can't be won. When you get home, tell your leaders that there are people here who are weary of fighting and want to talk."

The Syndic CEO paused. "When our facilities at Dilawa were mothballed about twenty years ago, it was judged uneconomical to remove the stockpiled materials at the mining facilities there. A lot of things were left in place. Just in case you have need of supplies after you leave here."

The window blanked, and Geary leaned back, thinking.

"Can we trust her?" Desjani wondered.

"I don't know. Where's Co-President Rione?"

"In her stateroom, I think."

"Shoot her a copy of that and ask for her assessment." Desjani's mouth twitched, and she hesitated just enough for Geary to see. "Never mind. I'll do it."

Five minutes later Rione was on the bridge. "I think she's being honest."

"She wants to talk peace, and expects us to defeat this Syndic flotilla, and told us where we can find raw materials to resupply the auxiliaries," Geary pointed out. "If the Syndic authorities find out any of that, they'll have her head off in a heartbeat."

Rione nodded to Geary, her face thoughtful. "This implies a higher degree of rot within the Syndic hierarchy than we expected. A star-system CEO telling us directly that she no longer supports the war."

"She's also sympathizing with us against her own forces," Desjani pointed out to Geary, seeming to be torn between gratitude and revulsion.

Instead of replying to her, Rione spoke to Geary. "The Syndic fleet has been a critical part of the mechanism by which the leaders of the Syndicate Worlds have maintained control over their territory. Anyone trying to display any independence would find warships arriving to enforce the will of their Executive Council. The more damage you do to that fleet, the greater the opportunity for local leaders such as this one to act on their own."

"That fleet is nonetheless made up of their own people," Desjani told Geary. "The fact that she's apparently willing to cheer us on against them should play a role in our assessment of her."

Rione shook her head as she addressed Geary again. "A hypernet-bypassed star system probably has proportionally fewer citizens in the fleet and feels far less a part of the Syndicate Worlds as time has gone by."

Geary looked back at Desjani, only then realizing that both women were talking just to him and ignoring each other, as if they were in separate rooms and could only communicate directly with him.

Desjani shrugged slightly. "The Syndic CEO we saw is a politician, and I suppose a politician might feel less compunction about the sacrifices of military personnel."

That made Rione's jaw visibly tighten, but she still didn't look at Desjani. "You have *my* assessment, Captain Geary. Now if you will excuse me, I have other matters to attend to." She swung around and left the bridge.

Geary pressed the fingertips of one hand against his forehead for a moment in an attempt to push away an impending headache. "Captain Desjani," he murmured so only she could hear, "I would appreciate it if you refrained from engaging in open combat with Co-President Rione."

"Open combat?" Desjani replied in similar low tones. "I don't understand, sir."

He gave her a sharp look, but Desjani was eyeing him with what was surely pretended innocent puzzlement. "I really don't want to go into details."

"I'm afraid you'll have to, sir."

Desjani might consider him guided by the living stars when it came to command of the fleet, but when it came to dealing with Rione, she obviously had a different opinion. "Just try to act like she's in the same room with you."

"She's not, sir. She left the bridge."

"Are you mocking me, Captain Desjani?"

"No, sir. I would never do that, sir." Perfectly serious, as far as he could tell.

It was clearly time to withdraw from the engagement. He couldn't go into more detail or get angry without drawing attention from the watch-standers on the bridge, and he didn't need that. "Thank you, Captain Desjani. I'm very happy to hear that. I have enough other things to worry about."

Desjani at least looked a little regretful as Geary left, trying to catch up with Rione. He suspected she'd had some other important insights to share, and he wanted to ask Rione something.

She wasn't moving fast, so he caught up with her halfway down the passageway. "Tell me the truth," Geary requested. "Is the Alliance that badly off as well? Is the Alliance ready to crack?"

"Why do you ask?" Rione's tone was as unemotional as ever.

"Because you didn't seem happy at the evidence of how bad things are for the Syndics. You've told me the Alliance military is unhappy with the Alliance government, you've told me that everyone is tired of war, but is it as bad as here in Syndic space? Is the Alliance threatening to fall apart?"

Rione stopped walking, her gaze directed at the deck, then slowly nodded without looking at him. "A century of war, John Geary. We can't be beaten, neither can they, but both sides can push until they fracture."

"That's why you came along on this expedition? Not just because you were afraid that Bloch might try to become a dictator, but because you were sure that he'd succeed, that the war-weary citizens of the Alliance would follow him because they'd lost belief in the Alliance."

"Bloch would not have succeeded," Rione stated calmly. "He would have died."

"You would have killed him." She nodded. "Bloch must have known what you intended. He must have had precautions in place against you."

"He did." A very small smile flicked on and off Rione's face. "They wouldn't have been enough."

Geary stared at her. "And what would have happened to you?"

"I'm not certain. It wouldn't have mattered. What counted was stopping a dictator in his tracks."

He couldn't spot any trace of mockery or dishonesty in her. Rione meant it. "You were willing to die in order to make sure he was dead. Victoria, sometimes you scare the hell out of me."

"Sometimes I scare the hell out of me." She still seemed absolutely serious. "I told you, John Geary. I believed the man I loved had died in this war. I've had nothing else to live for since then but my devotion to the Alliance. If the Alliance itself was about to crumble, then I'd have nothing left at all. My husband died for the Alliance, and if necessary, I could as well."

"Why didn't you tell me this right from the start?"

Rione watched him for a moment before answering. "Because if you were someone in the mold of Admiral Bloch, you didn't need encouraging. But if you were truly like Black Jack, you wouldn't believe me, because the idea of the Alliance falling apart would have been too hard for you to accept. You needed to see enough for yourself to understand how bad things are. And I did tell you things, though you may not always have recognized it." Rione shook her head. "I sounded you out, I watched you, I did what I had to do in order to influence your attitudes toward the way things are now."

"What you had to do?" The phrase sounded cold even for Rione. "You told me once that you didn't sleep with me just to influence me."

Her eyes stayed on his. "That wasn't the only reason, no. But it was part of it. Satisfied? You got my body, I got yours, and in the dark watches of the night I whispered to you about the need to protect the Alliance from those who would destroy it in the name of saving it. Oh, I enjoyed the sex. I admit that freely. But the day came when I knew that I no longer need fear you, and when I knew that my feelings were beginning to betray the husband I still love and who may still live. I didn't give you to her because I'm noble, John Geary. I did it for myself, and because I'd done what I needed to do."

He didn't believe all of that. Rione's posture and expression hadn't changed, but he remembered the drunken words she'd once spoken, and he noticed that even while dispassionately justifying all she had done, Rione still didn't say Tanya Desjani's name. "You haven't *given* me to anybody, let alone Captain Desjani."

"You may have to lie to yourself, John Geary, but give me some credit."

"Why are you staying on *Dauntless*, then? There are plenty of surviving ships from the Callas Republic to which you could transfer."

"Because you'll need me close when we get home. Not as a threat, as an ally. I know how the political leaders of the Alliance will react to you. Black Jack has returned, the savior of the fleet and the Alliance. You won't take what some of them will offer in exchange for more power for themselves. You won't do what others of them will fear, taking all power for yourself. No, John Geary," Rione insisted, "you will stand atop the bulwarks of the Alliance and defend it against all enemies, both those inside and those outside, because that's who you are, someone out of a simpler past. And I will help you against those inside who seek to use you or act against you out of fear."

"Against me? Do you think I'll be in danger from the political leadership of the Alliance?"

"If I had been on the Governing Council when you returned, I would have argued for your immediate arrest and isolation under the public deception of your being on some secret mission. Because I would have thought you were someone in the mold of Admiral Bloch or Captain Falco. I've learned different, and I will tell the other senators what I know. Believe me, you will need me," Rione declared. "Even those politicians who dislike me, and there are plenty of those, know that I will not betray the Alliance. My words will matter to all of them."

Geary looked away, rubbing the back of his neck with one hand and trying to think. No matter how complex getting this fleet home in one piece had always been, life once the fleet got home had seemed so simple. Resign his commission, go somewhere he wouldn't be recognized, try to hide from the legend of Black Jack and the unrealistic, devout expectations of those who believed he had been sent by the living stars themselves to this fleet to save it and the Alliance. He'd kept focused on that to keep everything from overwhelming him, even as the idea of walking away from this fleet and its people felt less and less right. Now he had to admit that at the very least he'd have more problems to deal with before he could leave these responsibilities behind. "Thank you, Victoria. I'm sure your help will be critical."

She shook her head. "Don't thank me. I'm not doing it for you."

"Thanks, anyway. Do you want to discuss the upcoming battle?"

"You'll be fine. You always are."

His temper threatened to explode. "Dammit, the last thing I or anyone else in this fleet needs is for me to become overconfident! I'm going to try to minimize our losses, but this battle will not be simple or easy or painless!"

Rione smiled in an infuriating manner. "See? You already know that. You don't need me to tell you. Anything else?"

"Yes," Geary stated between gritted teeth. "How about whether we should go to Anahalt or Dilawa afterward?"

Rione spread her hands in a dismissive gesture. "Follow your instincts, Captain Geary. They're much better than mine, at least while we're still in Syndic space."

"I'd still like your opinion on whether or not we can trust that Syndic CEO."

"Of course you can't. But that doesn't mean she isn't being truthful this time. See if what she said about Dilawa matches the Syndic star-system records we've captured." Rione turned to go, then spoke over her shoulder. "That's my political advice. If you want military advice, go ask your captain for her opinion. It'll give you two another professional opportunity to huddle close together."

He watched Rione walk away, without saying anything else that might have just invited another parting shot.

FOUR hours until contact with the Syndics. The Alliance fleet and the Syndic flotilla were less than fifty light-minutes apart, each force moving at point one light speed, their combined rate of closure at the point two light speed maximum for effective targeting. He could now see what the Syndic ships had been doing just less than an hour earlier, just as they could see the status of the Alliance fleet that long ago. It was still too early to set his combat formation, too early to let the Syndic commander know how Geary planned to meet the enemy.

"Captain Geary? There's something we need to show you."

He acknowledged the message from Captain Desjani and headed for the compartment she'd called from, trying not to look apprehensive as he passed members of *Dauntless*'s crew. Despite the need to concentrate on the upcoming battle, Geary had been constantly distracted by worries about what his internal enemies might do. It sounded like they must have tried striking again.

The compartment proved to be one of the primary-systems control stations, apparently confirming his fears. As the hatch sealed behind him, Geary saw Desjani, the lieutenant commander who was *Dauntless*'s systems-security officer, and the virtual presence of Captain Cresida. "What is it this time?"

Desjani and the lieutenant commander both looked at Cresida, who gestured toward some of the system modules behind her. "I'd been thinking, sir," Cresida began. "Trying to figure out how the aliens could be tracking us. The business with the worms got me wondering about our systems, about whether anything else could be hidden in them."

Geary frowned. "The aliens? This isn't about a new worm generated from somewhere within the fleet?"

"No, sir. We found something that couldn't have come from internal sources. We had to get Captain Desjani's systems-security officer involved."

"It *couldn't* have come from the inside?" Geary gave Desjani and her systems-security officer a puzzled look. "But you found something else?"

Cresida nodded. "Yes, sir. What I was wondering was, if something else *was* there, something that let the aliens track our movements, how could it still be hidden? It would have to be something unlike anything we've used or tried to use if our security scans missed it. So I've been looking at different things, just off-the-wall stuff, seeing if anything unusual or unexpected showed up anywhere inside our systems."

Desjani's systems-security officer tapped a control, and a virtual display popped up beside him, showing a weird image of what looked vaguely like overlapping waves with fluctuating boundaries. "This shows commands being sent through the navigational system, sir," he explained. "Not the code, but the actual electron signal propagation. It's a representation, of course, rendered in terms understandable to us. What Captain Cresida found was that the commands had something else piggybacking on them." He indicated the fluctuating tops and sides.

Cresida pointed to them as well. "I don't know how they do it, but somehow they're encoding a worm using self-sustaining probability modulation on a quantum scale. Every particle making up this signal has quantum characteristics, of course. Well, the aliens have imprinted some kind of program on those characteristics. I know it's not natural because there should be probabilistic variation in how these actions are occurring on the quantum boundaries of the particles making up the signal. There isn't. It's following patterns. We can't tell what those patterns do, or how they do it, but it's definitely something that shouldn't be there."

Desjani nodded toward the display. "We think we've found our alien spy, Captain Geary."

"I'll be damned. This is in the navigational systems?"

"And the communications systems. We're still screening the other systems but haven't found anything like it, yet."

Geary stared at the display, amazed. "It's set up to know where we're going and tell someone else. Can this thing send messages at faster-than-light speeds?"

Cresida made a frustrated gesture. "I don't know! I don't know how it works at all, let alone what it can do. I just know it's not supposed to be there."

The lieutenant commander spoke up. "Naturally, none of

our security programs or firewalls could spot this. It's, uh, alien to them, if you'll pardon the term."

"There's nothing we can do about it?" Geary demanded. "We just have to leave this thing infesting our systems?"

That drew a fierce smile from Cresida. "No, sir. I may not know how it works, but I know how to kill it."

"That's the first time I ever heard you talk like a Marine, Captain Cresida. How do we kill it?"

Cresida indicated the wavery boundaries again. "I'm sure we can generate quantum wave patterns that have opposite characteristics to these waves. In effect, using destructive interference to cancel out the modulated overlays. We don't have to know what the pattern does or how it's sustained to create a very short-lived negative image of it. Once the overlays go to a zero probability state, none of them should reappear except in rare random pieces that couldn't possibly function."

Geary frowned in puzzlement. "How could even random pieces reappear if they've been reduced to zero probability?"

"It's . . . a quantum thing, sir. It doesn't make sense to us, but that's how things work on that level."

The systems-security officer nodded. "In effect, sir, Captain Cresida has suggested creating an antiviral program using quantum-probability-pattern detection and cancellation. It's a totally new concept, but the actual creation of the program is well within our capabilities."

"Thank you, Captain Cresida. I don't think I'm exaggerating when I say that all humanity is in your debt. I want Lieutenant Iger in intelligence briefed on this, too. Any ideas how it got into our systems?"

The others exchanged glances, then Desjani answered. "I've been thinking about it since Captain Cresida showed me this. You suspect the hypernet gates were the products of aliens' technology, sir. *Dauntless*, like every other ship in the fleet, has an Alliance hypernet key on board that carries its own operating system."

Cresida's eyes widened. "Which interfaces with the ship's navigational system. You could be right. We'll get into the keys and see what we can find."

The systems-security officer frowned this time. "But if it is coming from the hypernet key, do we dare sanitize the key? It could somehow bear on the proper functioning of the key."

"Very good point," Cresida agreed. "We'd have to tread very carefully there. But we can set up an antiviral screen between the key and the rest of the ship's systems once we get the program working."

"Do it now," Geary commanded. "If you need anything, and you're not getting it, make sure I know."

"Yes, sir, but I'd like to wait until after the battle to start."

"The battle?" Geary almost slapped his own forehead. Between concerns about internal enemies and hostile aliens, the actual looming battle had slipped his mind for a moment. "Yes, of course, after the battle. And if anything else about this comes up that doesn't have to be dealt with until after that, wait to tell me." *I can't risk being that badly distracted again. A lot of ships in this fleet could die if I'm not focused on the most imminent threat.* What Cresida had found wouldn't have any effect on the outcome of this engagement, but it would make a very big long-term difference in the aliens' ability to intervene again on the side of the Syndics. *We're figuring out your tricks, you bastards. And when we've figured out enough of them, we're going to discuss this war with you and what humans do to nonhumans who try to manipulate them.*

ONE hour to engagement range if both forces continued on their current course and speed vectors. Now Geary could see the Syndic formation as of twelve minutes ago, still in its rectangular box shape, one of the short sides facing the Alliance fleet like a hammerhead rushing to strike. "Ready?" he asked Desjani.

"Now?" Her eyes were already locked on the enemy formation.

"Yeah, I couldn't do it earlier without acting uncharacteristically, but I need to give the Syndic CEO commanding that flotilla time to see what I'm doing so I'll have time to see how they react." Geary tapped his controls. "All units in the Alliance fleet, assume stations in Formation Echo Four at time three zero, formation stations to form relative to flagship *Dauntless*."

At time three zero, the big Formation Delta the fleet had been in broke apart, warships weaving everywhere in a complex dance as they proceeded to stations in five subformations. "This is like the formation you used in Lakota the first time," Rione noted, as the shapes became apparent.

"Sort of," Geary confirmed. "The coin-shaped subformations are very flexible. I can pivot each of them easily because of the shape and the smaller size. But they'll be arrayed differently than in the Echo Five we used at Lakota." Four coins were forming up in a diamond shape, their broad sides facing the enemy. In the open center of the diamond but farther back, a larger coin centered on *Dauntless* also faced the enemy.

"Are the auxiliaries bait again?

"No. I'm trying to protect them. I've got them in the back of my part of the formation because I have to do something with them, and if the Syndics try to go after our auxiliaries there, they'll have to run a very nasty gauntlet to get near them."

He waited, everyone waited, as the minutes crawled by and the Syndics raced closer. Surely the Syndic commander wouldn't simply charge up the middle. But the Syndic wasn't maneuvering, wasn't aiming for one part of the Alliance fleet. Twenty minutes to contact. Fifteen minutes to contact. Was the Syndic paralyzed with indecision, stupid, or carefully waiting until the last possible moment to shift his formation's course?

It was getting too close, and the Syndic box could still veer up, down, or to the side against any single Alliance subformation. Geary knew he couldn't wait any longer. He mentally split the difference between possible Syndic actions, figuring out Alliance maneuvers that were particularly tricky because of the way momentum would affect course vectors after changes in heading. Hoping he'd gotten it right, he called out orders. "Formation Echo Four Two, turn together and alter course to port zero eight five degrees up one zero degrees at time one five." That would cause Echo Four Two to change from a flat formation like an on-rushing wall with all ships facing forward, into a knife-edge with the ships facing the thin edge, slicing left and up across the space the Syndic flotilla should cross about the same time. "Formation Echo Four Three, turn together and alter course to starboard zero eight one degrees, down one zero degrees at time one six." The same thing, only with the sub-formation on the left side of the diamond slicing to the right and down.

He had to take a breath before calling the next two orders. "Formation Echo Four Four, turn together and alter course up zero nine zero degrees at time one seven. Formation Echo Four Five, turn together and alter course down zero nine five degrees at time one eight." That would bring the top and bottom of the diamond slashing across the center as well.

Now for the biggest single portion of the fleet, the large trailing formation containing *Dauntless* and the auxiliaries. "Formation Echo Four One, pivot down zero nine zero degrees around flagship *Dauntless* as guide and alter course up zero one zero degrees at time two zero. All units in the Alliance fleet fire missiles and hell lances as the enemy enters engagement envelopes."

Desjani raised both eyebrows as she absorbed the orders. "If he keeps coming up the middle, we'll nail him."

"Let's hope he does." Geary stared at his display, where the Syndics were charging closer at tens of thousands of kilometers per second. His image of the enemy was now almost real-time, only a few seconds delayed by the time required for light to cross the distance between opposing forces. "Damn. There he goes." The ships in the Syndic box had all angled upward slightly at the last possible moment, aiming to hit the Alliance subformation at the top of the diamond.

But that formation wasn't there anymore, already turning, momentum carrying it in a wide curve down and toward the Syndics. A Syndic barrage of missiles followed by grapeshot tore toward the expected location of the Alliance subformation, but instead of meeting the Alliance ships the grapeshot met empty space. The Syndic missiles curved into stern chases, trying to catch up with targets that had dodged to one side.

But the Syndic flotilla had made a much smaller course change, so that successive Alliance subformations had crossed near the path of the Syndics moments before the enemy, volleying out missiles of their own. Most of the Alliance specters smashed into the leading edges of the Syndic formation, wreaking havoc with the lighter warships and pummeling the battleships and battle cruisers in that part of the Syndic box.

"Damn," Geary repeated under his breath. The change in the Syndic course hadn't been very big, but it had been enough. The Alliance subformations had avoided getting hit by the Syndics, but were also out of hell-lance range as the Syndics cleared the missile barrage. At least he hadn't wasted any of his fleet's limited supply of grapeshot.

The same wouldn't be true as the Syndic box encountered the big trailing Alliance formation. The Alliance auxiliaries, which had been at the back of the formation, had pivoted to the top as the Alliance wall rotated flat and angled upward, protecting them from the fire of the Syndic warships that would pass just under the Alliance ships. "You called this one dead-on," Desjani murmured, her eyes still fixed on her display.

"Maybe too close," Geary replied, hastily triggering his command circuit. "Alliance ships in formation Echo Four One, employ all weapons, including grapeshot."

Dauntless and the other Alliance warships with her hurled out their missiles, followed by tightly packed fields of ball bearings. The Syndic box actually had more warships in it than the Alliance formation with *Dauntless*, but almost every Alliance ship in the flat-coin formation could engage the Syndics, whereas only the upper layers of the Syndic box could fire on the enemy.

The warships in the upper part of the Syndic box staggered as they hit wave after wave of Alliance missiles, followed by wave after wave of grapeshot as the length of the enemy formation shot past under the length of the Alliance almost horizontal plane, the formations almost touching as the rear of the Alliance warships passed the enemy. The Syndics hadn't had time to reload the missile launchers they'd used against the first Alliance subformation, but pumped out their own barrage of grapeshot.

In the tiny fraction of a second in which this was happening, hell lances also flashed out, hitting shields weakened by earlier hits and warships whose shields had suffered failures under the blows.

Geary knew he couldn't take time to evaluate the results of the clash, so even as *Dauntless* was still shuddering from hits and her watch-standers were calling out damage reports, he sent out more orders. "Formation Echo Four Two, turn starboard one one zero degrees up zero two degrees at time two four. Formation Echo Four Three turn port one one eight degrees up one six degrees at time two four. Formation Echo Four Four turn starboard zero five degrees down one three one degrees at time two five. Formation Echo Four Five turn starboard zero eight degrees up one five two degrees at time two five." He gasped a breath and kept going. "Formation Echo Four One, turn starboard zero three degrees up one six zero degrees at time two five."

The combined maneuvers should all bring the five pieces of the Alliance fleet up, down, over, and around and back toward the Syndic box. As he saw what the Syndics were doing, he'd have to adjust his orders, but for now it was enough to order his ships onto the right general headings.

Finally, with a moment to check the results of the encounter, Geary steadied himself as he checked the ship status reports. Most of the Syndic missiles that had chased Formation Echo Four Five had been destroyed by Alliance defenses as they tried to catch up with their targets, but a number had made it through. The heavy cruiser *Gusset* had lost propulsion, the light cruisers *Kote* and *Caltrop* had been knocked out, the destroyer *Flail* blown apart by several hits, and the battle cruisers *Intrepid* and *Courageous* had suffered damage but were staying with the formation.

The brutal exchange of fire between Echo Four One and the Syndic box had cost the Syndics more than it had the Alliance, but the destroyers *Ndziga* and *Tabar* had been destroyed, the light cruiser *Cercle* riddled into wreckage, and the heavy cruisers *Armet* and *Schischak* both put out of commission. The scout battleship *Braveheart* had lost all of its propulsion and weapons and fallen away from the formation as well. Many other Alliance ships had taken damage, though the battleships had naturally suffered the least.

The front edges of the Syndic formation had taken the brunt of missile volleys, then the top had fought the close engagement with Echo Four One. The Alliance advantage in numbers had told, particularly against the most heavily outnumbered Syndic light cruisers and HuKs. Of the twenty-five light cruisers the Syndic force had entered the battle with, twelve were destroyed or too badly damaged to fight, while the Syndic's forty-two HuKs had lost almost twenty of their number. Five Syndic heavy cruisers were out of the battle. Best of all, four Syndic battle cruisers were out of action, one destroyed and three badly torn up. In addition, one Syndic battleship had lost most of its propulsion and was falling back as the Syndic formation began curving to one side for another strike at the Alliance ships.

I bungled that, Geary thought bitterly. *The Syndic commander reacted so late I couldn't concentrate my attack properly.*

Desjani seemed cheerful, though. "Look at the damage on them! They won't be able to survive another run like that."

Geary didn't answer, focusing on the movement of the Syndics. They were still coming around in the huge turn necessary when ships were moving at point one light speed, but he felt certain they were aiming to hit Echo Four One again, perhaps hoping to get some shots at the Alliance auxiliaries this time. He snapped out orders to the other four formations, bringing them in to cross the track the Syndics would follow to intercept Echo Four One once more, his tone drawing a wary look from Desjani.

This time he'd guessed right. As the tattered Syndic box came toward Echo Four One from port and slightly below, the other four Alliance subformations ripped past close ahead of it in quick succession, each pass inflicting more damage on the leading Syndic units so that the front of the Syndic box kept getting shredded and replaced by the warships behind it. More enemy heavy cruisers, light cruisers, and HuKs exploded, broke apart, or simply fell away with critical systems destroyed. Two more Syndic battle cruisers reeled out of the formation, followed by a third, while the forwardmost Syndic battleships took more and more hits.

The Syndics could only hit back at each Alliance formation once, and while they scored some hits, they failed to inflict serious damage on any ships.

"Echo Four One," Geary ordered harshly, "turn port zero eight degrees up one four degrees at time four three."

The Syndic box kept on course. Either the Syndic commander hadn't spotted the Alliance maneuver in time or his flagship had been damaged and couldn't communicate orders quickly enough. The Alliance formation centered on *Dauntless* swept over the top edge of the frayed front of the Syndic box, this time able to repeatedly hit the Syndic ships there while taking much less fire in return.

Desjani uttered a small whoop of pleasure as a Syndic battleship exploded in the wake of Echo Four One's firing pass, followed by the core overloads of another battleship and one of the surviving battle cruisers.

But Geary just stared at his display, trying to rebuild his picture of events and how to bring the different pieces of everything together again. The Syndics were coming around to starboard now, angling slightly down. Alliance fleet subformations were swinging outward on four widely different vectors, their distances from the flagship varying. Geary tried to keep it all straight, tried to coordinate the actions of his subformations, and found it slipping away. He'd been rattled by his failure to call the maneuvers right on the first pass, and now the movements and the necessary maneuvers through different levels of time delay had grown too hard to grasp. But he couldn't just release the fleet for general pursuit. Not yet. All of his ships would swarm toward the Syndic flotilla in a wild melee that would drastically increase the risk of collision and negate a lot of his advantages in numbers and firepower. Nor could he count on handing the movements of the subformations over to the artificial intelligence in the maneuvering system, because that would focus on predictable highest-probability moves and therefore be predictable itself as well as probably in error.

He didn't realize he was staring wordlessly at his display, trying to get his mind around the complexity of the situation, as precious seconds ticked by. But then Rione was hissing a question in his ear. "What's wrong? Our losses aren't that bad."

"Too complicated," Geary whispered. "Can't coordinate . . ."

"Then trust your subordinates, Captain Geary!" Rione whispered back angrily. "Let the commanders of your subformations maneuver their own forces while you handle this one!"

Damn. She's right. Why do I think I have to do this myself? I chose subformation commanders I could trust to do a good job, and now I'm not trusting them. "Captain Duellos, Captain Tulev, Captain Badaya, Captain Cresida, maneuver your subformations independently to engage the enemy."

The complexity overwhelming him shrank to manageable levels as Geary's problem narrowed down to maneuvering his own piece of the fleet and keeping an eye on what the other subformations were doing. He swallowed, feeling in control of the situation again, then realized he'd regained control of everything by not trying to control everything personally. *Remember that. This isn't a one-person show. You were starting to think you were Black Jack, weren't you?* he chided himself. "Echo Four One, turn port one seven five degrees, down two one degrees at time five seven."

Absurdly, even though the battle was continuing, everyone on *Dauntless*'s bridge seemed to relax. It took Geary a moment to realize that his own anger and distress had been throwing off the others. He forced himself to look around with a smile. "Well done so far. Let's finish the job."

Captain Desjani completed ordering some priorities for repairing the damage *Dauntless* had taken in the first encounters with the enemy, then smiled at him like a lioness who was anticipating kills. "They should have run after the first pass. If we can get their formation to break now, their remaining units won't last long."

"Maybe we can help that along." Geary gestured to Desjani. "Can I get a circuit up to contact the Syndic flotilla?"

Desjani raised one eyebrow, then pointed a finger at her communications watch-stander, who tapped rapidly for a moment and nodded in confirmation, holding up four fingers. "You have it, sir. Channel four."

Letting out a calming breath, Geary activated the circuit, trying to speak with casual confidence. "To all warships in the Syndicate Worlds' flotilla engaged with the Alliance fleet, this is Captain John Geary, acting commander of the Alliance fleet. You are doubtless expecting reinforcements in the form of the large Syndicate Worlds' force this fleet encountered at Lakota about two weeks ago. Be advised that we destroyed that force in its entirety. It won't be showing up here or anywhere else. I urge you to surrender now and avoid further senseless loss of life."

That brought another smile from Desjani. "You're probably going to hurt their morale."

"That's the idea."

"I'll see what more *Dauntless* can do to hurt them physically." Echo Four One had come around again, approaching the frayed Syndic formation at a high angle this time.

Before Echo Four One could reach the Syndics, Echo Four Three and Echo Four Five hit the front of the battered box again, leaving another enemy battleship drifting in their wake.

"Use the rest of the grapeshot," Desjani ordered her combat-systems officer as Echo Four One and the Syndic formation raced toward each other again.

Another flash of contact, then Geary watched the fleet's sensors evaluating damage to the Syndics as Echo Four Two and Echo Four Four came in from above and below the Syndic box. The three remaining Syndic battle cruisers had lost all shields and were lashing out frantically at extreme range as the next two Alliance subformations approached. Only six heavy cruisers remained with the box, the rest of their number scattered in various states of destruction along the path the Syndic formation had taken through space. Five light cruisers and a dozen HuKs also had survived. The core of the Syndic formation remained its battleships, five of which were still in good shape.

Geary barely had time to hope that the commanders of Echo Four Two and Echo Four Four didn't push their luck too far against the five battleships when his subformations made their latest firing runs, tearing past so close to the Syndics that Geary felt a momentary spurt of fear.

In the wake of the latest Alliance assault, one more Syndic battleship staggered away from the box formation and two of the three battle cruisers were gone. But *Courageous*, *Incredible*, and *Illustrious* had taken serious damage, the heavy cruiser *Gusoku* had blown up, and the destroyers *Cestus* and *Balta* were also gone. "This battle is not going well," Geary muttered to himself.

But Desjani heard. "The Syndics aren't making mistakes," she agreed. "But it won't save them. One more firing run—"

"They're breaking!" the operations watch-stander shouted exuberantly.

"Thank you, Mr. Gaciones," Desjani replied. "I can hear without you yelling."

As the embarrassed watch-stander turned back to his duties, Geary watched on his display as what was left of the Syndic box finally disintegrated. Two of the battleships stayed together, and three HuKs clung to their protection, but every other Syndic ship bolted in different directions, seeking to outrun any Alliance pursuit.

That simplified things. "All ships in Echo Four Two, Echo Four Three, Echo Four Four, and Echo Four Five, general pursuit. Break formation and engage any enemy targets of opportunity. Echo Four One will engage the two battleships that have remained in company."

Which was easier said than done given the time and space

needed to turn the warships of Echo Four One, but the Syndic battleships were too close and too cumbersome to be able to outrun pursuit. As Echo Four One swung around, Geary watched the rest of his subformations fragment so fast it looked like they'd been blown apart by some huge blast. Individual Alliance warships locked on to Syndic warships and leaped onto firing runs, each surviving Syndic ship becoming the target of many Alliance strikes. On the display, the projected paths of the Alliance warships formed a tangled web from which the Syndics were frantically trying to escape.

"What the hell are *Brilliant* and *Inspire* doing?" Desjani demanded of no one in particular.

Geary looked. The two battle cruisers had broken away from their formation and from *Opportune*, the other battle cruiser in their division, and were accelerating toward intercepts with the two Syndic battleships. His anger at the costs of this engagement flared up again. *We've already lost enough ships today, but those idiots are ignoring my orders and going one-on-one with battleships.*

"They'll get there well ahead of us," Desjani protested, her disappointment clear. "But why? They can't take down even one of those battleships on their own."

"No," Geary agreed. He tapped his controls harder than usual. "*Brilliant, Inspire,* this is Captain Geary. Break off your firing run on the pair of Syndic battleships."

He waited. He checked the distance and how much time it would take his message to reach those two battle cruisers and for an answer to come. But no reply came, and both battle cruisers continued on their charge. Then he realized that *Opportune* had come around and was trying to catch up with *Brilliant* and *Inspire* as she also headed for an intercept of the Syndic battleships. This time he needed several slow breaths to calm himself before calling the ships again. "*Brilliant, Inspire,* and *Opportune,* you are ordered to immediately break off your firing pass on the two Syndic battleships."

More time passed as Echo Four One lined up for its own run on the Syndic battleships. "There's not enough time to get another message to them," Desjani noted.

Geary felt his jaw hurting and tried to relax it as he watched three battle cruisers conducting a senseless charge against superior forces.

Brilliant and *Inspire* shot past the two Syndic battleships, concentrating their fire on one of the battleships and passing close enough to unleash their null fields as well as hell lances and what must be their last grapeshot. The shields on the targeted battleship flared repeatedly but held until the second null field penetrated enough to take a chunk out of one propulsion unit and slow the battleship.

But the Syndics had also concentrated their heavier fire, and *Brilliant* staggered away with very serious damage, its own propulsion systems shot up and most weapons out of commission.

Then *Opportune* came in alone, one battle cruiser facing the fire of two battleships. Syndic hell lances crashed the Alliance battle cruiser's shields, then ripped into *Opportune*. Only momentum saved the ship as she tumbled away from the Syndic warships, horribly damaged.

"If *Opportune*'s commanding officer is still alive, I'm going to kill him," Geary vowed, thinking of how many Alliance sailors must have just died on that ship for no reason.

"Six months ago I might have applauded him," Desjani remarked in wondering tones. "Now I see how senseless it was. What's the point of bravery that only aids the enemy in destroying you?" Her voice changed, hardening. "All right, *Dauntless*," she called out to her bridge, "let's make those Syndics sorry for what they did to *Opportune*."

The three battle cruisers had weakened the shields on the Syndic battleships, though taking much worse harm in exchange. The warships of Echo Four One now hit the Syndics over and over again as the formation raced past, knocking the battleships' shields out completely, the four Alliance battleships with Echo Four One administering the death-blows that turned one of the Syndic battleships into drifting wreckage and knocked out most of the systems on the other.

"All warships in Echo Four One, general pursuit. Break formation and engage targets of opportunity." Geary switched to an internal circuit. "Lieutenant Iger, I want to know if any of the escape pods out there hold any Syndic CEOs. See what you can find out."

It had been a messy, painful battle. But the Alliance fleet had still paid far less than the Syndics. As he watched the wreck of *Opportune* tumble through space, Geary couldn't find much comfort in that.

ELEVEN

"WE can't save *Opportune*." Captain Tyrosian shook her head unhappily. "Too much damage, too many systems out. Even if you wanted to tow her, we'd have to linger here for several days reinforcing damaged parts of the hull, or the ship would break apart."

Geary checked a report that he'd already brought up, listing casualties in the fleet. *Opportune*'s commanding officer and executive officer were dead, along with close to 40 percent of the rest of her crew. He looked at the deck for a moment, not having to fight down anger now because he was filled with despair at the waste. Then he nodded. "We'll scuttle her. Get anything off her that we can pull off easily and that we'll need for the other battle cruisers. You've got four hours while the rest of the crew is evacuated."

"Yes, sir. What about *Braveheart*?" Tyrosian asked. "We're not sure why she's still in one piece and expect what's left to come apart at the first stress, but I have to ask."

"Yeah. We'll blow up *Braveheart*, too." The scout battleship division was now down to a single ship, *Exemplar*. "How about the other badly damaged ships?"

Tyrosian frowned as she looked to one side, checking reports on her own display. "Heavy cruisers *Gusset* and *Schischak* are already under way again though they won't be combat-capable for a while, and *Gusset* really needs a major yard period to repair her damage. Light cruiser *Caltrop* has lost a lot of systems but can keep up with the fleet. Four of the battle cruisers, *Courageous*, *Illustrious*, *Brilliant*, and *Intrepid*, have a lot of damage. *Courageous* and *Brilliant* in particular are barely combat-capable, but we've repaired enough propulsion units on them."

"Thank you, Captain Tyrosian." Geary slumped backward as Tyrosian's image vanished, thinking about the fact that of the four battle cruisers Tyrosian had just mentioned, three were commanded by senior captains who were also in charge of battle-cruiser divisions. Clearly the old spirit of *damn the grapeshot, full speed ahead* was still alive and well even among people he thought knew better by now. At least the fact that the Alliance fleet had retained possession of the field of battle allowed those ships to be recovered. If the fleet had been forced to retreat, all four of those battle cruisers would have been lost, too.

His stateroom hatch alert chimed, and Captain Desjani entered, looking worn but triumphant. Geary had to remember that by the standards of battles in the last several decades even this victory he thought of as costly was actually quite cheap. "We've got a Syndic CEO, Captain Geary," Desjani reported. "Not the one in overall command, who died on one of the battle cruisers that blew up, but her second in command."

"I guess we should be grateful that a Syndic commander who made so few mistakes won't be around to fight anymore," Geary noted. "How badly was *Dauntless* hurt?"

Desjani's triumph faded into pain. "Twenty-five dead, three others critically injured, but we hope we can save them. We lost an entire hell-lance battery, and I'm not sure we can get it working again no matter how much duct tape and prayer we use."

Geary nodded, feeling a little numb. "If you want anyone off *Opportune* to make up for *Dauntless*'s losses, let me know."

This time Desjani grimaced. "*Opportune* is a write-off? Damn. I saw that her captain is dead."

"Thanks to following the example of Captains Caligo and Kila on *Brilliant* and *Inspire*," Geary added bitterly.

"If I may ask, sir, what are you thinking of doing about that?"

He gave her a searching look. It sounded like Desjani had carefully phrased her question. "I have a nasty suspicion that you're going to tell me that the fleet thinks they did something admirable."

Desjani hesitated, then nodded. "Yes, sir. Closing on the enemy with no regard for the odds, that sort of thing. In the eyes of the fleet, they were justified in disregarding your orders."

"Meaning the fleet would be appalled if I disciplined them." Geary shook his head. "I thought . . ."

"That we'd learned?" Desjani asked. "We are learning, sir. But we need to keep that spirit of being willing to fight no matter what, too. And you know how hard it can be to change what you believe in. This is the opposite of what Casia and Yin did. They disobeyed orders so they could *avoid* battle. Caligo and Kila disobeyed orders so they could fight. Everyone condemned Casia and Yin, but if you try to treat Caligo and Kila as if they did the same, very few will agree with you. I respectfully suggest you tread carefully in dealing with them, sir."

"Yeah. Thanks for the good advice." A very-high-profile action during a battle, one designed to draw admiration from the fleet as a whole, and one which lured a fellow ship to its destruction as the price of that admiration. He didn't like where that line of thought led, that Caligo's and Kila's behavior bore some disturbing resemblances to the thinking of whoever had planted worms in the fleet. But that wasn't even close to being evidence of their involvement in that sabotage. He needed to think this through, discuss it with Rione. "It's not like I didn't make plenty of mistakes myself this time."

Desjani frowned at him. "The first pass didn't work out perfectly, but everything else went right." He didn't answer, and she frowned deeper. "Sir, you keep telling me that you're not perfect, but right now I can tell that you're condemning yourself for not being perfect. With all due respect, you're being inconsistent and overly hard on yourself."

For some reason Geary found himself smiling crookedly at her. "With all due respect? How would you say that if you weren't being respectful?"

"I'd tell you that you were being an idiot and that you can't afford to let a misstep destroy your confidence. Sir. Which of course I'm not saying."

"Because that wouldn't be respectful?" Geary asked. "It sounds like something I should listen to, though. Thanks. Where's this Syndic CEO?"

"His escape pod was picked up by *Kururi*, which is bringing him to *Dauntless*."

"Good. Please ask Lieutenant Iger to let me know when our visitor is ready for a chat with me. I'd like you there, too." Desjani nodded. "And Co-President Rione."

Desjani's expression closed down completely. "Yes, sir."

He'd figured out that when Desjani said "yes, sir" to him, it could mean a lot of different things, but agreement wasn't one of them. "Tanya, she's an important ally. She understands things we don't. She's a politician. This Syndic we're going to be dealing with is also a politician."

"So they speak the same language," Desjani stated in a way that made it clear that she thought Rione and the Syndic CEO shared many other qualities. "I understand why she might be useful, then. I will inform Lieutenant Iger of your wishes, sir."

THE Syndic CEO in the interrogation room was doing his best to put up a good front, doubtless worried that video of him might be broadcast to the Syndicate Worlds for propaganda purposes. His impeccably tailored uniform bore signs of the CEO's escape from his last ship, and his appearance was rumpled even though his haircut still looked like it had cost as much as a destroyer. Geary glanced at Lieutenant Iger. "Find out anything?"

Iger nodded, a small smile showing. "Yes, sir. He didn't say anything, of course, but I tracked his reactions, including his brain scans as he listened to my questions. He denied knowing anything about an alien intelligence, but I saw fear spikes when I asked."

"Fear?"

"Yes, sir," Iger repeated firmly. "No doubt at all. *This* CEO, at least, is frightened of those things."

"Are we sure it's not the question that frightened him?" Rione asked. "The possibility that he might give away a very important secret?"

"Or just that we know enough to ask the question," Desjani added.

Iger nodded respectfully to both women. "I asked the question different ways, Madam Co-President, and watched exactly what parts of his brain lit up. Captain Desjani, his nervousness did increase a great deal when I started asking those questions, but that registered differently than just concern over us knowing. See these records?" The lieutenant tapped controls and brought up images of the Syndic CEO's brain, images that hovered in the air before them. "See here? That's the area concerned with personal safety. This area reacts to deception planning, which is when he's working out a lie. You can see how as I asked variations on the questions, his reactions differed." The images flared and dimmed in different areas. "He's got a very deep-seated fear when the topic is raised, something that triggers some of the most ancient portions of the human mind."

"Fear of the unknown, fear of the stranger?" Geary asked.

"That sort of thing, yes, sir," Iger agreed.

"But outwardly he's claiming to know nothing."

"Yes, sir."

Geary looked over at Rione and Desjani. "I think I should go in there and talk to him. Lieutenant Iger can monitor his reactions. Should one or both of you go with me?"

Desjani shook her head. "I'd rather watch from here, sir. It's hard enough to keep from busting through that wall and locking my hands around the neck of that Syndic bastard as it is."

Rione frowned, though in thought rather than directing the expression at Desjani. "I think you should try just you first, Captain Geary. One-on-one, he may be a little more prone to speak. If it seems right, I can always come in and apply whatever pressure or encouragement an Alliance politician can add."

"All right." Iger came close to him and, with a mumbled apology, carefully attached something tiny behind one of Geary's ears. "What's that?"

"A short-range comm link operating on a frequency that won't interfere with the interrogation equipment," Iger explained. "We'll provide you with whatever the equipment shows of the Syndic's reactions as you speak to him. It's effectively invisible, though if the CEO knows anything at all about interrogations, he'll assume you've got a link to whoever is monitoring him."

A few seconds later, Geary stepped into the interrogation room, sealing the hatch behind him. The CEO sat in one of the two chairs the room boasted, both fastened securely to the deck. As Geary walked toward him, the CEO stood up, his movements abrupt with fear. "I am an officer of the Syndicate Worlds, and—"

Geary held up one hand palm out in a forestalling gesture, and the CEO broke off his speech but remained standing. "I've heard variations on that plenty of times," Geary informed the CEO. "It doesn't seem to have changed much in the last century."

That made the CEO twitch slightly in spite of himself. "I'm aware that you have identified yourself as Captain John Geary, but—"

"But, nothing," Geary broke in. "I know your superiors have already done a positive ID on me and confirmed who I am." He sat down, trying to look totally confident, and gestured the CEO to sit again. After a moment, the CEO did, his body staying stiff. "It's past time we stopped playing games, CEO Cafiro. These particular games have cost both the Alliance and the Syndicate Worlds terribly in terms of lives lost and resources wasted in a war you can't hope to win."

"The Syndicate Worlds will not yield," the CEO insisted.

"And neither will the Alliance. After almost a century, I assume everybody has figured that one out. So what's the point? What are you fighting for, CEO Cafiro?"

Cafiro gave Geary a worried look. "For the Syndicate Worlds."

"Really?" Geary leaned forward slightly. "Then why are you doing what the alien intelligence on the other side of Syndicate Worlds' space wants you to do?"

The CEO stared at Geary. "There isn't any such thing."

Lie, Lieutenant Iger's voice came to Geary like a whisper in his ear.

He hadn't really needed that to know it was a lie. "I won't bother going through all of the evidence we've acquired. Some of it the Syndicate Worlds probably aren't aware of." Let the Syndic CEO worry about that. "But we know they're there, and we know the Executive Council of the Syndicate Worlds made a deal with them to attack the Alliance, and we know the aliens double-crossed your Executive Council and instead left you to fight us alone." That all added up to a lot of educated guesses rather than known facts, but Geary wasn't going to admit uncertainty at this point.

The Syndic stared back at him, and even Geary could spot the outward signs of his distress without the help of Iger's equipment. "I don't know what you're talking about."

Partial lie, but he also seemed shocked when you mentioned the double cross. He may not have been aware of that.

Geary gave the Syndic CEO a doubtful look and shook his head. "I understand your name is Niko Cafiro. Second Level Executive Grade. That's fairly high-ranking." CEO Cafiro watched Geary with obvious wariness but stayed silent. "High-ranking enough to be second in command of the flotilla we destroyed in this star system." This time the Syndic's eyes reflected anger and fear. "We've pretty much evened the odds, CEO Cafiro," Geary stated. "The Syndicate Worlds can't confront us with overwhelming superiority right now. We've destroyed too many of your ships in the last few months."

He's hiding something, Iger's voice whispered. *When you spoke of how many ships the Syndics had, it triggered a cascade of mental reactions.*

Meaning what? That more Syndic ships than expected were actually out there, or that this CEO was just thinking about the battles in which the Syndics had lost so many ships and not wanting to show any reaction that might confirm Geary's statement? "We're close to the border with the Alliance," Geary continued. "A few more jumps, and we'll be in a Syndicate Worlds' border system. From there we'll get home."

That finally drew an overt reaction. "Your fleet will be destroyed."

"I'm going to get this fleet home," Geary repeated evenly.

"Everything the Syndicate Worlds has left will meet you in one of the border star systems and stop you," Cafiro insisted, though his voice lacked conviction. "This fleet won't make it back to Alliance space."

"Maybe they'll meet me," Geary agreed. "But the Syndicate Worlds haven't had a lot of luck with stopping this fleet so far. Besides, you know as well as I do that I don't need to get the entire fleet home to tip the balance in this war. I only need to get *one* ship back to Alliance space. The ship carrying the key to the Syndicate Worlds' hypernet." CEO Cafiro couldn't stop a flinch. "You don't know which ship that is. How are the Syndicate Worlds going to stop that *one ship* from jumping for Alliance space? And once that one ship gets home," Geary emphasized, leaning a bit closer, "the Alliance will be able to duplicate that key, and the Syndicate Worlds will have to destroy their gates one by one to keep the Alliance from using them. It grants the Alliance a huge advantage, and you know what can happen when a hypernet gate is destroyed, don't you?"

It had been a shot in the dark, but Cafiro looked away, visibly upset. "I thought Effroen should have been told."

"Effroen?"

"The CEO directing the forces left to defend Lakota. She had orders to keep you from using the hypernet gate at all costs, but even though those of us with some inside knowledge of what had happened at Sancere were worried about what would happen if Lakota's hypernet gate was destroyed, we were overruled."

He seems to be sincere, Iger advised Geary. *There's some anger spikes as memory areas light up, consistent with recalling events that upset him.*

Geary nodded at the Syndic. "Your superiors seem to be willing to run a lot of risks. Very big risks, like the one that got this fleet trapped deep in Syndic territory."

"It . . . it wasn't *my* plan."

"The ambush in the Syndicate Worlds' home system? The double traitor who offered the Alliance fleet that hypernet key so it would rush into the ambush?"

"Yes! I never would have taken such a risk."

Geary shook his head. "It looked like a sure thing. You'd have taken it. But it backfired."

"Because of you!" Cafiro yelled, suddenly red-faced and openly furious. "If you hadn't shown up—" He stopped speaking, his flush fading rapidly as his face paled with fear.

"Yeah," Geary agreed. "I showed up." The Syndic CEO swallowed and stared at him. "Let's think about it. Someone, if that's the right word for members of an intelligent nonhuman species, tricked the Syndicate Worlds into starting this war. Your Executive Council screwed up royally and has refused to admit it. Now, the Alliance will soon have the means to nullify the Syndicate Worlds' hypernet system because your Executive Council screwed up royally *again*. They started the war, and now they're about to lose it. And you're remaining loyal to them when you could be talking about ways to minimize the damage."

Cafiro plainly did think about it, his eyes shifting before he finally spoke. "Are you . . . negotiating?"

"I'm just asking you to consider alternatives."

"For the good of the Syndicate Worlds."

"Right." Geary nodded, keeping his face calm.

"You want the war to end?" Cafiro challenged.

"You and I both know that humanity faces another enemy. Maybe it's about time we stopped killing each other the way that enemy has tricked us into doing."

More thinking, Cafiro avoiding Geary's eyes again for several seconds. "How can we know you'll keep your word?"

"There's proof of that in every star system this fleet has traversed since we left the Syndic home system. Don't try to pretend you haven't heard."

CEO Cafiro pushed his palms tightly together, pressing the tips of his fingers to his mouth as he thought again. "It's not enough. Not now. I tell you honestly, as long as there's any chance that you can be stopped, no one will move against the current membership of the Executive Council."

He's telling the truth, Lieutenant Iger reported in an astonished voice.

"And when this fleet does make it home?"

The Syndic CEO eyed Geary. "Then the failure will be huge, the costs incalculable, the consequences too serious to contemplate. Even then, the current membership of the Executive Council won't negotiate. They can't afford to because that would assign the failure to them."

Geary nodded, remembering how Rione had stated the same thing.

"But," Cafiro added, his face hard, "after something like that, the rest of the Syndicate Worlds would not be willing to sacrifice themselves to protect the Executive Council from its failures."

Ask him if that means revolt, or new members of the Council, Rione urged.

Geary nodded as if to Cafiro, but also to Rione's words. "Are you saying there'd be a revolt, or that we'd be dealing with new members of the Council?"

Cafiro's eyes shifted. "I don't know."

Lie, Iger advised.

"Let's say it's new members," Geary pressed. "Will they be willing to negotiate an end to this war?"

"Under those conditions? I think so. Depending on the terms."

Truth, Iger stated.

"Would they work with us to deal with the aliens and stop pretending they don't exist?"

"Yes, I—" Cafiro flushed red again, this time with apparent self-anger at having finally blurted out an admission that he knew of the aliens.

"We both already knew the truth," Geary said. "We want the same thing. An end to a senseless war and a united front against something that threatens humanity. That should be grounds for working together."

The CEO nodded once.

Appeal to his self-interest! Rione demanded. *Not the best interests of humanity or the Syndicate Worlds! His self-interest! He didn't become a Syndic CEO by being self-sacrificing!*

She had a point. Geary forced a small smile. "Of course, when I speak of working together, I'm talking about with someone we know. Someone who understands the issues."

His brain's reward centers are lighting up, Iger observed.

Cafiro nodded again, this time much more firmly. "As you say, we need to think in terms of mutual benefit."

"Naturally," Geary replied in an even voice, though he wanted to spit. Why couldn't Rione have done this directly? But she would have been tarred like any other current Alliance leader with all the hatred and distrust engendered by decade after decade of war. He, the outsider even now, had a different status. But he didn't know the right words, and Rione wasn't feeding them to him, maybe assuming he'd somehow know them. Maybe he did. Geary dredged up memories of a superior officer he'd suffered under for a few years, a man who had nearly driven him from the fleet with his politicking and attempts to manipulate those around him. He just had to remember the sort of things that he had said. "The Alliance needs the right people to work with," Geary stated, emphasizing the word "right" just enough.

Cafiro almost smiled, but his eyes lit with eagerness. "Yes. I know others who could work with me. With us."

Cafiro favored Geary with a tense smile. "Of course, there's not much I can do as a prisoner."

"It seems we understand each other." More than Geary wanted to. But then this particular Syndic CEO had been ambitious and power-driven, or he wouldn't have been second in command of that flotilla. It followed that he'd react this way when offered the sort of deal Geary had implied. Other Syndic CEOs, perhaps less self-centered and more loyal to things other than their personal bottom line (like the CEO in charge of Cavalos Star System), would be far better leaders to deal with. But Geary had to use the weapons he had available.

Even very distasteful weapons. Weapons that were negotiating for their own freedom but hadn't bothered yet to ask about the fates of other Syndic survivors from the flotilla that had been destroyed. Geary tried to keep his face calm even as he sympathized with Desjani's desire to choke this Syndic CEO until his eyes popped. "I think it will benefit all concerned if you are released." *Before I decide to let Desjani in here so we can strangle you together.* He couldn't resist mentioning the other Syndic survivors in a pointed reminder. "We've taken no other prisoners here. Some of the escape pods from destroyed Syndicate Worlds' warships are damaged but appear able to reach safety."

"Ah . . . of course," Cafiro agreed after a brief hesitation.

"The Syndicate Worlds will be hearing from us, CEO Cafiro. After this fleet gets home." Geary stood up to end the conversation and left the room.

"He's nervous," Lieutenant Iger remarked when Geary rejoined the others. "Doubtless wondering whether he's really going to be released."

"Will he really stir up trouble for the Syndics if we let him go?" Geary asked Iger and Rione. Both of them nodded. "Then get him off this ship, please, Lieutenant Iger."

"Yes, sir. He'll be back in his escape pod and relaunched within half an hour."

Geary led Desjani and Rione out of the intelligence spaces. "I think I'd rather deal with the aliens," he remarked, not sure how much he was joking.

"You might," Rione replied with absolute seriousness. "If our speculations are right, these aliens acted against us and the Syndics because of their experiences with the Syndic leadership. They might simply want to be left alone or to feel secure against us. Remove the threat of human aggression, and those aliens would have an immense amount of space available to them on their other borders."

Desjani, talking as if speaking to herself, gazed down the passageway. "Unless there's something else on *their* other borders."

Geary frowned, then felt a sudden pang of worry. "If there's one nonhuman intelligence out there . . ."

"There could be more. Almost certainly are more," Desjani murmured. She looked at Geary. "We have to understand this enemy, and that's a very important possibility. *They* might feel penned between potential foes. They might even be fighting a war or wars unimaginably far away from our own battles with the Syndics. Maybe they need to keep us tied down because of that, because they need to protect their flanks. Maybe that means we've got potential allies against these creatures. Or even worse potential enemies."

Rione looked like she'd swallowed something unpleasant. "That's a real possibility. We have no way of knowing if it's true. There's too damned much we don't know."

"We've learned a lot. We'll learn more." He hoped that was true, anyway.

THE expanding balls of debris that had been the wrecks of *Opportune*, *Braveheart*, the heavy cruiser *Armet*, and the light cruiser *Cercle* were well behind the Alliance fleet now as it proceeded toward the jump point for Anahalt and Dilawa. Geary had kept the fleet's speed down to point zero four light to make it easier for badly damaged ships like *Courageous* and *Brilliant* to keep up, hoping they'd soon get more propulsion units repaired. No more attempts to plant worms in fleet systems had occurred. Geary wondered if that was because those responsible for the earlier attempts were busy dealing with damage to their ships, or were trying to find new ways to plant the worms, or were rethinking that tactic after the previous attempts had backfired by alienating most of the fleet. It seemed very unlikely that they'd given up.

He still wasn't certain which star to jump to next. Nor did he feel like thinking of that at the moment. The fleet had lost a lot of personnel as well as several ships in the latest battle. He'd spent a long time in the fleet at peace, a hundred years ago, and fought one hopeless battle before going into survival sleep. Others had fought countless battles during the next century, growing accustomed to losing ships and men and women in large numbers. Geary had kept trying to avoid dealing with that but realized he couldn't keep it up. He had to accept the cost that even victories required, and he needed to call up the personnel records, which would tell him the private prices the people he knew now had paid before he had known them. He owed that to them.

Geary called up the personnel files and read through them. Captain Jaylen Cresida. Home world Madira. Her first fleet assignment had been as gunnery officer on the destroyer *Shakujo*. Married five years ago to another fleet officer. Widowed three years ago when her husband had died aboard the battle cruiser *Invincible* when the ship was destroyed while defending the Alliance star system of Kana against a Syndic attack. Not the same *Invincible* that this fleet had lost at Ilion, but the previous ship to bear that same name.

Cresida had told him that if she died, she had someone waiting for her.

Geary closed his eyes for a moment, trying to dull the pain inside as he read the dry report. Then he read more, forcing himself to confront the costs of this war that had changed the Alliance he knew and helped forge the personalities of the people around him.

Cresida's mother and brother were also casualties of the war, the mother dead when Jaylen had been only twelve. The older brother had died a year before Cresida joined the fleet. Not wanting to tally the losses through the generation before that, Geary stopped looking back through the file.

Steeling himself, Geary pulled up Captain Duellos's file. His wife was a research scientist in a star system safely back from the front line, but Duellos's father and an uncle had died in the war. His oldest daughter would be eligible for call-up by the draft next year.

Captain Tulev had lost his wife and three children to a Syndic bombardment of their home world.

And Captain Desjani. She'd told him that her parents were still both alive, and that was so. Desjani did also have the uncle she'd spoken of a few times. But she'd never mentioned the aunt who'd died in ground fighting on a Syndic world. Nor the younger brother dead six years ago in his first combat engagement.

He remembered the young Syndic boy with whom Desjani had spoken when the refugees from Wendig were brought aboard, the way Desjani had treated the boy and the way she'd looked at him as he moved to defend his family. Had she seen her little brother in that boy?

Geary spent a long time staring at the display, then punched in the other commands he'd never had the nerve to face. The records of what had happened to his family.

Gearys popped up. A lot of them. He'd left no wife or children behind, something for which he'd often given thanks. But he'd had a brother and a sister, cousins, an aunt. Most of them had children. Many of those had ended up in the fleet. Geary remembered his grandnephew's bitter words, that it was expected that Gearys would join the fleet. A lot of them had done that, and a lot had died.

He was still sitting there, trying to take it in, when his hatch alarm sounded. "Come in."

Captain Desjani entered, then halted, watching him. "What's wrong?"

"Just . . . reviewing some files."

She hesitated for only a moment, then came around behind him to read over his shoulder. Desjani was silent for so long that Geary began wondering what to do, then he heard her speak softly. "Haven't you seen these before?"

"No. I didn't want to."

"We've all paid a price in this war. Your family has paid more than its share."

"Because of me," Geary ground out. Desjani didn't answer, apparently unwilling to deny something she had to know was true. "Why didn't you ever tell me about your brother?"

She was quiet again for a while. "It's not something I talk about."

"I'm very, very sorry. You know I would've listened."

The reply took a moment to come. "Yes, and I know you would've understood. But I thought you had enough things to worry about. My family's losses aren't special."

"Yes, they are," Geary objected. "Every single person is special. A hundred years of this, a century of life after life cut short in a war that's gone nowhere. What a damned waste."

"Yes." He felt Desjani's hand rest on his shoulder and squeeze lightly, the gesture of a comrade sharing pain, and maybe something more.

Geary brought his own hand up to cover hers and grip it. "Thanks."

"You need everything we can give you."

Suddenly it all felt like too much. His responsibilities, the pain the war had brought to so many, the feelings for Desjani that he had to keep as hidden as possible. He had to get *Dauntless* home, he had to get that Syndic hypernet key back to the Alliance, but he had to do so much more as well. People expected him to do so much more. Geary felt as if he would drown under the pressure, his only lifeline the hand resting on his shoulder. He dropped his grasp and stood up, facing her. "Tanya . . ."

"Yes," she repeated, though he wasn't sure if she knew what it was he couldn't say, or if she knew and was trying to deflect it. "It's so much for one man to carry. You will end it, though," Desjani stated firmly. "You'll end this war, you'll save this fleet and the Alliance."

Every word felt like a nail in his coffin. "For the love of my ancestors, please don't give me that speech!"

"It's not a speech," Desjani insisted.

"Yes, it is! It's a fantasy about who I am and what I can do!"

"No. It's true. Look what you've done already!" Desjani gestured to the display. "You can stop this. I know it must be hard to be chosen by the living stars for such a mission, but you can do it!"

"You have no idea how it feels to have that kind of demand placed on you!"

"I see the effect it has on you, but I know you can handle it. You wouldn't have been chosen otherwise."

"Maybe somebody made a mistake!" Geary almost yelled. "Maybe I'm not able to save the entire damned universe by myself!"

"You're not alone!" Desjani was clearly upset now, her face as she gazed at him twisted with hope, fear, and something deeper, all jumbled together.

"It sure feels like it!" Geary swung his own angry hand toward the display now behind him. "All of those dead, and people expecting me to end that. How can anyone accomplish that? I can't do this!" Had he ever actually said those last four words to anyone, or had the thought only echoed inside him since he'd been forced to assume command of this fleet?

"What else do you need from me?" she asked desperately. "Of course you need help. Tell me, and it's yours. I'll do anything." Desjani looked appalled as the last words slipped out, and she stared at Geary.

His despair drained away as Geary stared back at her. Something that had been at least partly hidden now lay in the open between them. "Anything?"

"I didn't—" She swallowed and spoke with obviously forced calm. "I'm without honor now. I know that."

"Stop it, Tanya. You've got honor to spare."

"An honorable woman would not feel this way about her commanding officer! She wouldn't speak of it. She would not be willing to—" Desjani bit off her words and stared frantically at Geary again.

He could reach out and have her. Right this very moment.

Geary looked down at his hands, thinking of the price so many others had already paid. He'd been willing to use Victoria Rione when she'd offered herself to him, just as Rione had used him. But he couldn't do that to Tanya Desjani. Even though Desjani and almost everyone else would excuse him for it, justifying to themselves whatever was done by the hero sent from the past. But he couldn't do that to her. The very thought of it revolted him. That, more than anything, told him that his feelings for her were real, that he wasn't just reaching out again for any safe port when the storms of his responsibilities grew too rough. "I won't take your honor," he whispered.

"You already have it," Desjani replied in agonized tones.

"No. I'll take nothing from you that you don't freely choose to give."

"It's *given*. I swear I didn't seek that, I swear I tried to fight it, but it has happened."

Geary looked up again and saw her despair. "Either we'll live to reach Alliance space, or we'll die on the way. If we live . . ."

Desjani nodded. "I can resign my commission. It won't be enough to return my honor or erase the burden I've put on your own, but—"

"Resign your commission? Tanya, you live to be a fleet officer! You love it! I can't allow you to give that up on my account!"

"An officer who cannot carry out her duties according to regulations is required to—" Desjani began, her face now stiff.

"*I'll* resign," Geary broke in. "As soon as we get home. I never wanted this responsibility, and once I get this fleet home, no one can demand more of me. Once I'm no longer a fleet officer, your honor can't be questioned, and—"

"*No!*" Desjani now appeared horrified as she gazed at him. "*You can't!* You have a mission!"

"I never asked or wanted—"

"It was given to you! Because the living stars knew you could do it!" Desjani backed away, shaking her head. "I can't allow my feelings to influence you this way. Too many people are depending upon you. If I caused you to shirk that mission, I would surely be damned by them and deserving of it. Say you won't do that. Say you didn't mean it." He looked back at her silently. "Say it! If you do not, I swear I shall get this ship home to Alliance space, then go as far from you as human space allows!" Geary struggled for words, and Desjani took another step backward. "If the temptation I offer you has to be removed from this ship now, I'll do that. I'll do whatever I must."

He finally found his voice again. "No. Please. You're *Dauntless's* commanding officer. You belong on her. I . . . I promise you I won't resign until this war is over." The words felt acidic in his mouth, the thing he had never wanted to accept even though he knew so many expected it of him.

"Your promise should not be to me," Desjani replied, her face and voice calmer now.

"It is," he insisted. "I've avoided making it because it scared the hell out of me. But the thought of not seeing you scared me more. Congratulations."

"I . . . I didn't—"

"No, you didn't. You never would have tried to manipulate me on purpose." Unlike Victoria Rione, he realized. "I made the choice. I'll carry out the mission. As long as you don't resign *your* commission. I need you with me if I'm going to have any chance of succeeding. And when my mission is done, and I'm no longer in command of this fleet, I'll finally say the words that I wish I could say to you now."

Desjani nodded to him. "Thank you, Captain Geary. I knew you'd do what you had to do."

"As opposed to what I want to do right now."

Amazingly, she laughed. "If you and I did what we wanted to do at this very moment, we'd be different people. But hard as it is, I must stand here instead of stepping closer to you. Much closer. No. You have my honor, I have your promise. If the gift of my honor gives you the strength to do what you must, it's a small price for me to pay."

"You think of it as a price, then?" Geary asked.

Desjani nodded as her laughter faded. "My honor is the thing of greatest value that I possess. That I used to possess.

I know you will not use it against me, and I know it is safe in your hands. But there have been times when it felt like my honor was all I had left. I regret losing it."

"Then I promise you that I will keep your honor safe until I can return it."

"But . . . it was given. To my shame . . . but it was given."

Geary shook his head. "I want to return your honor, and you want me to keep it. There's a way to do both if that's what you want."

"How could I have both—?" She seemed shocked, looking away for a moment before focusing back on him. "You mean that?"

"I can't come out and say how I feel, just like you can't, not until this war is over and I'm no longer your commanding officer, but I swear on the honor of my ancestors that I meant it."

Desjani blinked, swallowed again, then gave Geary a stern look. "You must know something, Captain John Geary. Right now you are my fleet commander, and I do as you say and defer to you. You are on a divine mission, and while that lasts, I will follow you to hell itself on your command. But when all is done and the war is over, a man would come to me with my honor and himself. Not like any other man, not even then, but a man, and I will not be subordinate to any man in my own life or my own home. I will only have a man as a partner, an equal, to be beside me in all things. Any man must agree to that if he someday wishes to share a life with Tanya Desjani."

Geary nodded. "Any man who really knew Tanya Desjani would gladly commit to those conditions and promise to honor them."

She gazed back at him, then smiled. "It is very hard, and I fear that it'll be harder still before all is done. But when the day comes that your mission is fulfilled, I will accept my honor back and all that comes with it."

All he had to do was get the fleet the rest of the way home and win the war that had been raging for a century. But he'd never thought he could get this far, do what he'd been able to do. If he could somehow end the war, end the deaths . . .

And, for the first time since he'd been awakened from survival sleep, he knew without any doubt that he had something other than duty to live for. They'd talked around it, they might never again discuss it even indirectly while the war lasted, but they each knew how the other felt and what they'd promised each other. "In that case, Captain Desjani, let's take a look at the star display and figure out our next move on the way home. We've got a fleet to save and a war to end."